THE
WILD RED DAWN

PART ONE OF
'Jack Tucker of Exmoor'
A FAMILY SAGA 1815–1875

Paddy King-Fretts

ryelands

First published in Great Britain in 2008

Copyright © 2008 Paddy King-Fretts

British Library Cataloguing-in-Publication Data
A CIP record for this title is available from the British Library

ISBN 978 09556477 3 4

HALSGROVE
Halsgrove House
Ryelands Industrial Estate, Bagley Road,
Wellington, Somerset TA21 9PZ
Tel: 01823 653777
Fax: 01823 216796
email: sales@halsgrove.com
website: www.halsgrove.com

Printed and bound in Great Britain by Short Run Press Ltd, Exeter

Front cover illustration
'Dawn over Dunkery' **by Jack Hoar**
Tel: 01769 572131 e-mail: jackhoar@hotmail.com

Author's Note

'The country is called Exmore……a filthy barren ground, so it is.'
DANIEL DEFOE (1661-1731).

So…..why this book?

In August 1818, the wild uninhabited Exmoor Forest was purchased by a Mr John Knight, a dynamic and immensely wealthy Iron Master from the Midlands. Over the next forty years or so Knight, followed by his son Frederic, struggled to develop the moor and searched for copper and iron ore of which there appeared to be abundant evidence. They broke the land, built farms and roads then appointed tenants to run their new properties, all the while prospecting for the elusive minerals.

My family farmed on Exmoor for more than fifty years and, when children, we were assailed by stories of what the Knights had achieved and their herculean efforts. It was a saga that fired the imagination and we were forever wondering what life must have been like for those involved. There were countless tales of the desperate struggle, of hardship, of tragedy and heroic endeavour but still no *'humanisme'*. It required a family to bring personalities to life but I could find none…so I decided to develop my own and build around it the stories we learned all those years ago. The family is called Tucker and they hail from Molland, a small village on the southern slopes of the moor. *Jack Tucker of Exmoor* is their story, all four generations of it.

I read avidly, gradually choreographing the life and times of the Tuckers in and around the factual evidence I found, in particular, the story of the Knights. The very business would have taxed many to the extreme. Take it all back to the brutal lifestyle of the pre-Victoria era (public hangings, deportation, man traps, duelling, smuggling and highwaymen), throw in a love story that crashed through the rigid strata of society and one has the makings of a powerful saga.

The development of my story has not been without its problems. Often the evidence was conflicting and I had to consider the most likely option. Occasionally the correct date frustrated and I had to expand or contract accordingly. For example, duelling purists might quibble over the date of the Tucker–Knight duel. However, in 1845, a Lt Hawkey R.M. killed a Mr Seton after the latter seduced his wife. He was tried at Winchester and acquitted to much public acclaim so I am not far off the mark.

Names – always difficult! The fictitious characters were easy enough and I have used unashamedly the Devon names I know so well. The Tuckers, Bawdens, Thornes, Vellacotts etc live on today and in abundance. The great names of Exmoor, though, presented a problem which research itself overcame.

3

Initially I was uneasy at taking the liberty of using the names of well known families yet the more I delved into local history the more apparent it became that the Luttrells, Aclands, Chichesters, indeed the Knights themselves, were men of great compassion and benevolence and were synonymous with the development of the moor. However they, too, are essential to my story. A glance at what the Luttrells did for Dunster, the Aclands for those around Holnicote or what Frederic Knight accomplished at Simonsbath bears testimony to their goodness and vision. And in any case, if I chose not to use some, what about the others? Where would I stop? My conscience is thus clear.

I have included also a number of well known characters of the day. Parson Jack Russell hunted Exmoor throughout this period and would undoubtedly have known them all, as would the Reverend William Thornton of Simonsbath and Dr Charles Collyns of Dulverton. Burgess committed his foul murder as described and Alfred Tennyson may well have come to Exmoor to seek inspiration as did Wordsworth and Coleridge.

But back to the book. In order to get the very best out of the material available I decided to select, enlarge, add to and rearrange many historical and geographical facts. Soon after the publication of *Far from the Madding Crowd*, Hardy read *Lorna Doone* (where Blackmore had done just this) and commented that he found it an exquisite way of describing things and wished that he had read it before considering the kind of work he had just attempted. If it was good enough for them then it is most certainly good enough for me! That said I have made every effort to read into the hearts and minds of those who broke and first inhabited the heights of Exmoor.

The Knights themselves had a hard time of it, pouring in an immense fortune. By today's standards, the purchase of the moor itself would have set John Knight back something in the region of £10m (he paid £50k in 1818 when a head groom was earning 75p a week). His purchase of extra land would have been about the same again and he put a similar amount into the development of the area and his search for minerals. John Knight's first wife died early while Frederic's only son predeceased him without leaving an heir. A further considerable, and expected, family fortune did not materialise and, in the later stages of their great adventure, the family was bedevilled by lawsuits flying to and fro - money, inevitably, being the root cause. These were real events. However there was never a Kenton Knight – the villain of my piece, who you will meet in due course, is a purely fictitious character.

All this and much more emerges in *Jack Tucker of Exmoor* but it is the Tuckers themselves who will capture and hold your imagination. Their fortunes and their trials between Waterloo and Victoria becoming Queen Empress of India will, I hope, bring to you something of early Exmoor.

Paddy King-Fretts,
South Molton.

The Tuckers

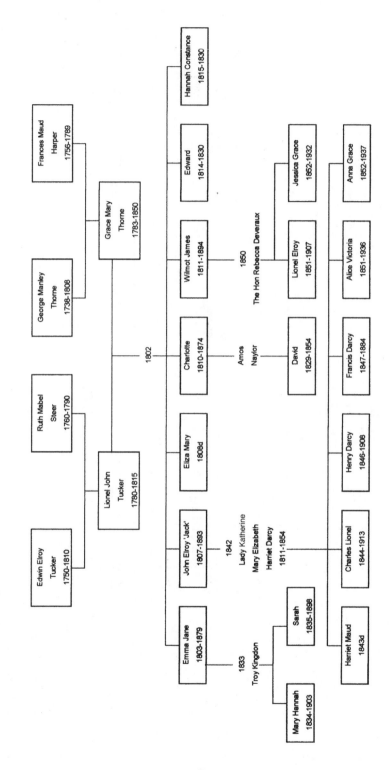

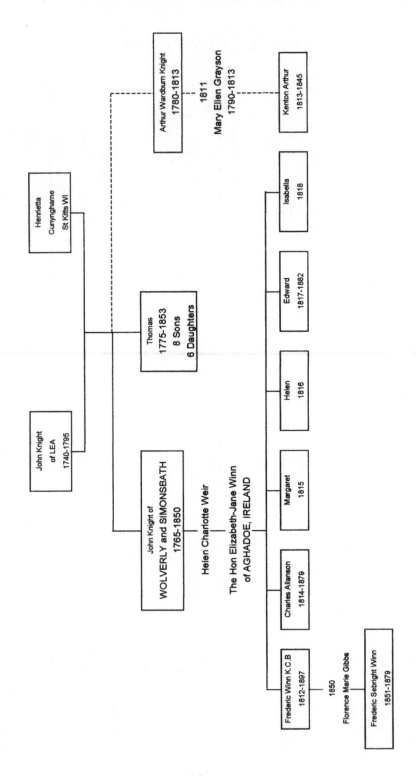

The Knights

Henrietta
Cunynghame
St Kitts WI

John Knight
of LEA
1740-1795

Arthur Wardburn Knight
1780-1813

1811

Mary Ellen Grayson
1790-1813

Kenton Arthur
1813-1845

Thomas
1775-1853
8 Sons
6 Daughters

John Knight of
WOLVERLY and SIMONSBATH
1765-1850

Helen Charlotte Weir

The Hon Elizabeth-Jane Winn
of AGHADOE, IRELAND

Isabella
1818

Edward
1817-1882

Helen
1816

Margaret
1815

Charles Allanson
1814-1879

Frederic Winn K.C.B
1812-1897

1850

Florence Marie Gibbs

Frederic Sebright Winn
1851-1879

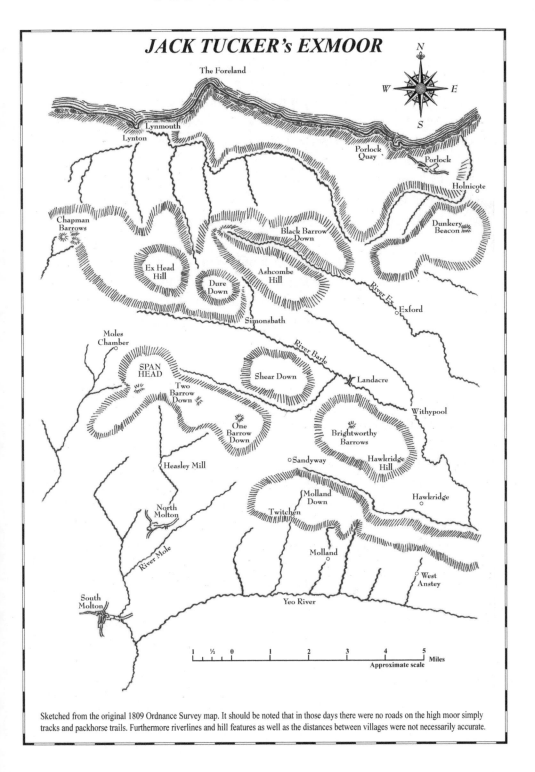

JACK TUCKER's EXMOOR

The Foreland

N
W E
S

Lynmouth
Lynton
Porlock Quay
Porlock
Holnicote

Chapman Barrows
Black Barrow Down
Dunkery Beacon

Ex Head Hill
Dure Down
Ashcombe Hill
River Ex
Exford

Simonsbath

Moles Chamber
River Barle

SPAN HEAD
Shear Down
Landacre
Withypool

Two Barrow Down
One Barrow Down
Brightworthy Barrows
Hawkridge Hill

Heasley Mill
Sandyway
Hawkridge

North Molton
Molland Down
Twitchen

River Mole
Molland
West Anstey

South Molton
Yeo River

1 ½ 0   1   2   3   4   5
Miles
Approximate scale

Sketched from the original 1809 Ordnance Survey map. It should be noted that in those days there were no roads on the high moor simply tracks and packhorse trails. Furthermore riverlines and hill features as well as the distances between villages were not necessarily accurate.

Principal Characters

(less those covered by the two family trees)

APPLETON, MRS JANET. Housekeeper to the Knight family.

CHAPPLE, MISS ENID. Governess to the Knight children.

DARCY, LADY KATHERINE MARY ELIZABETH HARRIET. The Duke and Duchess of Northborough's elder daughter.

ESDAILE, SIR JAMES. Chaiman of Esdaile's Bank, Lombard St, London. Banker to the Knight family.

GRANT, LEONARD. Gardener-handyman to Mr Knight and a close friend of Jack Tucker.

MORGAN, DURNFORD. Merchant banker from Esdaile's.

NORTHBOROUGH, THE DUKE AND DUCHESS OF. Friends of John Knight.

PARKER, MR BERNARD. Mr Knight's Head butler.

PRESTON, LORD HERBERT. Heir to the Duke of Northborough and friend of Kenton Knight.

Others of note

ACLAND, SIR THOMAS. Baronet, landowner and M.P. Wife Lydia, sons Charles and James.

BAMFYLDE, SIR CHARLES. North Devon landowner and father of Roger, a friend of Frederic Knight.

BARCLAY, SIR CRISPIN. Senior partner of Barclay's Agricultural Banking, Lombard St, London.

BRADDON, JOSIAH. Highwayman from Exford and father of Meg, a scullery maid.

BURGE, DAVY. A Brendon farmer and part-time smuggler.

CHICHESTER, COLONEL GILES. Master of Arlington Court.

COLLYNS, DR CHARLES PALK. A well known doctor and benefactor from Dulverton.

COWARD, HECTOR. Mr Knight's groom and a close friend of Jack Tucker. Husband of Nancy.

EXTON, MICHAEL. A contender for Exmoor from Dulverton. Husband of Donna Maria Josephine.

FANSHAWE, SGT BRACK. The Royal North Devon Hussars, Barnstaple.

FROBISHER, LORD GEOFFREY AND LADY. Landowner and M.P. from Filleigh.

FROUDE, THE REV JOHN. Vicar of Molland and Knowstone.

GOLDBERG, JACOB. Errant banker from The Barnstaple Bank.

GOVIER, ORWELL. John Knight's head groom at Lynton.

HARPER, JED. Old sea-dog. Father of Luke, smuggler and swordsman. Uncle of Jasper, a highwayman.

HAVERS, EBENEZER. Mining surveyor from Consett's of Durham.

LOOSEMORE, FRED. A Molland farmer and husband of Tilly.

LUTTRELL, JOHN. Bachelor and Master of Dunster Castle.

NAYLOR, AMOS. Foreman at Heathcoat's factory, Tiverton.

ORCHARD, JESSICA. Member of the Hartland family.

QUICK, MARY. Elizabeth-Jane Knight's lady's maid.

RAWLE, SARAH. Lady Darcy's lady's maid.

RUSSELL, PARSON JACK. Well known Exmoor hunting parson.

STRONG, MRS MABEL. Cook to Mr and Mrs Knight at Lynton and Simonsbath.

TARR, ABEL. Second butler to the Knights.

THORNE, BEN. Molland shepherd and son of Walter.

Webber, Dan. Groom to Mr Knight and a close friend of Jack Tucker.

Prologue

1815

May, that year saw the French army marching towards Belgium. Meanwhile in South West England the government had just conducted its final survey of the Royal Forest of Exmoor. These events, though totally unconnected, combined to shape the destiny of two very different families.

*

The man, he knew, would never change and he marvelled at his spirit. Always scheming, always planning his next enterprise, the fifty year-old Iron Master rarely relaxed. His energy drove him on remorselessly, exhausting those around him.

"So that's it. You've seen our Exmoor then?" Colonel Giles Chichester, Master of Arlington Court, calmly observed his friend pacing the room in front of him. "And as wild and desolate as the day God made it...I'll be bound." The diminutive, shrew-like host grinned mischievously, screwing up his eyes at the thought.

"Oh, not so bad...not so bad." The visitor inclined his head then shook it slowly is if assembling his thoughts. "Aha, no." Chuckling to himself, he wagged a finger admonishingly at the very suggestion that what he had seen had not been to his liking. But the mind behind the glowering features was racing. The subject had come up earlier when they were still at the table, when Chichester had let slip to the others that his old friend, John Knight from Worcestershire, was down to look over the Crown Allotment.

*

Only last year, the lease of wardenship had expired and one option for the government was to sell. Giles Chichester had passed word to his friend and Knight had moved with his customary speed, coming down the very same week with his agent, Raimond Maxwell. Maxwell ran Knight's estates in Wales and along the Borders where much of the rough, higher land was similar to Exmoor. The two men had spent days riding the moor together.

He had learned much this evening already but the ladies had now retired, leaving the men to amuse themselves. Most had wandered off, some to the library others to the gunroom with the butler. There were just the three of them, Chichester, the young Sir Thomas Acland and himself.

Knight continued to prowl restlessly. As he moved so he slipped his hand under the black, rolled collar of his finely spun silk jacket and rubbed the point of his shoulder. The injury, where the heavy smelting ladle had caught him a glancing blow all those years ago, still hurt, the more so when his mind was running free. But his family knew the signs: the pulsing vein on his left temple and the sudden change in his voice warned them to let well alone.

From where he was, even with the doors closed, Knight could hear the quintet in the hall serenading the ladies as they sat chatting. He was tone deaf: he hated the noise, tolerating it only for the sake of his young wife. Time and again Elizabeth-Jane had forced him to suffer without complaint while small groups of sombrely clad females, their faces screwed tight in concentration, scraped mournfully away. It all irritated him intensely and, as his fingers found the old wound again, he scowled.

Conversation around the table earlier had been concerned with the looming French crisis. It had been agreed that Liverpool and his Tories had taken far too long to prepare the nation for the contest that was sure to come. Even now, Napoleon appeared to be ready while here in England too little had been done and now there was pandemonium. Talk this evening had been earnest and hushed with none of the usual banter. Mothers and aunts, their eyes darting anxiously from one speaker to the next, sat fingering their jewellery as they listened to the predictions.

For Knight the crisis was different. Already immensely wealthy, his forges at Morton and Bridgewood, together with the furnace lines at Flaxley, were working night and day. The recent Peninsular campaign had seen to that. Cutlers and armourers throughout the Midlands demanded everything he could produce and Knight, ever the opportunist, had been happy to oblige. But now he was bored: his mind was turning to other things including the rapidly changing agricultural scene. The countryside, Maxwell urged, was ripe for development and Chichester's letter had alerted him. Several times this week he had seen evidence of old workings. The land, it seemed, had much to offer.

＊

"Yes, it *is* rough, *very* rough for sure but...well, I'd say something could be done." Knight remained guarded. The two had known each other since boyhood and Chichester had warned him that others here tonight harboured thoughts similar to his own.

"It'll be hard to tame the virgin moor, y'know. Damned hard." Chichester, his thin back hunched, shook his head then half turned in his chair. "Eh, Tom? You've tried it often enough around Dunster and Porlock, haven't you now? The devil's own job, is it not?" Knight glanced up at the casually tossed question, watching the young man's reaction and waiting on his reply.

"Gave up long ago." The Acland estates at Holnicote bordered the eastern edge of the moor. Before dinner the tall, exquisitely dressed Member for Devon had confided to Knight that he intended to reapply for the lease of the moor or, failing that, make an offer to buy the land outright. So why this indifference?

11

Was the man trying to bluff his way past him or what? Even as his eyes moved from one to the other, John Knight's eyebrows furrowed together. Something had to be in the wind or was all the earlier proud talk simply trailing the coat? Perhaps the jockeying for position had begun already.

"Can't be as bad as all that…surely not?" Knight's nonchalant tone disguised the thrust of his question. Hands clasped, Chichester sat back. The tips of their blades, so it seemed, had just touched.

"We-ell…all right, but you've gotta know the country," the young baronet rose and joined him. "It's wonderful up there at this time of year but come winter it's a different world."

"Hardly worse than the Beacons, sir…or the upper Malverns for that." John Knight pushed back his wild mane of greying hair. Such pronouncements irritated him. Most of those at the dinner table lived with vast staffs and every luxury known to man, yet they had all impressed upon him how hard life would be as though he was incapable of looking after himself. In addition to Acland, there were the others: a Lord Frobisher from Filleigh and a Mr Exton, some self-acclaimed shipping merchant from Dulverton. Both had been observing him closely during dinner, taking in his every word yet neither was aware he knew of their own interest. Knight shrugged demonstratively and adjusted his cuffs. "Anyway, there'll be plenty to do…plenty."

"Well, there's the hunting and you're a hunting man, I hear?" Although dusk, Acland seemed to be peering into the gardens at nothing in particular.

"Indeed, yes … most certainly. The Wheatland, mainly, up in Worcestershire … damn good they are too." Knight rested an elbow on the mantelpiece.

"And what about the family?" Acland turned towards him, his large, expressive eyes now searching Knight's. "It's desolate up there and you'd have to have 'em on side, you know. Not so sure my lot would make a go of it. I mean…it'd be difficult to imagine Lydia and the youngsters tucked away up in those hills. I dunno." He shrugged as though a suitable answer escaped him then turned back to the business of the deepening gloom beyond the French windows. "The place's empty…really it is. Not a soul anywhere…nothing," he continued as if talking to his own image in the glass. "No one to call on or pass the time of day. No gossip, no coffeehousing." Only then did he look up again. "Nothing at all…hardly a soul to be seen fer weeks on end."

"Then I'll build for 'em…farms, homesteads, even *villages* if needs be." Knight grinned, now relishing the inquisition. "And once the place's up and away, we'll play hard as well. The streams are teeming with trout. Saw 'em yesterday…salmon, too, no doubt." He looked from one to the other. "No…Elizabeth-Jane'll come. It *will* take a special sort, I agree, but she's one o' the best. Born to it, she was. Aghadoe in Kerry's a match for anything I've seen up there…she'll love it."

"So what're yer plans?" Acland remained staring into the dusk.

"Nothing," he snapped, straightening himself. "Nothing whatsoever." Chichester and Acland started, alarmed at the sudden change of tone. "All this is *years* away yet…years and anything can happen," he growled, pushing himself away from the fire. "Anyway, war's in the air right now an' the country's got to get itself through the next few months or there'll be merry hell to pay."

"For sure…for sure," Chichester mused, still surprised at his friend's reaction. Sensing the sudden tension, he hesitated before crouching low as though preparing to spring from his seat. "Right, come on." He banged the arms of his chair and stood briskly. "Suggest we away to the ladies. Eh? Can't do much more about the damned French in here."

2.

Knight waited in the hall. Giles Chichester had arranged the evening especially for him so he might get sight of the opposition and, for that, he was appreciative. But now he was tired and it was time to retire. The musicians had done their worst and gone on their way, dismissed mercifully by his host before the night was done.

Earlier their return to the drawing room had gone better than he dared hope. Long ago his father had warned him that it was often the ladies of those he had to compete against who presented the most danger. Study them, the old man had counselled, study them closely and tonight he had done just that. At dinner, his hostess had placed him near Lady Frobisher. He had been outside her immediate orbit yet close enough for that penetrating voice. Twice he had caught her looking his way and could see she was trying to fathom him out. She had sat assessing him clinically as a dealer might look over a fresh horse and it had grated. Then later, when Elizabeth-Jane took his arm, she had warned him that Catherine Frobisher had been pressing her about her husband's intentions. Paternal advice and his canny sixth sense had served well; that together with what his wife reported made him even more wary.

But there was money there. He could see it on her head, around her neck and on her fingers. Giles Chichester had mentioned the Frobisher fortunes when he told him that it was she, the Countess, who wanted ownership of the moors far more than her man. His Lordship, poor fellow, would no doubt be obliged to bid high; just how high remained to be seen.

Mrs Exton, however, was different. The young Donna Maria Josephine was perhaps a mite too short and a little on the plump side but it mattered not. She was an attractive little thing with her dark Catalan features that radiated humanity to whomsoever she addressed herself. Guests and hosts alike gravitated towards her, drawn irresistibly by her *joie de vivre* and it had amused him when the Frobisher camp had been deserted, albeit temporarily, in favour of the bubbly little Spaniard. No, the evening had gone well but now only the two of them and the Aclands remained. She and her husband were an engaging couple, however he was unlikely to pose a serious threat. But Knight had to be sure.

"Sir Thomas, a brief word if I may." His hand went to the other's shoulder and they turned away together. "Permit me." The Iron Master paused, glanced down at his feet reflectively before looking up again. "Permit me, sir, but I feel I must be honest with you." Again he checked. "Should this Exmoor business develop, I'm more than likely to be having a go myself...you heard that at dinner of course. Giles happened to mention your own interest and I feel you should know my situation."

Acland's head barely moved. It was the directness of the remark that caught him and Knight pressed his point. "It'll all be done very fairly and properly, no doubt...tenders submitted before a select committee and so on." He waited, reaching under his jacket for the point of his shoulder. "But should it ever come to this...I'd hate for there to be any ill feeling between us."

"No, no...my dear fellow." Acland's surprise took him a step back. "Absolutely not and I'm most grateful for you making your position so clear."

Knight bowed. "All right, and my thanks to you but one can never be too sure on these occasions...acrimony creeps around out there, does it not? But look, what I would wish you to know is this...should I go for it and *should* I be fortunate enough to succeed then I would be looking to increase my holding up there even further, to purchase more than just what might be on offer." Once again he paused. "Your estates border those of the Crown. Yes?" He watched Acland studying him. "So...if by chance you ever felt inclined to release any land adjacent to that owned by the Crown, I would be most interested. Should you come to any such decision, sir, then I would ask you to see me first."

Acland took a deep breath. Knight's face had told him nothing. "You mean you'd be interested in buying me out, sir? Is that what you're saying?" The two men stood motionless. Nothing moved save for the rise and fall of their dress shirts.

"Put like that, and for whatever you may care to offer...*yes*. Exactly that." John Knight lifted his chin but his eyes held Acland's. "I would indeed be more than interested to hear about any such ideas. And I'd be generous, y'know, sir. More than generous, in fact." The voice had softened. "On that point you can rest assured. Should it ever come to this then I'd see you well." Knight rolled his left shoulder. "It's just a thought for you to keep in mind...something to keep tucked away. Mmm?"

But it was no idle thought. Even as the Aclands were taking their leave, John Knight's mind was made up. Exmoor, he determined, would be his no matter who or what stood in his way. All of it and more.

Chapter One

A man, mounted well, could ride from Arlington to Molland in less than a day but a carter might take three, and then only if his cart was no more than half full. Whichever route they chose, the great western prow of Exmoor Forest rose up above and beyond them to the north, the highest of the folds sometimes in sunlight but more often shrouded in mist.

Most of the year the land lay deserted. It was adjudged to be a wild and desolate place, forsaken by travellers; a safe refuge for those who feared the law or who wished to be forgotten by the rest of the world. Only in the late spring, some time after the curlews and plovers had returned to their nesting grounds, would shepherds and drovers move up with their flocks to graze the pastures. By the time the autumn harvest below had been gathered they had come back down again.

But this year it was different. Just as the shepherds were setting out, gallopers appeared in the villages, sent urgently into every corner of Devon by the Lord Lieutenant. Their task was to convey news from France, together with instructions as to what precautions were to be taken should the country be invaded. If they could be found, soldiers who had been discharged the year before were recalled to the colours, as were those who had been granted leave of absence. In Plymouth and Torbay the press was out. In Barnstaple, Tiverton and Crediton the Militia assembled. In Exeter the Yeomanry was called to arms.

Everywhere an anxious, scurrying bustle spread across the land. Once parliament knew for certain that the French army had rallied to Napoleon and that the King had fled Paris, it moved with commendable speed. But it had left matters desperately late.

✳

"The man has left Paris...even now he's on the move." The knuckles of the hand gripping the edge of the pulpit were white, the other was shaking. "I'm afraid to have to tell you but it's war. Once again, we are at war with France."

Squire Courtenay sighed and looked up from the papers on the lectern in front of him. "The very devil himself, this...this evil Corsican tyrant and his Marshals are heading for Belgium even as I am speaking to you. Our noble Duke of Wellington is barring their path near Brussels and will not let them pass...of that we can be quite sure. However, the situation is about as grave as it can be."

Two months earlier, as soon as his escape from Elba was discovered, Napoleon had been outlawed by the Congress of Vienna. The good folk of Molland knew nothing about such matters, neither did they understand why they should become involved now. A mighty clash of arms was inevitable and word had come from London that the counties of southern England were to prepare themselves. Molland, like Arlington and everywhere else, had to be ready.

George Courtenay removed his spectacles carefully and rubbed his eyes before surveying the rows of faces looking up at him. The church of St Mary's was packed, and so it should be, the toll bell having rung for an hour. His mind went back to a similar occasion ten years earlier when Napoleon Bonaparte stood at Boulogne with his army, ready to invade.

It had been the squire's duty then, as charged by the Deputy Lieutenant, to read out the Schedules for Conductors and Overseers so that each member of the community knew what had to be done in the event of an invasion. Now he was doing it again. The villagers, he knew, would be as uncomprehending today as they were then. He sighed wearily, replaced his spectacles and read on.

And he was right; it was all quite beyond them. Their tiny world, bounded on one side by high, forbidding moorland and on others by the lush Devon countryside, was not equipped to embrace great matters of state. A day's walk or cart ride for the villagers was South Molton or Tiverton, Barnstaple perhaps, but no further. Exeter and Taunton were for the rich only, while anything further afield was the world of travellers and storytellers.

Molland, as it had done since the Normans built the church, looked after itself and was happy to let the world pass by. The villagers wanted for nothing. Food, shoes and clothes, bread and ale, their homes and farms even; all were the result of their own endeavours. The seasons came and went; there were fairs and feast days, ox roasts and dances. Sometimes the village made merry and sometimes it mourned.

Everybody in Molland knew everybody else and everyone had his place. The village had its own life, the inhabitants answering only to the squire, the vicar and the Almighty himself. Today, though, something was amiss. They had heard rumours but now they came to hear the news as they had been bidden, every one of them packed into the tiny church.

✳

"Squire don't sound none too 'appy," Farmer Rumbelow leant forward. The head in front nodded, unable to escape the hoarse whisper. Fred Loosemore, small boned and ruddy faced and with his hair tied neatly, half turned.

"Aye," he craned his neck backwards. "His lad went off last week...from Lunnon." He swung further round until he could see the hooked nose and black eyebrows behind him. "Went straight off, so 'e did...out to Belgium or some place...went with his regiment."

"Same as they two Steer boys…an' John Pugsley's lad."

"Aye…dare say." Loosemore studied the beady eyes and turned back, adjusting the collar of his smock. Behind them both, a large family squeezed into the next box-pew. Grace Tucker had left her two youngest at home but the other four sat cramped and irritable, dire threats having committed them to sullen silence.

"Stop it," she hissed. "Stay still an' be'ave…us'll be gone in a few minutes." The four year-old, dark and brooding, sat hunched glaring back at his mother. On seeing the conflict, his elder brother smirked provocatively and swung his bare feet. The boy, just eight, sat at the end of the pew, beyond their father and elder sister, while the youngest, no more than a toddler, stood on his father's thigh with one arm around his neck and stared intrusively at the faces behind.

Lionel Tucker listened intently, well aware that those around him had not the slightest idea of what might come to pass. He knew exactly. He had seen it often enough before but now there was to be more of it and, for him, there was no choice.

Grace smiled at her daughter but it was a sad smile. The squire's words were the confirmation she had been dreading. Once Lionel had gone, her lonely battle for survival would begin. She, too, had known war. For almost three years when Lionel was in Spain, she had been left to fend for herself and had prayed that that would be the end of it. Now she would have to go through it all again. The eternal waiting for news, the rumours and the loneliness…just sitting at home and not knowing; all that would be hard to bear. She took hold of her daughter's hand. Emma smiled back and leant against her mother's shoulder.

*

"Ah, Tucker." Squire Courtenay, his address over, stood in the church porch acknowledging the villagers as they filed past. "Congratulations are in order, so they tell me." He smiled genially, almost respectfully, at the figure in front of him, then glanced down at the boy who held his father's hand.

"Oh yes, we were *so* pleased to hear, Corporal Tucker…er…Corporal of Horse now, is it not?" Matilda Courtenay blushed self-consciously. "Oh dear, Captain Courtenay explained what it all meant and it sounds *very* important. He's gone already. His company left last week."

She laughed awkwardly again, this time flustered by the steady gaze of the blue-grey eyes. There was indeed something about the man, something rather special – the finely chiselled features, aquiline nose and handsome mouth. The tall Life Guardsman, seemingly taller than her son, was a far cry from the run-of-the-mill farmhand, yet he was a Devon man, born and bred. "Thank you, ma'am," Tucker inclined his head graciously.

17

"How's the wound now, Tucker? Salamanca wasn't it?" Courtenay felt behind his own back as if to show he knew where the sabre had cut. "Nasty business that…very unpleasant. Took some time as well, eh?"

"Talevera actually, sir." Tucker turned back to the squire. "Way back in o' nine, believe it or not. When we were with the Third Dragoons…the Prince of Wales's. But it's fine now, sir, the back, that is. Fine thank you."

"Well, good luck, my man," Courtenay took his hand again. "We'd heard you'll be off in a couple of days or so and no wonder, the Duke's screaming for every man he can get, what? Oh…and Tucker." The older man leant forward, turning away from his wife. "Look, should anything happen…I mean, you know. Not that it will, of course, but if…well…we'll see to things back here. Your wife's in very good hands, ye know."

"Aye, sir, and thank you for that." He nodded appreciatively and moved on, edging through the crowded porch and into the warmth of the spring sunshine. The villagers stood talking in groups, their voices little more than urgent whispers. Lionel and Grace eased their way past, nodding politely yet eager to be on their own. As soon as they were clear they stepped out for there was much to be done and precious little time.

Even as she took her husband's arm, three of their four children ran ahead to the lychgate but not Jack. The older boy stopped short, turned and waited, watching his father's every move as they approached him. He had been quiet all day. First one hand then the other took hold of the arm which he pressed hard against his cheek. He looked up to catch his father's eye but turned away suddenly, ashamed of his own tears.

2.

Old Walter Thorne lay in the sun with his legs apart and a blue linen kerchief over his face. The top of his chest, under its mat of grizzled, white hair, had been scalded pink by the midday sun. His tankard had toppled where he had let it fall and was now visited by a lone wasp busying itself with the last drops of cider. Lionel Tucker, lying with his back towards the recumbent figure, shook with silent mirth and took the stalk from his mouth. "Yer Dad's away, Ben," he nodded in the direction of the snores. "Away with the fairies."

"Aye…let's us know an' all." Ben Thorne, swarthy and dark jowled, smacked angrily at an insect on his leg then inspected the mess. "Can't abide the sun, father can't?" He tipped his felt hat to the back of his head. "Good job us've finished pullin' they docks an' thistles, eh Fred?"

"Bootiful job." Fred Loosemore jumped down from the wagon. They had been working since sunrise and, after their lunch, would work on until the cool of the day. "What with this y'ere weather comin' on, 'tis a good job done … beautiful. Tilly'n Grace'll be here directly with summat to eat." The carters and farmhands lay silently together, some basking in the heat, others sheltering under the blackthorn hedge, each alone with his thoughts. Devon men, one and all, they were not prone to panic or alarm yet they were worried. Like everyone else, they had heard the news. The squire had spoken of war, and of those about to leave the village once more for some strange sounding place to fight against people they knew nothing about.

"Be off early then, Lionel?" Ben Thorne hawked noisily then scratched under his smock, gazing idly to where the far hedge ran down to the river.

"Cock crow." Lionel leant back on one elbow. "Away by four anyways…gotta be. Orders are to meet up with some lancers and Redcoats at Tiverton afore six, then kick on for Taunton." He paused to pick at a tooth. "Should be several there, then us'll be movin' on to the London road…pick up a number more from Dene Gate then stop for the night at Ilminster."

"Cuh…there'll be several of yer then?" He looked at Lionel vacantly with one hand raised to shield the sun. "Thought 'twas only a few…just you an' one or two others, like."

"No, 'tis nuthin' like that, Ben. Nuthin' like that at all. There'll be hundreds of 'em, literally hundreds…right up and down the country. Old Nosey's bin 'ollering fer every man 'e can get." Lionel sat looking at the others who had stirred and were listening. "An' you should see the state of some of 'em, tho'…some of they lot back at barracks. Cuh, I dunno."

"Rubbish, eh?"

"Aye…dragged right up from the bottom. Just kids, too, mostly. Old Man'll go daft when 'e sees that lot."

"Be seein' the other lads will yer…you know, Alf an' Charlie Steer, or Garth?" The carter wiped the back of his neck. "They'm s'posed to have gone on last week, weren't they?"

"Doubt I will," Tucker pulled at another grass. "There's too many of 'em…far too many. Might see Garth, I s'pose. Seeing he's with the Yeomanry. Aye…could be seeing 'im."

The three men turned to study the commotion in the ditch. It was Old Walter. The retired carter gurgled and coughed throatily before struggling on to his elbows. "What d'yer reckon, lad? Cor, dearie me," he yawned noisily then wiped at his mouth. "Come to much, will it, Lionel? This Boney bloke…he's some boy, 'e is."

"Can't say," Lionel shrugged. "Wish 'e'd give over, though…we've all had enough, that's fer sure."

"Pack it in, lad...pack it in when's done an' finished with." Ben Thorne asserted. "Stop home here with Gracie an' the littl'uns. You've done yer bit an'more, you 'ave, boy. That job's comin' up at the stables, isn't it?"

"Aye, so I've heard," Lionel Tucker nodded thoughtfully. "Squire Courtenay's talked of another, an' all...down West Anstey way. Oh aye, there's work to be had...plenty of that."

Lunch, when Tilly Loosemore and Grace Tucker brought it in the donkey cart, was a noisy affair. The children ran amongst them all shouting excitedly, the boys rolling and tumbling in the hedgerow, the girls crying out to be left in peace before running after the others again. Lionel took his leave early.

He hated farewells and his friends knew it. One by one their rough hands took his, shoulders were clasped, heads pulled towards one another and backs slapped. When Ben Thorne flicked the reins, Tilly wept, unable to look at the Tuckers as the haywain lurched through the narrow gateway. Even Old Walter blinked and turned away as he let go of Lionel's hand.

3.

He slipped away from the cottage as he said he would, just his wife and the two eldest up to see him go. Grace adjusted his service tunic under the leather belt, Jack rubbed yet more fat onto the blade of his cavalry sword then knelt to buckle his father's spurs. Emma stood alone by the open window, watching intently and shivering, her shoulders hunched against the dawn chill. Both fists were at her mouth. The time had come.

"Farewell, my son." The boy offered his hand awkwardly but Lionel pulled the child into him. Emma came too, a locket and chain in her hand. He saw it was the one he had given her when he came back from Spain and took it reluctantly, his other arm holding her close. He turned towards Grace noticing her tightly drawn mouth and the tears in her soft brown eyes.

"'Twon't be long, my love...can't be long this time." He reached over Jack and drew his wife towards him, the four standing huddled together, shaken by each others' sobs. "Come, m'dears. Come now." Lionel lifted his head. "Must be away or I'll be late...come now," he whispered, stepping carefully away from his children's arms. "It won't be long...then I'm 'ome fer good, promise."

He strode briskly towards the stables not daring to look back. Further down the valley a low mist hung over the river. Somewhere a cuckoo was calling. The sun, although not yet warming the Exmoor hills, was on its way, rising inexorably towards the horizon, sweeping before it the last remnants of night.

✳

Across the Channel and three hundred miles to the south a pair of mallards sprang from the water. A low mist covered the River Vaucoule where it turned sluggishly by the large clump of willows. Here, too, a cuckoo was calling but the French standard at the masthead of Chateau Crespieres hung limp in the morning calm.

The first meeting would be in an hour's time and it would be an important one; momentous decisions would have to be made. As the lean, redheaded figure strode purposefully along the bank, head bowed in thought, more duck rose. For Michel Ney, Marshal of France and Prince of the Moskowa, and for count-less others, the long march towards Belgium would begin today.

4.

The two men picked their way through the soft mud. One cursed as water splashed on to his black boots and white buckskins. It had been raining hard all night and for much of the day before as well. "Get Blacker going with his whetstone." Lionel Tucker turned to the Corporal. "Listen, I want a double point on all the swords, d'you hear. They say it'll probably be the Cuirassiers against us and they've got body armour...it'll be spearing as well as slicing today, my friend."

"Aye, staff...no problem." Corporal Chambers stopped, still in the mud. "Goin' to be like that, will it? One of those?" The man checked himself. "Hey, staff, seen the new officer they've sent us, have you? The cornet, the one that's come down from Brussels...nort but a young boy" His rugged face looked haggard. Sleep had been impossible, the rumours coming back down the road from Quatre Bras and the weather had kept them on edge. Three nights earlier they had been billeted in the village of Waterloo but had been told to move on. The squadron had managed to squeeze themselves into a straggly hazel copse to the north of the road but of life's creature comforts there had been no sign. Men and horses were sodden to the very skin and now chilled to the bone. They were hungry and they were apprehensive about what lay ahead.

"'Ere, come on, keep moving my son." Tucker pushed the man forward. "The lads have got to be sorted...only a couple of hours now, and we'll be in the saddle." He coughed and spat. "But go on...we knew one was on the way. What's up with him then?"

"Nuthin'. No, all right 'e is but can't be no more'n seventeen."

"Poor little toad." Tucker grimaced. "What sort of chance has 'e got, for Christ's sake? Picked a right day to start earning his keep, didn't he? The French are good...damned good, an' they're going to fight like hell today." He paused and looked round. "Now then, hang on a minute...." He stopped again, this time the two of them watching the three troopers struggling with armfuls of fodder.

He took the corporal's arm. "Get over there an' get the swords going now, will yer...an' get the bivouacs down and away. Tell Crowley and that other fella...

Burnett. Tell 'im I want all the fires out sharpish. Right?" Lionel Tucker looked across the waterlogged campsite. "There's two or three over there, look...I want cloaks rolled and saddle bags packed. After that it's work on the horses, all the way in." He walked on, looking up as a skein of geese winged their way overhead, then stopped by the first charger.

The big bay was hungry mad, snuffling noisily on the flat of his hand hoping for the taste of some morsel or other. He ran his hands down the neck and across the withers; the line of ribs were clearly visible, the bones hard and sharp. The coat, once healthy and glistening, had lost its sheen.

"Steady, old thing," he whispered, his cheek against the soft muzzle. "Get you through this an' we'll be home again. Eh? We'll see to it...eh...there now." As his hand moved down the body, the animal lifted its hind leg obediently, turning to see what was happening. Tucker picked at the mud then bent to sniff. The hard frog had softened.

"Ugh...." He scowled and wrinkled his nose before gently lowering the hoof and patting the animal's rump. Half the horses had the painful infection and there was little to be done until they were clear of the water and mud. Tucker looked up. "How're their feet down there, Smith? Bloody thrush, here look...this'uns got it bad an' all."

The trooper smiled warmly. He and his Corporal of Horse had served together for years. Smith should have had tapes on his arm by now but there had been problems, several of them down the years. "Fine, staff. I've checked all the ones on this line. Just seeing if I can do anything with this cut here." The two bent down to examine the torn flesh. "I've had sulphur and lard on it...not sure whether to bandage it or not."

"Leave it open." Tucker stood back to check the animal. "Aye, let it breathe and we'll see what she's like later...if she's still with us that is." He patted her chest and shook his head. "Poor old things, eh...they know summats up, same as we do, an' they just stand waiting for us. Loyal as anything, they are...man couldn't ask for more." The mare pushed her head against him. "All she wants is a meadow of grass and a youngster running beside her. Don't you, dear, eh...and we've got to go and give 'er this."

"D'you reckon it'll be hard, today?" The trooper, his hair cropped short, looked up quizzically. "I mean...you know, real hard, like?"

"Biggest yet...so they say." The smile was grim. "And the French'll be coming right at us...Boney knows its all or nuthin this time. They reckon he'll start with the guns about midday." Tucker paused. "How're the lads, Smudge?"

"Same as ever." The trooper shrugged aware that his old nickname had been used. "Y'know...some of 'em made one hell of a racket last night...bit o' drink an' that. Others quiet...keepin' pretty much to themselves, like. Everyone knows what's coming." Their eyes met. "Even the youngsters…couple 'ere not seventeen so they reckon. Came in last night…after you'd gone."

"Judas be damned," Tucker shook his head. "Sixteen years old. I've a daughter not far off that…dear God."

"Aye, never get's no better, does it?" The old trooper scratched his head. "We must've bin right bloody daft signing on for this lot. Jus' look at it will yer." As far as they could see, columns and groups of men and horses were stirring in the dawn light. The smoke from hundreds of damp fires hung still and heavy in the air, as though pressed low by the clouds above. At last, at last it had stopped raining but that was all. There was no wind to dry them, the trees were not moving and voices carried across the landscape. They knew that, even now and barely a mile away, the French were forming up. Thousands upon thousands of men on both sides, all waiting and watching each one wondering what the day would bring. Nobody, so it seemed, in their right mind could have volunteered for this. "Christ, we must've bin mad…jus' look at the state of it all."

Lionel Tucker walked slowly towards the line of bivouacs, now being packed away. Some of his men were no more than boys yet that one chance remark about Emma had sent a sharp pang lancing through him. His hand went under his tunic to where her locket lay against the warmth of his throat. Grace and the children…Molland and Exmoor…Ben Thorne and Fred Loosemore; he could see them all so clearly yet they were a whole world away. What would he have given to be there with them just now? Still, just a couple of months or so they reckoned, but even that was long enough. He swallowed and lifted his forage cap to wipe at his cheek then took in a lungful of air.

5.

"All right, just this one, then no more tonight." Regimental Surgeon Macey grumbled to himself as he reached behind him to re-tie the blood-soaked apron. He had been working since dawn. Now, grey with fatigue, the second shift of assistants were as exhausted as their predecessors. Their arms, tunics, faces even, were covered with blood from the endless succession of wounded that had been brought into the makeshift hospital.

"Orderly, get rid of this lot," he kicked out at the half-barrel under the operating table, now full to the brim with shards of flesh and remnants of shattered limbs.

"Smithson." The surgeon called over his shoulder then nodded towards the table in front of him. "Get that lamp over here…*here*, look. Come on," he barked hoarsely. "Get a bloody move on."

Macey bent over his pile of bloodied instruments. "Right, let's see we've got everything. Bone-saw…forceps…amputating knife." He was checking aloud to himself, picking up the tools of his trade one at a time. "Knife's blunt," he muttered. "Blunt as hell, dammit. Too late...too late. Now then...scalpel... probes...hooks," he continued. "Right then, bring him in."

The surgeon turned to a second tub, pushed aside the yellowy-grey scum and scrubbed vigorously at the nails of one hand. "Above the knee, you say? Then I'll need three to hold him...so get yourselves in here." He peered at the body on the operating table. "Now'n, lad. What's yer name? Eh?" Macey leant forward, listening with his head inclined.

"Couldn't tell us, sir," the first man interrupted. "Bloody robbers got there first. Took everything, they did. All 'is uniform...the lot. Stripped 'im half naked except fer 'is one boot...bastards!" The man laughed and shook his head. "Looks odd really, don'it...just the one leg like that. Lookin' at 'im though, I reckon 'e were a cavalryman, sir...Life Guards most like. They was operatin' down there. Sods cut his ring finger off, an' all." He held up the wounded man's hand to show where the robber's knife had severed the finger at the second joint.

Macey shrugged. "Spoils of war, lad," he sighed. "So much for our fellow man...I've seen it all." The three men stretched the wounded soldier flat on the blood soaked cloth. One of them lay across his chest, gripping the far side of the table, the second held his right leg while the third held down the putrefying stump of the left knee.

"No...no...please God, no." The words were spat as the head thrashed from side to side.

"Right, here we go," the surgeon grunted, bending over the shattered leg. He cut quickly, the six inch blade of the amputating knife slicing through the swollen flesh around the wound, exposing the splintered bone. The man lying across the chest glanced nonchalantly as the mouth in front of him gaped wide before each shriek. The three of them had to fight hard to control the body bucking and twisting under their weight.

"Bone-saw," Macey cried, holding out his hand and moving aside so that one of his assistants could reach the arterial flow of blood. The second man stifled a yawn as he watched the saw grating back and forth, biting ever deeper into the white bone. The surgeon's hands moved quickly, rolling the flaps of skin together under the wound. He took the curved needle from his mouth, checked the silk then sewed swiftly.

"Show me the face wound," he commanded, pushing the first man to one side. "Sponge," he called before bending low to swab at the bone between ear and mouth.

Suddenly he stopped and stood up. "No, it's hopeless...useless," he said to no one in particular. "Gangrene in the stump, half his face cut away and the crows've had his eyes." He shook his head. "There's no point…get him out to the waiting room."

*

Three hours later, Corporal of Horse Lionel John Tucker died, alone and unattended. His left leg had been shattered by grape shot seconds after a French cuirass had slashed down the side of his face, peeling flesh from bone. His horse, shot from under him in the wild charge, had somersaulted, pinning his body. For two days he had lain there trapped, drifting in and out of consciousness, his cries going unheard.

The robbers had got there first and done their gruesome worst, taking even the child's locket hanging from the thin chain around his neck. One of them had forced it open only to hurl it aside in disgust when he found nothing more than a lock of fair hair. Then came the birds, cautiously to begin with but then hopping closer with their heads cocked warily. Eventually one had jumped onto his head, crowing triumphantly before the beak drove down.

Chapter Two

"Never noticed that before." John Knight, hands behind his back, nodded towards the window. "Over there, across the street. It lies north-south." He had arrived early. Lunch was still half an hour away and he had accepted his host's invitation to wait with him.

It had been the church that caught his eye. He had been looking down on the tangled mass of carts and carriages locked helplessly with other street vehicles and hand carts as they tried to push past each other in the narrow spaces between the hawkers and vendors. The hubbub, punctuated by shouts and loud cries, forced him to raise his voice even though the windows were closed. London, he noted grimly, was grinding to a halt. They would have to dig it up and start again. Lombard Street, ancient, cobbled and little more than an open drain, could not cope with the modern traffic. The elegant lines and steeple of the Wren building rose like a symbol of peace and calm amidst the mayhem.

"Church of St Edmund the King and Martyr." Sir James Esdaile sat back in his studded moroccan leather chair. "S'posed to be the only one in London like that...whole of England some say." He had left Knight deep in thought, reflecting carefully so he hoped, on his last question. This sudden remark from the window had taken him unawares.

"Mmm." Knight rolled his shoulder and bent to look closer. "Put the main door on the street so you fellas can get in easily." He turned and saw the banker's surprise. "Oh yes, to beg God's forgiveness while robbing the rest of us blind, eh?" He smiled wryly. "Come on, Esdaile, you know me better than that." Knight put his hands on the back of the armchair and leant towards the portly little banker. "You lot never change. But listen...I've got plenty enough capital in *hand*, for God's sake. Hardly need to come along with the begging bowl, do I now? Just called out of courtesy, damn it."

Once more the room fell silent. It irritated Knight that he was never able to quite read his banker's mind. James Esdaile gave nothing away, least of all money. His face, with that sallow flesh pulled tight across the high cheek bones, reminded him of the dockland Chinese, the more so when his dark hair was slicked back like it was today. His eyes, as usual, were screwed half shut and now quite devoid of emotion, gave no clue as to what lay behind the mask.

"Not the point, my dear good man." Esdaile sighed and inclined his head. Knight had seen the baleful expression before and knew the banker was getting into his stride. "Look, it's still an awful lot of money and we've checked with the Barnstaple Bank on land values." He paused. "You're proposing to put down a very high bid, ye know...way over the top. And for *what?*"

"Because I want the place," Knight snapped. He stood up straight and felt for

26

his shoulder. "I can afford it and that's that." The two men turned at the soft knock on the door. Durnford Morgan, tall, fair haired and a mite stooped, his face creased seemingly with worry, slid into the room. The heavy door, blackened with age, clunked shut behind him. Knight studied the new arrival. So here was Esdaile's blue-eyed boy. He acknowledged the deferential nod of his head and distanced himself from the two men, far enough to offer them privacy yet close enough to hear. Esdaile had told him about the younger man and his family's connections with exiled French nobility.

The banker had asked Morgan to bring in the business of the day. Luncheon at the George and Vulture, only a short walk from where they stood, would be sure to continue late into the afternoon and he wanted his desk cleared of business beforehand. Knight, Esdaile sensed, was in one of his more difficult moods and would have to be handled carefully. For weeks they had been discussing the expansion of his four biggest iron foundries and now, suddenly and without warning, he was talking about some madcap venture in the wilds of the south-west, buying great tracts of mountain and bog. But Knight was not mad, far from it, so there had to be something behind it all. Whatever it was the man's tail was up and, as he reached for the file Morgan was offering, Esdaile pursed his lips.

Morgan summarised swiftly, sometimes leaning forward to point out details of figures, highlighting discrepancies and explaining the more complex accounting procedures. He placed the files in front of his master one at a time, removing them deftly once matters had been concluded. Only twice, when Esdaile asked his advice, did he speak forcefully. Knight continued to stare at the chaos in the street outside but his head was cocked.

"What to do, eh?" Esdaile tapped the red folder he was balancing in his hand. "What to do with this fella, Stainforth? Look at the mess he's in, for Heaven's sake." Knight could imagine the round, screwed up face searching Morgan's for clues.

"Sorry, John," the banker called across the room. "Just got to get these bits and pieces out of the way." The figure at the window half raised a hand. "Now then," he turned back to Morgan. "What's your view?"

"Call in the loan, sir. All of it." Morgan was adamant. "We have to while his assets still cover the mortgage.

"A bit hard, don't you think?" Esdaile spoke quietly, his head moving from side to side as he weighed the matter. "Money's tight, just now...an' going to get tighter still. The wars have bled us white...all of us, and we don't want a name for breaking those who need us the most, y'know."

"We can't afford not to." Knight listened as the younger man stood his ground. Morgan was hard, all right, and he smiled cynically. Those slender, long-fingered hands and the soft, cultured voice had never known hardship. The estates around Pelham Hall near Woodstock had kept young Morgan and his family well insulated from the harsh realities of life. The boy had never felt the cold fear of debt, had never been forced to beg for a loan. Indifference to the woes of others came naturally.

"Hmm. I'll think…let me ponder awhile." Esdaile glanced at Knight, his face breaking into one of his wide, cat-like smiles. "Apologies again, John. Wretched things take time, y'know." He rose nonetheless, pulling at his cuffs. "But all right, that's enough for now, Morgan. Get across to the tavern, will you. Make sure everything's ready and look after Sir Crispin if he's there. We're upstairs at the back…the little green room."

"And see to my team on the way, would you." John Knight stepped back from the window and cleared his throat. "The blue brougham just across the street, there look…the four-wheeler. Tell Jenkins, he's the taller of the two in my green livery, tell him to get round to Cornhill and to tuck himself in behind Saint Michael's. Wait there 'til I call. What say you, James…four?"

"No later." Esdaile turned, allowing the steward to help him into his smooth, sea-blue redingote, then turned back to face the man while his servant adjusted the tassel fastenings and brushed at the cloth. He took his top hat, cane and grey gloves. Knight had no idea where the banker found the latest fashion but the three quarter length coat and new fangled grey trousers did nothing for the squat figure. And the high, silk hat, crammed hard down, squashed his face. Sir James Esdaile, he considered, looked like a bloated and overdressed frog.

Far better, he thought, and more practical too, were his own traditional pantaloons and long, brown cavalier boots for getting around the City. At least the muck, human and animal, was kept from the clothes. He waited until the second steward had adjusted his cloak then followed his host down the wide marble staircase and out into the street.

✳

Morgan met them as they emerged from Birching Lane where it ran into the broader Cornhill, stepping back as Esdaile brushed aside a barefoot waif selling flowers. As they turned, Knight caught sight of Gresham's Exchange, standing proud and massive, high above the roofline and bathed in sunlight. "Sir Crispin's already there," Morgan advised. "And smoking one of his favourite clays as usual." He grinned and rubbed his hands, remembering how his master detested the thick, cloying smoke. "Allow me to lead the way, gentlemen."

Knight knew the room well and grinned warmly at the sight of Sir Crispin seated by the coal fire. 'Farmer' Barclay, head of Barclay, Tritton and Company, always dressed for the countryside, in deference to the many landowners who rang the heavy bell outside his Lombard Street offices. His Lincoln green jacket, faced with russet lapels sat easily on his broad shoulders, while beneath, a yellow, colourfully embroidered silk waistcoat strained against its buttons. His grey-brown hair, longer now than Knight could remember, was tied untidily, allowing several loose strands to fall on to his collar. All that plus his full nose and bushy, red eyebrows, completed the picture of a prosperous yeoman farmer.

But he was none of that. Sir Crispin Barclay was one of London's most astute agricultural bankers and that was why Esdaile had asked him to join them for lunch. Knight observed drily to himself that the meal of West Country trout followed by a shoulder of venison set the scene admirably.

They ate and drank quickly, small talk and gossip punctuating the short silences. Knight knew they were set on dissuading him from his rural adventure and he did not have long to wait. "'Tis more than enough money, John." Barclay, leaning back to allow the waiter access to the table, coughed loudly then drew in a deep lungful of the warm, smoke-filled air before coughing again louder still. The effort made him groan and he wiped his eyes, before drawing on his pipe once more. "We've had a look," the deep voice wheezed squeakily between his gasps. "Young Cutliffe from Barnstaple's been up there an' we've got his report."

There was a silence. Knight stared into the fire and it was Esdaile who spoke. "D'you really want to take on both at once, John...your foundries *and* this Exmoor place?" He grimaced and waved away Barclay's cloud of smoke before continuing. "Yer time and effort'll be divided, y' know, and that's dangerous." Knight sniffed. "The iron works must come first...surely to God?"

"What's the opposition, John?" Barclay heaved his bulky frame from the chair, stretched for the bottle of port and helped himself. "D'you know who they are and what sort of hand they've got?"

"Three of 'em, at least." Knight sat deep and long in his chair, lying almost with his hands thrust into his pockets and his legs outstretched. He was scowling, hating the searching questions. Some of his hair had fallen forward, half covering his face. "The Barnstaple Bank reckon there'll be more hats than that...eight maybe, a dozen even."

"Numbers don't matter." Barclay wagged a large, hairy finger. "'Tis *who* they are that counts. Once we know that, we'll know what they've got, *then* we'll know how best to play things."

"That's where young Morgan can come in." Esdaile, still perched on the edge of his dining chair, looked from one to the other. Knight glanced his way, not lifting his head but raising both eyebrows to see better. "We're sending him to the Barnstaple Bank...we're their agents up here as it happens and they've asked us for help. The new North Devon Bank...that's Pyke and Law," he nodded to Barclay. "They're starting to make merging noises and Barnstaple have asked us to investigate."

"Morgan? Him? What can he do?" Knight tipped his head back and drained his glass. "Still wet behind the ears from what I can see."

"Don't bet on it." Esdaile saw Barclay smile. "Sharp as a costermonger and got a damned good brain at that. Ambitious too."

"Arrogant young beggar as well," Knight struggled up in his chair. He had heard that Morgan was soon due in North Devon and had it in mind to ask for his assistance but Esdaile had come to his rescue. He needed a financial spy, somebody to go ferreting around the West Country banking world. It had to be somebody sharp, someone who knew how the system worked, where the deposits and shadow accounts lay, how assets were liquidated and how long it all took to amass substantial capital. It needed to be somebody discreet; discreet yet ruthless. Morgan had the right air about him he had to admit and he grunted. "Ambitious you say, James? What's he want then? Looks like he's got most of it."

"Aha no, not our young Mr Durnford Morgan. He's after going up north…up to your part of the world, in fact. That's where he and the other youngsters see all the action. Steam, rail cars, canals, mines…a whole new world and new opportunities. They all feel too constrained down here…too many old fogeys like you an' me and they want to get on. That's him…that's what the boy's after." Knight said nothing. Still hunched and still frowning, he concentrated on the empty glass he was twiddling between his fingers.

"Now then, John…land values." Barclay glowered in concentration as he scraped at the bowl of his pipe with a silver fruit knife. "We reckon ten shillings an acre's about right, perhaps up to a guinea for the very best but no more. That's *land* value mind, anything else there and it'll increase, of course. But there's nothing more than bog and sedge up there…is there?" He blew into the bowl and cocked an eye in Esdaile's direction, the two of them watching as Knight crossed and uncrossed his legs. "Or d'ye know something we don't?"

"I'll have the answer soon enough." The words came slowly. "If you want to know, I'm getting a mineral survey done…right now as it happens." He sat up and swept back his hair. Now it was his turn. "There's been a whole deal of mining down there…since way back. Roman times, so we hear. What I don't yet know is whether they're just a few tired old seams or," he paused and looked up. "Or whether the place is draped over a whole mountain of the stuff…ore and tin, and copper perhaps."

"When will you know?" Esdaile stared at Knight, his face creased and with his eyes all but shut as though he was looking into the sun. Barclay sucked on his pipe.

"Can't say for sure." Suddenly, Knight stood and stretched. "Could be a year or so before we know for sure but the place will have gone by then. Just don't know." He threw up his hands. "But listen to me, can you imagine what that land would be worth if it *was* sitting on top of deposits like that...half of it, even? Can you *imagine?* Why it'd make all the mines in Cornwall lumped together look like nothing. And *that*, my friends, is why I'm going for the place." He paused for a moment. "I could do with some help to be sure but...well, I can manage all right. But then..." Knight looked from one to the other. "Or d'you want in with me?"

He had trumped them. They were cornered and he could see it at once. Any hopes of them getting him to back off now had gone. He had turned the discussion around and the bankers sensed a deal; a deal that could do them all very well. "But what if there's nothing there?" Barclay spoke quietly, a note of uncertainty creeping into his voice. "There might be little or nothing up there, John. Perhaps nothing at all."

"Then we lose." Knight's voice was harsh. "You, James and me...we all lose, the three of us together, but I stand to lose the lion's share." The two bankers looked at each other and Esdaile spoke first.

"I'll get something drawn up," he suggested, nodding slowly as he tapped the ends of his fingers together. "Just a rough draft at this stage but something to work from. Eh? What shall we say...a third each?"

"No," Knight shook his head. "Not at all. Fifty two to me and twenty four to each of you...then you can never hold it against me."

They both turned to Barclay who was sittting very still. "Mmm, all right. Let's see it on paper first though," he murmured. "Sounds interesting enough...let's have a look."

2.

Reg Vellacott rammed the long tapwhip into its holder, hauled himself to his feet and stepped wearily to the ground. Removing his high top hat, he mopped the sweat from his face and blew. It was just one o'clock on a cloudless June afternoon and the sun was blazing down. The heavily built coachman was far hotter than was good for him; his mouth was paper dry and his mind set on that jug of ale.

"'Tis Molland, Ladies and Gentlemen," he called over his shoulder to the coach behind him. "Ten minutes, that's all we've got, then we're on to Barnstaple. Just ten minutes mind." As he slipped the fob watch back into his waistcoat pocket, he glanced across to where the ostler's lads were already washing down the four bays. Loosening his collar, he limped towards the front door of The London Inn, wondering how he was going to break the news. Behind him the passengers alighted more slowly. One of them, a tall, slim young man with a slight stoop, dressed elegantly and with his fair hair well pomaded, moved into the shade and stood alone.

"*Albert.*" Vellacott leant against the front doorframe, his body heaving after the

31

climb up the cobbled steps from the road. He hawked loudly then peered into the gloomy interior. The air was cool but the smell of sour ale was sharp and his nose wrinkled. "Come on there, lad," he chuckled at the approaching shadow. "Show us a step…got a right raging thirst 'ere. 'Tis devilish hot out there." The landlord waited patiently as the red-faced coachman leaned further and further back to catch every last drop of the cool bitter, then held his hand for the empty tankard.

"Listen, Albert." The coachman gasped and his eyes bulged as he fought for air. "Here's the mail. Right? Now 'en, there's summat in y'ere I don't much care for." Bailey watched as he rummaged deep into the mailbag before reappearing with a well-sealed buff envelope. "Here now," he said quietly. "I've delivered several of these today, three back in Dulverton…an' one at Anstey. 'Tis bad news, I'm telling you. Bad news, that's what 'tis."

"'Bout the battle two weeks back? Waterloo was it?" The landlord watched as Vellacott nodded. "Who's it for then?" Bailey leant forward to peer at the address then stood aghast. "*Cuh*…I'll be beggared…'tis Grace, Grace Tucker," he whispered hoarsely. "Our Gracie down at Mill Cottage. About 'er Lionel, eh? D'you suppose that's what's 'tis about?"

"'Fraid so, if that's his name," the coachman replied. "Casualties from the battle, that's what they're writing about. Could be he's just hurt bad, mind." He paused then shook his head. "But who'd go writing about that sort of thing?"

✳

Albert Bailey weighed the envelope carefully. He looked down at the name again, willing it to disappear, then glanced up, shading his eyes against the brightness. Further up the village street and set back on a rise was the church and he could see the door was open. Earlier there had been a funeral and the vicar would still be there. Bailey sighed and pulled a solemn face before tackling the long climb.

The Reverend John Froude, Vicar of St Mary's, Molland, hurried fussily down the aisle, muttering to himself as his cassock billowed behind him. Greetings over he listened earnestly as the landlord explained himself. "True as I'm standing here, vicar," Bailey spluttered. "'Tis more'n likely, an' I reckon someone should be with the lass when 'er opens it. Someone what knows about these things."

"You're meaning me, I suppose," Froude's eyebrows rose in anticipation. "Is that it, Albert?"

"Reckon so, vicar. Well…I mean, you know how 'tis. If 'tis bad news, then perhaps you should be there, like."

"Yes…quite so," Froude was frowning. "Right, thank you, Albert. I'd better get round right away."

❉

As he approached the cottage, Parson Froude heard the sound of laughter and children's voices. He called out, as he always did, and the three of them rushed towards him. The eldest, a girl of twelve, reached him first and stopped suddenly before looking down shyly. She was dressed simply in a faded cotton dress and had woven a string of daisies between her long flaxen locks. Her cheeks were flushed and her eyes shining as though she and the others had been playing.

"Hello, Emma, it's only me," Froude smiled encouragingly. "Is you mother there? I wonder if I might have a word." The barefoot girl leapt away calling out for the parson to follow her.

"Ah, Mrs Tucker." Froude cleared his throat. "Good afternoon, how nice. May I perhaps…might I come in for a moment?" Grace Tucker brushed a heavy strand of hair back from her cheek. She was thin, worn and tired yet glanced sharply at the visitor. Immediately suspicious, her eyes were at once wide and alert.

"Yes, yes…come in, vicar, please do. Sorry about the mess," she muttered, waving her arm. "'Tis a bit difficult on me own, just now." She caught her breath, suddenly afraid of what might have brought him. "'Tis easier when Lionel's here. No news, I s'pose?" her eyebrows lifted anxiously.

"Nothing definite yet," Froude ducked under the low portal. The dark, musty interior reeked heavily of wood ash and over-cooked food. "Now then…I've got something for you…I think we ought to see it now. Is there somewhere where we can sit…just quietly for a minute or two?"

Grace motioned for him to wait, then called softly to her three older children, the ones he had met outside. Two glanced at the parson, the boy with straw hair who was still breathing heavily smiled cheerily. The third merely sniffed and watched his mother intently as she began to scrape at a large honeycomb. Bending low under the far door, she ushered them outside handing a spoon to each child, stooping low to say something he could not hear.

Balancing a toddler on one hip, she dragged a bench to the table and sat, sweeping at the flies. "You've come about Lionel, haven't you?" she queried, surprised at the calmness of her own voice. "I can tell, you know. That's why you're here, isn't it?"

"I'm none too sure about that, Mrs Tucker." Froude replied, studying the letter in his hand. "But, look, we had this come for you today. It's from London and the mail brought several of them along the way. Shall I open it and see what it says?" The young woman let her eyes fall and nodded but her hands were clenched tight. "Yes," she whispered. "Tell me what they have to say…all of it mind."

The parson tore open the seal, unfolded the letter, then turned it to read the formal hand. "*It is with the deepest regret that I am bound to inform you.........*" He read on swiftly, his heart having jumped at the shock.

"Well?" Grace Tucker looked up. "It's Lionel, isn't it. Has he been hurt or summat...summat like that?"

"Yes, I'm afraid so," he replied. "I'm afraid it's bad news." He paused, still reading the letter but now chosing his own words. "I'm so sorry... but Lionel fell at Waterloo. He was killed in the great battle...killed in action and they've buried him out there with the others." He reached out and took her hand, gently rubbing his thumb across her knuckles. Their eyes met. "I'm sorry," he said quietly, "So very sorry. They say he died instantly, killed by a musket ball. He wouldn't have known anything, that's what they say."

"*No*," she gasped. "Oh no...dear God no." Grace sat staring at him, motionless, her face drained of colour. Once she looked down and shook her head but no more than that. Even the child in her lap was quiet, simply raising one tiny fist to wipe at the dirt around its mouth. The three she had sent outside crept back and were standing silently by the door, licking the remnants of honey from their spoons.

At last she spoke out. "What am I to do?" she muttered, shaking her head. "There's six here to feed and clothe. Where's the keep coming from?" She shrugged helplessly. "What's to come of us, vicar?" she appealed, her voice suddenly raised higher. "What are we to do...now he's bin...now he's gone? He has, y'know an' it'll be winter soon. Then what?"

3.

Parker, Knight's butler, had been waiting for the riders. His master had insisted on it. As the three approached the house, riding slowly up the gravelled drive, the tall butler noted the fine clothes of the man in front and the quality of his mount. Even before he pulled up, a footman, summoned by his white glove, ran forward to hold the horse's head. Parker now stepped from the door way. "Welcome to Castle Heights, sir. A good journey, I trust?"

"Thank you, yes." Durnford Morgan dismounted, eased his limbs then stood for a moment to take in the view. At first Lynton had seemed perched almost at the summit of the steep valley but he could see now how far they had descended as they rode through the town. The view from the front entrance made him catch his breath.

Across the valley the mighty coastline of North Devon rose cathedral-like from the shoreline. Gulls wheeled and called, soaring ever upwards on the wind that took them high above to where the rough pasture fell steeply before meeting the sheer cliff face. The sea, azure blue today, shimmered and dazzled in the bright autumn sunlight. Hundreds of feet below the house, small waves broke silently against the black rocks.

"Yes, indeed." As soon as his cloak had been taken, Morgan stretched again then handed over his hat and crop before turning to look at the house. It was big, bigger than any of the others lining the high cliff-top ridge, yet not big enough for Knight. He had heard him muttering about having to live in a kennel where his style was cramped but, to Morgan's eyes, the place was substantial with the three floors of tall windows pushing the turreted roof way above the trees.

He could see the old part quite clearly. The northern quarter had been constructed more ruggedly where the solid, rough-hewn masonry and the round tower with its own tiled roof gave lie to its age. Somewhere over there, deep down inside so the Master claimed, Cromwell's men did terrible things to their Royalist prisoners. One room, little more than a cellar with a grill, was avoided by all except the boldest, even in broad daylight. Yet, in spite of the grim history, Morgan could see that somebody must have loved it here; somebody with an eye for the beauty of the location and with a small fortune to spend. Whoever had named the house Castle Heights, he thought, had chosen well.

The young banker turned back to the butler. "See to my men, would you. They'll need food and drink…the same for the horses. 'Twas a hard ride up there." The two outriders, by now dismounted, waited patiently. One of the mounts, black but for a narrow blaze, tossed its head in frustration, sending flecks of white foam spraying. Men and animals were wet with sweat.

"That's all in hand, sir," Parker rose on his toes. "There'll be victuals for the men inside and the stables will see to the horses. Now, sir, be pleased to follow me if you will." He turned to lead the way. "Mr Knight is expecting you."

✻

"Aha…excellent, excellent." John Knight rose in greeting, noting how Morgan strode confidently into the room, before bringing his heels together and bowing formally. "Excellent, well done indeed…and in good time too." Knight indicated the tall bracket clock as he took Morgan's hand. "Now then," he spun round. "Now then, Havers. We must stop I'm afraid but we'll go through the figures again…all of them, and this afternoon at that."

"Very good, sir." On hearing his instructions, the nearest and oldest of the three men behind him nodded eagerly. "That'll give us time enough to adjust the drawings and we can have a look at those figures you wanted to see again. And thank you, sir." The others began to gather up the maps and papers from where Knight's mahogany desk and the long refectory table had been pulled together.

"Indeed, indeed." Knight caught the butler's eye. "Oh, and Parker. Mr Havers and his team'll be ready for some lunch no doubt. And…another bottle of that canary if you will…some dried fruit and a few small sweet cakes." He glanced at his visitor then at the clock. "Mr Morgan's ready for a little sustenance right now, no doubt, and we'll be taking lunch on the hour."

"Thank you, sir." Knight motioned Morgan to one of the two leather chairs by the window after which the questions came fast. Morgan had been advised to have his answers ready and to be prepared to jump from one subject to the next, then back again. It was the way the industrialist's mind worked, racing first in one direction then another. Never, he was warned, must he allow this to irritate him neither should he forget what had been discussed earlier: the Iron Master never did.

"And the countryside?" Knight swept back his hair. "What d'ya make of it?"

"I have to say it's the devil's very own up there, sir." Morgan gave a little laugh. "Wild as wild can be, never seen anything like it...very glad to have the two guards along with me. I can see why the bank insisted on it."

"See anyone, did you? Riders, shepherds...anything like that?"

"Only at Simons...er, Simons...."

"*Sim*-onsbath," Knight interrupted. "Pronounce the first part *sym* like *hymn*, so they do. Can't think why, but that's the way of things in these parts."

"Yes, that's it," Morgan nodded. "A few fellas around the big house up there. Used to be a tavern, so one of my two told me. And a mighty big one, too, but God knows who used the place, it's miles from anywhere." He paused as the butler set the drinks on the table. "Just moorland and bog as far as you can see. One or two folk about as we pushed on over Brendon common but that was all."

"Aye," Knight got up and went to the window. Morgan watched him look out, peering this way and that, all the while pulling at his collar. "And that's the way it's going to be," he muttered before falling silent again. "*Anyway.*" Morgan started at the sudden change in tone as Knight turned to face him. "I've not paid for you to be here on a riding holiday, that's fer sure. Good job you've seen the place though, but now it's time for business. What have you for me? What news?" He flopped heavily into the second deep chair and stared at his visitor. "Eh? Tell me all you've found...who am I up against?"

Morgan, although ready and well briefed about the man, sensed danger. He had not seen it in Lombard Street but now, as soon as the subject of his opponents was broached, the man's whole attitude changed. No longer the genial host, John Knight was now the hunter. His senses were alert, he scented the wind hungrily. He was dangerous and Morgan could feel the man's eyes on him. "Four thus far, sir." The young banker cleared his throat.

"Go on." The voice was soft.

"Sir Thomas Acland...you know about already, I believe, sir." Knight remained still. "All our enquiries show him to be a much respected member of local society. Farms well, looks after his tenants and those who work for him. Wants to extend his estates. Can't do it near Killerton, his Exeter home...land prices there're too high so he's going to try at Holnicote, just off the moor, here, near Porlock. But...if he cannot do that then he may consolidate his assets around Killerton, their home near Exeter." Morgan eased the map he had brought towards Knight and pointed.

Knight waved it away. "His bid?"

"Not sure, yet," Morgan saw the frown. "I've yet to get to the Exeter Bank. We're working on it but it'll take a bit of time. My guess is that he will make a bid in line with land values."

"I've not invited you here to make guesses." Morgan looked down. "I want facts...facts, you understand. Who's next?"

"Frobisher, sir. From Filliegh, just outside South Molton."

"And?" Knight was barely audible. He remembered the man vaguely but his wife better.

"Very much the same, sir. Lord Frobisher's highly regarded also, both locally and in town. He has considerable assets though and we know he's very keen to make a strong bid. Has several ideas on how the land could be developed. He's also a great sporting man. Financially a very different proposition to Acland and likely to be more powerful. We think he could come in at a very high price...say four or five times over the odds."

"How so?"

"Bencroft of the North Devon Bank told us. He's been instructed to move assets down this way from London. The family has considerable stakes in sugar. Very lucrative but risky and a hefty contingency fund's always wise but, an' here's the point, they've withdrawn heavily from that and are holding the capital separately...enough to give them a very good hand." Morgan bit his lip. Knight, now slumped in his chair, remained still. "Shall I go on, sir?" A finger moved.

"We feel sure that, if either of these two come in, it will be done properly and with secure capital...exactly how much we have yet to determine. But, from now on, things get more difficult...messy in fact. We have a Mr Michael Exton from Pixton near Dulverton and a man called Branquehurst. Comes from Sussex but lives close to Taunton.

"Tell me."

"Both look slippery as eels and we're beginning to feel sure both have something of a record." Knight looked up. "Exton first. Likes to give himself some sort of a title but the College of Arms couldn't come up with anything…no trace of a lineage or deed poll. He's married to a Spaniard. She has some title or other and the money. Exton, or Repton as we think he is, was a shipowner, or a seafarer to be more precise. Recruited his sailors from the Cadiz area, hordes of them living around the naval base."

"How the devil d'you know all this?" Knight struggled to sit upright.

"Marcus Tritton, sir. Nephew of Alwyn Tritton, Sir Crispin Barclay's partner. Our man, Exton, came to see them about buying land. Asked to pay in silver…he'd got ingots of the stuff. Told them it was his wife's family money. They smelt a rat and it got traced to two ships in his name. They used to operate in the Caribbean against Spanish shipping."

"A goddamned freebooter," Knight shook his head and stood frowning. "Well I'll be damned." He quite failed to see how that bright, chubby little wife could have given herself to such a man.

"Worse than that, sir…treachery. Had to get out fast a few years back. Reckoned he might get a pat on the back over here seeing the Spanish fought at Trafalgar. He did, until Barclay and Tritton began to dig a bit deeper."

"I'll be damned," Knight stroked his chin. "I'll be damned. And the other fella …what's his name?"

"Branquehurst, sir. Another maritime tale but a seedy one. Pure luck this time. A Captain Andrew King, now retired as Harbour Master at Falmouth, dug up a lot of old records when they were clearing one of the warehouse offices. Falmouth used to be a supply depot for the fleet…one of the Commissioners' dockyards. Fiddling the books was a pastime then but, unfortunately for our man, King remembered being at the wrong end of it all. Nigh on starved them out, so he did…and on the Victory at that. King was one of Nelson's lieutenants apparently. Sent a report to the Admiralty who passed it on to Marshal's, the Navy's bankers. Branquehurst's name came up and they're cross referring the ledgers right now."

"Who knows about these two?" Knight had levered himself out of his chair and was pacing the room. Morgan watched as the older man scratched savagely under his long hair before trying, with both arms raised, to smooth it back.

"Nobody, sir. Well, certainly not down here." Knight said nothing. Morgan remained seated, his mind racing as to what his host might ask next.

"You'll be staying for lunch, sir? Yes?"

The young banker saw his chance. Thus far he had not enjoyed himself one bit.

It had felt as though Knight's mind had been boring into his and it had left him nervous. The idea of being trapped at the table where further interrogation was inevitable did not appeal. He would take his instructions and get away from the place. "Er, to be honest, sir and with my most heartfelt thanks for your kind offer but we should be on our way. Really, we must…there's a long, hard ride ahead and we've our own provisions that will suffice."

Knight nodded. Morgan paused before going on. "But your requirements first, sir, if you please. There is still some way to go and I need to be clear as to how you would wish me to proceed."

"Right, now hear this." Once again the sheer force of the voice startled the banker. "Leave the first two well alone. D'you hear? That they are men of honour there's no doubt, and I know well enough with whom I'm having to deal. No more enquiries…nothing." He cut the air with his hand. "Nothing at all. They'll be my neighbours here and they're men whose acquaintance I'll value. Now…these others." Knight frowned and scratched at his head again. "We'll let them run…they're but small men and of little consequence." He waved his hand. "Give them plenty of line but find out what you can. I want to know all there is to know about 'em. D'you hear? How they pin their cravats, even…how they take their snuff. Everything." His finger jabbed angrily. "D'you hear me, young man?" Morgan nodded. He had heard quite clearly.

"So…go from here, get your nose to the ground and don't lift it until I tell you. You've done me well thus far. Do me well, Morgan, and I'll see *you* well. I know most bankers in the City but I know every one of those damned villians up north, every man jack of them and most of their fathers too. Do me well, young man, and I'll see you on your way. But *listen*." Morgan stiffened. "Go…carefully. Word drifts with the wind in the world of business and we'd not wish for that. Knight clapped him on the shoulder. "On your way and safely now."

4.

Morning service was over. The Reverend Froude stood in the porch of St Mary's south door, beaming and shaking hands with those taking their leave. Above him the bells rang out across the Molland countryside and the flag of St George fluttered defiantly from the masthead. Sunday April 23rd, always a popular day for worship, had been designated a day of national thanksgiving.

Napoleon, now incarcerated forever on a small island in the South Atlantic, was no longer a threat and, for that, all England rejoiced. The church had been filled to capacity and the congregation waited patiently to pay their respects. Some talked quietly together, others watched idly as the captain of the bell ringers worked his team behind the ancient font. The winter of sixteen had been long and hard but spring had come at last and with it new hope to a country wearied beyond measure by more than twenty years at war.

Grace Tucker walked slowly down the church path with her two eldest children beside her. For her there was little to celebrate and nothing to cheer. As she reached the line of cottages near the lychgate, she looked anxiously for Ben Thorne and Jason Hawkins, the moorland shepherds, who were to take her two children to their new life.

The carter smiled encouragingly but it was of little comfort; the decision to split the family had been a terrible one and Grace had had no choice. The pay of a Corporal of Horse in the Life Guards might not have been much, but to her and the young family it had been more than adequate. Since Lionel had gone, the struggle had been hopeless and Parson Froude had arranged for the two children to go into the service of a wealthy family at Lynton. She knew little of Lynton and nothing at all about the family called Knight except for what Froude had told her.

And now the moment she had been dreading more than she knew possible had arrived. "Have you got all your things in the box, Emma dear?" She spoke softly lest those around should hear her voice. The young girl nodded. Her eyes were shining for, to her and Jack, the prospect of leaving home promised to be a great adventure. For days now they had been thinking of nothing else.

"Yes, mama." The girl held out her arms. "Shush now. Don't cry, mama. We'll be fine, you'll see. Really we will...we'll be fine."

"God bless you, my darling child." Grace, her arms drawn tightly round the tall, fair-haired girl, wept unashamedly on her daughter's shoulder. For a few moments they clung together then Grace pulled back. "Go on now, dear," she choked. "Go on...climb up on the cart with the others."

"Bye, bye, mother." Jack pulled at her hand. "Don't worry about us." Grace crouched down beside the boy. Although just nine, his eyes were Lionel's; the nose, the mouth and the chin also. Her son to whom she was now having to bid farewell was the very incarnation of the husband she had lost.

"Good bye, Jack," she whispered, stroking back his fair hair. "Try to remember all your father used to tell you, and you'll grow up to be a fine man...a very fine man. Look after your sister." With that she pulled the boy to her and held him tightly. "God be with you, dearest." She kissed his cheek then, for a moment, buried her face in his hair. "I'll be thinking of you, always. You know that."

"Me, too, mother. Bye now." With that he climbed alongside his sister, the two of them beaming with excitement with their legs dangling over the back rail so their feet could swing freely. The horses, side by side, leant forward taking the strain and the wheels began to grate forward. They waved and called out until the cart turned the corner and began the long climb out of the village.

*

The first leg of their journey took all day. Three times they stopped, once for lunch then twice more by ice-cold moorland streams to drink and to rest the horses. By the time they began the long descent off the moor, the sun had settled low in the west and a damp mist had spread like a wraith across the valley beneath them. Slowly, with the two horses backing against the weight of the cart, they descended towards the river. The large stone house tucked away in the trees came into view long before they reached the narrow, arched bridge. By then the sun had gone altogether, leaving the grey outline of their destination in deep shadow.

Once across, the pull up the track was steep and the two children stared apprehensively as the cart ground towards the driveway. Ahead of them, the pale, soft lights of oil lamps were flickering in several of the tall windows. Others were dark and lifeless making the house seem mysteriously quiet and as though it was staring back at them as they approached. They had reached Simonsbath where they were to spend their first night away from home.

"Round the back, you'll be," Ben Thorne announced. "Jenny Squires, that's the name of the lady who's looking after you. Works in the big house so she does. A fine lady an' all so don't go causing no trouble mind." Less than an hour later it was dark.

*

Next morning, as the packhorse train moved up the track and headed further north, they looked out of their wicker panniers onto a countryside quite different from anything they had known. Everywhere, as far as they could see, the land was wild and unbroken, the dun-coloured rushes and sedge covering the young, green shoots of bracken. From time to time they saw herds of ponies and twice glimpsed deer in the deep combes. Above them curlews and lapwings wheeled and called out but there were no sheep or cattle as in the farms around Molland, no trees, no lanes and no hedges. To their young eyes the great expanse of the unbroken moor seemed eternal, the countryside remote, empty and forbidding.

It took them hours to reach the highest ground then longer still to cross the rough, barren moors. High above Exe Head, the land levelled then undulated gently for mile after mile before beginning its long descent to the sea. "Lynton ahead!" The cry went up. "Straight ahead...down there, look. Just over an hour to go."

"That's where we're going, Emms," Jack pointed, standing up in his pannier and staring at the first line of houses in the distance. "Which one do you think is ours?" he asked quietly. "I wonder what the people there are going to be like."

"Don't know," she answered. "But it's scary, Jack, isn't it. I hope they're nice. D'you think they will be? Kind, I mean?"

"Oh, I should think so." He thought for a moment. "Or they wouldn't have asked for us otherwise, would they?"

"Don't know," said Emma again, quietly this time. "But I hope so." Suddenly, and without any warning, the great adventure had taken on a new twist. Home was a long way away and the rows of houses that stared back up at them were full of people they had not met. They had never seen so many buildings before and sat looking in bewilderment at everyone talking loudly or shouting to each other or hurrying in and out of the shops. Just past the church the road dipped sharply before coming to an open field. Behind them and on the high slopes, a few cottages nestled together but the largest houses were set in their own grounds along the edge of the cliffs overlooking the sea.

＊

"You Tucker?" A surly, lank-haired youth sporting a straw hat and wearing leather boots with no stockings looked on indifferently as the two children got out of their panniers. "*Oi...you Tucker*, I said?" He repeated his question, louder this time and nudged at Emma's box with his foot as he did so.

"Yes, I'm Emma Tucker," she replied. "And this is my brother, Jack."

"Hmm," he snorted. "Then pick up yer things and follow me." Without another word he set off across the field and up the slope towards the largest house of all. Emma could barely keep up with him while Jack, struggling with his own box, soon fell behind in the evening gloom. She turned and waited for him.

"I'm all right, Emms," he gasped. "I can manage, honestly." He looked up at his sister and smiled bravely.

Chapter Three

The grey-bearded beggar tightened the cord around his old military overcoat and looked around uneasily. Paternosta Row had turned bitterly cold. He could hear the sound of revelry from the tavern further down the cobbled alleyway and, each time the door of the Three Tuns opened, noise and light escaped into the deserted street. It was only then that he was able to see how the softly falling snow had begun to settle. One glance at the window above the front door of The Barnstaple Bank was enough to convince him that business for the day was dead.

As he bent once more, this time to collect his cap and blanket, he shivered violently: just two groats and a few pence. By now the ovens in Pastry Lane would be warming the walls so, slowly and relying heavily on his stick, he hobbled on his way.

*

Inside the bank, business had long since closed, yet voices could be heard coming from the front room on the second floor, home of the ledger clerks. Last month there had been three but since Jacob Goldberg's sudden departure, the two remaining had found their evening freedom rudely curtailed.

"I don't *care*, there has to be more moved across to Sundry Debtors." Durnford Morgan, the collar of his three quarter length woollen jacket turned up against the chill, prodded at the unwilling fire. "We've seen the discrepancies," he sniffed. "Page after page of them. Tally the last ones again."

The clerks glanced at one another then bent their heads once more, peering closely at the lines of figures. It was difficult to see for the ochre pages of the ledger parchment were barely discernible in the candlelight. "We've found twelve guineas, thus far, sir, and we've yet to check the smaller accounts." Luke Tanner, the older of the two, looked up hopefully.

"No," Durnford Morgan shook his head vigorously. "Nowhere near good enough, and in any case it's not just the sum itself…I want to *pin* the man beyond doubt. *That*'s the problem. Figures themselves don't always tally but it's the difference between human error and embezzlement that I'm after. That's what we need."

"We can show proof for six, seven maybe."

"Not enough, dammit." Morgan's voice cracked. "I want to stick twenty-five guineas on the blaggard. Twenty-five guineas and he'll hang." The smaller youth, dark-haired and skinny, stared. His mouth opened as if to say something but he thought better of it and moved his ledger closer to the light. "You, Burton." Morgan held out his hand. "Let me see the Principal Account

Holders' ledger. Over there, look...come on, come on." He stretched further, grunting as he snatched at the book then turned up the wick until the lamp began to smoke. After that, all three, save for the occasional cough or muttered curse, worked on silently just as they had done for the last month.

Jacob Goldberg had left The Barnstaple Bank without notice. It had taken Barnstaple more than two weeks to discover he had moved to Elliot, Bloom and Schoenbaum, a small farmers' bank in Canal Street, close to Taunton's livestock market. A week after his disappearance the accounting errors began to appear, the first spotted by young Burton.

Morgan based himself in lodgings at Paternosta Row. At first only Crane the bank manager knew his business, but word soon spread about the tall stranger from London and it was Goldberg's sudden departure which prompted the initial enquiries. The manager appeared resigned to the loss of his clerk. "A clever boy, a worker, too. Never afraid to put in the extra hours." Morgan listened impassively and unimpressed but heard him out. He had to for there was no choice.

"They're all the same, that lot...one uncle's a rabbi, supposedly. Another one's bin made Sammy Elliot's second partner in the Taunton branch." Morgan raised his head. "Typical yiddishers...pulling in all the talent and sticking together like that. Not so much as a word to anyone else." Morgan no longer heard him. "Never could trust that lot," the voice droned on. "Books are too tidy, always have the answers...too clever by half."

By now Morgan was on his feet. The elderly and hesitant Crane had given him the lead he was seeking and suddenly he saw it all. He was more than certain and it was Marcus Tritton who confirmed that Barclay, Tritton and Co were agents for the Jewish bankers. Then, as more discrepancies came to light, Morgan moved. He became like a man possessed, pushing himself and the two clerks late into the night, Sundays included.

Again and again, they went through the books, Morgan driving and goading; his own hours at the desk the longest of all. Tanner cursed and Burton snivelled. Statements from customers were called in, every entry and transaction in the bankbooks was checked against the customers' ledgers. Holdings with Friendly Societies and Mutual Agencies were cross referred. Deposits and withdrawals from both the bank and private investors were reconciled, interest shadings also. Column was balanced with column, page with page, book against book.

Twice Morgan caught the mail to London, once to Bristol and twice he rode to Exeter. The very name of the bank was at stake. Should word of fraudulent practices get out, a mere hint even, the bank would be doomed. Pride and a deep anger drove him on.

But there was something else: Taunton intrigued him. Closer to Exmoor than any other town of note, it was the local centre for commerce and trade. It seemed natural to him that landowners and men of means wishing to live near the moor would make use of the facilities on offer. Instinct told him so but he had to be sure, and for weeks he had been seeking the opening he needed. Now it was there. Time, he knew, was against him. Rumours were that the Crown Commissioners now intended to sell Exmoor later in the year and that the Treasury had concurred with their decision.

It took them two months but, finally, their work was done. The close scrutiny of the books had revealed the full extent of the bank's losses. Copies of the relevant ledgers were made, affidavits drawn up and sworn in court. He was ready.

❋

Morgan glared at the young clerk behind the counter. "Well, who *has* been left in charge of the place?" There was something complacent about the sallow youth that annoyed him, something disturbing about the little black cap on the back of his head.

"Sabbath has begun, sir." The clerk shrugged and pointed out of the window. "Friday evening, see. It's gone dusk and we're closed until Monday. So sorry." Morgan caught the smirk.

"Mr Goldberg, then?"

The boy hunched his shoulders. "He'll be busy just now."

His face quite expressionless, Morgan took off his gloves and reached into his fob pocket. "Then pray present him with this will you." The clerk held out his hand and glanced at the embossed card. Casually and without looking up, he placed it in one of the pigeonholes.

"Here, you." Morgan leant over the desk. "Listen to me," the voice hissed. "I'm here on business, serious business…and I've come a long way. Not from your friendly little Barnstaple bank but from London…Lombard Street. Right? Were Mr Goldberg ever to know you dared treat me like this, you'd be out…out into the cold of the night."

The youth rose quickly, his eyes taking in the finely cut clothes of the man in front of him. "Get on your way…*now* and present my compliments. Mr Goldberg would wish to know that a Mr Durnford Morgan has called on behalf of Sir James Esdaile and Sir Crispin Barclay. Both names he will know well."

❋

The banker from London had taken no chances. One of those who rode with him he left in the outer office with the clerk, two more remained outside, one at either door.

All afternoon Jacob Goldberg had been bored. It was late but he had to remain until the end, as was the wont of the duty cashier. Remain there he had but now it was time. He had scarcely begun to clear his desk when, all of a sudden, there was this. He scowled and rounded on the clerk then threw down his papers, but he knew there was no way out. The man had to be seen and that would make him later still.

He received his visitor coldly, motioning him to a chair while making a point of checking his timepiece. Morgan stepped forward and offered his hand, noticing the soft dampness of the one he took in return. He smiled pleasantly and sat, but the face confronting him was surly. It was florid also, the dark, heavy lidded eyes staring balefully, full of impatience.

Morgan continued to smile but only to himself. He began slowly, explaining why it was necessary to interview those who decided to terminate their contract. Goldberg shrugged, concurring that such a procedure was no more than sound banking practise. Morgan deferred, making much of searching through his saddlebag before producing the ledgers. These he laid before Goldberg, inquiring courteously if he might care to check the signatures. Twice at the end of each book, if he would be so kind, and once on each page, thereby verifying they had been checked and were in order.

He then placed the letter of confirmation by the ledgers. This, he explained, was but a short statement declaring the books and ledgers maintained by Goldberg to be a true and accurate record of all transactions. Goldberg signed, resentful at this lack of trust.

"Well, that seems to be almost everything." The banker returned to the ledgers. Then, as Goldberg began to collect up his papers once more, Morgan frowned as though searching his mind. "It's just that…" he appeared hesitant. "Dear me…I don't appear to see any sign of witness signatures. They don't appear to be here."

"There was no time," Goldberg rose sharply. "But now you have mine, do you not? Enough surely? And seeing as you are content that the books are in order, I must ask that this meeting is closed."

"Yes, of course, I'm so sorry." Morgan rose also and looked down. "Your task was indeed a busy one." Goldberg shrugged indifferently then moved quickly to avoid Morgan as he bent forward. "So I daresay that might account for the missing two hundred and seventy-five guineas."

Goldberg's head jerked up. "How *dare* you." The two stared at one another across the desk until, finally, the jew looked away, first at the door then back at Morgan once more. "How *dare* you imply that there might have been…."

"Em-*bezzelment*? Is that what it's called or is it known simply as plain theft? Not only by me, Goldberg. Not only me, by a long way." Morgan reached into his saddlebag. "Might I suggest we sit," he motioned. Goldberg made a move towards his coat.

"No, Goldberg. I suggest not." Morgan took his chair once more. "I have the building well covered and we have all night in front of us if needs be…until Monday, if it takes us that long. Furthermore I have here the original accounts plus letters from two leading London banks."

Goldberg sat heavily, Morgan watching as the fingers of one hand wrestled with those of the other. Even so the man remained defiant. "You can prove nothing. I'm a man of honour and this is a gross insult. I shall pursue any further such allegations through the courts. Kindly leave this premises and take your men with you. Go on," he urged. "Kindly do as I ask."

Morgan ignored him. "Of course you must protect your integrity…that is your right, Goldberg." Crossing one leg over the other, he nodded sagely. "However, court proceedings are already in hand, you should know. Not here but in London…we have taken the liberty. I advise you to dwell carefully on the fact that no court, not even the Crown Court is likely to pronounce against the word of two independent Lombard Street banks, whose financial integrity is beyond any doubt. The sum in question is but a pittance to them" He paused, holding up his hands. "What would be in it for them?

"But for you or for me, Goldberg, the money is no insignificant matter. Oh, no. It is a considerable sum, more than your life's worth, in fact…literally…and we both know that. Come on, now, think. And if that's not enough we have all this further evidence." Morgan tapped the saddlebag. Goldberg moistened his lips.

"Debtors and embezzlers, Goldberg, go to Newgate…the debtors' prison… even before their trial. Once behind bars they come face to face with a some-what less than attractive cross-section of society which has lost everything it ever had yet which fights tooth and claw for very life itself. It is not a happy place to be. They quarrel and rage among themselves yet, for all that, they remain united against one common enemy…the financial institutions who secured their downfall and those who run them…*bankers*." Goldberg sat, head lowered.

"Us, we bankers, are not popular in there, you should understand. Not at all welcome. In fact they detest the likes of you and me with an awfulness it is hard to imagine. And that is where you will go, Goldberg. A veritable Daniel you will be, locked in a den of animals worse than any that ever lived. *And*…d'you know *what*?" Goldberg jumped in alarm as Morgan's hand crashed on to the desk. "The last banker they threw into the debtors' cell had the clothes torn from him. That done, they beat him, after that they raped him…sodomised him for two days until he could no longer cry out. Then…as a final gesture of their goodwill, they held his head in a bucket of sewage and drowned him."

The room was very quiet. "It's not possible…just not possible." Goldberg whispered, all fight now gone. "What do you want of me?" He looked up pleadingly with the first lines of sweat beginning to run down his face. "What is it you want from me, Morgan? Tell me, for God's sake." Morgan saw his hand reach out for his own but failed to withdraw it before the man had grasped his wrist. "What d'you want, Morgan?"

Morgan scowled, wiping himself where the man had clutched at him. "We'll talk about the money later…but first Branquehurst. Does the name mean anything?" Goldberg stared and Morgan stared back. "You'd do well to think hard and think well, Goldberg. So?"

"Yes, yes. Dorian Branquehurst…commodity broker…fleet victualler…now retired and a very wealthy man."

"Quite so." Morgan sat back. "And what of his banking details?"

"But, I couldn't do that. It's not…."

"Forget even attempting to recall any virtues you once considered yours." Now Morgan stood. "You'll tell me everything there is to know about the man. *Everything*. We'll begin with his account, then continue until I tell you to stop. And as for absconding…I would not advise it. We have a Bankers' Search out even now and you're a marked man. Life on the run out there is hard and winter at its most unforgiving." Morgan paused. "Armed gangs, hungry ex-military men roam the highways and a fat little banker would be easy prey."

*

A month later, Goldberg took his chance but not before Morgan had received a letter back from his friend Marcus Tritton. It began by assuring him that Barclay, Tritton and Co were most certainly the London agents for Elliot and Schoenbaum. He went on to verify, as Morgan had requested, that a Mr Jacob Goldberg had applied for a position with the Taunton branch several weeks earlier. Any information that Morgan might be able to provide concerning Mr Goldberg would, he could guarantee, be treated with the greatest of respect.

Furthermore, he was able to confirm that a number of clients had indeed placed their business with Taunton recently. Among the enclosed list of those with substantial accounts was a Mr Dorian Branquehurst. It was his hope that the answers he had given to his earlier letter might be of some use.

2.

Emma, sitting on the edge of the bed with her feet swinging free, smiled at the girl across the room. Becky Randle had been at Castle Heights for more than two months, arriving with a number of other servants to prepare the mansion.

Mr Knight had stayed on several occasions already but was soon to move in permanently, bringing with him his family. Well developed for her age, Becky was slightly older than Emma but not quite as tall. Her eyes, darker even than her hair that fell in a mass of ringlets, searched Emma's face eagerly. "Well?" she asked. "What do you think? Not too bad here, is it?"

"It's unbelievable," Emma replied, shaking her head. Next to her own bed a second iron cot had been made up, the two separated by an elderly wooden dresser where someone had placed an oil lamp with a chipped glass. On the white cloth lay a leather-bound Bible whilst under the window, a large china basin and water jug had been put on top of the clothes chest. "Look at this, Becky," she marvelled, touching the small square of matting on the floor with her foot. "A *carpet*. I've never had anything like this before. It's...it's, well it's lovely."

Jumping from the bed, she crossed over to the window and looked down. Beyond the fields at the back of the house, she could see the buildings where the packhorse train had first brought them to Lynton. Her eyes followed the smoke from the forge chimney as it raced flat across the fields, hurried on by the strong sea breeze before disappearing into the trees. To her left, and past the gardens, she could see the coach house and stable yard and behind them the steep, wooded land above the cliffs. There was no sign of Jack.

Standing on tiptoe, she craned her neck, trying to see the shoreline but it was way down under the high ground beyond the stables and hidden behind a line of beeches, stunted and bent almost double by Atlantic gales. "That's Lynmouth way down there," Becky explained, reading her thoughts. "We go down sometimes. Only way down's by a steep track. They say they're going to build a bigger one soon so that carts and things can get up, but nothing's happened yet. D'you ride?"

"Yes," she nodded, her eyes suddenly brightening. "Father taught us as soon as we were old enough. I'm not bad but Jack's very good."

"We all have to ride here, but I don't like it," Becky pulled a face and curled a finger in her hair. "Everything comes up to Lynton like that...or you have to walk," she grumbled. "There's talk in the house of teaching the children when they're down. Young Master Frederic, as he's known, he's the eldest. He's coming with his mother, his nanny and governess. You know about the family, d'you?"

"A bit...are there lots of them?" Emma quizzed.

"Two lots, really. Mr and Mrs Knight have got their own. She's his second wife, mind. Comes from Ireland, I think. Ever so nice, she is. Elizabeth or Elizabeth-Jane," she added hurriedly. Both giggled.

Well, after Frederic there's Charles. Frederic's five...well, I think he is, an'

Charles's about three. Then there's Margaret and baby Isabelle or Isabella as she's called. Them's all theirs but then there's Kenton."

"*Who?* What's different about him, then?"

"Kenton, they call 'im. Doesn't belong to them…well, not really. His Dad were a cousin or summat of Mr Knight. Only what I heard mind. Well, he and his Mum were killed in a big fire. About two years ago, up London way."

"Poor little thing,"

"He's all right now…a little bit younger than Frederic but different, mind."

"What d'you mean?"

"Shouts and screams a lot. Always fighting or teasing the others. Proper little so-and-so, 'e is."

For a moment the two girls sat in silence. "What d'you think of Mrs Strong, then?"

Emma thought for a moment. Earlier in the day, after the house staff had break-fasted in the pantry, Charlotte, the second parlour maid, had taken Emma to meet Mrs Strong, the cook, who had come down from Worcestershire to join the household. As was their custom, Mrs Strong and Mr Parker, the butler, had taken their breakfast alone in the senior staff room. After their meal, Charlotte was told to bring in the new girl. Emma had been terrified.

"The name's Emma isn't it? Emma Tucker?" Mrs Strong asked, lowering her newspaper and peering over her half-moon spectacles. Patting the neat bun of grey hair behind her head, she looked Emma up and down in silence.

"Yes please, ma'am," Emma replied nervously, studying the floor with her hands clasped tightly in front of her.

"Well, look at me girl," the voice was brusque. "There's no need to stand there like that. As long as you do your work, you'll be fine." Mrs Strong sat back in her chair. "This is a big house and a busy one, too. Mr Knight's a very impor-tant gentleman, always filling his home with visitors when he's here."

She paused, observing Emma who looked back timidly. "Mmm, you're a pretty child, that's for sure, but we've got to get you properly dressed. Can't be seen around like that," she waved disdainfully at Emma's ill-fitting uniform. "We'll get Charlotte to take you up to the seamstress in the village. And you'll be needing a mob cap and some new shoes," she added, pointing at Emma's feet. "Look at those things…we'll have them burned."

"Thank you, ma'am," Emma smiled meekly at the formidable woman in front of her. Although Mrs Strong looked severe, Emma had detected the hint of a twinkle behind the spectacles. Last night Becky had told her about the cook, warning her about the fearsome temper. In the last month alone, three girls from the village had been sent packing. Nothing but the best was good enough, Becky had cautioned, but she was fair and looked after those who worked for her. When things got really bad, Mr Parker kept well out of the way and it was rumoured that even Mr Knight himself was afraid to go near until life had quietened down once more. Becky had giggled helplessly.

"Now then." Mrs Strong folded her paper then put it down before pushing herself to her feet. Emma was surprised at how small she was, even shorter than herself. "The first thing you should know is that you call me Mrs Strong not ma'am. That's for Mrs Knight and her lady guests...an' you'll be curtseying to them as well. And when there're real ladies here you'll call them M'lady...we'll tell you about that when the time comes."

She took off her spectacles and wiped them. "And Mrs Appelton, when she's here, is Mrs Appelton and Mr Parker's Mr Parker. Only if they speak t'you, that is. We do things properly here. Mrs Appelton sees to Mr and Mrs Knight and Mr Parker looks after the front of the house. The kitchens and the back area belong to me. Becky and Charlotte will show you how things are done and where everything is. Your place is out there in the scullery." She nodded towards the far door. "You take your meals in the staff room with the others and you use the back stairs to your room. I want to see you keep yourself clean and tidy...to work hard and mind your place."

"Yes, ma'am, I mean yes Mrs Strong," she added hurriedly, blushing at her mistake.

"That's all right, girl. Now away you go and get on with learning about what's what at Castle Heights. That's all."

"Thank you, Mrs Strong." Emma backed towards the door then fled to find Becky. She could not believe her luck. She had a bed to herself, three meals a day, some new clothes and had found a friend.

"Well, go on," Becky urged. "You haven't told me what you think of Mrs Strong."

"Oh, sorry," laughed Emma. "I was day dreaming. Mmm, she was all right, not nearly as bad as I thought."

3.

John Knight smiled at the memory. "Now steady, dear." Her words had rung loud in his ears. "It's not yours *yet*...and remember, anything can happen." He was certain he would not be outbid but, were that to be the case, he would buy it straight back from the new man. Ask him his price and pay it. But Elizabeth-

Jane was right – as she so often was. "Don't take *anything* for granted, dearest. You're too...too impetuous." She had touched the end of his nose. "And don't do anything until I'm down there with you."

Exmoor was not yet his and he had to guard against his optimism. He knew it and it irked him all the more. He wanted to get on, get out there to begin planning and building, shaping the land. Twice Morgan had reported back to him. There were now six of them in the field and, barring any late entries, he knew them all. Three were of no consequence yet two disturbed him and he had to get the measure of them. But he couldn't just sit there and wait, he convinced himself. He would go mad. He had to get out and prepare what he had determined already was to be his. Elizabeth-Jane would soon be down with the children and he wanted to show her his plans.

*

"Come on...come on." Knight glared at Parker. "Where's that Havers fellow? Chase him out or we'll be late. It's gone half past five already." The grooms, hard at work since before the spring dawn, had brought the horses to the front of the house, two for each man, their second to be ridden quietly by light-weight stable lads until they were needed. Knight watched as Orwell Govier, the head groom, instructed his charges. Two were new, one, a mere boy of ten or so, was riding his own favourite, Queenie, a deep-chested bay. The lad looked composed and the mare appeared quiet and easy in his hands.

"Simonsbath first." Knight pressed the silk top hat over his ears, pulling his hair clear of the jacket collar. He rose again to pull his black frock coat from under his seat.

"We'll take a look at the house and farm up there, Maxwell...see what's what and what you reckon they're worth." Durnford Morgan could see the optimism and confidence in the man. He was behaving as if the purchase had been made already and his mind was racing ahead. "Havers? Oh, there you are. Look now, you'd better get on...up to those old mine-workings. 'Bout a mile upstream from the house. Cornham and Burcombe...you've read the reports?"

"Aye, sir...they look promising and all." Ebenezer Havers, hollow eyed and black bearded and one of the best mining surveyors in the north of England had been loaned from the Durham iron works at Consett. He and two others had been living in Lynton from where, just as Knight had ordered, they had carried out a survey of every known mine-work on Exmoor. "I'll move then, sir. The others've gone on already with lamps and ropes. We can show you what we've found."

He looked squarely at Knight; the two men had worked together before. Knight nodded, then watched as Havers, not the most elegant of horsemen, bounced away clumsily on the trotting pony, his long legs protruding beneath the animal's belly. Unashamed and unafraid, he turned and raised his arm in salute, calling out something they could not hear. The whole party, Knight, guests and stable lads laughed together and waved back.

As Knight rode so he talked about the land. Maxwell knew his master well and was ready with answers to the endless questions about the soil, about plough- ing and burning, about fencing in the land and reseeding. John Knight, he now knew, was intending to break the moor and develop a whole colony of farm- steads up in the wilds: it was to be his New World.

From time to time Knight rounded on Morgan, telling him to take note of the figures they had discussed, figures that needed to be checked and analysed. Twice, when they stopped, Morgan dismounted hurriedly and wrote fast, least the details escape him. Maxwell wrote too, noting their discussions and check- ing calculations. Only the man himself remained mounted, walking his horse to and fro, always impatient to get on.

"Go and check the old farm, there." Knight pointed to the rough, single-storied collection of buildings. "Then get on your way, you've plenty to do." Maxwell swung off the track, leaving Morgan alone as his master's company. They had reached Simonsbath and the two rode up to the old house.

"Wonderful." Knight stood in the saddle and gazed in awe at the mellowed features. Peat smoke rose lazily from one of the chimneys and, somewhere behind the buildings, a dog barked. Morgan shuddered. To him it looked awful; the very idea of living in such a desolate, Godforsaken place was madness itself.

"See how they've done it in an E-shape." Knight, reins loose, pointed towards the manor. "Over there…each wing comes forward, as does the floor above the front door in the middle there." He checked for a moment, staring at the build- ing. "You know…they say it was built around the time of the Civil War but I've a mind it's earlier 'n that, and a good deal so. Look at *that*," he pointed. "*That*…and that over there. They're all pure Elizabethan, every bit of them.

Morgan could see his mind was set. "Will you leave it as it is, sir? Keep the character of the place?"

"Keep the character, yes…to be sure." His eyes were still on the house. "I'll keep the shape and style but enlarge and deepen it. Lift the roof off and begin from the ground up. There's space enough," he laughed. "That's one thing we've got up here…space and more space." He rode slowly towards the bridge, Morgan following. "It's a wonderful spot, y'know." Knight turned in his saddle. "Here…right here where we're standing now is damned near the centre of the whole moor. Nothing for miles, thank the Lord, yet we can get to anywhere we like. Did you realise that?"

Morgan laughed and shook his head. "It's all news, sir, all news, but a geogra- phy lesson at that.

"Huh, needs decent roads though but see here," he stood and pointed. "Over the bridge there and you're off to the south…the Moltons and all that, away up that track. Exford's away over there," he turned again. "Barnstaple out there, that way…the track along the river there, and Lynton out over the back," he jerked a thumb over his shoulder. "The manor stands where the tracks meet…it commands the place." He saw Morgan's bewildered look.

"Not your sort of country, lad? Not enough life an' action, eh?"

"I'll have to say that, sir."

"Ah, but it's what I love…and Elizabeth-Jane, too. 'Tis like her beloved Ireland." Morgan watched as he peered this way and that. "She's seen it out here and loves it…God bless her. Aye…here's where, I'll be." Knight saw the expression on his face. "And why not?" he laughed. "London one week, Worcestershire the next, then the midlands, then up north. Always problems to solve, always work to push forward and decisions to make."

He took off his hat and scratched his head. "Arguing, pleading, fighting, bargaining…meetings…drive on, drive on, drive on," his voice tailed off. "Then back to this…can you not see it, the peace and quiet? Can you not feel nature's calming hand?"

*

They reached Havers and his men in less than half an hour. "What news?" Knight leapt from his mount, throwing the reins to one of the lads. "What d'you think?"

"It's in very poor shape." Havers shook his head. "If the deposits are there, we'll need to rebuild the leading shaft and all the adits. See here, sir…this way." He took the lantern and, Knight followed, picking his way carefully past the workings and into the dark interior. "There…and there, look. Mind as you go, sir." Haver's voice echoed off the tomb-like walls as he swung the lamp for Knight to see the broken timbers and rock falls no more than a few yards inside the main drift.

As they moved forward, the sound of their boots swishing through the stream was magnified. Water dripped noisily from the roof into deeper pools. Daylight shone brightly from the entrance behind them but ahead they could see nothing save what the pale glow from the lamp picked out. Knight held up his hand; more water could be heard in the distance. "Underground, sir." Havers had seen his questing look. "We went forward earlier but it gets worse. A place like this needs maintenance. We'll need pumps, constantly…and the new steam ones at that."

"What are the deposits like?" They had emerged into the light once more and Knight held up his hands to shield his eyes. Even in the short distance they had gone, his boots were muddied to the tops and his coat badly marked.

"Not so bad," Havers crouched by the pieces of rock laid out on the horse rug. "See here…Devonian red…what we call arenaceous and argillaceous. Found them inside an' there's more to be had, that's fer sure. And here, copper. Not much, mind, but good quality. Whoever was here before certainly knew what they were after."

"It'll be worth a go then? Eh?" Knight stood, hands on hips. Morgan could see he was anxious.

"Well." Havers clambered slowly to his feet, still studying the samples they had collected. "'Tis *very* early days yet…*very* early." He stroked his beard then bent to examine them all once more. "But…from what we've seen today, I'm keen to have a damn good go." He glanced up at Knight. "It'd be worth it, every penny, sir. If what I think might be down there, *is* there…then my answer's yes. Most certainly."

"Then tell me for sure," Knight commanded. "I need an answer, Havers, and a true one at that. How long have we got…two months?" he turned to Morgan and saw his nod. "Get it by then, sooner if you can. I need to know, *have* to know. Do what you will, man. Move out here if you must, stay at the house. Do whatever…but let me know." Havers, head bowed, pursed his lips and nodded. He, too, knew his man.

"Right, what's next? Withypool? Then we'll change horses here an' now." Knight strode across to where one of the lads held his horse. The fair-haired boy looked up and smiled as he handed over the reins. "Well done, lad." Knight gave the boy his hat and crop then took hold of the reins. "A mighty big horse for a young'un like you. What's yer name, boy?"

"Tucker, sir. Jack Tucker." The lad moved to hold the stirrup. As he settled into the saddle and took back his hat, Knight paused to glance down at the lad once more before reaching out for his crop. The boy, still grinning, looked back at him, direct and unafraid.

4.

It took them no more than an hour, for the horses were fresh and the going good. Knight knew The Royal Oak; three years ago he had stayed there when Chichester had first called him down. Morgan knew it too, resting there when Knight sent him to check the bounds on the map. They rode slowly into the village, determined to save the horses, for the ride home promised to be long and hard.

*

"We're in the small bar, through at the back." Morgan ducked his head low and held the door. "I'll check the horses. What do you think sir...an hour?"

"Lets not hurry." Knight, his back to the fire, allowed the waiter to take his coat. As Morgan turned back, another party, two men and a women, pressed past him. Morgan frowned, certain in his own mind that he had booked the room where he and his master could talk undisturbed. Two minutes later he was back. Knight had not moved and the three newcomers were facing him. Something was wrong.

"Morgan, this gentleman, here, claims to have reserved the room." Knight spoke softly. His eyes moved from the man in front of him.

"No matter, no matter." The stranger shrugged, gesticulating then stopped suddenly. "My pardon, sir, but have we not met before? It's your face, sir, that and your voice."

"I cannot recall the honour, sir." Knight's voice had softened even further and Morgan watched closely. The stranger paused and wiped his neck, his confidence momentarily gone.

"We-ll, 'tis no matter that's for sure. There's room for us all." He laughed. "Pray be my guest, sir."

"*Your* guest." Knight pulled in his chin and looked down in surprise at the stout, shorter man. Even from where he stood, Morgan sensed trouble. The dark stubble shading the stranger's cheeks and the heavy jowls forcing themselves over his collar signalled danger. Even his stance, stocky legs apart with hands on hips, boded ill. The second man, younger and with short reddish hair, was taking off his coat. The woman stood quite still.

"Most certainly...nothing could give me more pleasure. Now, allow me, sir...Exton's the name, Sir Michael Exton." Knight moved slowly to take the proffered hand. "And now, permit me to introduce my wife...Donna Maria Josephine." Knight bowed. The woman, Morgan noted, in a gesture of arrogant indifference, barely lowered her head in acknowledgement.

"My pleasure...sir...madam. Knight's the name, Mr John Knight from Worcestershire and London. Allow me to present my companion...Mr Durnford Morgan, also from London."

In those few words, Morgan saw his master's hand. Knight had recognised the man, the one man on the list they had not been able to trace save for what Marcus Tritton had passed on earlier. Furthermore he had just heard the man talking about them meeting before and he had heard from Knight about his young Spanish wife. For all he knew, his master had indeed come across him but his signal was plain enough. He, Knight, would feign no knowledge of the man or his intentions. Let him make all the moves, Knight was telling him. But Exton, he could see, remained puzzled as if he was now more certain than ever

56

they had met before.

"Taking the air, sir, or just passing through?" Knight cocked an eyebrow. "'Tis a fine day for both, I'd say."

"No, neither." Exton took a glass from the tray, then signalled the waiter to serve the others. "Our home's near here. Pixton Park...close by Dulverton. We've land there." Exton wiped his mouth. "You familiar with the area yourself, sir?" Morgan watched as the second man stood back respectfully, allowing Exton's wife a better position near the fire. He noted the workmanlike cut of his jacket and breeches. A land agent or advisor, he thought to himself, confident that Knight would have assessed likewise.

"Not at all, sir. Strangers, both of us, We're here for the scenery and to sound out hunting prospects." Knight was playing him, trying to draw him out for belligerent, aggressive men were often braggarts. "A short stay only, just a week then we must away." Knight looked at his glass; that, at least, was true enough. "Wild country here. Not to be trifled with, d'you not think?"

"I'm up here to see." Exton rose on his toes then tugged at his collar, pleased enough with himself and happy to be holding court. "There's land to be had up here, y'know. The Crown's had enough of this wilderness. Got themselves into a terrible mess what with tenants and suitors here, there and everywhere."

"Really." Knight rolled his left shoulder. Morgan could see the vein on his cheek pulsing. "But who'd want such a place and what to do with it all?"

"Break it." Exton drained his glass and looked across to his man. "'Twould take time and money but it could be done. Eh, Harris?" The second man nodded, Knight raised his eyebrows.

"And that's your plan, sir? Goodness me." He shook his head in wonder. "Would cost a fortune, surely to God but then the land up here's worthless, is it not?" He frowned. "What d'you suppose...I know nothing of these matters, but what do suppose a man would have to pay for such a wilderness?" Knight never got the answer he sought. Even as he was speaking the door opened and two serving girls brought in their meal.

"Uh...huh," Exton turned back to Knight. While one hand held his plate of food the other was raised in triumph. "Oh yes, I remember now...*Arlington*... Arlington Court. That's where, sir. That's where we met, a fair while back now."

"Ye-es...yes...I believe I do recall now." Knight was speaking softly again. "Sir Michael Exton, you said? *Sir* Michael Exton. The name itself I recall, but that is all...yes, that is all." From where he stood, Morgan could see Exton's face. The challenge had struck home.

"Be that so, sir," the man blustered on, chewing as he spoke. "And you, good sir, if I remember rightly you were down to look at the moorland as well were you not? To see the King's bargain...no?"

"Aha, *looking*, yes, but that is all. As I said before, I'm a hunting man." Knight smiled but his eyes had no warmth. "They tell me the hounds up here can run the whole day through and now I've seen the place I can well believe it."

They did not remain long, excusing themselves for the ride home. Exton, both men knew, had his own form of capital; in addition he exuded a presumptuous self-confidence. Knight was angry, not so much that he had come across a rival he had considered a danger and one whom he had no wish to see again, but because Exton's bullish optimism mirrored his own and it stung. It worried him. It was as Elizabeth-Jane had said and now he had seen in another what others must see in him. Furthermore he, himself, had said too much and that concerned him as well. And what was more, Donna Maria had chosen to say nothing. Had she, he wondered, remembered the conversation around the dinner table at Arlington? It rankled deeply and, as they rode, he brooded. But it was the warning he needed.

*

"What say, you, Morgan?" Knight had pulled up at the head of a narrow valley, holding his hat against the stiff breeze blowing across the high ridge. The view to the north was magnificent. Exmoor tumbled away from them, downwards and onwards, fold upon fold of open countryside with only the last few hundred feet to the coast lost from view. Far away, across the wave-flecked, grey-green sea they could see the coastline of Wales where the high crests of the mountains behind were no more than distant smudges. As Queenie moved forward to drink from the spring, he let the reins go slack.

"Exton, sir?" Morgan had no idea what had been going through his mind.

"No, no...I've seen him already. Too much, in fact." Knight, his answer dismissing the man as inconsequential, tipped back his hat and blew heavily into his maroon and yellow kerchief. "I'm talking about the whole damn thing, buying the place...what's it all worth?" He turned, sniffing and wiping his nose, one hand on the back of his saddle. "You've seen and heard it all...listened to Maxwell, watched Havers and his men doing their stuff. What's it all to be?" he waived one arm airily. "How much am I going to have to pay?"

Morgan saw the jumble of figures rising and falling before him. He knew he was bound to reply and that Knight would challenge his answer but there was much to put into the equation. "Well, sir," he hesitated. "Land values first, then the mining potential." He drew the back of his hand across his mouth. "Then there're the others to consider...Frobisher, Exton and, perhaps, Branquehurst. You're going to have to pay hard, I fear."

Knight nodded. "Maxwell reckons the land itself's around seven thousand pounds. What do you think…five times as much, six perhaps."

"*No.*" Knight glanced sharply at the abrupt reply, then smiled, remembering the Morgan he had watched in Esdaile's office. "More like seven times, sir. A good seven times. Frobisher and Branquehurst have limits but Exton…now here might be a problem."

"*Seven* times, eh…*seven* times." He caught up the reins when his horse, now watered, moved forward to graze. "That's hard, Morgan. Very hard."

"Harder even to beat, sir…and that's what's going to count on the day."

Chapter Four

"And you should be aware that Mr Knight has plans to sell Lea Castle." Janet Appelton, forty years-old, spinster and housekeeper to the family for seven years, looked down the table. "It makes things tidier that way. Wolverley House will remain, of course, but I have been told to arrange a full staff here at Castle Heights."

Mr Parker, his neck tight and uncomfortable between the high wings of his collar, stared at his hands. His face was grim and he shook his head sadly. He had enjoyed his time at Lea and would miss the bustle of where he had started out as under footman to the old Mr John. Things had been different then with Mr Savoury, the house steward, in charge.

Mrs Strong, on the other hand, sat back with one arm thrown across the back of her chair. Her glasses were dangling from her mouth. She preferred it here by the sea and her face creased into a smile. Mrs Appelton paused and picked up her notes. The housekeeper had gathered the senior staff together prior to the arrival of the family. Abel Tarr, the young second butler sat next to the cook, beyond him Mary Quick, Mrs Knight's lady's maid. Opposite her and next to Parker was the diminutive and balding Saul Fraser, valet to the master.

"We must expect Mrs Knight and the children any time after tomorrow midday…and certainly before dark. They came down from Bristol today and are spending tonight at The George in South Molton. Miss Chapple, the governess will be joining us also…she'll be upstairs of course, taking her meals in the nursery or with the family when they see fit." Parker glanced at her but said nothing.

"The remaining house-servants, seven in all I believe, will be in the junior staff room." She glanced at the cook. Janet Appleton, rather *Mrs* Appelton and known as such by everyone in spite of her single marital status, was the second daughter of a Kidderminster apothecary. Brought up strictly and well educated, she had never been found by the right man and had chosen her own course through life, joining the house soon after John Knight's second marriage.

Age, she knew, was beginning to take its toll and, were it not for the close friendship of Mrs Strong, her lonely existence would have been lonelier still. She remained wary of men, many of whom made little attempt to disguise their jealousy of her position. Parker, Mr Bernard Parker in particular, she found difficult with his hauteur and his stifling, autocratic manner that too often infringed on her own sphere of influence. Angular rather than tall, she held her head high with her severely swept-back hair adding further to the daunting image.

"From today I am assuming responsibility for the housekeeping books, settling

60

all bills and seeing to the wages...in fact *all* financial matters." Parker, she noticed, showed no emotion at all but he would have resented the change, of that she was sure. "I will leave the engaging and dismissal of all internal male staff to Mr Parker but I will deal with the head groom and head gardener regarding the outside staff."

"The silver, Mrs Appelton?" Parker raised his head, inwardly bridling at the authority of the woman.

"Yes, as before, that will be your domain. We'll go through the inventory, then I'll leave the keys with you."

Parker lowered his head in acknowledgement then looked up again. "And the beer money, Mrs Appelton...and the silver fund?" His face was expressionless.

"And that's yours, too...thank you, for that." The housekeeper snatched at her notes. "And just as at Lea, I'll ask you to handle everything to do with reception and visitors...if you would be so kind. Now, Mrs Strong." The cook hurriedly replaced her spectacles. "As we discussed in the kitchen, I have decided that I will leave all the bottling, pickling and preserves to you, as well as the cakes and pastries."

"That's fine, Mrs Appelton...and thank you. We've room enough here for all of that."

"Good, so that just leaves me to say that I'm delighted we're all together at last. We need to be for I've been promised busy times ahead. Mr Knight, he's...well, anxious about a number of things at the moment. Now then, Mrs Strong, dinner?"

"Whenever you say Mrs Appelton."

"The family are dining at eight-thirty, yes? Very well, the staff will have prayers in the junior staff room at seven, then carve. *So*," she glanced around the table, "I will look forward to your company here at half past the hour. Oh...and one more thing." The five faces looked up. "I want to see the new staff one at a time in here after breakfast. That is all." Chairs scraped as she left the room with her head a touch higher than appeared comfortable.

✳

"A very good afternoon, madam." Parker waited until the footman had helped her to alight, then bowed and stepped forward. "And good to see you again, ma'am. A pleasant journey, I trust?"

"Thank you Parker but, goodness, we're all so glad to be here at last. Mr Knight at home?"

"Staghunting madam." Parker smiled. "Mr Lucas's hounds are on Brendon common today. He asked me to assure you that he'll be home well before dark." He accompanied her to the door. "Everything here's in order, madam. Mrs Appelton will see you in the day sitting room at your convenience."

"Thank you again. See the children and their staff to their apartments, would you." Elizabeth-Jane Knight nodded at Parker then turned, smiling at the figure that had appeared. "Why Mary...*here* you are. All well, I hope?"

"Indeed ma'am," Mary Quick bobbed neatly. "Your boxes arrived yesterday and your rooms're all ready. Would you care to follow me?"

*

Elizabeth-Jane unpinned her hat, threw it on to the poster bed and flopped beside it. "Oh, at last, at last...it's *so* lovely to be here, and this time it's for good. What's to do? How many do we have for dinner tonight?"

"Twelve, ma'am. I put your copy of the seating plan on the dressing table. There, look. You'll have the vicar on one side. Ever so tall he is...and the master of the hunt on the other." Elizabeth-Jane got up and scrutinised the names.

"So, what d'you suggest I wear?"

"Well, ma'am. Seeing not everything's here yet...coming tomorrow they are, so the stables say. An' seeing it's one of yer favourites, I've laid out the full satin and muslin dress, the one with the train an' the green trimming. An' I thought the white crepe cap, that one with flowers'd be nice...oh, an' yer buff gloves of course."

Elizabeth-Jane, tall, twenty-eight and the mother of five patted her flat stomach. "Perfect...and I'll have the cream slippers. Unpin my hair, will you." She turned and sat at the dressing table, lowering her head to enable her maid to unclip the double row of pearls. Watching Mary through a hand mirror, she began to hum an Irish lullaby.

"Mary," she stopped suddenly and raised her head, long strands of loose hair falling to her shoulders. "It's going to be fun here, isn't it. The staff...are they all happy?"

"Oh yes, ma'am. Well, most of them anyways." She nodded, meeting her eyes in the mirror. "Always a few grumblers mind. Not sure Mr Parker's too happy."

"Oh him...old stuffed-shirt," Elizabeth-Jane caught her maid's eye and they both laughed. "He'll come round. You wait 'til we get the house full." She lowered her head again, her mind going back to the moors they had crossed earlier and how much they reminded her of her beloved Kerry.

It was there that John, more than twice her age, had courted her and sworn that, were she to give him her hand, he would find somewhere just as beautiful, somewhere just as romantic. They had laughed at the time, wondering where such a place could be. Now she knew and she smiled to herself, remembering his vow and how he had picked her up in his arms when she nodded her acceptance. She was shy then, as shy as any girl of seventeen would be.

2.

In spite of the sea breeze lifting the curtains, the August night was hot.

John Knight, half awake then half asleep, tossed and turned. He was worried and had been for days. The sale of Exmoor by the Crown was little over a week away and he had been confident, too confident perhaps. But now, in the back of his mind, a small worm of doubt gnawed ceaselessly at his insouiance. Two names - Exton and Branquehurst – had been haunting him; now they were mocking.

An hour before cockcrow he threw back the sheets, struggled from his bed and stood unsteadily by the heavy curtains. "What's the matter, dear?" Elizabeth-Jane half rose. "Are you not well?"

"Can't sleep, damn it," Knight muttered. "Where's Morgan's room?"

"*What?*" She sat up straight, scrabbling for the flint. "For God's *sake*, John. Why *him, now*?" The wick caught. "And at this hour. What's on your mind?" Her eyes followed the nightgowned figure as it made it's way to the door. "The second door on the left...the west wing. But John, dear...."

"Damn boy...won't do as I tell him," Knight was fumbling for the chair by the armoire. "Thinks he knows it all. Too easy by half on those villains out there." He continued to grope. "My cap, where's my cap, God dammit...and my house shoes?"

"*John.*" Elizabeth-Jane was beside him. "*Not* now, dearest...not now. 'Twill be light before long...and you'll be able to think more clearly. It'll be easier...come back to bed."

"Let me be, dear. There's work to be done...I *have* to get things moving. I must drive him on...time's against us." He kissed her forehead, holding her head gently. "Worry not...have faith, my love, have faith."

✳

Morgan heard the footsteps. As soon as they stopped outside his door, he was out of his bed, flint scratching against metal until the lamp-flame took. He knew at once who it was and it did not surprise him.

For weeks, Knight had been brooding, demanding ever more information about his opponents, proof of what they knew already, even promises that what he had been told was true. He was by the door when it opened. *"Ah,"* Knight stepped back. "So you're awake too, Morgan." He stood framed in the doorway, a ghostly figure in his white cap and gown, and now somewhat abashed. "Forgive me, at this early hour, but we have to talk."

"Indeed, sir, indeed. Be pleased to come in." Even as he reached for his coat, the younger man sensed the change. "Now…where would you wish. In here, sir, or down below…the study perhaps." He held the lamp high and started in surprise. The heavily-shadowed face that stared back was not the one he knew. Instead, he saw an old man whose face was drawn and haggard and whose eyes had sunk deep. The hair was standing out wildly from under the cap giving the impression of a living corpse, one whose strength and purpose had gone. Morgan caught his breath then gave the answer himself. "Here, sir. Take a seat, will you. 'Tis warm enough in here. Now then, what is your wish at this hour?"

"Exton and…Branquehurst." As he sat in the offered chair, his voice groaned the names wearily. "They're varmints, the two of 'em, Morgan. Nothing but a pair of villains and 'tis not right they should stand in our way." He sat nervously with his hands together, clasped tight like the man on edge that he was.

"Indeed, sir, indeed." Morgan sat beside him, peering closely at the face behind the lamp. Was it possible that these were the same features that had glared so defiantly a month ago, ordering him to leave the two imposters well alone. *"Let them run,"* the voice had growled dismissively. *"They're small beer…little men of no consequence."* Now *he* looked the hunted one. Something had changed: he was no longer the man of even a week ago. "Have you had news, sir?" Morgan placed the lamp on the covered table between them. "Do you know more than we've found already?"

"Yes…I mean, no." The hesitant voice again. Morgan stared, now thoroughly alarmed. Knight, the great industrial mogul of middle England, the dynamic Iron Master who held the livelihood of thousands in his hand, seemed bereft of energy. He had shrunk: that awesome presence had vanished leaving just the husk of a little old man. "Listen…you remember we…I told you just the other day to think no more of them, to forget about them." Morgan nodded, watching closely as Knight looked down, toying with the buttons on his gown.

"It was Exton that did it." Knight looked up sharply. "That chance meeting at the inn…I saw him for what he was." He pulled off his nightcap then scratched hard at his mane. "Dangerous, he is…dangerous like a snake, and a liar to boot…all this Sir Michael nonsense."

"Then we should act as I suggested, sir. Straight away after first light. A letter to the Second Sea Lord at the Admiralty and another to the Court of Saint James…to His Excellency, The Ambassador of Spain. We must expose the rascals for what they are and let those who are seeking them do what they will.

We spoke of it all, sir...remember?"

"I know, I know." He sounded resigned. "It's just that such action as this seems so...so...well, to do that would look as though I were unable to run my own affairs...as if I was touting for support when this is a fight I must win, and win by myself." The words out, Knight looked up, some of the vigour had returned to his face. "We must see them off ourselves, d'you hear. See them off with what we ourselves have found, not get others to do our dirty work. That would be cheap...a foul almost, and something I could never countenance.

"Then, I shall write to the two men themselves." Knight glanced up at the strength in the younger man's voice. "I have all the evidence we need, more than enough. If they have nothing to fear then they'll continue to fight...if not, if their gaff spar is blown then their race is run. They cannot continue, they would not have the courage."

"Have we time, boy?" Knight's face was searching his. "Is there time for games such as this?"

"To be sure." Morgan rose relieved. It was what he had been seeking permission to do. Time and again he had pressed his master for action. Knight, he was certain, had seen the danger but had been unwilling to act. He had considered such a move to be a mark of weakness, something beneath his dignity and he had prevaricated.

"They both live locally, so they'll receive the letters this very day. I'll phrase them so there's no doubt...even half of what we know will suffice. Fear not, sir." His hand reached for Knight's shoulder. "There *will* be no challenge, I assure you, sir, no fighting back. They would not dare...the evidence we have on them alone will break their resolve."

Morgan leant against the door. Knight had not said much, simply risen and taken his leave. What was it, he wondered, that the man could have seen or heard to force such a change. What was it that had, at last, brought him to his senses. He shrugged and pushed himself away from the door.

Knight turned the corner of the corridor and stood, one hand against the wall steadying himself in the darkness. He could feel his strength returning, the blood coursing back through his body once again. It had been a whole week since her arrival, since he saw the happiness on her face as she came down the main staircase to meet him; that laughter in her eyes and the outstretched arms. He remembered how his heart had surged with the sheer joy. To see his young wife thus was more than he ever dared hope for and, in that instant, he was determined that the moors would be theirs at whatever the price and whatever it took. Even now that memory of her made him smile.

He took a deep breath, felt in front of him tentatively and moved slowly along the wall.

3.

"Thank you." Raimond Maxwell took his seat in the hotel lobby. Two others were there but the remaining seats had yet to be filled. It was quiet, unlike outside in the main square where a small, noisy crowd had gathered. Maxwell recognised Sir Thomas Acland's agent but not the one sitting reading who chose to ignore them. He took out his watch and saw there were five minutes remaining then watched casually as a liveried waiter opened the brass-handled door at the far end of the corridor. Cocking an ear, he listened to catch the voices inside the room until the door was pulled shut.

Jameson, Acland's man caught his eye and smiled but the man in the chair read on, his head bowed as if he had no care. Maxwell got up and studied the hunting print over the desk then the pattern of mounted fox masks and pads nailed to the wall. He had just begun it all over again when the front door crashed open. All three jumped. In the sunlight beyond, Maxwell could see the tightly pressed faces, straining for a glimpse at who or what lay inside South Molton's George Hotel.

"No more tenders gentlemen." The Yeomanry sergeant, sabre drawn and head held high, looked down from under the peak of his cap. "That's it…just seven bids but only you three gentlemen here for the result. That's all." They watched as he marched briskly to the end of the corridor and knocked. As he did so the town clock struck midday.

Almost immediately the door opened again. "The result gentlemen." The Town Crier read quietly from the parchment. He was a large, heavy man, red-faced and pompous and he spoke with a hoarse voice that was more used to shouting. "As it pleases the Crown Commissioners acting for and on behalf of His Most Excellent Majesty King George the Third, all bids tendered within the time allotted and having been perused by the said Commissioners, the same have been pleased to make the following announcement." He pulled on his scarlet collar and raised himself up further.

"The allotment, known as the Royal Forest of Exmoor and given in right of the Crown, has been purchased by Mr John Knight of Wolverley Hall, Worcestershire and of 52 Portland Place, London for the figure of fifty thousand pounds. The said…."

Maxwell did not wait to hear more. By the time the Town Crier had opened the front door to face the crowd and make public the news, he was running to the stables at the bottom of the hotel yard. "'Tis ours," he gasped. "Ours, by God. Ride with the news…ride fast to Lynton." Maxwell clapped the man on his shoulder. "Go straight to Castle Heights…you'll find the master waiting there."

✳

66

"Abel...Abel...go for the Master and Mrs Knight." Mrs Strong stood panting in the doorway. "Go on, *quickly*...there's news from South Molton. He's there, the galloper, look...waiting all excited at the back door." She waved her hand in the man's direction, gulping for air at the same time. "Oh, my dear soul...'tis wonderful, wonderful...."

"What is it?"   "What's the news?" Chairs scraped back hurriedly. "Tell us quickly....what is it?" All three in the room spoke at once.

"It's *ours*," Mrs Strong gasped, her eyes wide. "The master's done it...see the galloper's face. The moor is ours. He's *won*. Oh...Mary," she swept Mrs Knight's maid into her arms. Mrs Appelton stood beaming, waiting for Mrs Strong. Mary Quick hugged them both at the same time.

Parker turned slowly from the window. His face was stern. "Oh, come on, Mr Parker, be *happy*...it's wonderful news." Janet Appelton clapped her hands. "It's marvellous, we're here to stay."

"There's work to be done, Mrs Appelton." Parker reached for his coat, as the others made for the door. "The master will be pleased and will wish to celebrate his good news...of that there can be no doubt."

Mrs Strong held back, waiting until the voices faded down the corridor. "You didn't want it to be like this, did you dear? You were hoping...maybe, we'd be going back up north again, weren't you?" She smiled kindly and took the butler's arm. "Don't be angry, Bernard. Not now. 'Tis what the master wanted, you know that. Don't let him see you all down like this...not just now."

Parker stared at her then lowered his head. "Well," his voice was thin. "It's our job to serve the master wherever he is...Wolverley, London, here...or wherever he chooses. That's his choice but...." He stopped suddenly, knowing the cook was watching him. "But, yes...since you ask." He paused and nodded to himself. "Och, never mind," he laughed drily, glancing back at her. "Come on now, away to the others...I've to see to the master. He'll be calling for me."

The butler heard them as soon as he came into the hall. Elizabeth-Jane and Mrs Appleton were chattering excitedly together. The children appeared at the top of the stairs and made their way down accompanied by their nanny and a parlour maid. The eldest, a pale child of about six, was dressed in a scarlet silk shirt and navy blue knickerbockers. His mass of tight black curls bobbed as he jumped the last steps.

"Come on, come on everyone." John Knight's voice boomed from the terrace. The front door burst open. "Parker...ah, there you are. Champagne, my man, champagne...let's be having it right away. Great news, what?"

"Excellent news indeed, sir. My congratulations." The butler's face gave nothing away.

"Oh, Parker, this is marvellous…you must be thrilled." Elizabeth-Jane took the youngest of her children from her nanny's arms.

"Very exciting, madam." He could see they were all delighted. "I'm sure you must be overjoyed." It was not within his remit to demonstrate emotion and he remained impassive.

"What is it Papa? What is it?" The two eldest boys struggled for possession of their father's hand.

"Parker, tell them to round everyone up." Knight patted his shoulder then bent and ruffled the boys' hair. "House, stables, ground staff, all of them…be here…no, wait a minute. Out in front, there's more room outside." He rubbed his hands together vigorously. "Outside in half an hour and I'll confirm it all myself."

"Very good, sir. And the drinks now?"

"Yes, yes." The two men looked at each other but it was Knight who looked down. His face fell. "Oh, Parker…oh dear…oh dear. I can read your mind you know. I can tell by your face. I know what you were after. You were hoping that maybe…perhaps…."

"The memory goes back a long way, sir. They were very good days up there, were they not? Happy times indeed."

"I know, I know but I'll need you here, my man." Knight had lowered his voice. "Need you badly, you know. There's so much to be done." Parker caught his look of concern. "D'you think…."

"You can rely on me, sir. You know that…there'll never be a problem there."

4.

Jack took time to adjust to his new way of life. It should have been easy for there was plenty enough room in the spacious loft above the stables and Kathy Govier, wife of the head groom, begged pieces of furniture from the house. But, new and smaller than the other stable lads, his early days were wretched and folorn.

Two of the older lads, Nathan Westcott, the one who had met them at the forge when they arrived, and Wesley Cross, took what bedding he had been given. He was forced to sleep in the hay, curled up in a horse blanket. Sometimes they taunted him, sometimes they bullied: whenever they could, they stole his ration of food. There was no one to turn to and he was a long way from home.

*

The first years were hard, the next worse but he survived and when Cross left and Westcott ran away to sea, his confidence returned. He grew tall for his age and his body filled.

He watched and he learned, and he made new friends. Hector Coward, the second gardener, a year older, taller and strongly built showed him how to make kites from thick paper and pieces of wood. They would fly them from the cliff edge where the kites rose high, lifted by winds that rushed up the cliffs from the shore below.

Ruben Corwen, the slow talking farrier, taught him how to listen for the different ringing tones as his mighty arms beat hammer against anvil. The boy learned how to help by keeping the coal fire filled while waiting for the horses to be shod, how to work the bellows and hold spare shoeing nails ready for Ruben to place in his mouth as he bent over the iron shoes when they were still glowing red.

Orwell Govier was the head groom. Diminutive and hawk-faced, he was a Lynton man, quite unable to remember when he first sat on a horse. Orwell's elder brother said that it was some time before he was three. But he was six, Orwell Govier remembered, when he started cleaning harnesses and oiling hooves at the livery stables behind The Rising Sun. He could, he declared with certainty, tell a horseman when he saw one. "Young or old, expert or novice, it mattered not," Orwell decreed. "If 'tis there, 'tis there." Young Tucker, he announced assuredly, was born to ride. The horses, he declared, knew it too.

*

Winter passed and in the spring three foals were born. Orwell gave Jack the task of tending the youngsters. One afternoon, just after he had changed the water in the boxes, Jack noticed a small boy standing alone. Looking closer he saw the youngster was finely dressed in a bottle-green velvet suit with lace collar and cuffs. The tiny shoes on his feet had silver buckles and his ink-black hair surrounded a dark blue velvet cap in a ring of tight curls.

The child was watching him shyly with one finger in his mouth. When Jack moved to pass, he took his finger out. "What's your name?" Jack barely heard him, but he stopped and bent down.

"My name's Jack, sir. Jack Tucker." He smiled at the boy who stared back, inquisitively. "And who are you, might I ask?"

"Frederic," he whispered, almost inaudibly. "I'm Frederic Knight. Please may I see the horses?"

"Ah," said Jack, standing up. "I know who you are, young sir. Your papa is master here, isn't he, now? Come on then, let's see what we can find." The boy slipped a warm, damp hand into his and clung tightly as they made their way across the yard to the line of foaling boxes. Jack bent and lifted him, then held him against the door so he could peer inside.

"Oh, Master Frederic, there you are." The shrill voice made them turn. "Oh, my dear soul, we've been searching for you all over the place. Where've you bin?" The housemaid, with her hips swaying heavily, was running awkwardly, holding her cap to her head. "What you doing way down here? Come away with me now. Come on. Come away, this instant."

Frederic clung to Jack. The tears came with the shout. "Leave me alone, you," he wailed, pushing at her hand. "I'm six now and I want to stay here. Leave me *alone*," he screeched. "I want to see the horses."

"Come on, Master Frederic," Jack coaxed gently. "You'd best be doing what they want. Perhaps your mother'll let you come down again. We'll see to that," he looked at the maid. "I'll show you round proper then. We've got kittens in the hay over the horses and chickens in coops round the back." The boy had stopped crying and was looking from one to the other. His eyes were still wet.

"D'you think so, Ruth?" Frederic looked at the maid. "Can I really? D'you think mama will let me come down and see them…the kittens and things?" His face swung back to Jack's, one arm still around his neck. "You'll be here, won't you Jack?" he asked anxiously. "Say you will."

"I'll be here, Master Frederic. No fear of that." Jack lowered him to the ground. "I'm here every day," he laughed.

*

"So, that's the lad, Govier?" John Knight leant over the paddock fence with one foot on the bottom rail. "Been here a while, yes?"

"Aye, sir. That's him. He's got a beautiful seat…a natural horseman if ever I saw one."

Jack coaxed the tall chestnut around the perimeter then turned sharply, urging the animal towards the line of timber fences. "Round again, Jack," Orwell called loudly. "Take a straighter line this time, lad. Collect 'im up, an' ride 'im well into them." He looked at Knight. "Course, you've heard about his father, sir?"

"Yes," he replied, watching the boy. "A fine man and a gallant soldier, so I hear. Young Freddie's met the lad…can't stop talking about him. Goes on about him the whole time…drives us all mad, especially young Kenton."

Orwell Govier watched closely. "Right, Jack. That'll do for Cutlass," he called. "Take him in and bring on Queenie. Check that cut on her leg first, mind."

He turned back to Knight. "Well, beggin' your pardon, sir, but I reckon it's time to be thinking of getting young Master Frederic up and away. I'd like to see him make a start. I'll watch the boy carefully then, once we're happy, and if you agree, there's no better person to look after him than young Jack here...be rising twelve soon, so he will. I've watched 'em together and he's real gentle with the boy. Takes proper care of him."

*

John Knight, a careful man not prone to taking chances, liked to have a second horse with him whenever he rode out from Castle Heights and Jack, being so light, was appointed to ride behind him. Sometimes he would lead a third horse and after several hours of hard riding they would stop for Knight to select a fresh mount. The boy would then be tasked to ride home alone on the tired animal.

All this time Jack was learning about the high moors, how to recognise areas of soft, marshy ground that could trap a horse and rider, sucking them down before swallowing them altogether. He learned to follow the tracks left by sheep and deer who knew instinctively how to pick a safe route through the dangerous, waterlogged bogs. Orwell Govier taught him how to judge the weather pattern and foretell sudden changes when, without warning, clouds would roll in from the west, covering the moor in a thick, damp mist that swirled around in an eerie silence. "Soon as they mists start coming in you need to have your wits about you," he warned.

"Never wait 'til it's all round you...'twill be too late. Soon as you see it coming, take a line on where you're going and keep to it," he cautioned. "If you're really lost then make for lower ground, sooner or later you'll reach farmland then the farm itself. Never stay up there, never...you'll get nowhere 'cept into a bog," he said with a laugh.

He began to ride further afield on his own, sometimes leading two or even three horses. It was not long before he found the steep track that ran down behind Castle Heights through the woods to Mars Hill then on down again to the harbour at Lynmouth and the harbour. He told Frederic what he had seen and they rode down together.

"Come down with us, papa," Frederic begged his father. "You never take me with you. Come and see the ships and all the fish they catch." Knight promised his son he would and kept to his word.

Jack lead the way. They dropped sharply on to the slender shelf at Mars Hill, then plunged down the cliff path again before emerging from the woods. "Look, Papa," Frederic shrilled excitedly. "They smoke the fish there...don't they, Jack? And look over there, that's where they put them in salt."

They watched as baskets of fish were unloaded from the small herring drifters before being carried across the quayside. There, women would stand in a line laughing and joking as they gutted the catch in the bright sunlight.

"Tell me, Jack," Knight queried. "Is the way we came today the only route down?"

"No, sir. There's the packhorse trail…over there, sir, look." He stood and pointed. "There's talk of another road to be built, but there's no sign of it yet." Knight did not reply but stood silently in his saddle, staring up the steep gorge to where the two Lyn rivers met a short distance behind a line of fishermen's cottages. Riding to the harbour's edge he asked about the depth of draft and how the tides and winds affected the approaches to the harbour.

Eventually he returned. His hat was off and he was scratching his head. "I have it mind to use this harbour." The two boys followed him as he continued his search for a route. "But we're going to have to find a better way up than this or else build a way ourselves. All right," he gave the high cliffs a final glance. "Come on Jack, take us away up home. There's work to be done and tomorrow it's out to Simonsbath."

5.

Katherine Mary Elizabeth Harriet Darcy stood a little apart from the others. She was bored. The north facing lawns of Castle Heights were already in shadow, while the tall oaks beyond the beech hedge were keeping all but the last of the sun from the grass. Her father, George Preston the fourth Duke of Northborough was out riding the moor with his host, John Knight. As soon as the result of the sale was known in August, Elizabeth-Jane had begged her husband to invite their guests to stay so they could show them Exmoor and tell them their plans.

Amelia, the Duke's wife, held her skirt with one hand and leant forward about to throw the quoit. "But there's nothing to do, mama." Katherine, the eldest of her three children walked towards her. "You promised we could go down to the beach. You said we could," she pleaded.

"No, Katherine. Not today, it's far too late. Oh…tch, look at that will you." The rope fell short and the Duchess went forward to collect the quoits from the coloured pins that somebody had pushed into the grass. "We're going to go down there tomorrow, with papa and Mr Knight, so let's not hear any more of it tonight." She watched as Lizzie, the most sensitive of her three children, lowered her head. Katherine, she noticed, glared defiantly

"Hush. I can hear them now." Elizabeth-Jane held up a hand. "Listen…horses. That's them…they're back. Freddy, you and Kenton run on with the girls. Tell papa not to be long…remind him we've got the musicians coming in and dinner's going to be early. He's promised to be there."

*

The two men had alighted already, the horses taken from them by the waiting grooms. "Yes, that's right. Both dog carts...round to the front at nine." John Knight stood with his hands on his hips. "Lord Northborough and I'll have second horses...we'll ride on after the picnic. And get ponies ready for Frederic and Kenton...and one for Lady Katherine."

"Very good, sir." Orwell Govier nodded. "And the same the next day as well?" Knight paused, chin in hand, before nodding.

Jack lead Cutlass slowly. The fine horse had been ridden hard and his flanks and saddle patch were still steaming. The boy stopped, then stooped low to feel carefully down each leg before lifting the hooves one at a time to check. The animal, still blowing, stood patiently with its tired head low. But suddenly it was up again, alert with ears pricked. Jack turned.

"Have you seen my papa and the others?" Jack looked at the face under the straw hat. He knew exactly who she was for Govier had warned everyone about their arrival.

"Yes, m'lady." He struggled to tidy his hair. "They're all up in the yard...by the boxes, ma'am." Katherine smiled back at the friendly face.

"D'you ride him yourself?" She took a step closer.

"Only for the master, m'lady. Only when he wants a second horse, like."

"Oh, so will you be coming out with us tomorrow then...out to the picnic?" She looked at him hopefully with her head on one side.

"'Spect so, m'lady. That's if Mr Govier says so," he shrugged, still smiling and unaware that they were talking so freely.

She paused. "And you might come riding as well...with us I mean?"

"Don't 'spect so, m'lady," Jack shrugged again. "My job's to bring out the horses, that's all."

"Oh, I see." For a moment she seemed disappointed but smiled again briefly before turning and running towards the stable block, skipping as she went. He watched her go. There was something about her that reminded him of his own sister. It was the hazel eyes and the long brown hair...and the soft voice. He sighed and led the tired horse back to its box. How fine it would be if Emma could be dressed like that.

Chapter Five

"Come *in*." Durnford Morgan turned, still adjusting his white tie.

"Compliments of Mrs Knight, sir...dinner will be ready shortly." Abel Tarr stood in the bedroom doorway. His sharply receding ginger hair made the second butler's face seem rounder than it actually was and when he smiled, which was often, his rosy cheeks positively glowed. He had been looking after the banker since his arrival a week earlier and the two men had taken an immediate liking to one another. As usual, he was grinning.

"Right, look...see to my tails, will you...quick now." Tarr took the ivory-handled brush and began to tidy the taller man's evening dress. "Who've we got this evening, Tarr? Just Mrs Knight and myself again?" He asked the question nonchalantly, busying himself with his gold cuff links. Several times, after he had been alone with his hostess, he had seen the expression on his servant's face. It was an amused, quizzical look, as if the man was trying to read his mind and was wanting to know more. He wondered if Elizabeth-Jane's thoughts ran similarly. The very idea intrigued him but, if she did, she had given no sign.

"Not this evening, sir. Miss Chapple's back from Bristol and will be taking dinner with you." Morgan's disappointment was tinged with relief. The more he had been alone with Elizabeth-Jane this week, the more he had felt drawn towards her, irresistibly so, but this evening it would have to be different. The thin, mouse-haired governess, surely a lost cause to the hungriest of men, would be sitting there, ears picking up every nuance, every intimation in what was being said. Each gesture, glance and tiny signal would be marked carefully. He would have to force all emotion from his mind, concentrating instead on his food and the woman's meaningless prattle.

For almost a week John Knight had been absent, dashing away with Maxwell to check something or other, forever seeking more land to purchase or tracking down Havers to question his findings. He, Durnford Morgan, had been left back at Castle Heights with orders to see to the books. He had taken himself off to Barnstaple, as instructed by Knight, only to return later. The Master had warned him that he, too, would be hurrying back as soon as possible.

That would be tomorrow when Elizabeth-Jane would be reunited with her elderly, tempestuous husband. Their situation intrigued him. She was an alluring woman, beautiful in her own winsome way yet lonely, of that he was sure. She had to be; her husband, more than twice her age, left her alone for days at a time, weeks even, when she was miles from anything or anyone that might amuse. She must surely crave company and attention but there was no one. What man could fail to notice, wondering who or what it was she missed most? And who would not have felt the devil on his shoulder?

"I'm on my way…go tell her I'm coming this instant," Morgan ushered Tarr to the door, then ducked back to tidy his hair and feed his watch chain into place before hurrying after him. At the top of the stairs he paused, listening intently as the soft plaintive notes of Mozart's *Fantasy in D* floated up through the hall to where he stood. She was playing again and he closed his eyes, inwardly groaning with pleasure. His heart, he could feel, had begun to beat faster.

＊

"Elementary numeracy and simple literary skills…no more than that." Enid Chapple sat back. "It'll be easy, Mrs Knight. I suggest we make a start as soon as we can. Three lessons a week should be quite adequate." The small talk had bored him but the woman herself had surprised him; he had to admit. Morgan looked again. This evening Enid Chapple was buoyant and alive, her eyes actually shining as she laughed. Her dress, plain yet well fitting, did her no harm. She might even have begun to look faintly attractive. An effort had been made but for whom or for what cause he had no idea.

Throughout the meal Elizabeth-Jane had talked continuously to the governess about educating the staff, about Freddy and Kenton's progress and of the latest fashion in the Bristol shops. No longer dowdy and withdrawn, Miss Chapple had led the conversation and her mistress was happy for that to be so.

"Let us adjourn." As Elizabeth-Jane rose so Tarr moved to open the door through to the hall. "Please excuse us, Mr Morgan," she looked up and smiled at the figure already standing beside her chair. "Pray join us in the music room when you're ready, we shall not be long." She turned to the butler. "Take the drinks and dried fruits there too, if you will."

"Will you play for us?" Morgan caught her eye.

"Ha, Mr Morgan…I was wondering if you might ask." She tapped his wrist with her fan. "We'll see…we'll see. It's been a long day and I'm tired but, Tarr, light up the candelabra, will you…the tall one next to the piano."

Morgan waited, first in the dining room, where he sat alone finishing his glass, one leg crossed over the other, his eyes making contact with those staring down from the portraits high on the walls. Hearing no sound he got up and strolled leisurely through the hall and into the music room where he stopped by the piano to tinker idly with the keys.

"Oh dear, oh dear, Enid's lost to us both," Elizabeth-Jane, skirts raised in front of her, swept into the room. "Wouldn't come down," she protested. "I tried to entice her, but no."

Morgan caught the scent of her freshly applied perfume. "Try as I might but she said she was tired…something about a long day tomorrow." Elizabeth-Jane stopped in front of him. "Perhaps that's our cue…a quick glass of canary. Port for you, yes? Then one last piece." She moved towards the piano but checked herself. "*I* know" she smiled over her shoulder. "Let me surprise you…John Field, the father of the nocturne…and an Irishman at that. Let me see now."

Morgan watched from his place by the fire. Sitting erect with her hair swept back before falling in long ringlets, Elizabeth-Jane stared at the score in front of her, her eyes wide with intensity and her lips slightly parted. She paused composing herself, then slowly, as she began to play, her whole body moved. Fearful of distracting her, he placed his glass down carefully on the mantel-piece and stood quietly.

The woman was in love with the music, her every movement as sensuous as the sounds of the notes she was playing, her expression changing with the rise and fall of tempo and passion. Slowly, and as silently as he was able, he stole closer, as close as he dared until he was standing behind her, looking down at the music that held her attention.

He watched carefully then leant forward half over her and reached out. Without thinking, she nodded. Morgan turned the page, secured the sheet and stood back. She played on; again his hand reached out. Once more she nodded, this time smiling in acknowledgement. They continued together until he held the page for the last time, waiting for the music to end.

"Well, well, well…Mr Morgan." Elizabeth-Jane reached up and caught his hand. As she leant back, craning her neck round to see him, her body brushed his. "Now *that's* something I never knew. And, my goodness, you read well." Her hand fell away.

"Since I was a boy," he cleared his throat and coughed lightly. "Do excuse me for intruding…our mother taught us at home. We all learned…we had to but I loved it." Elizabeth-Jane looked away; for a moment neither spoke. "Please, play on," his voice was little more than a whisper. "It was beautiful…quite beautiful."

"Just one more." Her voice was low. "And it must be the last." She turned back to the piano, searching through the music until she found what she was looking for, then adjusted the stool. Morgan looked on as her hands flicked through the music then watched her eyes as they studied the work. Softly, one hand at a time and with her head moving in unison, she began again, this time it was the hauntingly slow movement of Beethoven's *Pathetique* that filled the room.

Morgan swallowed. He had not moved and felt her against him whenever she leant back. She would have known he was there. He watched, first the music, then the soft whiteness of the top of her breasts rising and falling under the rows of pearls. He reached out for the page but she shook her head closing the book herself and playing on instinctively. Gently and tenderly he rested his hand on her shoulder, almost at once sensing her stir under his touch then move with him as his fingers crept towards the nape of her neck.

"What are you doing?" She had stopped and was staring straight ahead. Her body was quite still. "You're testing me, aren't you?" she half turned, but did not look at him. "Aren't you?" One hand reached up and closed over his.

"Testing myself," he muttered, curling one finger through hers.

"It's neither the time nor place." Shaking her head, Elizabeth-Jane rose and turned towards him. "I'm married," she whispered. "And I'm a mother, too...and the mistress of this house."

"I know," he whispered back. "That's why I've waited so long."

She smiled and looked down at the studs on his shirt. He watched her face, his eyes lingering as they searched for some clue. For a moment they stood close, neither moving.

"You're wicked, Mr Morgan...Mr Durnford Morgan, but I appreciate your sentiments." Elizabeth-Jane looked up and straightened his tie. "Thank you," she whispered. "But come...the servants will wonder why we're so quiet."

✳

The two doors closed, one after the other. Somewhere a drawer was pushed shut, somewhere else a shoe fell to the floor and a chair was pulled across boards then silence spread throughout the house. Ten minutes later a door on the landing opened. She moved slowly and silently across the open space, picking her way carefully before turning down the corridor. At one point a floorboard creaked and she froze, terrified of being found and waited several minutes before daring to go further. By then her whole body was shivering.

Even as she opened the bedroom door she heard him stir. She knew he had been waiting for her, ready and expectant, and warming the bed. Neither said a word. As she slipped between the sheets she felt the strong, muscular arms close around her thin body pulling her towards him. She could smell the animal earthiness of the man and the sour drink on his breath. "Bernard," she breathed. "Oh, Bernard." Reaching out hungrily, Enid Chapple pulled his head down then wriggled further underneath the butler's warm, hard body.

2.

"So you reckon I'll be in trouble with Sir James Esdaile, d'you? Is that it, sir?" Knight glanced at Morgan, a look of scorn on his face. "Too many promissory notes going out of my accounts? Eh?"

The four men sat in the morning room. Morgan had been back to The

77

Barnstaple Bank where he found a letter demanding his immediate attention. It was in Sir James's hand and what he had to say made him read it again, then a third time as he sat in the window overlooking Paternosta Row.

The bank, Sir James had written, while retaining every confidence in their much respected and highly esteemed client, Mr John Knight, was, nonetheless, becoming increasingly concerned. Seeing that Barclay, Tritton and Co were involved closely, he, Sir James Esdaile, had discussed the matter personally with Sir Crispin Barclay. While the banks had been happy to release funds covering expenditure to date, it was noted that the outflow of capital had been substantial. Lombard Street was desirous of information concerning Mr John Knight's future intentions, in particular his proposals for reconstituting the accounts at his earliest convenience.

There was no need, Sir James went on, to bring the matter directly to the attention of Mr Knight himself, rather an informative and urgent reply from the recipient should be forwarded to him in person. Sir James Esdaile had every confidence in his representative while he, on behalf of Esdaile's of London, remained his most obedient servant.

Morgan pulled a long face. Knight would not be pleased, the less so as he had numerous plans afoot, most of which would require further and extensive capital outlay. Were such ideas to be brought to the attention of Sir James, then he, Durnford Morgan, would lie squarely in the middle of what would undoubtedly become a noisy and unseemly dispute and the idea was not appealling.

∗

"Well, sir, hardly trouble," Morgan gave a little laugh. "However, as I am your bank's representative, I considered it only prudent that we should take stock of the present financial situation. We've...rather you have moved with uncommon speed, sir, and, from what you say, there is still some way to go." Morgan looked across the table. Raimond Maxwell glanced at his master then nodded in agreement. Havers, cautious as always, stared back at him, his face lugubrious but otherwise devoid of expresion.

"Right." Knight rubbed his shoulder and frowned. "So, London's bin screaming and yelling have they? Hmmph...don't bother to answer me...I can tell. Well, I'm not having any of that wretched crowd up there telling me what to do. They're terrified of getting their feet wet, that lot. Lily livered, so they are." The voice was harsh. "None of them've bin near the place, dammit...an' they can't go preaching the gospel like that...not at me anyway."

"Quite so, sir." Morgan had been ready for the tirade, in fact he had warned the others to be prepared. But then Knight, he surmised, knew only too well that the banks would want to know how matters stood. "Might I suggest that we see first where we stand...then look ahead?"

"Hmmph." Knight scratched his mane. "You lot don't run me, ye know."

"Of course not, sir, but I think it only right that we should keep London informed…enough to satisfy them, at least." Knight remained silent. Watching him carefully out of the corner of his eye, Morgan opened the file in front of him. "Well, sir, if I might start. Now…we have secured the three thousand acres or so from Sir Thomas Acland." Morgan read from the sheet in front of him. "And at the same price per acre as you paid for the moor itself." Maxwell nodded.

"I know," Knight muttered sullenly, aware that the others had tried to get him to lower the price. "But I gave him my word and that's that."

"And the same with Sir Charles Bamfylde." Morgan pursed his lips. The price there had also been high, far too high, but this, he decided judiciously, was a point now best left unchallenged. "There are several smaller bits and pieces but, all in all, it looks as though the estate stands at around sixteen thousand acres."

"Don't forget all that we're buying from the Chichesters…Sir Arthur."

"Sir?" Morgan looked nonplussed.

"Oh, come on boy," Knight banged the table. "I told you weeks ago. Brendon…the manor there…Badgeworthy and all those other farms Then there's Simonsbath Manor itself, together with its own farm. For Heaven's sake, man, that's well over five thousand acres more…what've you been up to?"

Knight glared furiously. His eyebrows were puckered and his jaw jutted pugnaciously. "Sitting there with that mind of yours up in the clouds no doubt…what? Address yourself more diligently to matters that concern *me*, sir…that's what I'm paying you for."

Morgan looked down. He knew it would be coming and that he would be the most likely target of the wrath yet he cursed himself for forgetting that particular conversation; it was the one slip which had given Knight his chance. The man had often let his views concerning the calculating ways of bankers become known. He despised them for their wariness and lack of courage in seeing a project through and for their serpentine response to anything that might not be in their own best interest. Here, now, was his riposte.

The other two were busying themselves with the papers in front of them. It was Havers who brought up the subject of mineral rights. "Now *that's* important." Knight jabbed the table with his finger. "That's *most* important. Well said, sir. Well said."

"We have them for the Forest already, sir." Morgan paused, about to continue.

"I *know*." Knight's hand crashed down again. "But I want them *all*, dammit…I want every single acre I've got to be covered. What d'you s'pose would happen to Havers here," he waved a hand at the engineer. "What would we do if Havers came running in with a quarter of pure copper in his hands an' I've not got the development rights? Eh? What in hell's name do we do then?" He got up and walked to the window, leaving the three at the table to imagine the consequences. "Just make sure we have the mineral rights and mining options on everything." He turned. "On *everything*."

Morgan knew he had to continue and that Knight, however much he shouted and cursed, would know as well. It was his unenviable duty to press on. "We can do it all, sir," he had checked and rechecked the figures. "We can do everything here but…no more. I will order the necessary funds from London…they should be in Barnstaple in a week or so."

Knight glowered. His hair, always a wild tangle, now looked worse than ever, but he nodded nonetheless. He knew he had to hear Morgan out. "Anything after that will be up to you and Sir James, sir, but he'll wish to have further assets released and brought forward…the more so as you have been thinking of building roads and developing farms."

"And my rail tracks." Knight smirked mischievously, glancing from one to the other. "You'll not forget my railway…or the canal."

"Indeed, sir." Morgan winced. "But might I suggest we wait awhile…wait until we know a little more perhaps."

"After France, you mean?" Knight's fingers drummed challengingly on the top of the table.

"Exactly, sir." Even as he took a deep breath, Morgan saw the looks of surprise. "Yes, gentlemen. After we've been to France…but I must point out that what we're dealing with here is already an immense project, the likes of which only very few will have seen. And if I understand you correctly, sir," he glanced at the Iron Master, "This is only the beginning." Knight raised an eyebrow.

3.

"*Who*?" Mrs Strong looked up from her crochet. "Never heard of nothing like that before, I'm sure. Who d'you say he is?"

"The Surveyor General of Roads." Parker adjusted his jacket. "Arrived about three hours ago and the master's got him to work already…out there look." The cook joined the butler by the window. "Known each other for years, so they have…comes from Telford and Mr Knight's got him down here to talk about all these roads he's planning."

"Well I never…whatever they going to be doing next, Mr Parker? I don't know." She peered at the two figures in the drive then returned to her needle-work. "As if we haven't enough going on around here."

*

John Macadam, slight and almost bird like, crouched on the wet gravel. John Knight was beside him and the two peered closely at the stones on the drive-way. "We call it metalling," the older man, by now on all fours and impervious to the stones, looked at Knight. "First of all we build the foundations up with several layers of larger stones." He looked round, adjusting his grey wig. "Like those over there. But then, and here's the secret, my friend, we put a good layer of smaller stones and chippings on top...pack 'em in and roll 'em in tight...really crush 'em down."

He got to his feet and took the metal-rimmed wheel from the coachman. "Here we are...watch. As long as the top stones are smaller than an inch or so they'll be forced down by the sheer weight, binding together ever more closely under the pressure...watch." Knight leant forward to study the impact of the wheel on the rolled surface.

"But these ones here're too big and too loose...they just get pushed aside like a ship going through water." Knight nodded. "But if you get it right...smaller ones that're really well packed down, then the wheels ride over 'em. Far easier for wagons and animals." Knight stood and toyed with the wheel. "The surface'll take anything you care to put on it so long as we get the foundations solid enough. Like this, only deeper." Macadam stamped hard. "It'll cross anything...bog, sand, you name it."

The little engineer went on to explain how they were beginning to experiment with coal tar they had extracted from open seams. "If we can get *that* right, *then* we'll have something." He bent to pick up a handful of loose gravel. "This tar possesses qualities that bind everything together...solid. Makes it impossible for the surface to break up. It'll take anything...anything at all, and for ever." He brushed his hands together and laughed. "So that's it, John...and we're well pleased with it all thus far."

Knight stood, deep in thought, with his chin in one hand and one arm support-ing the other. "Dear God. it'll change everything," he muttered. "Why, it'll be a huge jump. You'll..."

"Get from Exeter to London in less than half the time," Macadam volunteered, both hands rubbing his wig to and fro across the top of his head. "And none of that rolling around and crashing in and out of ruts and pot holes all the time."

"Well." Knight blew slowly. "I'll be needing good roads here," he mused. "They're the sort of roads that're going to open up my country. *Huh*, dear God. Can you do it for me, John? Out here in the wilds?"

"To be sure," Macadam adjusted his coat as the two men walked towards the house. "So long as we can get the right machinery down here…the stone crushers an' rollers an' so on…and the skilled labour, of course. *But,*" he put a hand on Knight's arm. "It's an expensive business," he warned. "Damn me if it's not. We have to level the ground, raise it up in one place then make cuttings over there and so on."

"No matter, no matter. Come," Knight waved his guest forward. "I'll pay whatever it takes, it'll be worth every penny…got to be. It'll change the whole way of life up here."

4.

Age seemed unable to slow him. Away for a week in Hereford with Maxwell to purchase cattle, Knight went on by coach to Carlisle to see how they built walls. After that it was back to the iron foundries, where he met up with Havers and others to discuss mineral deposits, then on to Wales to look at sheep. Two weeks later he was in Norfolk talking about corn, then to London where he bullied the accountants and fought with his bankers.

The sixty year-old was relentless. "So they want a *wall?*" he stared at Maxwell who showed him the letter from the Crown Commissioners. "A wall around my land, eh?" He did not wait for the reply. "Right then. They shall have one, and a real one at that…none of yer dry stone walls. I'll give 'em a proper one, one that will last for a hundred years and more. That'll keep 'em out of our hair."

*

The winter of 1823 arrived early and when it came it was hard. Knight sent Elizabeth-Jane and the children to London, while he and most of his staff remained at Castle Heights. But he was restless, frustrated by the long drive out to where work had begun already on the roads and his wall.

"We're going to move up to Simonsbath, dammit," he declared. Even Parker was aghast. "I need to be right on top of it all…all that's going on. Can't see a blessed thing stuck away down here." A deputation came to see him. The house, they explained, was empty save for the builders who had made a start on the restoration plans he had ordered.

"Then throw 'em out," he yelled. "Tell them we need the place. Give them two weeks to make the place weather tight and we're moving in." It took them four. No matter how much he raged, the house and provisions had to be prepared to see the winter through. Enough wood, enough food, fodder for the animals, furniture and equipment for the house all had to be brought up from Lynton or South Molton, every item hauled painfully by oxcart or wagonette.

Even before the house had settled, Knight rode out to see progress on the estate, Jack riding behind him. His destination, that New Year's Day, was the southern edge of the moor. There, on a great shoulder of land, a gang of Irish labourers, sent over by Elizabeth-Jane's family, were working on a section of his wall.

For weeks the rain clouds had been rolling in from the Atlantic soaking the ground; but now the wind had veered north, bringing with it an icy blast from the Arctic. Bent low over the animals' shoulders and with their faces masked against the wind, the two riders reached the men at work. "Ahoy, there," Knight shouted into the wind. "How goes the wall? Is the foreman there?"

A team of six oxen, their legs hock deep in the freezing mud, were hauling a cartload of stones slowly along the line of posts. Every few yards the drover halted, allowing the men on the cart to throw off enough for the wallers to do their work. The man turned, struggling to keep his feet. His eyes were watering and his long hair flying in the wind as he stared, bearded and wild-eyed, at the two horsemen. "Away along de top, sorr. Up on de top, there look."

"How are you doing?" Knight bowed his head, holding onto his hat. "Cold enough for you?"

"Och, not so bad, sorr. Not so bad." The man, southern Irish like the rest of them, hawked and wiped his mouth. "'Tis ever the same in the hills." He rubbed his hands and turned back to the load of stones. Behind them a second cart was waiting to be called forward. The oxen stood patiently, tired after their long climb and their heads hung low. Behind them again, a third team was grinding up the rough track where the huge, dun-coloured beasts leant forward into their yokes. They were straining with exertion and blowing hard, for the quarries from where they had set out earlier were several miles away and more than a thousand feet below them.

Some of those working on the wall itself were stripped to their shirts, the sweat running freely as they laboured. Others struggled to shovel the water-logged earth into the gap between the two six-foot walls of stone. Beyond them yet more were digging ditches, packing the tufts of grass and earth sods they cut from the ground into place around the stonework.

"Afternoon there, sorr." Knight turned at the shout, watching the foreman leaning into the wind. He came up close and doffed his muddy bowler hat. "Hard going in all this water, sorr. No more'n twenty yards today, I'm afraid. I was hoping for more but..." he shook his head.

Knight looked down at the man whose rugged, weather beaten face was covered with a grey-flecked stubble and whose bare arms were exposed to the shrill wind. He bent down to speak but stopped as the man from Cork, wet from the waist down, heaved himself around to curse an idler who had caught his eye. "Beggin' yer pardon, sorr." He turned back and looked up at Knight. "Got to keep at 'em, you know."

"Thank you, Webber." The man was close but Knight still had to shout. "That's not far enough today, is it? Twenty yards won't get us far," a sudden gust made him snatch at his hat. "We're aiming for sixty at least…from each of the three sites, you know. You'll have to move on once you're away from here." He glanced at the ox team making its way towards them, then back at the work on the wall. "Tell me, man…can it be done? Can we do it?"

"No problem, sorr. No problem at all." Webber grinned and tucked in his open shirt. "We'll be getting more rock up directly. There's seven teams on the road just now and three more're coming out from North Molton in the morning. Two round trips each, that's nigh on sixty tons a day, seventy maybe. And I'll be keepin' the flat o' my hand behind them." Webber rubbed his hands together. "Have it too easy these days, so they do." The foreman spat contemptuously.

Knight touched his hat with his crop and rode on. Hard men one and all, he mused. But how dare those rotten bankers, sitting in their office fug, quibble about money for these men? How dare they! Do 'em a power of good to spend a few days up here themselves. See that fat little toad Esdaile and his cronies with picks and shovels in their hands. Ha! But then after the wall itself would come the hedges and banks in between, mile after mile of them criss-crossing his land between the farms. It was going to take time and it was going to take money whether those in London quibbled or not.

5.

Spring came late, and brutally so, like the wild winter before it. For weeks on end, storm after storm raged at the coast sending great rolling columns of stone-grey waves thundering against the wet, black cliffs, causing mountains of spray to be hurled high into the air. Birds, animals, trees and man himself all cowed before the full might of Mother Nature. The last and angriest storm of them all took four days to blow itself out. Only then, so it seemed, was the weather prepared to calm, making way grudgingly for the sun and the sea-blue April skies.

The day the storm abated, Jack took Frederic down to Lynmouth. News had arrived earlier that an Ilfracombe herring drifter had been dismasted before being driven helplessly on to the jagged rocks between Black Head and the point. And it was there, with help unable to reach her, that the 'Matilda Jane' had foundered. The crew, it was feared, had been lost.

But a giant sea was still running. As if disturbed by some primeval force, the waves now swollen and foam flecked and laden with seaweed and flotsam, swept in, rank upon rank, rising ever higher before they pounded against the jetty. Clouds of spray flew high and shingle crashed onto the harbour. Debris was still blowing wildly about and the air remained thick with brine.

He saw them at once, beyond the harbour wall. "Look, Master Frederic." Jack had to stand and shout against the wind. "A boat, look, and it's coming this way." They watched as the open rowing boat, its crew bent to their task, was lifted high on each giant swell as it swept underneath, before sinking out of sight in the troughs between.

"Should never 'ave been drifting near them rocks, last night." The boys turned quickly. The old face was rough and weather-beaten, the clothes those of a sailor. The left leg finished at the knee, leaving his weight to be supported by a broad wooden stump. As he walked so Jed Harper lurched and swung his hips. "An' what be you lads doing down here on a day like this?" Frederic's pony shied, blowing in alarm, but the old man was quicker and caught hold of the bridle before running his hand gently over the pony's ears. "Not afeared of old Jed, are ye?" he asked quietly. "Not afeared of old Jed, then?"

"Please, sir, what happened?" Frederic, unable to contain himself, was studying his leg.

"Oooh, that were all a long time back, lad." The old man grinned, his teeth keeping hold of his pipe. "Way back in…in," he paused looking down. "Oooh, way back in ninety-eight…aye, ninety-eight."

"And then, sir?" Frederic persisted. "Was it an accident…or something like that?"

"Aye, summat like that," Jed Harper replied slowly. He looked from one to the other then behind them, his face studying something way beyond. The boys turned, following his gaze. "Aboukir Bay." He paused, catching their eyes again. "Cap'n ordered us right in close so 'e did…less than a hundred yards from the Frenchie when she caught us amid ships."

"Go on," Jack gasped. "What happened?"

"Us took a broadside and that was the end of my leg. Shot away by the ball, clean as that." He chuckled suddenly. "But that's enough of that…you'd best away from here an' not be watchin' while they bring 'em ashore. Them should never ought to 'ave bin out there last night…no sir." Jed Harper patted the pony. "Be back tomorrow, maybe? Aye?" He looked at them. "The New Inn, back there. Ask for me, Jed Harper…that's my name. I'll be there, round the back most likely. Just ask."

✳

The next day they were there and the day after. Everyday for a week until Frederic went back to school, as soon as Jack's duties were done, they rode down to The New Inn where they sat listening to tales of the sea. In return they helped him stretch and roll the nets he had been mending, telling him about their own lives at Castle Heights.

"Listen, lad." Jed Harper turned to Jack. "For more'n a week now you've been hearing tales of fightin' and dyin' and all of that." Jack nodded expectantly. "Have yer never learned none of the skills yerself…of fighting? Have yer never felt the balance of a cutlass in yer hand or the whip of a rapier?" Jack shook his head. "Never loaded a pistol and fired? You should, you know…as any man your age should. Oh aye…'tis only right."

"No, never." The sixteen year-old, now on his own, shrugged his shoulders and blushed. "Never had the chance…but I'd like to, Jed. If that's what you're asking, I'd like that very much."

"Hmm." Harper wrinkled his nose. "Can't do nothing, meself, nowadays. But my boy, Luke…'ee can do all I've said, and more. Finer swordsman you won't find in all of Devon. Off the Levant, he were but 'e's home again now. But never go asking him nuthin'" The old man wagged a finger. "Don't go worryin' about things like that. He has his ways, does Luke, but 'e has a heart as well. He'll teach yer all 'e can, that's for sure, I'll see to that."

✳

A dark, brooding, black-bearded man with a mane of hair tied back in a well-greased pigtail, Luke was leaner than his father and taller. His eyes, themselves as black as coals, stared out from under bushy eyebrows and his beard was neatly trimmed. "Stand up." The order came quietly. Jack stood as Luke walked round him slowly, then back again, as a man might look at a horse. "Turn slow." Jack did as he was bid. "Can yer dance?"

"No?" Jack's mouth opened.

"You'll need to dance on yer feet when a man's at yer throat with a sword," Luke countered. "See here." He walked quickly to the sack by his father's feet, drew out two swords, and laid one side-on across the other. Then he stepped between them. "See my feet…see how they go. Don't worry 'bout me, just see my feet." He checked the tail of his hair then shook his sleeves loose before nipping them back. "Now see here." Both hands were clasped behind him.

First he stepped slowly, one foot here, the other there, each lifted gently but never down together. Then he moved faster and Jack watched fascinated as the tall man skipped, danced and kicked. He crossed and uncrossed his feet, turned and doubled back, his feet stepping nimbly between the blades. Faster and faster he went, spinning and twisting, back and forth from side to side, this way and that, his feet a blur but never once disturbing the blades.

"Three things yer need at sword play and yer need them all at once," he announced, scarcely out of breath. "You need yer feet, yer eyes and yer hands. Here, catch." Luke tossed a sword, hilt first to Jack who jumped, snatched at the blade and dropped it.

*

For three months Luke, at his father's request, taught Jack. Patiently, hour after hour until the sweat ran into their eyes, Luke showed him the moves, pleased enough at how quickly his pupil learned. Then, as the two men moved back and forth along the piste, he refined Jack's parries and lunges with the rapier, his cuts and slashes with the cutlass. Gradually it came.

They fought with blunted weapons on the hard ground behind the inn, their necks and bodies protected by heavy clothing and animal hides. Luke found he had to concentrate more and more, to fight longer and harder to keep ahead of the boy. Then Jack began to strike. Occasionally at first, then more often, he would break past Luke's guard to score a hit.

He found the pistol easier. "When you're fighting one to one, like in a duel, always come up fast with the muzzle then lower slowly. You'll make him panic and he'll fire too quick. Once that's done then he's yours for the taking. *Up*…and down like that." Luke checked his stance.

"Never pull on the trigger, squeeze gently like you would a baby's finger. Aim just below his throat…'tis both his widest part an' if yer pull low the ball still gets 'im."

It was August until they were done but the day came when Luke turned to his father. "The teachin's done," he muttered. "Can't help 'im no more now." He looked at Jack and gave the mere hint of a smile. "That's it, boy. Now 'tis practise, practise…or the real thing itself come the day. Up to you…can't 'elp you no more."

"Watch after your master, proper like. These be yer tools." Jed Harper beckoned Jack across. "Carry 'em proper and use 'em well…all the time, too," the old man continued. "'Tis every man's right to look after heself. Never get caught out there wi'out 'em. Only needs to 'appen once, then's all too late."

*

The following year the Knights moved out to Simonsbath.

There was still much work to be done, John Knight exclaimed, but pleasure to be had as well. Their many friends would be coming to stay. There would be balls and parties, fishing expeditions, falconry and hunting. In the summer there would be picnics and rides out on to the moor where he would show them what he was planning to do. Jack worked for his master; mainly at Simonsbath, he would sometimes be called back to Castle Heights nonetheless. Whenever he was in Lynton he would go searching for Luke. For hours, the two men would duel across the firm, flat piece of ground behind The New Inn.

Jack Tucker grew strong. His body became hard and his eyes keen. He learned to fear no man.

Chapter Six

"Mama, look. It's Mr Morgan." Edward Knight stood pointing from the rock pool where he and his two sisters were shrimping. The girls stood expectantly and followed his hand.

"Come on, Maggie." Isabella, nine, and a year older than her brother, jumped down onto the thin strip of sand between the rocks. "Let's see what he's brought us." The three raced towards the tall figure. He was picking his way carefully across the stream that meandered through the gritty sand after tumbling from the high cliffs. Once closer they slowed, hesitant until they saw him stop and reach into his bag, then ran forward again.

*

Lee Bay, tiny, isolated and almost cut off by grey-black cliffs, was little more than a thirty-minute ride from Castle Heights. Frederic and Kenton were allowed there alone but the two older boys were now away at school. The others, much to their chagrin, had to wait until the family came back to Lynton. Only then was it possible for them to return to their secret cove which lay hidden, surrounded by its towering ramparts and dark, forbidding caves.

John Knight had been gone for over a week and was now in Worcestershire. Elizabeth-Jane, bored and lonely in the late summer heat at Simonsbath, and desperate to escape the dust and noise of masons, had come down to the beach with the children and a party of servants. Lee Bay had always been a particular favourite of hers and today she had decided on a picnic, taking the Irish jaunting car and one of the dogcarts. She wanted peace: a number of things were disturbing her and she needed to think.

"Why Mr Morgan. What a pleasant surprise." She watched smiling as Durnford Morgan greeted the children, waving packets of Turkish sherbet above their outstretched hands. "You shouldn't have done that…really, there's no need, you know." She had forgotten how tall he was and today, with his coat thrown casually over his shoulder and his pale, wide-sleeved silk shirt half open, he looked even taller.

He was tanned and his tousled hair gave the usually impeccably dressed banker a raffish look. "But why here…and today?" she made to move until his hand waved her back. "I thought you had plans to remain in London? But, no matter…it's so nice to see you."

"Indeed, the pleasure is mine." Morgan smiled warmly then looked up and nodded to the footman and maid behind her. "What's this I hear, Miss Tucker?" he called across. "Great plans are afoot, are they not?"

"Indeed, sir and thank you." Both Carrick, the young footman, and Morgan caught her coy smile.

"*C'est pas vrai…pas possible,*" he gesticulated, feigning dejection, then shrugged and lifted his arms. "All the prettiest ones go like that, and pray who's the lucky man?"

"Troy Kingdon, sir." Emma, still smiling, adjusted her mobcap. "From Filleigh, near South Molton, sir."

"A fortunate man indeed…and my congratulations to you both." He nodded at her bob then turned back to Elizabeth-Jane.

"My pardon for such a liberty, but they told me at Castle Heights and I'm delighted for her." He spoke softly. Bending forward he took her hand and raised it until their eyes met. "Yes, London," he replied. "I had intended to stay…I *should* still be there, but I escaped," he laughed. "A letter from the master ordered me back…so what could I do?" he joked. "He has decided to visit France after all…determined to see what has to be done." As he steadied himself on the shingle, he caught her look. "I'll be with him, of course, but he's coming back here on Sunday and wants me to have our plans ready."

"What *is* all this about France?" Elizabeth-Jane motioned for him to sit on the rug beside her. "And what on earth is all this about *rail*ways and *canals* on the moor? They're building them all over England so…why off to France? Why not look at something here?" He could see she was unhappy.

"He's taking on too much." She paused, toying with a piece of driftwood, then looked up sharply, her eyes pleading. "He's simply driving himself into the ground. I…we miss him here, you know. He missed the boys going off to Charterhouse, then Maggie's birthday…her eleventh."

Morgan leant back on one elbow and pushed a hand through his hair. "You'll never stop him, I'm afraid." His eyes were seeking an explanation for this sudden outburst. "He's one of those rare men who simply goes on and on…triumph, success and wealth." He lifted a hand dismissively. "They only serve to drive him harder."

Elizabeth-Jane's mouth tightened and she looked out to where the rollers were breaking against the furthest jagged rocks. The tide was out and the distant sound of the waves boomed and echoed around the stillness of the cove. The short walk down from where he had left his horse with the carts and grooms had left him hot and she watched as he took out a silk handkerchief to wipe his forehead.

"Oh, I'm sorry, it's dreadfully hot here in the sun." She sat up and turned. "Emma," she cried, motioning to the maid. "We're going to get out of this heat for a while. Over there, look. Keep an eye on the children, we'll have lunch when we return…oh my goodness." She spun round with one hand to her mouth. "I never even asked you to stay, did I?" she laughed self-consciously. "I just assumed. But you will stay for some lunch, won't you? Please do."

"Nothing would give me greater pleasure. But right now…" he stood and took her hand as she rose. "A spot of shade for the weary traveller would be most welcome. The rocks over there, under the cliff…but we'll have to cross the stream." They walked slowly, Elizabeth-Jane picking her way across the firm, wet sand, one hand holding up her lilac and pink skirts, the other her parasol.

"And how are things up at Simonsbath?" His hand steadied her across the water. Tarr, himself back at Castle Heights, had told him how much she enjoyed coming back to Lynton where she could shop and meet up with those she knew.

"Ohhh…when it's all done it'll be fine…beautiful…wonderful. But right now it's dreadful." Elizabeth-Jane picked at some strands of seaweed with the tip of her parasol. She was searching for words and he waited. Suddenly she faced him. "Mr Morgan." He saw her glance towards the servants and children then back again. "I'm so glad you're here…I want to ask you something…but there's something else first." She looked down shyly.

"Well." He was studying her face. "Go on."

"Do you suppose, Mr Morgan that, when we are alone…that perhaps we might be somewhat less formal?" Her laugh was nervous. "Or is that too improper of me?"

"Why but…."

"No, no. Pray do not read anything into my request, it's nothing at all." Her finger wagged in caution. "It's just that, well…I'm on my own so much. Completely so, and I feel as though I'm shut away, trapped up there in some sort of cage…cut off from the world. Nobody talks to me. It's dreadful…*madam this, madam that… yes Mrs Knight, certainly Mrs Knight,*" she mimicked. "Sometimes I could scream…go mad even. There's no one with whom I can relax, no one," she paused. "Nobody at all and yet you seem…."

"I'm deeply honoured, Mrs..er…"

"Elizabeth-Jane, *please*, Durnford," she begged, unaware that it was she who had broken the spell. "I can't stand all this formality. Can we not relax, just the two of us, when we're together. It would mean so much to me. Now then," she turned briefly to check they were quite on their own. "Here we are…let's sit here, it's far cooler." She looked up and about, shielding her eyes. "The sun's behind the cliffs here, and no wonder. Those high ones…see how high they are."

"You said there was something else?" Morgan stood facing her. He had lifted

90

one foot on to the rock beside her and could see she was hesitant. "You can be assured that whatever it is on your mind will go no further...I give you my word."

"Mmm? Oh, I don't know." Her shoulders sagged. "Well," she took a deep breath. "Last week, I saw this letter. It was on his desk. I don't make a habit of prying so," she added hurriedly. "But I couldn't help it." Morgan nodded. "It was from his bank...*your* bank and curiosity overcame me."

"Ye-es."

"They're worried...aren't they? About his expenditures?" She searched his face and laughed drily. "Oh yes, I can see the answer on your face...it's written all over you. But I *have* to know, Durnford...I must know what's going on."

He told her all he knew. It was easy. Professional etiquette be blowed, her mind was in turmoil. He could see that everywhere she turned there were questions or problems. She needed his help and, even had he wanted to, he could not have left this tender, sensitive woman in suspense. And she was vulnerable too. Suddenly, there and then, he wanted to sweep her into his arms, press his lips against hers and console her. His desire for her was stronger than ever.

"But you need not worry," Morgan sat beside her. The band of rock was narrow and he eased himself carefully until their hips were touching yet she made no move. "Your husband has assets enough to cover every conceivable extrava-gance...and to do so ten times over should he so wish. But he's no fool, not by any means." Morgan's hand reached for hers and she let it rest. "Here he's gambling, but it's no fanciful whim of some madcap. He sees a good chance of a great return on his money...from the minerals he believes lie up there under the moor. That's why he's driving so hard."

"So...that's what all this talk about railways is for?" Elizabeth-Jane stared out to sea. "His schemes are getting more and more ambitious...where's it all going to end, for God's sake." Her head dropped. Morgan sensed her despair and his hand closed softly over hers. "Tell me about it, Durnford...please. You're away next week, is that not so? John tells me you're going off into the Pyrenees to see how they run their railroads with water. Can that really be?" She bent forward to shake grit from her shoe.

"Yes indeed." He could feel the warmth of her body under her skirts move against him. "We shall leave from Falmouth on Sunday and sail to Narbonne...the roads in France are still dreadful. From there we'll go to Carcassonne where we'll stay with some relatives of mine. They are among the few who survived the terrible purges...lost a deal of land but kept enough, and kept their heads into the bargain. Then on to see what Henri has to show us".

"And what of us back here?" she shrugged as though nobody cared. "And all the while I suppose I just have to sit and wait to see what will be."

"Don't worry, time will pass quickly, you know." He shook her hand gently. "You'll be all right...I could not bear to think of you otherwise." He looked at her but she avoided his glance, turning her head away nervously and fingering the gold necklace at her throat. He could see the flush on her skin and the soft contours under her blouse that rose and fell as she considered his words.

"D'you realise what I feel when I see you here alone, with just your children and the servants for company?" His voice had dropped. "Can you imagine my feelings, Elizabeth-Jane? Can you?"

"Stop." She looked away. "Please...say no more."

"But why? Does it hurt...or do my feelings, perhaps, find acceptance?"

"Yes, but not readily so." She glanced up, tilting her head back so she could see him from under the rim of her straw hat. She pursed her lips then moved a finger across the corner of her mouth. "I cannot...I must not allow such feelings to...."

"Torment you?"

"Yes, I mean *no*." She started at the strength in her own reply. "Oh dear, my pardon...I did not mean to raise my voice like that. Come, Durnford. Time for lunch, I can see them waiting for us. And try not to look at me as you did just now."

"Did I offend?"

"No, of course not but, come on, we must go." She stepped lightly from the rock, and laughed gaily as he jumped down beside her. Suddenly her body was alive once more. The moment, a difficult one, had passed but their emotions had not. She knew it and it was that which lifted her spirits. "It's just that looks such as you gave me are best kept hidden from prying eyes."

2.

John Knight did not enjoy France. It was too hot. The dry, burning heat of the Languedoc autumn was worse than anything he could remember. Thick dust hung in clouds above the tracks while the air was heavy and seemingly silent save for the constant chirping of crickets and cicadas. Their hosts, mindful of his age and of his soft white skin, rose at dawn then rested throughout the heat of the day but that, they could see, made their guest irritable and more impatient than ever.

At Chateau Corbain, he sat puzzled and remote as Durnford Morgan and his French relatives chattered and babbled endlessly. Sometimes a question would come his way and the room would fall silent as Morgan explained what had been asked. Rows of polite and expectant faces would stare owl-like down the table in silence as he gave his reply, then turn with one accord back to Morgan in order to hear what their guest had been saying. But that would be all and they would simply nod sagely or mutter incoherently, as they deferred politely.

Then they would turn back to continue their business, the tempo rising once more, leaving him lonelier and more isolated than before. Knight would scratch at his hair or pick at his teeth, even get up from the table to wander across the room and stare out of the windows. The guest, Morgan's relatives informed him, was restless and they had better get on their way.

※

The Canal du Midi impressed him. "When did they do all this?" Knight let the reins drop then took off his hat to wipe his brow and neck. "Sixteen-seventy or something?" He stared in amazement. "Dear God, and to think that we were still cleaning up London after the great fire." If they, the French, could do *that* all those years ago, he determined, then he could do it now.

"Here's how they control the flow of water." Morgan had remembered how Knight and the others used to deliberate the problem endlessly on the high moors behind Simonsbath. They dismounted to study the channels that Riquet, the French engineer, had created. Knight watched as the lock keeper explained, then listened intently as Morgan repeated what he had been told.

"It's much as we thought," he confirmed, referring to the plans they had studied earlier. "Any surplus from the catchment area simply overflows the sluice and falls back into the original stream. He says they get wild storms here…just as we do at home." Knight shrugged and they rode on.

"And here's the feeder stream they built, linking water from the lake to the main canal."

Knight rode along the edge of the narrow waterway, leaning over and peering down. "'Tis nothing," he remarked sourly. "Just a few yards wide and a couple of feet deep."

"Yes, but a little more than that, sir, surely. It's twenty miles long and twists and turns through the countryside, at a constant gradient of one in five hundred or so." Morgan pulled up. "And isn't that exactly what you're after on the top of Exmoor? Something similar to this, perhaps, yet only half as long."

"That's it, that's it." Knight brooded on the matter then cheered. It would be a channel like this from the dam he was going to build, to the point where the water was needed to balance out the weight of his rail wagons.

His spirits rose, the more so as they approached the Pyrenees, winding them-selves further and further into a deep ravine-like valley, disappearing from one world before entering another. No longer the burnt, arid plains but great sheets of rock, around which the mountainsides were covered in black-green pine: a land of tumbling cascades, of sheep bells and wood smoke. They left the coach and took to horses with their baggage on the backs of mules behind them. The air became fresher, the mornings cold and clear. Every once in a while their track rounded a wide outcrop of rock, opening the view to reveal the ragged teeth of the distant Haut Pyrenees where the summits were already dusted with snow.

*

"*Monsieur*, permit me to introduce Monsieur Renee…Monsieur Jean-Paul Renee." Knight bowed, relieved that Henri Ascave's English was so good. "Monsieur Renee is the consultant engineer here in Cauterets. He will explain our *mecanismes. Oui?* After that we will ride to the top and examine the machinery. *Oui?*"

Knight could see it at once. Although longer and steeper than his own require-ments, the French engineers had utilised the weight of water to counterbalance wagons going either way, be they loaded or empty. "See here, Monsieur." Renee turned a small wheel causing the sluice to close, channelling the icy mountain water into a funnel. He watched as the wagon filled then rolled towards the incline, automatically pulling those behind under the piped water. "*Voila!* As many as we need until the trucks below are pulled up while these descend." An hour earlier they had ridden up in an empty wagon watching the guard control progress with a simple brake lever.

"So," Knight glanced at the wagons as they passed going the other way. "You are never left with too many wagons at either end…full or empty."

"*Exactement, monsieur.*" Renee beamed proudly. "Any problems and we simply uncouple as many as we need. They are pushed to one side then used later. *Comme ca,*" Renee pointed. Knight nodded thoughtfully. At the top he walked to the edge, then back, then along the line of wagons filled with limestone. He looked at the couplings, tested the brake system then worked the sluice and climbed the water tower. Renee and Ascave followed him, Morgan sketched and wrote.

"Can we see these going down?" he patted the leading truck.

"*Bien sur,*" Renee signalled and they watched as a mule was harnessed to the first truck. "Remember we always have two wagons full of water at the bottom or perhaps pieces of machinery we need up here…all of them ready to take the weight. The guard, you remember him, yes? He is in his wagon in front and will control the speed. There will be no problem…*pas du tout.*" John Knight was convinced. He had seen all he needed. There was nothing here the French had done that he could not do at home.

*

For months, Havers had been worried about getting the ore and other minerals off the moor just as Maxwell had been about getting lime for the land up the steep hills from the coast. And they had both spoken of thousands upon thousands of tons. As they rode over his land so they had wrestled with the problems, struggling helplessly about how to get steam trains to climb the gradients. It would be difficult enough for the engines themselves, he had seen them at Stockton and Derby, but for them also to pull heavy loads was out of the question.

Now he had his answers. On Exmoor he had the water, a never-ending supply, and now he knew how to control it. The top of the moor was flat, plenty enough scope for a canal and he had his port, not Lynton but the more sheltered Porlock Weir, further along the coast.

No sooner had they left than Knight immersed himself. Hour after hour he pestered Morgan to check his calculations, to prove his measurements and challenge his theories. France and the French, Knight considered, might be interesting enough, but what they had accomplished with their water-powered transport was far more so. He would see to it that what he had learned would be put to good use.

The bankers, he knew, would suck their teeth and create their usual irritating problems then sit back and wait, teasing him before allowing him access to his own money. He cursed them for it, but as the schooner pulled out of Port-la-Nouvelle he stepped back from the rail and inhaled deeply. Above him the sails rippled and flapped noisily until they filled. Morgan saw him grin to himself then roll his shoulder.

3.

John Knight laughed, stepped back and surveyed those already in the main drawing room. The atmosphere was buoyant. The air, even now hazy with cigar smoke and the aroma of fresh coffee, was filled with animated chatter. Men in their hunting pink or black tailcoats with white stocks at their throats and their ladies in winter finery were in a cheerful mood. Maids with trays of drinks, coffee and sweet cakes moved among them. Although now past ten o'clock, more guests, he knew, were still in the breakfast room.

The laughter and expectant buzz satisfied him, and well it might, for his formal invitations, scripted on vellum, had drawn together the flower of North Devon and West Somerset society. Last night they had danced, tonight they would dine, but today it was the turn of the hunt. Hounds had met here countless times in the past but this was the first time that he, master of Simonsbath Manor, was playing host.

"Best be on my way, sir." Knight turned at the hand on his arm. "They're kennelled up the road and will need a bit of a stretch before we put 'em to work."

"Eleven o'clock, eh Russell?" John Knight stood on tiptoe to see the bracket clock on the mantelpiece then smiled warmly. Any man who could hunt his own hounds three days a week then find time to ride with others; who could wine, dine and dance with the best of them and preach a good sermon on the Sabbath as well *must* know how to live. The parson from Swimbridge knew how to do just that and Knight had taken the young man to his heart.

"All right, my good man. I'll drive 'em out of here in good time...but give us something to talk about at dinner tonight. Eh? Don't fail me now."

"I'll do me level best, sir." Parson Jack Russell went on his way.

✳

"Where're you going to draw, vicar?" a voice called from the mounted field.

"Upstream about half a mile," Russell shouted over his shoulder, his horse now surrounded by the pack eager to get on with the chase. "Just beyond Simon's pool...up there, where they say the old fella used to bathe." He laughed and raised his horn then turned to John Knight and his party.

"Reckon you'd be better off on the far bank, gentlemen. I'll put them through the rushes over there and try to get him to break cover up that way." He waved towards the high ground beyond the river.

Parker watched from the front steps of the manor. He could see Frederic and Kenton riding with Tucker as his master had decreed they should. The two Acland boys were with them also and he could hear sounds of their laughter as one or other rose to demonstrate something or to make a point. He watched as Tucker led his charges away from the rest of the field, making their way past the master and his own party. He noticed how Knight called his young groom over and watched as they spoke easily together. He observed everything carefully before turning briskly and striding into the house.

He failed to hear the plaintive note of Russell's horn or his thin, high-pitched voice ringing out in the still air and he missed the sight of hounds drawing through the long rushes near the riverbank. None of that was of any interest and, in any case, he had seen enough.

Less than a minute later the first hound whimpered. There was a pause then a second spoke followed by a third then a fourth. Suddenly, the whole pack was in full cry, the great crash of hound music filling the deep combes and surrounding hillsides, echoing back and forth, up and down the valley. The horses threw up their heads, starting at the notes of Russell's horn, and began to pull impatiently. Across the hillside, other riders pressed forward and began the long climb towards Shear Down.

They galloped for an hour. Scrambling through bog, drumming hard over firm ground, man and boy racing against the other. On and on they went, everyone of them determined to see it through. But the wily, old fox outdid them all, saving himself by running to ground in a big earth above Landacre Bridge.

The youngsters left their ponies and ran forward to where the pack was crowding the entrance to the earth. Some of the pack wandered off satisfied with a job well done while others bayed disconsolately, their bodies mud-flecked and steaming in the cold air. Parson Russell forced his way through the melee, took off his cap and bent down to listen. They watched him stand, shake his head and shrug before putting the horn to his lips.

*

That evening, long after the party had returned to Simonsbath, Jack was working on alone. As soon as they had reached home, he had collected the horses, stabled them and let them cool before giving them their feed. Now, by the soft light of a lantern, he was checking them carefully, his charges already bedded down for the night. Save for their quiet chomping and their rummaging in the mangers or the occasional pull on a halter rope, the stables were silent. As he moved among them, he talked soothingly, examining each one as the shadows from his lamp played on the walls.

All of a sudden he stopped and listened. The horses had heard something in the darkness beyond and now stood motionless. Their jaws were quite still, their heads alert and they had turned towards the door with their ears pricked. As the latch clicked open one of them whinnied quietly.

Looking up Jack saw the figure of Parson Russell standing in the light of his own lamp. "Hello, young fella," he said cheerily, moving closer. "It's Tucker isn't it? Jack Tucker?" Jack nodded, wiped his palms on his breeches and clasped the outstretched hand. "Still working hard, I see."

"Oh aye, but it's not too bad, sir," Jack smiled. Standing back he ran his hand gently over the flank of the animal he was checking. "Sometimes 'tis the best time of day. All home safe and sound…bedded down for the night. And what brings you out here, sir? Can I help at all?" In the soft light of the lamp he could see a tall, athletic man with fine, handsome features, about ten years older than himself. Whenever the parson smiled, his eyes, half hidden by long sideburns, twinkled merrily and his face would crease into a wide grin. A fur-lined coat over a well-cut evening dress completed the picture.

"Oh…I thought I'd escape from dinner." Russell patted the animal's rump. "All money and politics in there," he grinned. "Whether the Duke of Wellington or Lord Grey is going to lead the Tories or whether Lord Melbourne will manage to get the Whigs back." Russell waved a hand dismissively. "Nearly came to blows, they did…you should've heard 'em." He paused. "Cuh, I dunno…anyway I asked Mr Parker…you know him, of course? Asked if you were about…much better out here than listening to all that."

"Aye, sir. Can imagine it is."

"But enough of that…listen. Long before dinner your master and I were talking about hunting and, now the old staghounds have gone, he wants me to bring my lot up whenever I can." Russell wiped his hands. "I'd have to kennel them here, mind you, but he's keen to show some sport for his friends." He leaned against an upright beam, worn smooth by years of animals rubbing against it. "He was saying how well you know the moor…better than anyone, he said. 'Tis magnificent country, for sure, but quite new to me and handling a pack up here's very different to the farming country down around Torrington and South Molton."

"Don't doubt it, sir," Jack laughed, bending to rub the wisp of straw down the mare's legs. "Molland, that's where I come from 's very different again."

"To be sure…but I said I'd do it," Russell continued. "I told him if I was going to make a proper job of it, I'd need to know the country. Well…he said he'd get you to show me the way. Where the good ground lies, the best cover and the most likely runs." Russell pushed himself away from the beam. "Could you do it, Jack? Show me the moor?"

"Well, sir," Jack stood up and brushed back his hair. "Can't say I knows it all, like, but it'd be a pleasure, sir. If Mr Knight can afford me the time then I'd like nothing better."

✻

Chanter, the second footman, came for Jack the next morning, picking his way carefully across the yard. Time only to clean his boots and tidy his clothes, Jack waited outside the scullery door until Abel Tarr led the way through the kitchens. They turned into a dark corridor where the second butler left him outside the staff room. There was no sign of Emma.

He could hear voices, but started nonetheless when the door opened suddenly, bathing him in sunlight from the far window. "He's here," Mrs Appelton called over her shoulder. "Knock and wait," she ordered before striding on her way.

"*Come,*" the voice rasped. Jack tidied his hair then entered the neat well-furnished room cautiously. He noticed the vase of daffodils on the bare table and the stacks of china on the shelves of the dresser at the far end. The air was a mixture of breakfast, soap and tobacco. The butler was by the bay window, staring out with his hands clasped behind him. Jack saw that his dark hair, oiled and well-slicked, fell short of his white collar.

"Excuse me, Mr Parker, sir. It's me, Jack Tucker…you sent for me." He spoke quietly.

"I *know.*" The butler swung round. His sallow face was lined and grim, his mouth a hard, thin line. Jack straightened himself. "I'm aware of that."

"Is there something…."

"Silence," Parker eased his shoulders. "I'll be doing the talking in here."

Jack, still unaware of why he had been summoned tried again. "But, Mr Parker…"

"*Hold your tongue.*" The butler came closer. "If I want you to speak, I'll ask." Jack, even now uncomprehending, watched the eyes surveying him. "Look at the very state of you, man…where do you think you are?" Parker had little time for those who worked outside. The stables to him were a dirty, unhealthy place, those who worked there coarse and uncouth. He had little time for any of it.

"I've had a complaint about you from Mr Knight." Parker, shorter than the figure in front of him, had to lift his head and it riled him. "He considers you've been getting too familiar with his guests…far too familiar, as though you consider yourself one of them. I've seen it myself, Tucker. Who the devil d'you think you are?"

Jack stared. "Let me tell you, boy. You're *not* one of them. Not now, nor ever will you be. Your place around here's outside this door." He pointed towards the kitchen. "Mr Knight and his friends are from a different class altogether…a different world. Those who come here, Tucker, are from the nobility or they're titled gentlefolk and come from grand homes, not some village hovel in…Molland or wherever." Jack swallowed.

"They were born that way and if they want you to speak, then they'll ask. You say your piece then step back to where you belong. That's the way things have been and that's the way they'll remain." The butler was breathing heavily. "Remember where you're from, boy, and remember your place in this house. I'll not be telling you again."

Jack watched him stalk back around the table. "D'you *hear*? Any more and you'll be on your way." Parker pushed out his jaw. "And it won't be on one of Mr Knight's horses either," he added. "You may go," he snapped. "Go on…leave the room." He turned back to the window.

"Thank you, sir," Jack spoke quietly but it was neither in fear nor shame. Parker had cut him, but not down to size and it was a sense of outrage that boiled. Who, or what, had led Parker to believe this - he had no idea. Perhaps it was the man himself. Whatever the reason, Jack knew he was marked.

As he left he pulled the door behind him. It shut a mite too hard.

Chapter Seven

The two men passed the junction of Cheapside and Bread Street within a few minutes of one another. Had they known this they would have arranged to meet and proceed together, for their destination was the same.

Sir Crispin Barclay had been for his usual morning stroll. But today a chill breeze had been sweeping up the river from Wapping and The Isle of Dogs encouraging him to step out as he turned back to the City and headed for Southwark Bridge. The morning was still young, young enough for the broken clouds above to be brushed by the pink dawn hue. He was tempted to turn left and make a quick detour around St Paul's, but the puddles and ruts in Cannon Street deterred him. James Esdaile would be at his desk already and eager to make a start.

John Knight, meanwhile, had left his brougham at Holborn Circus where the traffic was bad. He knew it was quite the wrong hour to traverse the City of London but he wanted to stretch his legs before the meeting. He took his time, easing his way purposefully through the pedestrian throng and stepped carefully to avoid the worst of the filth and sewage. Beggars, he knew, were attracted by his attire and more than once he rounded sharply on those who were pressing him too closely. He guessed that Esdaile would be waiting. The banker had called for the meeting after expressing his deep concern. Knight scoffed: the wretched little man was always concerned.

*

"We'll call him in a minute." Barclay nodded towards the door beyond which Raimond Maxwell and Ebenezer Havers were waiting. "Let's take the land business first," he suggested. "We'll need to have a look at the two projects separately." He adjusted his thin pince-nez that had been balancing askew on his nose then opened the folder. "You've seen all this of course, John? Eh?" Knight nodded, watching as he turned the pages deliberately, from time to time lifting his head to see under his glasses. Morgan had warned him that even Barclay had become uneasy.

"Page twelve, Crispin. The summaries are there." Esdaile, half hidden in the depths of his chair, wriggled himself upright. He craned forward to check where Barclay was pointing then swung the other way. "Morgan...get the supporting ledgers brought in, will you. And that book of estimates as well."

Knight glanced up as Morgan rose. The man had done him well, of that there was no doubt and he was pleased that his services were to be extended. Yet seeing him here made him wonder. How many times, he asked himself, would Morgan have furnished London with reports and opinions about his affairs, all no doubt expressed in his usual forceful manner. Would he have exaggerated, passing back news he suspected his masters wanted to hear or would he have played down the problems they had often discussed together in North Devon? There again, he might have decided that accuracy and honesty would serve his ambitions best.

But what did it matter? By now, it was too late and, in any case, the full extent of his plans would be divulged sooner or later. So, why not now? After all Morgan understood his mind better than all of them. Knight, with his chin resting on clenched fists, watched the two men examining the figures.

"You paid one hell of a price, John." Barclay closed the file and sat back. "They must have seen you coming, I reckon." He took off his glasses and rubbed his nose, then blinked and chuckled.

"I had to, for God's sake, and I warned you that I was going to go in high. We'd no idea who else was out there." He glanced angrily at the clerk who came in with the extra files.

"I know, and we were happy with that...but it all adds up to something over six pounds an acre. And that's a whole lot of money, y'know." Barclay paused. "You can get a tip-top farm in Anglia for under two pounds an acre...perhaps fifty shillings. One of a thousand acres...one with everything up and running, stock in the sheds, cows milking an' that...the lot for around two thousand pounds."

"The problem is this, John," Esdaile interrupted, pushing his file to one side. "This figure of yours is only the start point. Now...if we take Crispin's example here, we would be getting a handsome return the very next day...ricks to sell, lambs at the market and so on." Barclay could see the Iron Master bridling. "But here...on your Exmoor there is absolutely *nothing*." Knight wrestled himself around in his chair.

"I mean, first we have to put in the infrastructure...*build* the wretched places...*create* the fields. Then we have to find tenants, and God knows who'll want to live up there." Esdaile paused, smiling benignly. "So it's only after all that, and when they've got the place running, that we can hope to see something of a return. It's going to take years...*years*."

"Oh, for Heaven's sake." Knight thrust back his chair. "Why can't you all get it into your heads that I happen to have the funds...*all* of them. I've bought the place now; it's done. That's history for Heaven's sake...*but* I've got the capital to do everything else as well. It's not as though I've come grovelling around begging for a loan, damn you all." He eased his shoulder and stalked to the window. "Stop getting yourselves into a lather about something that's of no consequence...you're beginning to sound as though you're preparing me for something."

"Steady, old thing." Barclay soothed the hunched figure then raised a restraining hand to Esdaile. "You can do whatever you like with your money, of course you can, but it's *our* job as your bankers to give advice…to try and ensure that whatever we release is put to good use…reinvested wisely so you get a good return. It's our duty and, to be fair, we have a point."

He peered over his glasses at Knight's back. "The money for the land was one thing…as you say that's all in the past. Now, though, we've got to consider what's coming next…and there's an awful lot still to come." Barclay heaved himself laboriously out of his chair. "*Any*way, now's as good a time as any." He threw open the door and peered. "Come in Mr Maxwell, will you. We need to hear from you."

Knight returned to his chair and sat heavily.

Raimond Maxwell, so Morgan always thought, set out to impress. Punctilious and correct, he dressed more as a city man would when visiting the country, rather than a true countryman. He doubted if the plaid tweed suit over the bright, embroidered waistcoat had ever seen the Sussex Downs let alone the top of Exmoor and he watched unimpressed as the agent fussed uneasily with the files in front of him. The man was nervous.

Knight absorbed everything said. Half sitting, half lying in his deep chair, he had his legs pushed out and his hands thrust well into his pockets. His head, half hidden by hair, never moved until Maxwell rose to leave. "Almost exactly," the body growled. "But I'm planning on three or four farms more than he suggested…and up to twenty miles more of good road." Then he rose surprisingly fast, levering himself to his feet with a loud grunt. "Ye said it well, Maxwell, an' well done for that."

"So there you are," Knight turned exultantly. "A further twenty-five thousand pounds it's to be. That's what the man said. I told you so and you know the money's there, all of it."

"A little more than that, perhaps." To Morgan, Esdaile's grin was as inscrutable as ever. "A touch nearer forty, John, and that's quite a bit more. Forty thousand is my guess and to realise that we'll be looking to the Midlands…and to part with anything there will reduce your income substantially."

"What the devil's behind it all, John? Eh?" Barclay, his hair lying unkempt on the collar of his fawn jacket, leant forward. He blew loudly through his clay and opened his tobacco pouch. "I've never understood this sudden, massive investment into the unknown…and at this pace. It's not the John Knight I know." He rose and stood facing his client. "What's behind it all…eh?" The three bankers waited, Barclay frowning as he concentrated on his tobacco and pipe. Morgan tidied the files.

Knight shrugged. He moved to speak then shrugged again. "Times have changed." So quiet was he that Esdaile bent forward. "All my life I've driven hard…brushed aside anything and everything, let nothing or nobody stand in my way." He glanced at Barclay, who motioned him on. "But then…I lost Helen."

"Indeed…indeed." Barclay nodded knowingly, clearing the frog in his throat.

"Well, after that it got worse…became a man possessed, didn't I just? Lost myself in my work." As he half turned, the light from the window caught the strong face. "Like a drug it was…but it kept me from going mad. Well…life rushed by but…then came Elizabeth-Jane." Knight raised his arms and let them fall. All eyes were on him. "Then the children…and, all of a sudden, there was more to life. I'm not so young as I was, y'know…I'm never going to see sixty again but I've been blessed with the greatest of good fortune."

He came back to the table and picked up the files in front of Morgan. "That's what all this is about. For the woman who's brought so much to my life. I owe her everything. This Exmoor's my gift to her and our young…something they'll cherish long after I've gone. Exmoor's going to be ours if it takes every goddam bar of iron I've ever made. It's going to be a fine place where good men can toil honestly and live decently…breathe the clean air, feel the sun and wind. Not like those poor devils in the mines and factories." The words came softly but they were ground out. "So that's *why*, my friends." He held the files high then lowered them on to the table.

"Bravo, John…bravo." Crispin Barclay put his arm on Knight's shoulder. "I thought as much, dear friend, aye…thought 'twas something like that."

Morgan watched as Knight took his seat once more. Even as he was speaking, the man had changed, as had the mood in the room. His mind went back to the night at Castle Heights when Knight had come to him in the hours before dawn. It had been the same then. His frailty, his one weak spot was the love for his young wife, of that there could be no doubt. But what of her? Was she aware, he wondered, of the power she held over her man? Did she feel for him as he did for her, love him in the same way? And was this love of his purely spiritual or was it physical and passionate, such as any young woman would crave?

Morgan toyed with the quills in the inkstand. Perhaps all these gifts of land and property, of finery and the high life where Elizabeth-Jane ruled supreme, perhaps all this came in lieu of the love John Knight could no longer give. Perhaps he was buying her company, and perhaps she needed more.

✳

The dark sunken eyes of Ebenezer Havers that peered out from behind his black-grey beard brought no cheer. Aeacus from Hades' own kingdom, Morgan thought to himself. Sitting there crouched in his bulky, old-fashioned coat with his striped brown waistcoat and red necktie, his very presence was enough to dampen the spirits.

"None at all?" Esdaile peered at the man across the table. "*None*...can that really be so?"

"That's our appraisal, sir," Havers inclined his head. "We've been back time and again but there's little sign of potential...the lodes have been taken, all but worked out."

"But the chances are very fair...they must be."

"Aye, sir." He sniffed and wiped his nose. "There's always a chance but I've known of better ones left for dead."

"So we go *down*." Morgan saw Esdaile glance at Barclay, but Knight was adamant. "They can't have cleaned up, man. There must still be seams of high quality ore, and copper as well...deeper down."

"Aye, sir," Havers pulled on his beard then clenched his hands. "We know where we want to look...exploratory shafts, like, but there's water about and lots of it. You've seen for yourself, sir, and that means...."

"Pumps and drains," Knight exploded. "And you shall have them, I'll see to it. I want to make a start as soon as the roads are in. You should start preparing the plans and checking the estimates." They heard what else he had to say then showed him the door. All of them, Knight included, knew that while the cost of exploration would be high, the chances of success remained slight. They broke to eat then returned and worked on by lamplight, then broke off again to continue in the morning, vowing to conclude by midday.

Knight left London part satisfied, leaving his bankers to work out the detail on what they had agreed. He could go so far but no further, they told him. Shafts would be sunk, the line of the canal and railway would be prepared. Capital would be provided for that and for the roads and farms but no more until they were sure.

2.

Jack knew that the hard physical work with horses had made him slow and ponderous. His hands felt stiff and his feet leaden. He had to find Luke and fight with him before he lost his touch but The New Inn on the harbour front was crowded. As soon as he opened the taproom door, he felt the blast of noise and warm air.

For an hour he sat by himself watching quietly as the room grew ever more crowded and the smoke haze thicker. The fiddler had to stand to be heard then a drunk crashed off his stool. Two more, hairy and dirty, stood swaying, shouting the words of some song to each other. Everywhere there was laughter and merriment. Heads were thrown back, fingers were jabbed and tankards banged down.

Then suddenly he was there. Standing by the long curtain next to the door, Luke Harper had seen him already. Their eyes met and he beckoned.

Jack closed the door behind him, shutting out the light and the noise. The air was ice-cold. "Good to see, yer, Jack." Even in the quiet emptiness of the harbour, the voice was low. "Heard you was down...and I've been seeking yer." He took him by the shoulder and led him towards the low seawall. "I need yer help, man. Need it bad."

"Why me, Luke?" Jack peered more closely for the man's back was to the moon and his face no more than a dull shadow. "There's nort I can be doing for you, surely. Well...is there?" But he knew the answer and his pulse began to quicken.

"Listen." Luke paused. "I need another man. Right? I'm short of hands, wickedly short and it's fer tomorrow night." His voice was low. "There's a ketch from France due in...coming in on the tide. Half my team's away and I need someone...someone I can trust. Will you help?"

"Dear God." Jack froze. "Not that," he gasped. The two men looked at each other. "Smuggling, Luke, an' nothing less. An' yer know what happens to those they catch?" He looked away. "I can't, Luke." His voice was barely a whisper. "I've a job anyhow and I'm a law abiding man. Sounds soft and weak, I know." He could feel the smuggler's eyes. "Sorry, Luke, but there's my very life, too, for God's sake." Jack lifted his hands in appeal and shook his head. "I can't, Luke...I can't."

"Listen, Jack," Luke caught his arm urgently. "'Tis only this once, I'll not ask again. It's not for me, you know that...I get little enough from it all. It's for they that lives down here...there's *nothing* for 'em. No work like you've got up at the big house. *Nothing*, d'yer hear." Jack felt the fingers on his arm. "D'you know the price of a barrel of brandy? What it means to them down here?" Luke's grip tightened further. "The mouths it feeds, eh? D'you know what a run like this means to these folk?" He turned and spat. "They've got no other, Jack. They're helpless...*and* ye know it." He threw Jack's arm down.

The two stood in silence. Across the moonlit harbour, waves brushed gently against the shingle one by one before sinking back again. "Well?" He took his arm again. "Will ye do it, Jack? Will ye help?"

Jack shook himself free. As he walked to the edge of the jetty and stared down at the water, his shoulders were hunched. He couldn't do it, everything inside was telling him to walk away. He remembered his father's advice about respecting the law. And what was it old Jed had said? *'Once a smuggler, always a smuggler. Gets into yer blood and there's no going back.'* But he couldn't turn away. Already he owed much to the man and now, this evening, he was about to ask for more. And Luke had asked him as a friend, somebody he could trust. He had come to him for help.

The penalty was death: lifted high by the neck with body twisting and feet kicking; with eyes staring and tongue lolling until life had gone. He looked up at the sky and closed his eyes, thinking hard but now his heart was pounding. A powerful surge was coursing through his body, the same as sitting bareback over the steep and staring down before the gallop. It was a challenge, a thrill that dried the mouth, a thrill that excited. "All right," he breathed. "I'll not let you down, Luke...I could never do that. But just this once, mind, only once. And that's the bargain."

"Thanks, Jack. Here tomorrow, then...at eight. Can't say nothing now but I'll tell yer more then, when we're all together. Come, man...back inside or tongues'll get loose.

*

The night was bitterly cold, unusually so for November. Jack left the warmth of the forge, turned up his collar and made his way across the fields, his feet crunching on the early frost. At the gateways he slowed to pick his way past the puddles that had been coated with ice.

The old moon, no more than pale yellow was low in the east. It would be down by midnight and he wondered if Luke had asked the ketch to stand off until then or whether he would bring her in straightaway, making use of the light. For an hour he idled, checking the horses and sorting saddlery in the harness room until, at last, the clock on the stable tower chimed quarter to eight.

He approached the inn cautiously but there was no sound or movement from the taproom. Watching carefully, in particular one of the upstairs windows where the dull glow of a lamp was shining, he moved closer and crouched, listening for signs of life. He could hear the river behind him and, way beyond, the soft washing of the waves along the shoreline. Somewhere a dog barked, further off another replied but that was all.

Keeping to the shadows, he stole on, stopping again once more before moving out into the moonlight and standing in the open where they used to duel. "Jack." He turned slowly at his name. "Psst...here." It was Luke, no more than a shadow under the low eaves by the back door. The voice called again and he hurried across.

Standing in the entrance of the open doorway, he peered into the inky blackness of the taproom bar. There was a cough, the faint glow of a pipe and the sharpness of tobacco in the air. He knew he was being watched. He could even feel the presence of those already there but could see nothing. Then suddenly, no more than a yard away, his name was called. He knew the voice and stared into the blackness, but still nothing. "'Tis Hector...Hector Coward. Get in, quick." Even as the door closed behind him, voices began to mutter. Feet shuffled and bodies moved as the room relaxed once more.

They were all round him, ten, a dozen maybe but still it was black. He bent low, staring this way and that, one arm feeling the air in front of him. "Don't move." Jack strained his eyes in the direction of the voice then jumped back at the touch on his arm. "Over here. There's a bench. Steady now."

"So you're in this too." Jack muttered, squeezing himself between Hector and another figure. "And who else?" he whispered.

"Several in here, now. More outside and more up in the hills." Hector paused. "But one you'll know...Westcott, Nathan Westcott. Remember him from the stables? Ran off to sea, he did. Now works for Luke. Turned out not so bad."

"*Him*," Jack felt his body stiffen. The memories flooded back...the beatings, the duckings, the long, cold nights and the stolen food. "Je'es...*him*." He felt his anger rising.

"Aye but steady, lad." Jack felt Hector's hand. "Go easy now. Mended his ways, he has and don't go startin' nothing here." Once more the door opened and closed then a curtain was pulled across and the room fell silent save for the scratch of metal on flint as a lantern was lit and the wick turned low.

Le Coquillage was due off Lynmouth at eleven, shortly before the moon faded. They were to take two boats to bring in seventy kegs of brandy and wine. Luke spoke in a soft voice as the shapes around him craned forward to hear. Twenty pack ponies in two trains would meet the boats on the jetty then climb out of the harbour using the steep track up Countisbury Hill. Combe Farm, outside Brendon, was their destination. That done their work would be complete.

"Now then," Jack watched Luke's face as he spoke, where his throat and chin had been lit up by the lamp on the table under him. "I don't want no weapons. Right? The excise men have 'em, mind, but that's their good luck. If taken, do what you must with yer fists and yer boots but that's all." Jack felt his mouth open.

"We've got pickets up in the hills, so we're taking no chances." Some of those listening coughed or cleared their throats. "Two musket shots from the pickets an' the game's up. Just two...right? Then the others'll answer. If we hear that, then we use the track up the valley through the woods. Up to where the two rivers meet. 'Tis a maize bad track and as black as hell in they woods...but that's the way we'll go."

*

An hour later Jack was in the first boat.

Nathan Westcott gave the helmsman directions. For several minutes they saw nothing, just sat listening to the slow pull of oars, the creak of rowlocks and the gentle lapping of water under the bow. Once round Black Rock it was the two masked lanterns at the masthead that gave her away.

Jack rose gingerly, stumbling to keep his balance in the swell as he made his way to the centre of the boat. By the time he had stepped over legs and pressed carefully around bodies they were secure against the ketch, both boats rising and falling together. "Bloody Frenchies," a voice growled. The strange, bitter odour coming from the ship was powerful and several others cursed quietly.

"No more'n a peg o' garlic an' a drop o' wine." It was Westcott. Jack watched as he scrambled into the bows. "*Hey, hey,*" his voice was little more than a whisper. "*Salut, messieurs. Bon soir...ca va?*" Then he was gone, scrambling on board to greet the figures in the companionway.

Jack had never seen such a ship and stood fascinated, waiting patiently for the kegs to be unloaded. The first almost fell through his arms and he stumbled, gasping before passing it on. The second was as heavy, the third heavier still, chaffing the inside of his arms as he struggled with the weight.

"*Trente neuf...quarente. C'est tout...allez. Au revoir et bon chance!*" As they were cast off and began to drift apart, hands were raised in salute.

✳

The pack train had just begun to pick its way towards the bridge over the River Lyn when the two shots rang out. Even as they stood undecided, two more cracked loudly in reply, the echoes rolling back and forth high in the steep gorges above them. Jack turned at the sound of running feet.

"Davey!...Davey!" It was Luke. "Davey...Davey Burge!" The smuggler ran down the line of ponies until he found who he was looking for. "Forget Countisbury...take the old track along the river bank," he gasped. "The one down there. Hard going mind...and steep...so you'll have to go steady." He stopped, gulping for air. "Look out for the others...by the old camp...just off where the waters meet. And Davey...no weapons mind. No weapons." He paused again. "Us don't want none of they." And with that he was gone.

For a while nobody moved. Save for the heavy breathing there was silence. The men in the hills had seen something, now everyone was listening. One of the ponies blew, another shook itself. The men from Brendon had little time for authority and none at all for those they knew were on to them. But this was their livelihood and they did it for money. It had always been thus and tonight was no different.

Only after scouts had been put out in front did they move. The going became more difficult, especially for the ponies, laden down as they were. They soon slowed. Sliding on the loose, icy shale and knocking against rocks, they had to feel their way in the blackness, feet and legs of ponies and men stumbling and tripping. Twice they descended to the riverbank and twice they climbed steeply before they reached the clearing. Men dropped where they were, thankful for the cold ground, the ponies simply stood wherever they were left and bowed their heads. But the job was done and Jack, like the others, sat wearily while Burge talked with the horsemen who had met them.

*

Luke came a week later. It was during the quiet of the afternoon and they were alone in the stable yard. "Thanks for yer help, Jack. You were there when I needed yer...and I don't forget. 'Ere, look." He caught hold of Jack's hand and pressed his fingers around the leather purse. "'Tis yours and well earned at that."

"No, Luke." Jack stared at the expression on the smuggler's face. "No, I never came for money. Here." He held out the purse. "Honest, Luke. I came the other night 'cos you asked for help and you're a friend. Here take it."

"Don't be daft, man," Luke laughed and pushed his hand away. "And quit all that fancy, rich man's talk. You need it, boy...'tis nothing more than you deserve, same as all the others. His Majesty King George can do without it...you can't. Gid on."

3.

Elizabeth-Jane put the letter down and sauntered slowly across to the room. Outside, one of the gardeners was tidying the edges of the top lawn but she never noticed him. She stood quite still, for a minute at least without noticing anything at all before returning for the letter. This time she walked purposefully back to the window seat where she settled herself, leaning back against the curtains and half-turned towards the light. Even as she began to read it again, she could feel her heart beating.

Esdaile, she knew, had agreed that Morgan's stay in Barnstaple should be extended. Only a week ago, after they had all dined together at Portland Place, Morgan had expressed his hope that they might be able to meet again. She remembered his face when she let slip the fact that she would be staying in Barnstaple at the end of the month in order to complete her winter shopping. Simonsbath was too far for a round trip and she had decided to stay overnight, taking one of the maids with her.

*

Morgan, so he wrote, was beside himself with joy. It would indeed give him the greatest of pleasure to place at her disposal his lodgings in Paternosta Row. He would not entertain the idea of her staying alone in some hotel or other. In fact he had already taken the liberty of making the necessary arrangements. Mrs Dobbs, his landlady, would prepare his rooms while he himself would be happy to take temporary residence above the Old Coffee House, a comfortable gentlemen's retreat barely two minute's walk from his lodgings.

The only condition, his elegant and flowery hand stipulated, was that Mrs Knight would consider honouring him with her company for luncheon and dinner unless, of course, she had made alternative arrangements.

Her eyes closed. John would be home by then, however he knew of her plans. Cockrams, the Barnstaple dressmakers, had written to say that her orders were ready and they were waiting for her to call. That alone, with so much to be fitted and tried, would take a while, the more so as Nanette, the seamstress, insisted on perfection. Hebditch, the milliners could not be rushed either. Then there was the question of shoes, and boots for the new riding habit, the glovers, the haberdashers and the fan makers. It would take longer, two days not the one she had previously considered; nobody, she convinced herself, could deny her that. Her spirits soared.

Her letters took her an hour; the one to the bank alone requiring three attempts before she was satisfied. But she rose at last, yawned and stretched lazily then moved to the fireplace where she studied herself in the gilt mirror.

She peered closely, then stood back and tidied her velvet dress, allowing her hands to smooth the flat of her stomach as she stood on tiptoe, turning left and right to check her figure. Moistening a finger, she bent forward and dabbed gently at the rouge on her cheeks then toyed with her short curls before turning again to adjust her fichu. She smiled at herself appreciatively, as if the image she was admiring belonged to somebody she knew. For a moment she was lost in thought and sighed deeply. Then she hugged herself and twirled herself around like a dancer. Her body, she could feel, had come alive.

"Ah, Mary...and you, Emma," Elizabeth-Jane turned towards the two maids who had answered her call. "Here're the letters, look." She wrinkled her nose and waved at the bitter smoke from the sealing wax. "Ask Mr Parker to arrange for a galloper from the stables, would you. They must go to Barnstaple today, this very afternoon. Here, there're four...Cockrams, Hebditch...a Mrs Dobbs in Paternosta Row and one to The Barnstaple Bank."

"Very good, ma'am." Mary Quick stepped forward. Emma, new to the role and still under instruction, watched as the older maid checked the wax on the paper. "An' a drop more there, p'raps, ma'am...like that. There we are." She glanced at Elizabeth-Jane. "Best to be safe seeing as they'll be going in a saddle bag. Here...I can do it."

"I've decided that *you*'ll be with me next week, Emma." Elizabeth-Jane smiled at the look on her face. "Don't worry, I'm sure you can take good care of me for two nights. It'll be good for you...and we've got to see the seamstress about your trousseau, have we not?" She pulled a face playfully. "Yes indeed we have. We'll get it done while we can."

Emma shrugged and smiled nervously. "Won't be for a while yet, ma'am...but 'tis ever so kind." Her face had flushed with excitement.

"You'll be fine," Elizabeth-Jane put a hand on hers. "And in any case, Lady Frobisher specifically asked me for you. You'll be very happy down at Filleigh...not too far from here either, even less to Molland. And there's Mr *Kingdon,* of course," she laughed. Now then." Elizabeth-Jane closed her inkwells. "I must be away. Mary will show you what we need for our visit."

✱

"Oh, Mrs Knight, so it must be, ma'am. Please do come in." Mrs Dobbs, grey hair swept up, beamed happily. She had seen the double brougham, her eyes quickly taking in the green-liveried coachman, the footman and the pair of matching greys. "Go and tell them to bring in the luggage, my dear" she smiled at Emma. "Then come in yourself...your mistress is on the first floor.

"Now, ma'am, this way, please," Mrs Dobbs turned to lead the way up the narrow stairs. Elizabeth-Jane followed, acutely aware, as her hand moved up the banister rail, that this had been, and still was, the province of Durnford Morgan. It was as if she was intruding into forbidden territory, reminding her of the time when, as children, she and her sisters would creep into a prohibited room, curious, nervous but excited at what might be. "There we are, ma'am...in here."

Elizabeth-Jane went to the lattice window. "Gracious, not one church but two, I see," she opened the window and peered out. "But a pretty view nonetheless. Thank you, Mrs Dobbs." She turned to face her landlady. "It's charming...thank you."

Mrs Dobbs beamed and inclined her head. "But look here, ma'am...down over there...see?" She moved to the window. "There's Church Lane, look. Just past St Anne's chapel." Elizabeth-Jane followed her hand. "Mrs Horwood's down there...the Old Coffee House and that's where Mr Morgan's staying. Very comfortable it is...proper place for a gentleman."

As she looked, Elizabeth-Jane felt the landlady studying her, scrutinising her inquisitively. "Now then, ma'am, we've put your things from Cockrams through here...came in this morning." She followed the housekeeper into the smaller, brightly decorated and comfortable sitting room, noticing at once the chintz curtains and the line of china ornaments above the coal fire. Her clothes, still chalked and rough stitched, hung from the picture rails.

"How lovely," Elizabeth-Jane lifted the sleeve of the striped satin walking dress. "Oh, and look...the ball gown." She ran her fingers down the brocaded silk. "It's just as I asked and look at the colours…I'll have to powder my hair. How exciting," she laughed gaily. "What fun the fitting's going to be."

"Lovely, ma'am. Reel lovely. Now then," Mrs Dobbs, whatever thoughts on high fashion she might have, had something of importance to announce. "Oh, and by the way, ma'am…Mr Morgan said to tell you he'll be over to see you at seven o'clock. Sent his apologies but he can't get away no earlier." Elizabeth-Jane caught her look. "He's asked me to do dinner tonight, ma'am. Salmon, he suggested…told me it's one of your favourites. Baked with nutmeg and shallots…with one of my sauces that he likes." She paused, watching closely.

"That'll be down stairs, ma'am," she added, as though Elizabeth-Janes' silence had finalised the matter. "In the dining room, just the two of you. I'll see to the girl, ma'am. She'll be up on the top floor, along at the back and will sup with me." She paused. "Well then, I 'spect you could do with some tea and I'll bring a lamp."

"Thank you, Mrs Dobbs. Tea would be nice. And please tell Emma to be ready. I'll take a stroll into Boutport Street…to see the shops before it gets dark." She allowed the landlady to help her off with her velvet caped overcoat then undid her plumed silk bonnet. Once on her own, her eyes strayed again to the gardens where she half expected to see the tall, spare figure and his casual wave. In spite of all Mrs Dobbs's fussing and attention, her thrill of anticipation remained.

Where was he just now, she wondered, and what would he be thinking? Glancing at his watch perhaps…willing the time to pass? Or would he be engrossed in the business of the day, his mind concentrating furiously on ledgers and stocks; of profit margins, and of John, maybe? And what, she tried to imagine, would be Durnford Morgan's thoughts towards her husband now? Not, surely, as the all-powerful master he knew but as any other susceptible man whose wife he had arranged to meet secretly. The more she thought about him, the more intrigued she became.

＊

"So, really, it was much as we expected." Durnford Morgan, elbows on the table, leant forward and carefully moved the single candle to one side. It was the only one on the lace cloth. The others, together with the globe lamp had been placed around the room, cleverly lighting the walls and ceiling with a soft glow. "They both urged caution, tried to get him to take stock and slow the pace down."

While Morgan was thanking Mrs Dobbs for their meal and bidding her good-night, Elizabeth-Jane toyed with her glass. She had moved her chair away from the fire. The heavy beams of the little dining room seemed to hold the heat and she had removed her cotton shawl placing it on the oak sideboard.

"And?" She looked up hopefully, her eyes searching his for some answer other than the one she feared.

"We-ll, it might have been worse…a good deal worse in fact." Morgan raised his eyebrows catching her just she moistened her parted lips nervously, like a child. Then, still unaware of his gaze, she took up her napkin and dabbed daintily at the corners of her mouth. Her pale cream dress with the open Bruges lace-work balanced her complexion perfectly. The scarlet ribbons on her bodice and in her hair added further to her bidding. Her jewels sparkled. Everything, so Morgan thought, was perfect. She was beautiful and he adored her.

"Why are you looking at me like that?" she laughed then raised her glass to her lips, suddenly coquettish.

"I'm sorry…forgive me, my mind was far away," he lied.

"How far?"

"Oh, further than you could imagine." It was his turn to laugh. As he did so he blushed, afraid she had read his thoughts.

"So…." she was serious again. "What do you suppose we do? I've tried and tried again but he's impossible. He's not a young man and sometimes he's so stubborn…just won't listen or see sense, and then he gets angry, almost tyrannical. One minute I'm up on a pedestal, then…next I'm treated like a child."

"D'you love him?" The words tumbled out. Morgan glanced down as he reached for his glass, then up again. "I mean really…and with all your heart?"

"Now that's not fair, Durnford," Elizabeth-Jane looked suddenly defensive. "No woman's ever going to admit they don't love their husband…not at the dinner table anyway."

"I'm sorry," Morgan refilled his glass. "Do forgive me. It's just that we've talked about everything…well, almost everything and I couldn't help but ask. But please do forgive such an intrusion, it was most impertinent."

"Of course I forgive you," she looked down, embarrassed by the strength of his sudden apology and hesitated, frowning as she thought about how best to continue. "Ye-es, I do love him…in a way. He's a most wonderful man, and so kind to me. But he is so much older. Sometimes he's more like a father. I'm half his age, you know. Less, as it happens."

"He worships you. D'you realise that? Idolizes you, we can all see it."

"I know," she sighed. "And he's so good to all of us. Yet sometimes I feel he just can't understand how the children and I think. But…." she started to speak then fell silent. "A little more wine, please." He filled her glass then sat back, noticing her sudden inquiring look. "But why all this?" she smiled coyly.

"Come, Durnford, why are we talking like this…it's something very private, you know, a most personal secret." Morgan looked down. "And why *now?*" she persisted.

"Oh, I was just curious." He pulled a wry face and glanced up, catching her look.

"Why so? About me?" she shrugged.

"Yes, you." He leant forward, his elbows on the table once more and with his chin resting on his hands. "And more so even than when we last spoke." He took a deep breath and sighed. "You see…you've quite taken my heart, stolen it in fact."

He laughed nervously and checked himself, pursing his lips briefly. "I think…I think I've fallen in love with you, Elizabeth-Jane…and from the very first time we met." He reached out for her hand. "I have never felt like this before and that's the truth, I swear it is. But," he sighed and looked down. "From the beginning I knew then that you could never be mine…that you were his and it would always be that way. That is so…isn't it?"

"Yes…and I told you why," she murmured gently, her eyes searching his face. "It would be impossible, Durnford, and very, very wrong. She leant forward and cupped his hand in hers. "And we both know that," she whispered.

"So you *do* have feelings for me, then?" His look was intense. "If you knew it would be wrong then surely you speak for both of us…can that be so? Have you had such thoughts also…of me, and what might have been?"

She lowered her head, allowing the ringlets round her neck to fall forward. Then she nodded, slowly, taking her hands away from his. "Yes," she murmured. "I could not lie. I have but…oh, *God,* I don't know." A hand came to her mouth and when she looked up he saw the tears in her eyes. "I'm so sorry…I should not have said that. It was wrong. Even my *thoughts* were wrong and to speak of them like that worse still."

He listened, shaking his head slowly from side to side in disbelief. But he said nothing. "I suppose it was that day at Lee Bay," she went on before pausing to bite nervously on the edge of her lip. "It all began there, when I was alone…as always, dreadfully alone. But then, suddenly you were there, weren't you." She glanced at him. "I knew at once you would understand…at last there was someone to whom I could talk. It was so wonderful to have you there and, yes…I needed you. Just somebody…to hold on to…to put their arms around me and reassure me. "

He got up. "No, Durnford…it cannot be. Please…no."

"Just one, that's all I ask. One sweet kiss, no more than that…I promise. A mere keepsake of your thoughts…come."

She rose gracefully, taking his hand but with her eyes lowered. Slowly and tenderly he took her in his arms then lifted her chin until she was looking up at him. She was afraid; he could feel it in her body and saw it in her eyes as she searched his face. "Just one," he murmured as his hand went to her cheek.

"Just one," she whispered, closing her eyes. "But no more."

*

John Knight crossed the hall. There was no one in the day room, nor the drawing room either and it puzzled him. "Ah, Parker. Mrs Knight around?"

"Back tomorrow, sir." The butler drew himself up. "Mid-afternoon, sir. Before dark, so she said."

"*Tomorrow?* But why's that?" Knight scratched at his hair. "We'd agreed that she'd be away for one night only. And, I saw her maid a few minutes ago…Mary Quick. What's she doing here, then?"

"Mrs Knight didn't take her, sir. Took one of the younger girls, Emma Tucker."

"That's strange. Where's she staying then?"

"With acquaintances, I believe, sir. In town."

"Ac-*quaintances*…in *town*?" Knight put a hand to his chin and turned back to the drawing room, muttering to himself. "Acquaintances? Who do we know who lives there…in Barnstaple? There's only the bank, and who do we know there?"

He walked to the window but took no notice of the rain beating against the panes. Then over to the fireplace where he sat on the fender with his head bowed. Suddenly he was up again, pacing the long carpet; then he sat once more, this time heavily into a deep armchair.

For a time he was still, alone with his thoughts. When he tried to rise he struggled then struggled again, this time violently with his legs kicking out wildly. He managed to half rise but fell back clutching at his chest.

Parker was the first to hear his muffled cries.

Chapter Eight

Mr and Mrs Knight had all the servants assemble in the great hall. It was Boxing Day and, as was the tradition by now, it was the turn of the family to serve mulled wine to the gathering, complete with mince pies and frumity. Sprigs of holly and ivy decorated the pictures on the panelled walls and hung in long swags and tresses from the gallery. Faggots crackled and blazed in the open hearth while, in spite of John Knight's protestations, five lady members of the Porlock ensemble sat playing in the alcove beyond the stairs.

Elizabeth-Jane moved among the staff with a tray of felt purses tied with coloured ribbon. Frederic followed with a wicker hamper of wrapped gifts, Kenton and Edward with jugs of ale and wine. The other children took trays of sweet cakes and, as their mother had insisted, sought out the oldest and shyest. The master, stick still in hand, moved slowly and laboriously among the gathering.

*

Jack stood by the fire with Hector and Leonard. Dan Webber, one of the new lads, was with them. They had listened dutifully to John Knight's address but now, as soon as the company had relaxed, along came the more pressing business of the housemaids who were standing awkwardly together across the hall. Pleasantries apart however, nothing was going to be easy: Parker and Mrs Strong had seen to that.

"There ye go, man." Leonard nudged him. "That Meg, over there, see. Her's giving you the once over again." The big man, his face ruddy and glowing in the heat and his hair a startling mass of tight curls, winked. "Can't take her eyes off yer, an' all." He scratched at his chest then nodded to Hector Coward for support. "What's up then boy?" he taunted. "Scared...eh? S'posed to be a man, aren't yer?"

"Away with yer, Len." Jack, taller even than Leonard Grant but slimmer, ran his hand through his hair. "Nuthin' but talk...nort but kitchen prattle that is." He caught his friend's smirk. "Aye, that's all 'tis. On yer way, boy...and you Coward, sniggerin' on like that. Anyway, she's with Tom Smale, she is." Jack drained his tankard wondering if they had heard any rumours and waited for the dig. But none came so at least they didn't know everything. He smiled at the memory then caught the scullery maid's look.

"Here, Jack, there's yours somewhere." Frederic lifted the tray and peered at the labels. "Here you are," he nodded. "There...and there's yours, Hector...and you as well, Leonard."

"Thank you, Master Frederic." Only a month earlier, Jack had praised his horsemanship. Frederic, already a wild and daring rider, had been overjoyed

116

and they had become friends, firm friends, who often rode out together.

"Here, Jack, your glass."

"Whoa, Master Edward...that'll do me fine, sir...thank you."

"All the young around you as usual, Jack. What's your secret?" Elizabeth-Jane looked up at the head lad. He was as tall as Durnford Morgan but stood straighter. The hair, tied back with a black ribbon in the old fashioned way, was fair and straight. Already there was a strength in his face. Whenever he smiled his eyes creased and twinkled like those of an older man. The faded green shirt and buff jacket suited him as did the grey-brown knee breeches and white stockings.

She returned his smile, now aware of what Mary Quick had been saying about Emma's brother. But she nodded at the others also, laughing at Hector's quizzical look and Leonard Grant's huge bulk before her eyes turned back to Jack. "Hunting with us tomorrow?"

"No ma'am." He stood relaxed, casual and easy, yet his respect was there. She could see he knew why she had asked. "Mr Knight want's me to ride out with him, ma'am. Quiet like, just for an hour or so, that's all...doctor said not to do too much."

"Yes, be sure of that...don't let him stay out too long." For a moment her eyes dropped to the neat twist in his necktie. "Just you tell him from me," she warned.

"Aye, ma'am...I'll see to that." He held her gaze until she looked away again, wondering if it was true what they were saying. He had heard the rumours but chose to discount them, nonetheless. She was a fine lady and he was glad that the fellow from London had gone. Then he looked up and saw Meg again. She smiled but this time he was prepared and grinned back cheerily.

＊

It seemed so long ago but it was only two days. The yard had been bedded down and he had gone into the boiler house. Outside a chill wind had been buffeting the drizzle but inside it was hot. The air was thick with steam and the powerful scent of linseed that had been mixed with the mash now simmering in the copper vat.

He was tired but it was his turn to work late and the boiler had to be checked. Jacket off, he worked fast, bending down to rake away the spent ash before wriggling fresh logs on to the embers. Even with more water added the mixture was heavy and he took both hands to the ladle. It was oppressively hot with moisture running down the windows so he undid his shirt, pulled it from his waist then bent to wipe his face. It was just as he turned from the fire to

117

breathe more easily that a movement caught his eye. She was there again.

"Hullo, Jack." Meg Braddon had slipped inside and was leaning against the door. "Workin' late, are you? Thought it might be you. Phew," she pulled at the front of her blouse, fanning herself. "My, 'tis hot."

"Same as ever, Meg...you should know that in here." He turned back to the ladle, bending once more to wipe his brow. "Always like this when the boiler's fired up." Dan Webber had warned him, and he had been right. Tom Smale was seen as Meg's man but short, black-haired Tom was away and when he was gone Meg Braddon went hunting. Least, that's what they said. He had thought no more of it until a week ago when she had come into the stables.

He remembered how she had stood there with her hands on her hips and her head to one side watching him with that look of hers. Without a care in the world she had strolled over and caught him by his belt then dragged him towards her. Pulling him close, she had pressed herself against him, letting his body feel the full softness of hers. He had just stood there letting her have her way and he remembered how she had left him with her fat, wet kiss. That was it: she had chuckled and smirked but nothing had happened. That was Meg Braddon for you but Tom Smale still was away and she had come back.

"So what's up then?" Jack looked round again, lifting a shoulder to wipe at the sweat on his face. "Come to mess me about again, have you? Gid on, Meg, bain't got no time for that nonsense." But he had noticed how she was standing; even as he turned back to the boiler he could sense the thrill of her presence. Then she laughed.

"Ooh, I dunno...dunno, really," she teased. "Taking some scraps to the poultry and saw the lantern in 'ere. Thought it might be you." Bending low to place her basket down, she paused, long enough for his eyes to take in the fullness of her body swinging free under the thin blouse, and she knew he was watching.

Carefully and deliberately, by pushing with her buttock, she pressed the door shut. "No messin' tonight, boy," she drawled once the latch had clicked home. "No sir, not tonight." Then her hands came up to her blouse, kneading her breasts together and forcing them tight against the white cotton. She watched his face but now her pulse was racing too. "Eh, Jack?" For a moment he stood there with one foot on the vat step before turning back to knock the mash from the ladle.

"Come on, boy, I've seen yer these last few weeks. 'Ere, " she beckoned with her head. "Keep giving me the eye but not doin' nuthin'. Why for, then? 'Fraid Meg's goin' eat yer, or run and tell?" She pushed herself away from the door and sauntered towards him, swinging her hips slowly and fingering the buttons on her blouse. "D'you know a woman, Jack...a real woman? Eh?"

"'Ere, come on Meg," he backed away. "Not in here...not now." It was the bran sacks that caught his heel and he stumbled before falling backwards. He struggled to sit then reached out to pull himself up but she was too quick.

"Gid on, boy." She pounced and pushed him back then straddled his waist with her skirts lifted high. Her weight and her sudden strength surprised him and he lay for a moment, watching as she swept back her hair then cursed as it fell forward again. Her face was flushed, her eyes wide and urgent.

"Just shut yer noise, Jack Tucker," she gasped. "You're a big lad, aren't yer now?" Pinned by her weight, he raised his head as her fingers pulled at his belt. As she lifted herself to get at him more easily, her fat thighs, open and white, were thrusting towards him. "Come on. I've been waiting fer this...let's see if yer a man or no." Lifting herself again and reaching behind her, she began to pull at his breeches. "Gid on then," she gasped, wiping her mouth. "Do summat."

Suddenly he was alive, pulling and scrabbling to free her blouse. Holding his head in both hands, Meg bent forwards, forcing their mouths together before sitting back again. "Lift yerself, man," she grunted, struggling with his clothes. "Here," she panted, burying his face in the valley of her breasts. "Come on, now. That's better...that's it." As she pushed him down they fell back together before rolling into the straw. "Come on," she gasped as her thighs locked around him.

*

Jack lay still, fighting for breath in the hot steam. She had fallen across him exhausted and he struggled to free himself from her nakedness. She was ugly, he thought, coarse and fat as she lay there in a tangle with the remnants of her clothes in disarray. Her face was drained and blotchy and her hair matted and powdered with meal, but he helped her tidy herself until she was ready, dusting her down and picking straw from her hair. She had said nothing at the time, just pouted with her mouth as she bade him farewell.

Now, on Boxing Day in the great hall and in front of the whole household, it was his turn. Blowing her a kiss across the crowded hall, he raised his tankard and laughed quietly at the look on her face before she turned away.

2.

"I'll be off then, sir." Jack Russell turned to let Parker help him into his tan riding coat. "Charles Collyns is your man."

Knight, striding out once more rather than creeping about the place, as he put it, walked briskly onto the front terrace. "I'll take your word for it, my boy. That Dr Levens fella from Lynton was driving me mad." He rolled his shoulder and sniffed the spring air. "Would've had me in a chair for the rest of my life if I'd let him."

"Aye, well you're not out of it yet, ye know. The boys tell me you're still catching your breath." Russell, with his foot in the stirrup, hopped twice and was in the saddle. "Collyns'll advise you better than me, but a wee flutter of the heart like that...and there's a message. Somebody's telling you something." The family could laugh now but for three months they had watched in alarm as Knight fought to regain his strength. At first a nurse from Exeter had stayed at Simonsbath, then Elizabeth-Jane tended him.

Twice he had turned to her begging to hear that his worst fears about her were unfounded. Twice she had sat stroking his brow, listening to the voice that now pleaded rather than demanded. The third time she had been brusque with him, the Irish in her finally rebelling at his refusal to accept her word. Nobody, she protested, had behaved with more dignity and honour than Durnford Morgan. Nobody else had seen fit to call his integrity, or hers for that matter, into question.

If he wished to press his case, she remarked icily, then that was his affair but he would be doubting her word, and something precious between them would have gone forever. And there the matter had rested. Morgan was still in Barnstaple but came out to Simonsbath less frequently. Knight grew in strength, ever more reliant on his young wife, and ever more doting.

"You tell me I've met him?" Knight came up to the horse, perplexed and scratching his hair. "The one who carries that bag everywhere...the fella in black with the stovepipe topper? Yes? Who rides that lovely old cob?"

"The very one, sir, an', more often than not, he's got a terrier of mine in his bag along with everything else." Russell pulled the horse round. "One hell of a rider he is and a champion among men as well." The parson bent forward. "He's a great one for helping the needy, y'know...always around the villages seeing what's to be done."

"Aye, so you told me," Knight mused. "Tucker's family as well, eh? *Cambridge,* you said, wasn't it?"

"That's right. Ask him about it if you will but he'll probably say nort. He's a modest man for all that...keeps what he does to himself. Try Tom Acland...he knows about it and could tell you more." Knight watched as the parson settled himself then turned his horse and trotted briskly down to the bridge. He turned as Parker approached.

"Lunch is ready, sir...and the family are all present."

※

"It doesn't surprise me," Frederic toyed with his napkin ring. "You could always tell those sort at school. Honestly." He shrugged and reached for the butter. "There were some who just devoured their work...lived for the stuff.

120

The tutors picked them out and worked on them...kept them well away from the rest of us," he laughed. "Groomed them up for university and away they went."

"Lucky devils, every man jack of them." Kenton scowled and pulled in his chair. "The rest of us were just left to get on with it...the useless mouths."

"Go on, you loved it," Edward interjected.

"*No*, they weren't lucky." Frederic ignored Edward. "Gifted yes, but not luck as in cards or dice." He knew Kenton was jealous. "I mean, if you're born like that, it doesn't matter where you come from. Isn't that right, papa? I bet you that half the engineers and scientists working for you...half at least didn't come from public schools."

"Well, not half, but certainly some...and some of the very best what's more." Knight leant back to let Parker remove his plate. "There's a fellow called Newman in Rugby...works in the foundry there. A chemist, he is, runs my research department...as Welsh as Welsh can be. A brilliant man but God knows how he got there."

"What's wrong with being Welsh?" Kenton fingered his glass. "More wine please, Parker."

"Nothing at all." John Knight brushed at the crumbs on his waistcoat. "But the fellow came from nowhere...no family background, no money...nothing at all but there he is and doing me proud."

"Then somebody must have spotted him." Frederic, with his fine features crowned by a mass of black curls, had heard Jack speak about his own younger brother and how Dr Collyns had discovered him. Jack knew little, other than his brother had now left home and was away studying somewhere. "Just like Jack Tucker's brother, Wilmot. There you are...Dr Collyns found him and look where he is."

"Well that's certainly luck." Kenton wiped his mouth. "Luck and nothing other than that."

"No, you're wrong," Frederic leant forward. "The ability...the gift or whatever has got to be there, for goodness sake. Let's face it, Kenton, if you or I were picked up now and dumped in some university or other, we wouldn't have a hope...and we'd loathe it. The talent has to be there."

"Oh, for Heaven's sake, Frederic. Grow up." Kenton threw down his napkin. "Honestly, you and your Tuckers. Why...."

"Now that's *quite* enough," Elizabeth-Jane rapped the table. She had seen Parker wave the footmen out of the room. "We do *not* discuss such matters at the table...*ever*." Her look was enough. "You know that perfectly well. And in any case" she drew herself up. "But least of all do we want to suffer you two arguing again...you're too old for goodness sake."

"Right, Edward, come on." Knight rose heavily and stood with both fists on the table in order to catch his breath. He nodded at Parker who had taken hold of his chair. "Let's away and hear about this history you're after studying. Then I've got that doctor fellow coming." He shook his head. "Edinburgh's the other end of the world, you know, but...you're man enough now."

The others left also, leaving Frederic with Elizabeth-Jane. She alone understood her eldest son. Time and again he had spoken to her of the plight of the poor and of doing something for them. There had been trouble a year ago when he had resisted his father's wish to go up to Oxford, planning instead to fight the cause of the less fortunate. He had ridden to Holnicote and talked to Thomas Acland, then to Filleigh to dinner with Lord Frobisher: politics, it seemed, were to be his destiny, that and succeeding his father.

✳

"Well," the stethoscope was new and Dr Collyns twisted his head to free himself. "We're getting there, my friend...getting there." The large man sat again and tapped Knight's wrist. "Your heart's steadied, Richard Levens was right enough there. He's not such a bad fella, you know."

"Poof," Knight struggled to sit then adjusted his shirt. "Did nothing but bleed me dry and send me to bed. And as for that tincture muck...foxglove and lilies or whatever...wretched man near' did for me." He stood and tucked his shirt into his trousers. "D'you reckon you can deal with me all this way out, doctor? It's a bit off yer beaten track, I know, but I'd be more'n grateful."

"Don't see why not." Collyns rose and began to pack his bag. "I'm up here often enough. Perhaps I could call in every now and then." He pushed back the thin hair on his near-bald pate. "But on the condition you do as I say. Right? Dulverton's a way away from here and I don't want to come galloping over to find I've a *corpse* on my hands." He saw Knight start. "I'm serious now."

The older man grunted and reached for his coat. As they walked slowly down the ornate oak stairs together, talk turned to the new Poor Laws. The doctor had heard about Frederic. "I know, I know," Knight shook his head. "It's all very well but there's not much of a living to be made." They paused at the bottom. "He can't spend his life banging the drum on behalf of the poor. We've plans afoot to get him into the business up country...that's where he's needed most, he and the others as well."

"Look, sir." Collyns walked slowly, head down. "I don't know the lad yet but he's spoken of mightily well...as are they all, but perhaps industry's not for him. Perhaps he's no businessman at heart. Maybe he has a calling, you know…a calling for something else. He loves it down here and you should see him with hounds…young Russell 's hard pressed to keep his nose in front. You know…" Dr Collyns stopped and stroked his chin. "There really *is* a life for him here, is there not? You'll be thinking of stepping aside one day and…what finer young man could you wish for. Perhaps his calling's here…here on Exmoor."

"Ha, you're a canny man, Doctor," Knight held out his hand. "And you may well be right there. The boy and I've talked long enough and there's much in what you say…and a good deal of sense in it all as well. A safe journey now and I'll do as I'm bidden. You've my word on that."

3.

Parker was alone in the senior staff room. Mrs Appelton was serving tea in the day salon and there was over an hour before he had to fetch the wine from the cellar. It was hot and he sat at the long refectory table quietly, biting his nails and catching up with himself

Enid Chapple would be leaving at the end of the summer. It had been bound to come to this and, as he relaxed in the sun, he pulled thoughtfully on his ear, staring absently at the welsh dresser. It was warm and, with the sun taking hold, his lidded eyes began to close, like an old guard dog trying to drowse. What with Edward Knight now away at boarding school and Isabella, fourteen next month and destined for a private academy in Paris, there would be none of the family left to teach. He cursed and continued to stare absentmindedly.

There were no other houses in the area so Mrs Knight had arranged for Enid to go to a family in Barnstaple. She had been to see them and there had been tears. Would he come and visit her, she had begged. Some chance, but he promised he would try and the snivelling had stopped. The butler looked down at his nails and half-smiled to himself. Keep it that way until her departure, he resolved, and all would be well. He got up, went to the dresser and opened the lower cupboard.

The bottle, one of the consignment he had been told to order from Bristol, was at the back behind the plates and he had to bend double to find it. He slipped and he swore but eventually he stood again, grinning triumphantly and ignoring the lank strand of hair that had fallen down over his face. The cork, as he pulled it, squeaked and Parker swayed.

The cup on the fifth hook was his and he counted along the rack carefully, then counted again to make sure before lifting it off to blow at the dust. It was habit by now. Half filling the cup he drank fast, then shook his head and gasped as the gin burned its way down. Returning the bottle was not so easy but he managed somehow, groping clumsily for the shelf of the dresser as he hauled himself up again.

*

"And there's no need to carry on like that." Mrs Strong busied herself with her shopping basket. "I've warned you time and again and you won't take no notice. A man in your position should be ashamed of yourself."

"Don't you worry about me or my side of the house," Parker bridled theatrically. "Come the moment I'm wanted, Mrs Strong, and I'm there. Every time...you watch."

"Now, don't be silly." She rounded on the figure in the chair. "It's not right all this drinking and we...oh, my dear, there's the bell." Parker half rose and stumbled but the cook moved first and held his arm. "Abel, you go, dear. It's the day salon...Mrs Knight I expect. *Sit still.*" She put a hand on the butler's shoulder. "You're not going anywhere, Bernard...not in that state. Just wait until Tarr's back and he'll help you to your room.

The second butler hurried to check himself in the mirror then ran into the corridor. "It's not right this, Bernard." Mrs Strong pulled up the chair next to him. "Not right at all...an' there'll be trouble...we can all see that. Mrs Appelton knows something's wrong...you've got to try, you know."

"Aye, I know. But I'm fine...just fine." He rose and patted her hand, grumbling to himself about something or other.

✳

"Give you a call in an hour, Mr Parker, sir." Tarr jerked back as Parker slapped his hand away from the door handle. "Sorry, sir...just opening it for you. Making it easy, like."

"Away with you, boy," Parker swayed then steadied himself and swept back his hair. "See to it I'm woken by six...go on...away you go." He listened as the steps receded and waited again before opening the door to his room and shutting it quickly behind him.

"Come, dear, I've been watching and waiting for you...an hour at least." Enid Chapple, her wispy brown hair unpinned and straggly, rose from the narrow metal-framed bed. "I'm dining with them tonight so I'll have to change soon."

"Och, to hell," Parker let himself fall backwards on to the bed, blowing heavily but allowing the governess to untie his cravat. For a moment he stared at the thin, worried face in front of him, then blinked and closed his eyes.

"Let's have your coat, dear. Come on." He half sat allowing her to wrestle with his jacket then lay back once more, feeling her bony fingers on his waistcoat buttons. As she undressed him, she smiled lovingly and leant forward to stroke his forehead.

"I dunno." He sighed and placed his arms behind his head. "Sometimes I think you're better off out of it...well out of it."

"We *could* go together, couldn't we?" She began to unlace one of his shoes. "We did talk about it...remember? In Porlock that afternoon."

"Nah," he sneered, angry that she had remembered the time he made all those stupid suggestions. He was just leading her on and had never meant it like that but she had clung to the idea. A sharper man would have had his way with her without promising anything, he thought. A rich man would have simply bought her. True she had given herself willingly, too willingly, but she was not that sort and he often wondered why she had. It was as though she was working on him, trapping him with all this mewing and petting. Now he was stuck.

"I'm going to have to see the master through here first." Parker shut his eyes again. Would the woman never learn. "He's a great man...gets more an' more like old Mr John...and I couldn't be leaving him."

"That's no matter, my precious." Enid Chapple took off his socks then sat stroking his feet, taking them one at a time and running her hand up the inside of his leg. "But you've had enough, haven't you, dear? Keep saying you're fed up and it's time to move on." She smiled endearingly with her head on one side. "I find them difficult too, you know...all this entertaining and rushing about the place." She bent to kiss his toes. "I can see it's too much for you...poor you, never mind."

"No...the master's a fine man." Parker nodded to himslf. "She's all right, too...very fair an' all that, but I'll bet there was something going on with that banker...that Morgan fellow. I tried to get close but they were clever. He's coming back, you know." Parker propped himself on his elbows. "Would you believe it...the master's letting him back. Me, I'd have had him run out of town." He fell back and lay staring at the ceiling. "But maybe you're right...maybe it's time to move on...before anything happens here and that Frederic takes over."

"I thought you liked him, dear." Enid Chapple moved to sit by him then bent and kissed his cheek.

"Aye...he's no' bad but he's the favoured man...Freddy this an' Freddy that. The others never get a look in. And that poor lad, Kenton...they never let him forget he's not one of them."

"But he *is* difficult, that one." Enid sat back, her hand in Parker's. "Ever since he was little, always teasing or fighting...always. He used to make it difficult for himself then just scream."

"Fighting his corner," Parker laughed caustically. "Can't blame him for that, you know. See myself in him sometimes, I do...doesn't care for it out here in the wilds. *'There's nothing going on, Parker. Nothing to do out here.'* Doesn't like the gardens…nor any of that lot that work in the stables." Parker rubbed his stomach. "He's an eye for the girls tho' but there're not many of them around here…not his sort, anyway."

He struggled back on to one elbow. "That's one of the reasons they keep filling the house, you know. Nobody here so…wheel 'em in to keep the youngsters happy. That's why." He yawned heavily. "Got the Northboroughs coming again next month as well…the whole lot of 'em."

"They're nice."

"The old man's a good laugh…she's a right old strumpet though. Tries to run the place, she does."

"The young, I mean."

"Oh aye. The girls are right bits of crackling…but you can keep *him*…that young Lord Herbert."

"Isn't he friendly with Kenton though? You said they seem to get on."

"And so they do. There you are, see…give the lad half a chance an' Kenton's right friendly with all of them. Fancies both the Northborough girls…can't keep his eyes off that older one. Here," he sat up and squinted at the wall clock. "Come on…I've got to get on."

"Can I come back later?" she begged. "You know, I can be here…waiting for you."

"And warming the bed, eh?" Parker stood over her. She was plain, he could see that. Her hair was a mess, and her pinched little face was too thin. But she would do, somebody had broken her in and taught her well enough. "Aye…you see to that. Slip away early, mind, so they forget all about you."

"*You* won't though…will you, Bernard?" Enid rose and stroked back his hair. "You won't forget me, my precious." She could smell his breath but it made no odds. His looks were cruel and that was what she liked best; that and his lean body.

"Here, come on." Parker opened the door and nodded. "On yer way now…but don't make a noise."

4.

They had considered walking for a while. Whenever the metal-rimmed wheel hit a rock or large stone the jolt would rock the coach from side to side. Then they would lurch as the wheels slipped into a deep rut making the springs

126

creak alarmingly. Outside they could hear the jingle of harness and the voices of the coachmen and outriders. But they sat on, facing one another as the four-wheeler ground and slid over the rough track.

Although the worst of the moor was behind them, Arlington Court was still an hour away and Barnstaple an hour beyond that. The Duke of Northborough's head lolled against the beige silk cushions as he gazed out of the window. He liked the sound of the idea and his heavy body, encased in his blue tailcoat and taut, grey pantaloons, shook as he laughed. "'Tis a thought, John...quite a thought." He pulled on his walrus moustache and clutched at the ivory handrail, his little eyes popping at the very idea.

"Well...as ever, it's the women that do all the talking about these things...and the scheming, too." Knight eased himself into a more comfortable position. "Elizabeth-Jane mentioned that she and Amelia had been discussing it. Nothing certain mind, just a thought."

"An' a good one at that...mmm. Freddy an' Katherine, eh? Would make a damn fine couple, you know." The Duke coughed. "Financially very sound, as well. Eh? Of course, we'd do our level best to match whatever you put up for Freddy, John." The two men were silent.

"What d'you reckon you might be able to do?" Northborough knew well that he could never match the Knight fortunes. His bloodshot eyes may have been small but they focused on the figure opposite.

"He'll be coming into Wolverley of course...Elizabeth-Jane'll take the manor." Knight opened up his cutaway coat and pulled at his spotted cravat. "Then there're the businesses...pretty substantial just now and doing me well. An' the boy's my heir, so he'll be due the lion's share." He looked up expectantly.

"And right enough, too." The coach lurched again and Northborough swore but what he had heard pleased him. "Never did go along with sharing things out every whichway...that's what sons are for. Mind you, John, there's time enough yet...but then the lad's of age next year," Northborough mused. "An' twenty-one's hardly a boy, y'know."

"Right enough...an' Katherine's a step ahead."

"That's no matter." George Northborough leant forward and shouted above the rattle and squeaks of the coachwork. "It sounds fine...fine, but keep our damned women out of it. D'ye *hear*...keep 'em well away," he swept his hand back and forth. "They'll get the pair of 'em all worked up an' scare 'em to death." He thought for a moment. "And, d'you reckon...reckon they're keen on each other?"

"Ye-es," Knight mused. "She's a lovely gal...so're they both but funnily enough it seems to be young Kenton who makes all the running. Calf love probably...the boy's barely out of his teens."

"Young Lizzie's a thing or two to say about him...so Amelia tells me."

"Best idea's to let things run for a while," Knight surmised quietly. "Keep 'em happy and keep their mothers out of it."

"We'll get Freddy up to Blagdon for a bit of shooting."

"And up to town as well. Plenty to do there...an' Portland Place's fully staffed." The two passengers fell back into silence, both happy to ponder over what had been discussed. It would, it seemed, be a fine match.

*

"When's all this then?" Jack reined in Nimrod. Emperor and Caesar, the two draught horses behind him slowed while he slipped from the bare back to open the gate.

"Two weeks." Leonard Grant urged his mount forward leading two more heavy animals through the open gate. He rode loosely with his fawn smock lifted, allowing his baggy trousers to hang free. "Hector's cousin's put my name down."

"Still fightin' novice, are you?" Jack sprang lightly on to the gelding's back.

"Oh, aye." Leonard took off his felt hat and scratched his curls. "Gotta have had ten or more fights for the open...an' I've only had six. But Hector and they lot reckon I'd be all right."

"Get away." Jack urged his mount alongside his friend, the four harnessed carthorses now following them placidly. "You've bin wrestling as long as I've known you, Len. Near on fifteen years or so."

"Aye but they's talking of proper fights now...bouts when you's doin' it fer money, not just scrappin' about the place." Jack glanced at his friend. Leonard would be a hard man to beat. The strong back and trunk-like legs would keep him well balanced and then there were those massive arms. Time and again he had watched the man lifting sacks or spreading dung, working effortlessly while those around him were forced to stop and rest.

"Don't know much about it reelly." Leonard laughed shyly, lifting his eyebrows at the thought. "Hey, there we are look...beyond them trees. Cuh, look at they cart loads."

Ebeneezer Havers had been sinking a small shaft, just above the riverbank a mile downstream from Simonsbath. Two carts had been left there to be loaded with any deposits that needed further analysis. Now they were full and Jack had asked Leonard Grant to ride out with him and harness them up. The mine fascinated them both and Havers had promised to show them their progress.

"They're working up on the top, Jack. Over there…under the bank, out of the sun." Jack shaded his eyes. "Get this lot harnessed up and we'll take a look."

The two worked quickly. One by one the horses were backed between the shafts until each pair stood side by side. Leonard lifted the central and cross poles together while Jack attached the collars. Both then checked the chains of the wipple trees and crooks before running their hands over the leatherwork. The horses were ready, but the carters never got to see the mine.

"Hey up, Jack…trouble." Leonard pointed downstream. The two watched closely as the four riders approached, one of them trotting ahead. "That's Master Kenton out front, Master Frederic's stopping back with the ladies."

"Aye," Jack grimaced. "We'll be hearing summat or other in a minute, that's fer sure."

✳

"Did you check Lila's girth? The one Lady Elizabeth's riding." Kenton reined in.

"No, sir." Jack walked up to the horse. He could see the mare was hot. "One of the lads would have got her ready today, sir." He held out his hand to the animal's muzzle.

"Leave her alone," Kenton snapped angrily. "The wretched animal's had enough people messing her around today." Leonard watched Jack, then looked from one to the other. "Well, whoever it was has made a right mess of it…come and see for yourself." He wrenched at the mare's head. "Come on…hurry up"

"Aye, sir. Right away. " Jack turned. "Here Len, hang on to Nimrod." Then he saw his friend's face. "Steady on, lad," he muttered. "I know, I know…just take it easy."

"Bastard don't deserve a mule, he don't."

"Hey," Jack's voice was louder. "Keep yer peace, Len. I'll see to it…just mind the horses." By the time he reached the riders, Frederic had helped Lizzie to the ground. The two women had been riding sidesaddle and Lizzie stood awkwardly where the long skirt of her riding habit had been caught in the bracken. Jack could see that the stitching around the mare's girth leather had come loose: as soon as he pulled it, the buckle broke free.

"That should have been checked properly." Kenton had come up behind them.

"Come on, Kenton, it can happen to anyone. Always playing the sleuth…give 'em a chance." Frederic removed the saddle. "Now what, Lizzie?" he laughed. "No bareback antics in that habit."

"Begging your pardon, sir," Jack took the saddle. "Best ways, p'raps, might be for her ladyship to ride back with Leonard, there…that's if you don't mind m'lady." He looked round at the laughter and grinned sheepishly. "Honest, ma'am…there's room for two on the cart and we can put a coat on the seat."

"What about your saddles, Jack?"

"Us came bareback, Master Frederic, an' I wouldn't like to see her ladyship on either of they two…both a mite frisky."

"Go on Lizzie," Katherine giggled. "On the cart and we'll see you back in time for dinner."

"Don't worry, m'lady," Jack grinned. "Leonard here'll see you safe and we'll soon have one of the dog carts down to collect you." He returned her smile. "Honest, ma'am, 'tis the best way."

✳

Jack kept his distance. Ahead, the three riders rode together, separating only to cross and re-cross the river where bog and sedge forced them into the water. The sun was low but he was warm, even in his open shirt. He could hear the distant chatter but, as Orwell Govier had taught him, he reined back out of earshot.

Half a mile from home, Kenton Knight pushed on by himself so Frederic moved his horse alongside Katherine's. They were quiet for a while but he drew closer and, after glancing back over his shoulder, put his hand on the back of her saddle. Now an unwilling and uneasy witness, Jack drew further back yet kept his eyes on the two in front. He saw her push him away then watched again as he closed in once more, this time allowing their legs to touch. For a while they talked and laughed quietly together before she looked back again and pushed him away once more.

Suddenly, Frederic urged his horse forward, leaving her on her own. She pulled up and waited, half turning her mount. Jack stopped as well, then trotted slowly towards her. "Nuthin' wrong, m'lady?" He looked under the narrow-brimmed hat. The face that looked back was happy enough but there was something amiss.

"No…everything's fine, thank you." He glanced again, curious at the tone of her voice yet afraid to intrude. He saw the eyebrows rise and her shoulders sag despairingly. "Kenton…Master Kenton went off to get help for my sister. The two men just couldn't stop talking about it. Honestly, anyone would have thought she was half dead. *And*," she patted her horse's neck. "Freddy's just remembered that somebody called Dr Collyns is calling. He's got to see him about his papa."

She shrugged again, seemingly irritated at the situation. "So...there's just me, I'm afraid." But then she laughed lightly with a hand to her mouth, as if a moment had passed. "And I'm not much of a horseman at that," she declared now smiling bashfully. It was a pensive smile, almost sad in a way yet friendly enough, but that was all he could tell.

"My pleasure, m'lady...we won't be long now." He pulled off the cart track waiting for her to ride ahead.

"Oh, come on, for Heaven's sake. Lets ride together...it's Tucker, isn't it? I remember you now; Freddy's often talked about you."

She pulled alongside him. At first they were silent but then they talked. It should never have happened. Such familiarity would never have been countenanced: it was just not done. No lady ever engaged a mere servant in casual conversation like this and on her own, and with somebody else's groom at that. But talk they did and as they did, so their eyes met. It was impossible for them not to on so narrow a path. "It's wonderful coming here, you know. I really love Exmoor."

"Beautiful place, m'lady," he agreed politely catching her look and the brief smile before she glanced away. "Rough out here in the winter, mind."

"Does it snow a lot?"

"Aye, from time to time but 'tis the cold that gets to yer. Day after day...weeks on end sometimes."

"Still beautiful, I'm sure. I can just see it." She hesitated, wondering how he managed in the biting cold. "We'll...I'd like it here in winter, anyway." He knew she was looking at him but he rode on, head down as though searching for something in the brambles and long grass by the side of the track. Even then, he could feel her eyes on him.

He looked up. "Sorry, m'lady?"

"What?" she frowned. "What are you sorry about?"

"What you said, just then."

"What did I say?"

"Summat about winter, I think."

"Did I?"

"Yes, m'lady."

"What was that?"

"About liking it here in winter…aye, that's right."

"Did I? Really? Oh, come on, this is ridiculous," she laughed. "We're talking in riddles…Heaven knows why."

She could see he was puzzled but, like the good servant he was, he left the last word to her yet she didn't know how to continue. For a moment she was tongue-tied and confused about something, then she found herself looking at him again. It was his face, and the way he carried himself. Elizabeth-Jane had been right. She was only teasing when she said it but she confessed with a laugh that Tucker was her favourite. The tall, quiet one with the fine features and with his hair tied back. The one with the grey-blue eyes. The one who could ride like the wind and the one who Freddy adored.

She wanted to talk and she wanted him to talk back to her so she could hear the soft Devon burr in his voice. In fact she just wanted him to talk so she could watch while he spoke. She thought of making some excuse and stopping so they could spend a little more time together but decided against it. There was much she wanted to say but she dare not. The silence was tantalizing so she rode on ahead, the man behind now her servant again.

Chapter Nine

It was the lace in the man's boot that intrigued him so, with his head cocked to one side, the little dog studied it intently. Suddenly he crouched, growling fiercely and made ready to pounce but thought better of it. Instead he barked as loud as he could and promptly fell over, causing the four onlookers to burst out laughing.

"There you are, Jack." Parson Russell bent down and picked up the puppy, whose teeth were now savaging the fingers that held him. "That's as good as I'll ever get 'em...he'll do you proud." Jack took the animal then flinched as the puppy wriggled excitedly to reach up to his face. Scamp had arrived.

"Don't know what to say, sir." He looked from one to the other. "Just seems...."

"Say no more, Tucker." John Knight beamed. "We reckoned you'd enjoy the company of a fella like that and the Parson here wanted to remember all your hard work. Eh Jack?"

"Aye, that's right." Russell stroked the tiny brindle ear. "There's twenty years of breeding in there. Bit o' bull terrier, bit o' dachshund...and a bit of every-thing else," he laughed. "Afraid of nothing, these little chaps...neither man nor beast. Look after him, my boy, and you've a friend for life. Now then," he turned to Knight. "What about the morning, sir?"

"Hounds're meeting at eleven?" Knight looked at Jack then back to the parson. "Out on the Exford road by the gates at Honey Mead. So...let's have a think," he paused.

"Ten-thirty?" Parson Russell glanced at Jack.

"Best say ten, sir," Jack bit his lip. "Aye, ten I reckon. 'Twill give us a bit of time in hand."

"Right enough," Knight nodded. "And we'll have second horses...we can all ride out together. Tell the kennelman ten then." Jack turned as the two men walked towards the yard gate.

"I'll take mine at eight, Tucker." Jack stopped. "Make sure everything's ready and be sure you're on time."

"The master said ten, Master Kenton...and there's a good deal to be done beforehand, sir. There's the pack, don't forget."

"No matter. I'll be here at eight," Kenton Knight lifted his head. "Just see to it, will you." Jack stood and watched him go then walked into the tack room with the puppy held to his chest.

*

The hour before dawn was raw but they were up, mucking out and checking the horses by lantern. They had breakfasted even earlier, as soon as the parson's hounds began to sing. Jack felt slow, loury. Throughout the night the spectre of Kenton Knight had been preying on him. Time and again that pale scowling face had looked down, hectoring arrogantly as he lay half awake in the darkness, glaring back and determined to stare him out. He detested the fellow whose very presence around the yard stifled chatter and laughter.

He knew the man would be in the yard as he said, if only to make his point. It would have been simple to give him a horse, then stand back and let him ride out smug and satisfied that his authority had prevailed. But the master had given his orders. He half wished he had not for he would have preferred to face Kenton alone rather than shield behind the master's authority. The wretched youth, barely nineteen, would sense it and see it as a weakness. Hiding behind his master was the easy way and it riled him. He would have been seen as more of a man were he to face him alone.

But the orders had been clear – the horses were to be ready by ten o'clock - there could be no exceptions and, as he checked his charges, he was determined that that should be the case. Even so, and ready as he was, the sudden commotion at the far end of the yard made him start. His heart sank but his pulse quickened. Voices were raised in anger. As he made his way to the harness room door, he could hear the one he was waiting for.

And there he was, as hostile and demanding as ever. "Well, *why* the hell isn't it ready? I thought I made it clear, I wanted the animal ready by eight...*eight*, d'you hear." A lad was in front of him and his finger was jabbing angrily at the boy's chest. "*Now* look," he held out the watch in his other hand. "It's half the hour. What the devil's going on?"

"I'm sorry, Master Kenton," Jack tidied his shirt into his belt. "Your father's wishes were very clear, y'know, sir. He told me which ones he wanted and I've got the lads doin' just that. The horses've had their feed and are settling a'while...they'll be ready by ten." He sensed the other grooms watching. "Won't be long, now."

"I don't give a damn." Kenton Knight's face was flushed. "I've got myself ready and that's what I want...now." Jack met his glare. "I told you eight and that's it." He spun on his heels and walked towards the stable door.

"Sorry, Master Kenton." Jack side stepped him nimbly and stood barring the door. "The horses that are ready are for your father and the reverend...they're as he requested. Look, sir," Jack, his voice low, appealed to the face in front of him. "Perhaps we can talk...quietly like, just you and me. I'm sure we...."

"Oh, stuff and nonsense. I told you last night what I wanted. Didn't I make myself clear?"

"You did indeed, sir. But all instructions regarding the stables come to me from your father and nobody else. That's his ruling, Master Kenton, and I've to see they're obeyed." He looked at the younger man. "Tell you what, sir....we'll get Delilah. As I said, it won't take long."

"Oh, for *God's sake*." He went to push his way past but Jack stood his ground. The younger man stepped back, his anger now risen to livid hate. "Get out of my way, you," he hissed. "If you don't, I'll see you out of here."

"I'll move, Master Kenton, I'll move...just so long as you don't take any of your father's horses."

The face was white. His whole body was trembling and his fists were clenched. "*So...*Tucker. So...*that's* it, is it? Right...I'll speak to Parker." He wiped the spittle from his mouth. "We'll see about this." The eyes were glittering. "My God, we'll see." He turned and began to walk. "Damn you, man," he called over his shoulder before turning. "And damn you again."

The lads in the yard stood watching silently.

✳

"Heard there was a bit of a rumpus in the yard this morning, Tucker." John Knight stretched and stamped his feet. The two had met later to change horses. "What was all that about then?"

Jack paused. He had expected word to get back. His master must have heard before they left Simonsbath and it angered him to think it would have been playing on his mind, nagging away at him throughout the morning. "Well, sir. 'Twas all a bit difficult, I have to say." When he made his report he used the words he had prepared. He spoke carefully then dropped behind. Enough was enough, probably too much and the two rode on in silence.

"All right, Tucker. Thank you...thank you for that." The face that looked at Jack from under the top hat was set hard by the cold, only the grey hair was blowing free. "You were right...quite right." He reached for his shoulder. "Can't have the youngsters meddling with the stables behind my back."

He lowered his head then looked away, his eyes searching the distance as he sought the right words. Jack knew he was hurt and that what he had told him must have caused the grief. His own anger had driven him to say too much but he was determined his master should know and had chosen his words. Now it was too late.

"Keep an eye on the lad." Knight's voice had softened. "The boy...well, he's apt to go off like that now and then. Not like Freddy, y'know. They're different...very different. Young Kenton's different to all of 'em." Knight turned his horse, leant forward and patted its neck.

"He's a difficult lad, y'know, Tucker. Sometimes he's the softest and gentlest of them all...no one could ask for more love from a son. But then," his head shook slowly. "Then all of a sudden he'll change...quick as flash, just like that." Jack caught the sidelong glance and nodded. "A sudden crash like gunpowder it is...shouting and yelling...mother and sisters in tears." He smiled grimly. "Oh, I dunno...you've *no* idea. Nothing much we can do...that's the boy and that's that. Ah well," Knight checked himself then took up his reins. "Leave it to me. I'll do what needs to be done."

Knight rejoined the hunt and Jack rode slowly back to Simonsbath. The horse he had taken from his master was tired. After a while he dismounted, loosened the girth and walked beside the animal. It saddened and angered him to see the man upset by what had been said and that had been his fault. Why did he have to go and unburden himself like he had? He should have told him less, made light of the incident, dismissed it even. There was no need to colour it all like he did. What did it matter?

But too many around the yard had seen and heard it all. Word would be out in the kitchens and around the house...Emma, and Mary, Meg and Nelly Combes. Parker and Mrs Strong...all of them. The grooms, the gardeners and the labourers, they would all be talking.

It was the first time some of them had seen the blind rage of the man. Soon, if Frederic was to leave as he was considering, Kenton would be the eldest left at home. His father had chosen to give him loose rein, and he knew how to use it. Every time he dictated what had to be done, he went as far he could then pushed a little further. Men like him did that, it became their trademark.

2.

"About four o'clock every afternoon, sir." The guard's toothless grin forced a smile from Durnford Morgan. Even as the last of the rumbles from the blast echoed around the valley, his horse cantered on the spot with its head tossing and nostrils flaring as it tucked itself up before lashing out in rage. When the first charge had detonated in the Brayford quarries behind them, he had been hard pressed to contain the animal. And there had been several of them, one after the other, each one causing the horses to start.

"Hang on, sir, hang on tight...cuh, dearie me." The packhorse handler was laughing too.

"Let's press on out of here...get up and onto the high ground." Morgan looked round disdainfully. "Come on...they'll be better once we get going."

Morgan and his escorts had left The George after lunch. Less than four hours to Simonsbath they had been told and, once the long climb up to Fyldon Ridge was behind them, the landlord should be proved right. Sir James Esdaile had requested him to be present for the siting of Knight's railway and canal the following month. Knight, however, had asked him to go up earlier in order to discuss the first of his farms and some workers' cottages.

The fresh breeze off Hartland Point cooled the May air. It had been bright earlier, but high mares' tails now covered the sun and the older of the two guards predicted rain before nightfall. Dogs rushed at them as they passed the last of the dwellings, but already the open track ahead, no longer hemmed in by tall hedgerows, could be seen winding its way across the open moorland. They rode in silence, one guard on the high ground above them, the other half a mile in front.

Morgan's emotions were mixed. Esdaile had alerted him again to Knight's lavish spending. It had got worse not better, so he said, and Morgan had been ordered to make an early report. He had been out to Simonsbath twice only, the last time over a year ago and he was intrigued as to what he might find. Elizabeth-Jane would, no doubt, have decorated the house to her taste. He could imagine the curtains and drapes, even the wallpaper delicately matching the shades and pastels of her clothes. It would have been done tastefully, beautifully perhaps. And how, he wondered, would the lady of the house herself be enjoying life in the wilds.

It was six months since they met last at the Filleigh Ball. There they had danced twice and he remembered her now as if it were just a week ago. Her dark eyes, darker still when she smiled, were as beguiling as ever and he had agonized over the messages they were sending him. Promises, maybe, promises or was it merely her subtle adroitness. He had been tempted to find out for himself, testing himself at the same time but there had been no chance. In any case, she had warned him that eyes were watching and that tongues were ready to wag.

※

"Ahoy there…up ahead, look." Morgan started at the cry from the slope above them.

"Out front, sir." The pack handler came alongside him. "Guard's waving…seen summat, I 'spect."

"Keep on coming, sir." The second guard joined them. "Matt's seen summat…keep moving up." Morgan watched as the two men conferred. They waved ahead then everybody spoke.

"A cab of sorts."   "Wheel gone, by the looks."   "Someone's there."   "A guard most like."   "Two others as well, there."   "He's coming this way." "Stand off, Matt. Up on the higher ground…quick now."

Morgan recognised the dark green liveried coat and breeches. He had seen the man before, at Lynton, and knew at once to whom the carriage belonged. It could be none other, yet Simonsbath was more than two miles distant.

∗

He saw, immediately, that she was not badly hurt. Somebody, probably the coachman, before he had gone for help, had arranged the cushions and rugs against the inside of the carriage that was now tilted on its side against the bank.

"Durnford...My *God* it's you. *Oh*...how wonderful. Thank goodness for that." He caught her hand as she tried to stand. "Perry thought you might have been...."

"Robbers?" he suggested smiling at her look of relief. "Highwaymen or cut-throats, perhaps? Happily no, none of that...simply your loyal and faithful banker, ma'am," He bowed mischievously. "And about his lawful business at that." She remained as enchanting as ever, even in distress and with her hair half undone and her clothing disarrayed.

"Oh, thank Heavens," she breathed. "I'm so glad it's you. Yes, you're right...I knew you were coming. I should be home by now but the dressmakers in South Molton took ages this morning...far too long. We've a house full at Simonsbath, you know, and there are two more yet to join us but we were late and were hurrying...and now this." As she sat, she put her hands out to steady herself. "But fear not. Dankin has taken the horses on to fetch help. He's been gone an hour and they should be here soon. But you'll stay with me...yes? Here..." The half-turned carriage creaked and swayed as she made way for him to join her.

"Would you rather I did?" He asked the question in all seriousness yet she could see he was uncertain. "Or would you prefer that I left my two men here and pressed on to tell the household?"

"*No*," she pleaded. "Stay, I beg you. I'm safe enough and...well, I can think of nothing better...your company would be more than welcome." Elizabeth-Jane held out her lace-gloved hand. "And it's been so long, Durnford." He recognised at once her perfume and the fragrance of the pomade in her hair.

"Wait," he commanded gently then turned and ran to his men, his leather soles slipping on the wet grass between the heather. One guard he sent on with the pack handler, the other he ordered on to the high ground to join Knight's man. As he returned to the phaeton, the rain came; he felt it first on his cheeks then heard the soft rustle against the canvas hood. A gust of wind shook the carriage and he could see she was cold. "Here, take my cloak," he insisted, crouching low to place it round her shoulders.

"You know, I really am so pleased to see you." Elizabeth-Jane could feel his body against the cloak as he settled beside her. She felt secure, protected and safe once more and it was through his presence. The thought was sudden and comforting but it passed and she sighed, looking down before bending to rub the pain where her foot had kicked against the door.

"It's nothing," she murmured in reply to his query, but he had seen her wince.

"Here, allow me." He managed to kneel carefully, balancing himself against the carriage side.

"Yes, that's it," she flinched, drawing in her breath sharply as his thumb felt her ankle. "Just there, where you pressed."

"It's a knock," he announced. "No more than that but it's nasty and a little swollen. Nothing more as far as I can see…your foot moves easily enough but it needs to be bound." He left the carriage and ran again, slithering and stumbling as he went, this time to his own horse with the guards. The rain had stopped but he could see there was more on the way. Working quickly, he opened his saddlebag and rummaged around until he found the old silk shirt. He cut quickly with the guard's knife then tore the material, before picking his way back to the carriage.

✳

As he knelt to bandage her foot, he could feel her hand on his shoulder steadying herself. When he stood, still half bent in the cramped cab and with his hair ruffled and his face flushed with effort, she took his hand. "Thank you, Durnford." Her eyes were full of gratitude. Although she was in pain, there was warmth in her look, one of tenderness and, in that instant he was tempted to stoop down and take her in his arms. But he stood back instead, turning awkwardly to peer up through the carriage door for signs of the riders. Both felt the silence.

"You're quiet today," she remarked softly. "A very matter-of-fact Mr Morgan so we are…not on account of me, I trust."

"No," he replied, laughing at the suggestion. "That would never be so….I could never think like that." He ducked back inside to look at her and smiled shyly. His thoughts were muddled and had been since he had come across her in this situation, but now they were more so. Certainly Knight had remained distant when they last had met, leaving him to wonder what she might have told him. He had been expecting a difficult reception at the manor today, one in which he would have had to have made his own way, see to his master's business then depart with whatever good grace he could muster.

Yet here she was, as delightful and as forthcoming as ever, making light of this bizarre situation, even of her painful injury. Perhaps it was simply relief at not having fallen into bad hands or having suffered more seriously when the carriage toppled sideways. "It's just that…well, coming across you like this was a surprise…a shock even."

"Oh, come now, Durnford. That's not how a man of the world should react to the unexpected…a *pleasant* surprise, I sincerely hope…but nothing else. And what is this about being shocked? Mm?" He remained still, searching the far ridge. "Hardly an encounter to make you speechless, surely." He was as silent as if his mind was elsewhere.

"Durnford," her voice was cautious. "Tell me something would you."

"Of course…what's that?"

"Something has happened, hasn't it? Something…or someone has come between us." He made no answer. "Here." She leant across the seat and pulled at his coat tail before making room for him. "Come down and tell me. Quickly, while we have the chance…I have to know."

He bent back inside the cab to see her then caught her arm as she reached forward for support. They both heard the shout. "*Riders ahoy*…three of them and a carriage. *It's them*…aye, it's them from Simonsbath, all right."

"Tell me, quickly." Her hand slipped through the crook of his elbow.

"Nothing's been said, I promise you." Morgan looked down at her hand then up at her face. "Nobody has approached me about anything…yet there are those who would believe we have seen more of each other than perhaps we should…maybe their imagination has taken them further than that."

"John?"

He nodded. "And others, too."

"The children…surely not?"

"No, but the staff…that's as bad and more dangerous than you might suppose." He could feel her breathing faster. What he said had shocked her, disappointed her perhaps but she realised he had to tell her.

"Durnford?" He turned. As he did so she kissed his cheek softly. "Thank you," she whispered.

"'Tis nothing, I assure you." He felt the spot touched by her lips then put his fingers to his own. "I had to warn you. Coming across you like this has saved me from trying to find a few moments alone with you at Simonsbath…that would surely have been courting danger. No, I had to warn you…and fate has given me this chance."

"No…no, no, *no*." Elizabeth-Jane squeezed his arm. "My thanks are not for you warning me. No…it's because what you've just said has told me something about you. And because you're here with me now…that's why."

3.

Somewhere in the tall conifers beyond the border, a dove called softly. A little further away, its mate replied. A warbler bubbled and trilled in the gorse but otherwise it was quiet. The heat of the afternoon sun had driven everything into cover. It was June, late June, however it could have been high summer. Behind the wall, the gardeners talked and joked as they worked.

Isabella, now sixteen and as tall as her mother, sat on the children's swing, her long curls of auburn hair tucked under her wide-brimmed sunhat. Her arms and shoulders, where not covered by her white cotton dress, had caught the sun as had her cheeks and freckled nose. The swing was old, the wooden seat moss covered and the scuffed earth underneath had long since healed over. But it held her, squeaking rhythmically as she swung idly while looking down at her feet beneath her frilled pantalettes.

"When are they coming, mama?" Tarr had taken the tray of cakes and iced drinks, leaving mother and daughter to themselves.

"Who dear?" Elizabeth-Jane looked up. "The Northboroughs? Oh…August, well the end of July to be precise."

"And who before them?"

"The Naresmiths…then the Piggots." She returned to her book. Isabella continued to swing.

"And when are Maggie and Edward due back?"

"What? Oh, come on dear…I'm trying to read."

"Sorr-y." Bored and alone, she slipped from the seat. She would have loved to have gone and met the children who had moved into the labourers' cottages but it had been forbidden. They were rough she was told, they and their dogs. Last week two of the girls had smiled at her and she had smiled back. Then one of the farm boys, short and blonde with knee length breeches had stared, allowing his eyes to run over her body and making her blush. She remembered his face and the sudden thrill of excitement it had given her but she had not seen him since. She had asked for a maid of her own, someone to talk to, but was told she was too young, and the girls in the house avoided her.

The sound of men's laughter behind the wall made her turn. For a moment she was undecided but she remembered how Abbot, the bearded head gardener from Ilfracombe, had promised to show her his new glasshouse and garden frames. Twice she had gone searching for him but he had been away, now she could hear his voice.

The door in the wall opened with a shrill squeak before the metal handle clacked on the wood as it shut again. The three men looked round. "Why, hello there, Miss'abella." Leonard Grant and the others had long since given up trying to pronounce her name. Isabella had always liked Leonard. Years ago the big man used to take her by the hand when her brothers and sisters, all older and swifter, had rushed off together leaving her behind and in tears. It was ages since she had seen him.

"Come to see the new house? Eh?" He drove the fork hard into the bed and lifted his hat. "Didn't know you was home, right now, ma'am. 'Tis ever so quiet at the house so it is." He dusted his hands and walked over.

"It's too quiet, Mr Grant." Isabella smiled warmly but stopped, suddenly bashful. Kind and gentle though he was, she could not help but notice his open shirt and the strong, sunburned arms. She had heard the maids talking about the men often enough, mainly Dan Webber and Jack Tucker although Leonard Grant's name had been mentioned as well. She had thought nothing of it often wondering what it was about him that caught their eye. To her he had always been a friendly, brotherly figure. The maids' talk and their giggles had seemed out of place but no longer. "They'll all be home soon enough but…oh, I don't know." She shrugged and looked down, still bemused. "It's so boring here on my own."

"Come on then, ma'am, I 'spect Mr Abbot's working there now. Could do with a break, meself." He could see at once that the little girl in her had gone, Abel Tarr had told him so. Isabella Knight had changed and he knew he was walking beside a young woman, a pretty one at that, tall and elegant yet still fresh and innocent. He would not have been a man had he not sensed it. He tried to talk as he used to, like he did when she was a bubbly youngster but it was no use. She had changed.

"Still not taken to ridin' then?" Jack had told him how she remained nervous, preferring to walk or ride in one of the wagons.

"I'll never do it, Mr Grant." He grinned sympathetically. "All the others are so good. Off they go…galloping away and I can't…just can't do it." She shrugged and pouted, knowing he was looking at her. But today it was different. And she was aware of him, too, like she was with the farm boy last week.

"Same as me, ma'am. I'm no horseman to speak about. Should hear Jack Tucker and they others guffawing an' that when I'm up." He caught her smile and they both laughed, then they heard the shouting.

"*Look up,*" Reg Adams was pointing. "Little dog's come runnin' in…there look. *Comin' your way*…running all tucked up, scared o' summat."

Wide-eyed and glancing back as it came, the terrified creature ran to Leonard and cowered against his legs. Now Adams was shouting again and they could hear barking. Three larger dogs, wild and running free, ran into the garden, quartering the ground as they made their way towards them.

Before he could warn her, Isabella had knelt and snatched up the frightened animal then stood holding it in her arms. "Stay still, missy," Leonard warned before turning to face the dogs that were close and which were now running straight for them. *"Don't move,"* he cried. "Just stay where you are." Suddenly he crouched low facing them, shouting defiantly and waving his arms before throwing himself in front of the girl. One shied away, the others attacked.

Isabella screamed. Leonard struck out at the first and largest animal that had fastened on to his arm but then the second, a black lurcher, leaped at Isabella, the two of them falling together. Fighting off the dog on his arm and kicking it away, Leonard jumped at the dog on Isabella. Even as he beat it to the ground, the animal was snapping and biting viciously.

"Run, missy. *Run,"* he yelled. *"Reg…Reg…*here Reg." The first dog turned back and leapt at his face. The jaws closed but he felt no pain. *"Run,* missy…*just run,"* he shouted.

There were shouts from the stables, more from the garden. Reg Adams and Tora Abbot he could see through one eye and he knew others were there. One of the dogs at his feet, he could feel, was still moving so he stamped again and again with his boot. There was blood on his hands, more running down his shirt but of the dogs there was no sign of life. He crouched slowly, bending forward to steady himself before sitting on the ground when he toppled forward.

✳

"You'll keep your sight sure enough." Dr Collyns sat back. "Your cheek's badly scarred though. Here now, look in the mirror. There, you see…torn back like a piece of cloth it was, so we've sewn it back." The doctor bent to check his hand-iwork." The main thing is that the wounds're clean…all of them, the one on your arm as well. What the hell were they, for God's sake."

The doctor rose from the cot continuing to talk quietly. But Leonard no longer heard him for the opium had begun its work.

4.

"See that, Emms. That…over there." Jack pointed over his shoulder. "D'you know where we are?" He turned back to his sister, waiting for her reply. "It's called Kinsford now…the little stream we crossed when we were on our way over. Years ago…way back."

Simonsbath and the tearful farewells were behind them. For an hour his sister had ridden in silence, her mind seemingly a whirl of memories. Last night the other girls had feted her while this morning she had breakfasted with the senior staff in their room. Then, just before they rode off together, she went before the Knight family. She remembered how John Knight, the master himself, had got her flustered when he spoke about her in front of them all. There were the memories of Frederic and Edward's smiles, of Isabella's warm embrace and the presents from the lady of the house.

But now it was home to Molland, to her mother, to Wilmot, to Hannah and the others. Then it would be the wedding and after that Filleigh with Troy. Only twice over the years had she seen her mother, the last time three years ago in South Molton. Parson Froude had written on a number of occasions and they had written back but that had been all. Tonight, they would be together again, the first time since she and Jack left home and crossed the old King's Ford all those years ago.

∗

They saw the figure by the stone hut at the same time as he saw them. Emma watched as her brother dismounted and walked towards him; he had told her on the way up that the shepherds would be there. It was shearing time, and he saw them every summer. By now her brother was talking to him, arms were grasped and backs slapped. It must be him, she thought, the one he had told her about. Three more appeared and she could see it was Jason.

"Well, I'll be *damned*...see how you've grown an' all." Jason Hawkins looked older, far older than she imagined. His hair had receded from the top of his head and the face was thinner. His eyes had sunk deeper but the long pigtail was still there and his arms still swung with that funny rolling gait.

"*Married*, says Jack. *Married*...cor, I dunno." He looked up at her with one hand on her knee as his eyes searched her face. "*Cor*...fancy that...little Emma Tucker. Jest look at ye now. Come on, dear...down you come." She slipped easily into his arms and on to the ground. "Ben Thorne's lads are y'ere...Drew and Henry. An' Morley Holt. An 'tis dinner time, too...you've come just right, you have."

For the next hour, stories were swapped, the travellers eager for news of Molland, their family and friends who they could barely remember. When Jack rose to take his leave, it was Jason who made the suggestion. "'Ere, hang on...Morley and me's goin' back tonight. 'Tis best to ride all on together." Emma half listened, keen for them to be on their way. "Bin some tales of late," he warned. "Not much, mind, but 'tis best if us can ride together as far as Twitchen...'tis safer from then on." The shepherd paused, thinking for a moment. "Aye, that's best, Jack...four us's better than two.

∗

The party had crossed the Sandyway track and climbed on to the high ridge

144

above Twitchen when they saw them. It was Morley, riding ahead, who spotted them first.

"Two of 'em," Jack muttered, squinting into the distance. "Coming this way, an' all. See how they've turned." Now the horses could see them too. "Could be them," he continued. "They say there's a fella bin operating out of Chibbet Ford. Sometimes has another with 'im...an' Chibbet's over that way."

"Seems they're making this way." Morley Holt had joined him. "What d'you reckon?"

Jack stood in his stirrups, one hand on his saddle. His mind was racing. "Right..." he turned to the others. "Now then, listen. Reckon I'll get myself out there a fair way...'tween them and us. Jason, take the packpony and stay close to Emma." The older man took the rein then watched with the others as Jack unsheathed the carbine. His gun and his cutlass were now permanently with him."

"Who are they, Jack?" Emma looked from one to the other. "What's happening?"

"Hey, Jason." Ignoring her, Jack was looking up at the ridge behind them. "No use you being out there if they're armed. Get up there...take the horses and Emma. Keep right up on the high ground...up there, look.

"Jack, *stop*. Talk to me. What is it?" Emma's voice was raised. "Who are they for Heaven's sake?"

"Dunno, Emms." He was checking the carbine. "No one probably. Well, nobody bad, like...but 'tis best to be safe, just in case.

"And Morley." He turned again, searching for the second shepherd. "Best stay here abouts, 'tween me and Jason." The thin, serious face nodded. "Keep riding, all of you. Get up there, Jason. You and Emms, as high as you can...head for those trees.

"Jack," Emma held back. "For God's sake...they'll be armed as well."

"Don't worry." His voice was raised. "Keep moving. Stick to the high ground, up there with Jason. Go on...get up there."

Now on his own, he pulled ahead with his carbine resting on his thigh, all the while watching the two riders. They stopped, spoke briefly together then came on again, this time more slowly. They stopped again but now they were much closer.

He could clearly make out the straw hair beneath the tricorn hat and the russet coat, even the green waistcoat underneath, and what appeared to be the butt of the pistol in the waistband. The smaller, untidy rider in a dark frock coat was on something little more than a pony, but he had drawn his sword. They were coming for them, of that there was no doubt.

He watched as they split, the shorter man moving away down the valley to his right while the other, mounted on a heavy cob, worked his way up the slope to their left as though trying to get behind them. He could hear him urging on his horse. Two foxes working together but splitting so as to cut a lamb away from the ewe, he thought to himself. Luke's voice was in his ear. *'The nearest one's the most dangerous.'* He hesitated but just for a moment, wondering if that would be right. Then the voice came again. *'Always take him first, always.'*

"Right, Morley," he yelled. "Let's see him first…this one, over here." Spurring his horse forward, he rode hard towards the tricorn hat, now close behind Emma and Jason. "Stay where you are," he shouted. *"Stay…where…you…are."*

Jack saw the pistol as it was drawn, then fired himself. He never knew if he hit the man but he was still alive and still on his horse. He saw him turn away. His second barrel, he was certain, must have hit but still the man was there, now low in the saddle and galloping hard.

The gun was empty so he threw it down and drew his cutlass. The man had fled but Morley was after him. "See him away, Morley…see him away down the valley." He was standing in his stirrups, cheering his man, pointing with his cutlass. "Go on Morley…see him away…*see him awaaaaay.*"

He stopped, alert once more. The second man…where was he? The carbine could wait. Jack turned to see him working his way towards Emma and Jason. He could see the dark frock coat flapping as he rose at the trot. The shepherd was with his sister but it was not enough. He had to get to him but it was going to be close. Digging in his spurs, he hissed in the horse's ears, riding low on the big animal as it leapt forward. The man had a pistol but it was too late to stop now. Even as he flattened himself against his horse's mane, he saw the puff of black smoke.

Fired too soon, just as Luke said they would. The highwayman turned away but the pony was no match for John Knight's hunter and now it was his turn.

He rode him down then rose in his stirrups with cutlass raised just as the rider turned back to see where he was. Jack could see the grey-black stubble, even his badly stained teeth as the mouth opened to shout. Shouting and cursing with a wild, raging fury he swept the blade down and back, the feel of the strike telling him he had cut deep.

The man screamed and tried to double back but Jack swung his mount in a wide arc. The horse knew what had to be done and they charged in again. Once more he rose, standing high and lifting the cutlass. Behind the raised arm, he could see the eyes, wide with terror. His swing was savage and his shout loud.

This time the sharp jar told him he had struck bone. Again the scream, and the mad galloping down the slope.

Gently easing the horse, he turned back but his mount had sensed the violence and it reared, foam flecked and snorting before pulling strongly again, eager for more. Jack soothed the animal and slowed again, talking quietly before pulling up and jumping to the ground. Even then the gelding was not done. It backed away, pulled against him, wild-eyed and trembling, its flanks running with sweat.

"What have you done, Jack?" Emma reined in. "My God, there's blood on your sword."

"Had to be done." His chest was heaving as he struggled for breath. "Aye, 'tis blood fer sure," he gasped. "Not sure if 'twas the first one…but the second," he swallowed, still panting. "The second…oh aye, he's cut bad. 'Twas his own fault tho'…he fired first." He tore off his neckerchief, still fighting for air. "Aye," he panted. "The swine bled all right." And blood there was indeed as he saw when he began to wipe his blade.

*

At the bend where the track began to drop steeply into Molland, the two shepherds bade farewell, leaving Jack and Emma to approach the village on their own. They rode slowly and in silence before dismounting and walking. Every turn in the road, every building, every sight and sound brought back long distant memories. It all appeared to be so much smaller, so different to Lynton or the wilds of Simonsbath. They passed St Mary's church and The London Inn then turned down the lane. Again they slowed but this time they stopped.

Mill Cottage, the thatched roof collapsed and the windows empty, stood half hidden by brambles and undergrowth. "Goodness, " Emma whispered. "That's home…that's where we were born. Look at it." The sound of running feet made them turn.

Two youngsters, a youth of seventeen, and, behind him a girl, slightly younger, slowed to a stop. The four stared at each other. Emma began to walk towards them then threw out her arms and ran. They were home, after fifteen years. Edward and Hannah, no more than babies when they left, had come to find them.

Chapter Ten

"What an amazing sight...like the military on manoeuvres." Both riders slowed to a stop and regarded the cluster of tents beneath them. "What on earth's he gone and done all that for?" The man from the London and Derby Bank opened his brown and green jacket before scratching under his arm.

"The big presentation was yesterday." Durnford Morgan dismounted and checked his girth. "He's been working himself up to it for weeks. Heard there's been talk about his great scheme so he's decided to let people know what's afoot...and was determined to put on a good show."

"Told the world what he's going to do before we let him know if he can afford it, you mean. The landowners as well, eh?" Joseph Saunders, his reddish hair cropped monk-like, pulled on his long nose. Exmoor, so the portly forty-six year old had concluded, was a decidedly unlovely place in spite of the bright August day. It was warm but not hot. Overhead, rank upon rank of great white clouds, pushed on by the gentle south wind, sailed past serenely with their shadows racing across the countryside beneath. Sheep grazed peacefully, unconcerned about the tented invasion, raising their heads to stare only when curiosity presented itself.

✱

Joseph Saunders had never been this far west before, in fact he had never heard of the place until his masters had dispatched him to report on John Knight's project. That he was here at all was due, entirely, to Sir James Esdaile who he had first met two weeks previously.

London and Derby, one of four City banks financing railway projects through-out the Midlands, had been alerted by Esdaile that a client of his was embarking upon a venture necessitating the construction of a private line. Would the London and Derby, he requested, be so good as to produce for him their considered opinion on every aspect of the exercise but, in particular, the financial implications. Lunch that day, when Sir James had entertained him, had been a memorable occasion.

While he knew little about the countryside, and cared even less for what he saw, Saunders was well versed in the new and mysterious world of railways and steam locomotion. Furthermore, in spite of his appearance, he was also a shrewd and successful corporate financier. "Rather putting the cart before the horse, isn't he?"

"That's John Knight for you." Morgan swept back his hair that had become damp and matted under his top hat. "That's the way he's always done things. He scents an opportunity, makes his decision then hurls himself at it leaving the rest of us to tidy up behind him." The very thought of it made him laugh. "Canny though…and very rarely gets caught out. As far as yesterday's concerned, he just wanted to put the record straight…and who can blame him? But today's important."

"That's for sure…and this little lot's going to cost him, I reckon." Saunders dismounted, took off his jacket and loosened his cravat. "You can't go building railways up the side of a mountain and digging canals across the top of the world like this for free, y'know." He waved his arm airily over the route they had taken before applying his red and white spotted kerchief to his face and neck. "You just can't go doing that without spending a penny or two…a serious fortune if you're asking me. Can't be done." The two men stood contemplating the scene.

Morgan had been advised that the preliminary lines for the canal and railway had been cut and when he had ridden out with the family, Knight had shown him part of the routes. Even then, it was obvious that considerable capital would be needed and had urged the master to order a financial review before announcing his intentions and securing land leases. But here he was, once again, pushing on as hard as ever.

*

The campsite they were overlooking had been erected on a heather-clad spur overlooking the rolling farmland that fell away towards Porlock Bay more than half a mile away. Here the front of the green and white striped marquee stood facing the sea while, tucked inconspicuously around it, smaller bell tents and bivouacs had been erected for the servants. Blue wood smoke from the kitchen fires, some distance further away still, drifted towards the horse lines and carriage park. Morgan counted eight or ten ant-like figures moving about; a similar number, he knew, would be working or resting.

It was to this lonely spot that Knight intended to haul lime up the steep hillside, wagon by wagon, from the port of Porlock fourteen hundred feet below. The machinery for this task would be powered by gravity and water, the only permanent source of which came from the far end of the moor. Going down and out by the same route would be the ore and copper from his mines, beginning their long journey northwards to his Midland foundries. The material would be fetched and carried by a steam engine riding on rails across the top of the particular world for which Joseph Saunders had demonstrated so little affection.

Yesterday had been a day of presentations, wherein the master of Simonsbath laid bare his plans. He needed either to purchase or lease more land for the line of his railways, and for the reservoirs and leats channelling his water supply. Merchants and industrialists who might invest in his venture had been present but it was to the owners of the surrounding countryside that he had directed his attention.

"The principal's simple enough," Saunders muttered. "We've got several of these lines where water counterbalances whatever goes up or down. But see here," he pointed to the steeply sloping land. "It's all right if the gradient's constant but once it becomes variable then the problems begin. See that thatched building down there, to the left of the wood...see how the slope decreases. They'll have to dig a deep cutting, blast it out maybe...and that eats the money. You wait." He nodded knowingly and hitched at his buff breaches. "Wonderful spot, though...must be Wales over there, surely?"

"Porthcawl and Bridgend," Morgan answered. "And Barry over there. Coal and steel country...the old man's got business interests there as well." The two stood in silence, each taking in the view. "It'll be a shame in a way," Morgan continued. "Up here...Hawkcombe Head as it's known, must be one of the most beautiful corners of the moor. Can't really see a railway here, for God's sake, all those sheds, tracks and engines...pumping houses, trucks and all the rest of it."

"Well," Saunders took out his watch. "We're about to hear the truth from the experts. Just hope your master didn't promise the earth yesterday...or frighten 'em to death." Morgan watched him trying to avoid the teeth of his horse as he struggled back into the saddle. Fat men and fit horses, he considered, were an unlikely combination. "Damn sure not everybody in this part of the world wants to see the result of what he's planning to do."

*

The inside of the marquee, hot, airless and smelling more and more of damp canvas, seemed empty compared to the day before. The flowers, so carefully arranged by Elizabeth-Jane, had begun to wilt, tables and chairs were stacked in one corner and the carpets had been removed from the coir under-matting. John Knight sat near the entrance, leaning back in a wicker armchair at the head of a cloth-covered table. The steep slope running down to the cliffs above the harbour fell away in front of him.

Saul Ramsey, the leathery Scot from the Shropshire canal sat on one side, Saunders on the other. Opposite him, sitting hunched and nervous, was William Jessop, an engineer-surveyor from Rugby. Jessop, bespectacled and weasely-faced, had been recommended to Knight by Arthur James. The seventy year-old, a friend of Knight's father and now long since retired, sat at his shoulder.

They had been talking and talking. Theories had been challenged and figures disputed. At noon they stopped for lunch, served by Tarr and the footmen off silver brought out from Simonsbath. At one o'clock they began again. "Why for Heaven's sake?" Knight thumped the arm of his chair.

"Natural reasons." Ramsey, the canal man, walrus moustached and dressed in his beloved tartan trews, rose heavily. "The line of the canal is incredible, I'll tell yer that, sir…there're nay problems there. And exactly the right drop from Pik…Pink…."

"Pinkworthy, but they call it Pinkery up here," Knight waved him on.

"Aye, Pinkery." Ramsey pulled at the map in front of him. "We'll have to build a cutting just here, up beyond yer grand hoose…close to the head of the River Exe, to get the canal water onto the north side o' the valley. After that it's as flat all the way, flat as a millpond…marvellous, unique so it is. I've ne'er seen anything so level…ne'er."

"Well?" Knight lifted his hands. "That's half the battle surely?"

"Aye, but only one half." The Scot grinned ruefully. "The ground hereabouts is very spongy and there'll be a deal of natural soakage. Then there's plant life, animals and the weather itself…they're all thirsty and will be taking their share. And if that's nay enough the animals'll be crossing back and forth…breaking down the sides of the waterway." He pulled slowly on the ends of his moustache. "Ye see…fer a start, the flow from the pond will nay be great and it's a fair way to travel…fourteen miles in fact. An' what with the gradient we have it'll be travelling slowly…and vulnerable as it goes, ne'er mind the nine wee burns we've got to feed it along the way."

"No other way?" Knight saw Ramsay's frown.

"No other way, Mr Knight." He leant forward and pointed at the map. "For summat o' that length, sir, we're going to have to line the walls…stone sides and slate underneath. Nay very big, mind…six feet wide by three deep'll do it. An' you'll need a wee maintenance track no closer than six or eight feet from the walls. A leat like that'll last ye for ever…it'll be worth yer money, sir."

"How much?" Morgan watched Knight slump in his chair. He knew the sign.

"Difficult to say…but with the cutting, a thousand pounds maybe."

"Hmmm…but it can be done?"

"Oh, aye…nay problem, sir, and I mean just that…the geography's perfect."

Knight, head in hands as he thought, nodded slowly. "And the tracks?" He looked at the engineer. "You look as though there's bad news, Jessop" he growled. "Go on, man…tell us your worst."

"Only one, sir," Jessop wheezed as he spoke. "Straight in front of you." The others followed his finger. "It's the slope…not constant." Morgan glanced at Saunders. "If we go for it from here then the slope eases before it gets steeper again. The pulling power of the downward load is lost and it'll all grind to a halt."

"So?"

"Two solutions…either we cut into the slope…make a deep cutting to take off the lip or we do the journey in stages. Water counterbalance up the first steep bit from the harbour, then change tracks and haul the freight using water wheels…slow but steady."

"Isn't it marvellous," Knight grumbled, smiling cynically. "Always some goddamned problem…anything you try, there's always something. What's the cost, Jessop? Come on, keep the misery coming."

"Right, sir." Jessop cleared his throat and reached for his pocket book . "We, that's Mr James and myself, are of the opinion…." He turned the pages, searching for his figures. "Ah, here we are, right…all up…top tramway running, water connected and, if we were to go for the cutting…four thousand pounds."

"And the other way?"

"Less by five hundred pounds, sir, but complicated and a far slower turn-around."

"That's no good." He pulled himself up in the chair. "I've got more than twenty thousand acres over there and it'll be needing a couple of tons per acre at least…and that's annually, mind. What do you reckon, Mr Saunders?" The chair creaked as Knight turned to the banker. "How do the figures compare with your part of the world?"

"Very fair, sir, but we'd need to budget for a reserve."

"What?"

"The unexpected. All this is very new and we're right out on a limb down here. We'll have to get everything on site by road…such as they are down this way, or by boat, then drag it all up…tracks in, trucks, the engine in bits then reassemble it here…the buildings, the lot. It's pioneering stuff, sir, and we'd be mad not to cover for contingencies. Five thousand's my bet but I'd put a ring around six."

"*Six.*" Knight smiled grimly. "You bankers trying to price me out of business? Eh? Not some plot you've been hatching, is it?"

"No, sir," Saunders spoke quickly. "It's plain hard fact checked against similar projects."

"Can we do it?" Knight sat up and glanced around. "Morgan, where are you, man?"

"Here, sir. No, not as we are." Announcing the bad news was painful. "Sir

James asked me to tell you that four thousand was the limit…that's as things stand at the moment." He could see Knight's irritation. "And there's another thing, sir…both he and Sir Crispin feel strongly that it's time we had some good news from the mines. They're keen to see a return coming in…they reckon it's been time enough now to know the prospects."

"Havers?" Knight looked across expectantly. "What have you got for me?" There was no news. Morgan knew it; he had asked a week earlier and again two days ago. None of the exploratory works had yielded the results they had been expecting. Ebeneezer Havers made his report, everybody around the table was aware of the implications, nobody more so than the miner himself. He kept his eyes on Knight as he spoke then looked mournfully from one to the other. The only sounds were the servants' voices in the tents behind. Knight's head dropped.

"That's a shame." He was speaking to his hands in his lap. "We were hoping for better news, weren't we. News of *some*thing, anyway." He shrugged, muttering to himself. "How much longer d'you need, Havers?"

"Well," for a moment, the sad face flickered optimistically behind the black beard. "There're a number of options yet, you know. It'll cost, I'm afraid but…if I could have a free hand, there's a year's exploratory work still there…hard work at that but some good chances."

They watched Knight nod. "*So.*" He rose quickly, somehow suddenly revitalised. "Then this is the way we'll do it. Life's full of setbacks but there's more to be had from Exmoor than we've seen yet."

He spoke for an hour without a note in his hand. Everyone was questioned again, alternative suggestions were sought, discussed and discarded. Leaseholds would be taken, land purchase forced through. The lines of the canal and tramway were to be completed, but only the lines. Havers would continue to prospect, Maxwell press on with the farms and roads, Morgan would report to London.

John Knight's restless, driving energy took command. Many, himself included, left the windy, moorland hilltop convinced, but there were others who were not so sure.

2.

Fred Loosemore was happy, and when he was happy he whistled. At first he had been embarrassed and had tried to get away but Grace had persuaded him to stay. Now he was glad he had been there.

"Listen," she had cried with one finger in the air. "That's horses…isn't it? It's them…it has to be." They had both inclined their heads. "Yes," she started from the bench. "It's them. Yes it is…oh, I know it is."

"Be on my way then, Gracie." He had risen stiffly from the seat under the old plum tree where the two of them had sat chatting. "'Twill be a special moment for you, me dear...best be on your own."

"No, stay," she begged. "Oh please stay, Fred...please. It's bin so long, so very long, an' they're sure to remember you an' Tilly. Just for a few minutes...just to say hullo." He had little choice and remained in the shadow of the porch watching as the three horses came into the yard.

He would have passed the two for strangers in the street, so he would, but then he looked again. The young man was taller than his father, his hair a bit fairer and longer tied back like that, but he was Lionel all over, the living image of his old friend. The girl, too, was tall but he could see her mother. She was Gracie all right, even the way she carried her head and flicked back her hair.

As they walked up the path, he stepped further into the shadows. Grace was waiting half way down. Both hands were clenched with excitement and her shoulders were hunched expectedly. He could imagine her face. Three years she had told him, three long years since she had seen any of her children. Emma ran first, her arms open, then Jack, then Edward and Hannah. How Lionel would have loved it: oh would that he could have been there now with them all! They turned and Fred tried to step further back but stumbled and they saw him.

"Fred. Here, Fred," Grace spoke first. "They're here...here at last. Oh, Fred," she was laughing helplessly, clinging on to the arms of her children. "This is Emma and...Jack. They *do* remember you, I know they do." They laughed at the expression on his face then Emma hugged him, Jack shook him by the hand while the other went on to his shoulder. Lionel again; he had done that the very day he left them in the hay meadow.

*

He continued to whistle to himself as he backed the big shire between the shafts. "C'mon...c'mon, gently now," he coaxed softly. "Steady up, *steeaady*, now. Whoa!" He lifted one side of the shaft to the saddle chain, hooked it and checked the hames. Ducking under the animal's head, he secured the second side, ran his hand over the animal's shoulder then took hold of the cheekpiece. "Come on, Captain." Facing the animal, he walked backwards slowly, pausing to let the horse take up the strain.

Lionel had been a year younger than him...fifty-three this year he would have been, but Fred's mind went further back to when they were boys. The two had grown up together, played and worked together, gone courting together. He had been heartbroken when news of his death came through. But it was he who had first suggested that Grace should move out of the old cottage and into Luckworthy. As soon as the farm had come his way, he had gone to see her.

✳

"Some elderflower, vicar...'tis just about the last drop." Parson Froude had called on the Tuckers at Luckworthy with the wedding in mind. Grace fussed busily and proudly around him and her two eldest as they sat chatting. "An' a griddle cake as well. Come on, Emma...watch the tray, dear. 'Tis hot mind."

Later, when Froude took his leave, Jack accompanied him to his horse and held the animal's head waiting for him to mount. He was just about to do so but stopped. "A minute, Jack, if I might." He kept his voice low. "There's something I want you to know. I've something on my mind...been there for a while. Now's not the best of times perhaps, but...we're on our own and I'd like to tell you." He nodded and urged the horse forward. "Come on, let's walk a bit."

The two left the yard and turned down the farm track, ducking away from the worst of the briars and blackthorn. The parson, with his fair locks over the collar of his black frock coat, spoke carefully. Several weeks earlier, he explained, he had been dining at Bampton. An army man had been there, somebody he had never seen before, but he seemed amiable enough. After dinner, when talk turned to France, Froude told him he was from Molland and that the village had lost men there. "Claimed he was then the adjutant to the Second Life Guards.

"That's the officer responsible for keeping the records," he explained. "When I said we had a man killed at Waterloo, he asked me his name and I told him. Swore blind he knew your father, Jack...even described him." Froude put his arm on Jack's shoulder. "No doubt about it, he knew him all right.

"Couldn't remember his rank, mind you...nor even his squadron but knew he was a senior man...and a Devon man at that." Froude stopped. "It was after the meal, Jack. The ladies had left us and he came back again...pulled up the chair next to me. Must have bin on his mind. Told me that the surgeon had been unable to save him...your father, that is." Jack watched as the parson chose his words. "From what he told me, he could never have survived. But I'm afraid it's not quite as they wrote to your mother. I haven't told her of course," he added hastily.

"Go on, vicar," Jack slowed and put a hand on the horse's shoulder. "Tell me everything, sir. Don't go missing nothing out."

As Froude spoke he watched the younger man. His face was expressionless, devoid of any emotion. "All I can do is to tell you what the officer said. He told me that he died doing his duty," Froude said finally. "That particular charge...at a place called La Haye Sainte was a desperate one. But they routed the cream of the French...helped save the day." He paused. "Your father was there, Jack...right up there with them. You can be very proud of him."

Jack took in a deep breath, filled his cheeks and blew hard. Then he shook his head. His heart was pounding. His mind went back all those years to when his father used to tell him how the cavalry would charge. Sometimes Emma and Charlotte would be there and the three of them would sit at his feet listening.

They would hear how the horses would first walk in the long extended lines, then trot, harnesses jingling, and keep trotting until they were close. Then the bugles would sound the canter and then, last of all, would come the charge with the great surging roar of thousands of voices. How, like a deep, rumbling thunder of hooves, a hundred hunting fields in full cry together, the regiments would charge as one, turf flying, swords aloft, everybody around him, those same thousands, shouting and cheering as they went.

He could see his father riding hard down in the seat, urging his horse on, the long, white plumes streaming behind the helmets, the scarlet jackets and white cross belts and the high, black boots. Sometimes the Redcoats or Highlanders would cling to the stirrups as they charged and he could imagine the fierce, bewhiskered faces...he could hear the noise, see the glint of the long steel bayonets and the sabres of the cavalrymen drawn and ready for battle.

His father described the sound of a great clash of weapons like a mountain of cutlery cascading and crashing onto flagstones, then the huge, heaving, kicking tangle of horses and men, every one of them fighting mad for his life, the curses and the screams. That's how it must have been when his father last charged, just like that. That's when the Frenchman's cuirass would have swung and the canon thundered to topple his charger.

Froude looked at him anxiously. "You with me, Jack?" He caught his arm. "Not too upset, I hope?"

"No, sir. Not at all...not at all." Jack saw the surprise on his face. He knew the parson had been troubled by what he had said and smiled reassuringly. "No, sir. Father used to tell me about it...how they went at 'em...how they charged." Froude could see his face was flushed. "I know exactly how he must've felt, sir. Can't explain it, but I know. Just know and I can see it all. Thank you, sir...'twas very thoughtful of you." Jack held his horse while the parson pulled himself on to the saddle, settled quickly and tidied his coat.

*

Later that morning Fred Loosemore showed Jack the great barn where they were to hold the wedding feast. The hay and sacks of corn had been moved and tables set in long lines down the length of the room. There would be dancing on the threshing floor, he explained, the band from Tiverton staying on to play after the service.

From dawn on the day itself a pig and lamb were to be roasted, ready for the evening, turning on spits over a slow fire. There would be cider and beer and a cask of French wine from The London Inn, elderflower wine and sloe gin, perhaps a keg of brandy as well. The ladies of the village had arranged the meal and the older children were to serve those at the table.

There was so much to do and so little time. Then there was the cost of it all. That night Jack barely slept. Who, he wondered, was going to pay the bills, see to the church, the band and the dinner, the animals that were to be roasted and the drink? And the clothes, the flowers and other decorations? Such thoughts came hard in the middle of the night and he lay, turning and tossing restlessly, until the birds began to sing. If the truth were known, he wanted none of these problems. Weddings, even his sister's, were best left to others. There was a moment when, were he able, he would have taken his horses and fled back to the peace of Simonsbath.

But it was Emma's day and he rose early, determined to see to the tasks that lay ahead. He would have to challenge his mother about the money, force the truth from her. He had to know. Time and again he went to her but each time he stopped. She was so different now to the woman he knew when he was a child. Then she was strong, her wishes and demands were there to be obeyed, her scolding something to be feared. She was worldly then, knew what had to be done, how to feed them and find clothes for them all. She was there when they needed her, there when they needed her love.

All that, however, was long ago and time had changed everything. The rich, dark hair, once so thick, had thinned to a tired grey. Her face was lined, her spare frame stooped. She was smaller, too, or so she seemed. She had striven so hard, borne so much and must have grieved so deeply yet she had never complained. Now it was she who needed them. They, not her, would have to be gentle and he would have to be especially gentle now.

"Hullo, mother." She jumped as his arms encircled her from behind, his hard stubble pressed against her soft cheek. "Now listen. Everything seems to be nearly ready...there's nuthin' to worry about." He felt her nod. "But there *is* summat. There *is* summat I don't like too much." She was still for a moment then tried to struggle from him. He could feel her frail body helpless against his as she strove to free herself.

"Now then...tell me and tell me true, mother." She was still again, listening intently. "Where's the money coming from?" he whispered. "Who's paying for...for all this?" He waved a hand in front of her. She glanced down, for a moment uncertain, then sighed, her cheek once more against his.

"We'll manage somehow, Jack," she murmured. "Everyone's been very kind. They've told me there's no hurry and we'll get by one way or t'other." She tried to look at him and he let her go. "Why d'you ask, dear? It should be no worry of yours. Don't spoil things, Jack. Not today," she pleaded.

"Mother, it *is* my business...*all* of it. If I'm to give Emma to Troy and...well, I'm the man of the family now...I need to know these things, I have to. And in any

157

case," he stepped towards her. "Here...I've brought you this." He took her hand and pressed the small leather purse into her palm, one of his hands closing both hers around it.

"Shhh," he whispered, a finger to his lips. "Never breathe a word. Right? Never...I've earned it all," he grinned to himself. "It was all mine and now it's ours...ours to be spent as we want. And don't say a word...not a word." He bent down and kissed her forehead then hurried from the cottage.

He was miserable, his whole body felt burdened with guilt. It was nothing to do with the origin of the money, to hell with that. It was deceiving her, his own mother that hurt so. How that soft, brave smile would vanish were she ever to know the truth, how she would cast the purse aside in horror before wiping her hands on her apron. He could imagine how her face would be drawn down with grief. It would be his conscience that paid for the day, not the smuggler's gold. That was what was so hard to bear.

3.

Jack recalled little of the service except that it was a dull, windy morning causing those who were making the final preparations to curse their luck. He remembered the rows of smiling faces in the church glancing around to greet them as he led Emma towards Troy, the proud look on his mother's face and her cold hand as he took his place by her side, but not much else.

He had seen little of his sister since they had come back to Molland. She had been removed to Luckworthy by the women folk, hidden away to prepare for the day, one lady summoned from Anstey to do her hair, another, a cousin from Withypool, to do her flowers, while still more fussed around preparing the feast. He had felt unwanted, superfluous and was frustrated at not being involved more in the arrangements.

But there had been Wilmot. His mother had told him about what he had achieved but it meant little. He had heard it before from Dr Collyns but what his brother said amazed him. "It was pure luck...absolute luck," Wilmot explained. "The doctor had come to see mother and when he came out of her room he caught me rummaging through his bag. I was terrified, thought he would be furious but he just laughed and asked me why I was so interested."

Wilmot, as slim but darker and shorter than Jack, was nervous and shy for his twenty-two years. Jack watched him carefully as he spoke, at first unsettled by his fierce concentration. Dressed in his winged collar and dark suit, he seemed tense and uneasy, frowning and biting his nails, his words tumbling out in a rush. "I asked him about the potions and creams he had with him, what the instruments were for and that sort of thing." He paused while he thought, then suddenly laughed, his face brightening as he did so.

"Would you believe, he stopped what he was doing, pulled up a chair and

158

began asking me about what I'd read, what I knew...all that sort of thing, and what I wanted to do. Strange," he frowned again. "Seemed strange at the time."

Jack smiled, leant forward on the table and found himself caught up by his brother's urgency. "Go on, what then?" Wilmot sat back and looked down to pick at a thumbnail, his eyebrows raised.

"Well, nothing really...not for a bit anyway." He shrugged, suddenly embarrassed and turned anxiously. "Then, a month later he called to say he'd managed to get me a place at Dulverton school and from there I went on to Peter Blundell's in Tiverton...the school paid for everything." Wilmot glanced up, unsure how his brother would react.

"Then?"

"Cambridge," he laughed nervously. "They found me a place at Trinity to read mining and engineering."

Jack listened, fascinated but uncertain about what he was hearing. His brother spoke quickly, used fine words and sounded so assured. He spoke with an intensity he had not seen before. His grand way of speaking and fine clothes unsettled him, intimidated him even. As he listened, he studied him, unable to understand how one who looked so shy and uncertain could speak with such confidence.

"What're you going to do after Cambridge?" he asked, now leaning forward, eager to hear more. "There's not much place for that sort of thing here in North Devon."

"No, no, that's for sure." Wilmot looked away. He knew his elder brother could not understand. "It's not down here, Jack. It's all up further north, in the middle of England," he replied, now speaking rapidly again. "The world's going mad up there. Honestly...the mines, the mills, the textile industry, ship-building, you name it.

"All revolutionised by the steam engine. It's incredible...the power and the speed of everything. And yet, behind it all are our own natural resources...underground...the mines, right under our very feet...that's where the future lies. That's where I want to be. Honestly, there's nothing down here in this part of the world," he shrugged expansively. "It's all up there and *that's* where my future lies...I can't wait." Jack could see his mind was on matters a world away from Exmoor. Unlike himself and the others Wilmot was not a man of the land, he would never be satisfied with the steady routine of rural life.

Talk turned to Charlotte, their missing sister. Two years earlier there had been a child, born out of wedlock, whose father, so she claimed, was a weaver from

Tiverton. Despite pleas from the family she had followed the man home and now lived with him in a mill worker's cottage on the banks of the Exe close to the new woollen mills. Wilmot saw her occasionally. "From time to time, when I'm down but that's all," he muttered. "She seems happy enough but misses us...mother and the others. I know she does. It must have been hard for her to stay away today."

"Why's she not here today?" Jack would have given anything to have seen her. "Surely she knows we would have welcomed her here...child or no, for Heaven's sake. What would it have mattered on a day like this?"

"You never knew Lottie," his brother replied. "We loved her, really we did, but she was for ever carrying on...telling us all what was right and wrong, how to dress and how to behave. After you and Emms had gone, she was the eldest. She thought it was up to her to set an example." He paused.

"Well, mother needed all the help she could get," Jack countered defensively.

"I know, I know...but then, suddenly disaster," he shrugged helplessly. Where most would have smiled in compassion, Wilmot scowled, angry at the memory. "You can imagine how she must have felt. Had the child here at Luckworthy, a little boy...Davey, I think. The Loosemores were marvellous but she was determined to go her own way...to fend for herself and no one could make her change her mind. Mother was in despair but, 'twas no good. Her mind was made up."

∗

Jack found the evening no easier. Seated at the head of the table with his mother, he found himself among the Kingdons, none of whom he knew. He longed to shut himself away with the family, spending every precious moment he had in the little cottage with them before leaving the following morning. He would be leading two horses back and had decided to set out before dawn, crossing the Sandyway track while the world was still asleep.

He watched idly as the guests danced; turning, wheeling and clapping in time to the music, laughing away and calling out to each other. To him it looked a complicated and uncomfortable business and he could not understand how people took such pleasure in parading up and down like that. He knew it was his duty to ask people to dance but was happy enough to let the others do that, leaving him to talk at the table. It was the same at Simonsbath where Leonard and the others would rib him for sitting out the dances and jigs.

Emma and Hannah never left the floor. He could see how different they were, Emma tall and elegant, Hannah smaller and finer boned, perhaps the more beautiful of the two. Both had their father's striking features, both were lovely young women, so unlike the poor, dumpy Charlotte he had heard about. How his father would have loved to have been here, sitting quietly next to him and watching his daughters with their heads thrown back and their long hair flowing as they spun with their dresses and ribbons swirling behind them. He would have enjoyed that.

"Ja-ack?" Hannah had crept up behind him and stood listening as he chatted and drank with those around him. Reaching out with one arm, he caught her hand then made room as she slid onto the bench beside him. He felt her arm curl round his own.

"Hullo, my love...what're you up to, then?"

"Can I ask you something?" She hesitated, uncertain, then hugged his arm. "D'you suppose there might be something for me to do up at Simonsbath? Some sort of work? I'm seventeen, you know...that's quite old." She smiled shyly and squeezed him. "I mean we'd be together then, all the time, wouldn't we?" She rested her head against his shoulder.

Before he could reply the band began again. "Here, dance with me, Jack," she sat up and looked beseechingly, her eyes bright with excitement. "Just this one. Come on...please. Before you go...*quickly* or someone will come." She leapt to her feet, pulling him. A hand on his shoulder made him turn.

"Jack, listen. Dr Collyns is here," Wilmot pointed across the room. "Over there...see? He knows you and wants to see you."

"*Please*, Jack...just this one." Her voice was urgent.

"After this dance, Will," he smiled beseechingly. "Let us have this one...only this one."

"No, no." Wilmot frowned urgently and took his shoulder. "He's away in a minute. Come over now...come on." Jack saw the insistence on his face.

"Look, my love." He turned to his sister. "I'd best go, but I'll be back...I promise." He knew he had erred, even as he glanced over his shoulder and saw the angst on her face. Collyns could have waited a few minutes, but Hannah had been waiting all evening. It would have meant much to the girl and he would have been proud to have taken her on to the floor. She smiled bravely and raised her hand when he caught her eye. The sight of her made him curse himself.

He was surprised at the softness of the doctor's hands. "Aaah, yes...yes, of course," Collyns searched Jack's face. "Up at Simonsbath and out at Lynton too...with Parson Jack and the rest of them. But now, tell me," he turned back to those around him. "Does Mr Knight know what's happening to the deer up on the top? The poaching that's going on? It's terrible...*terrible*." Everybody listening nodded.

"We're going to have to bring these felons to order or the herd'll vanish. Happened before, you know…and it'll happen again." Collyns was enjoying his audience. "Soon as the hounds went, control of the herd went with 'em. It's the management of the herd that's so important and that's best left to the hunt…we need 'em back, that's what's got to be done."

Jack looked for Hannah. She had gone, so had his chance for them to have their dance. He cursed again, angry with himself for having jumped at Wilmot's assertion. As for Collyns? He had had no more than a nod and a word for him.

※

Later, after most of the guests had gone he went to the stables and prepared the horses. The wind had worsened and bed for him, he knew, was not to be. Ash from the fire was blowing across the yard, fat-smoke gusting everywhere. A few remained in the barn, either spread eagled across chairs, or huddled in small groups, burbling senselessly to each other. Two more slept by the fire, curled up like dogs with their bodies kept warm by the embers. The place was a mess.

Hannah came back for him, insisting that he go with her to the kitchen where she had made him broth and oatcakes. They sat together waiting for the hour before dawn, telling each other about their lives. He was drawn to the girl, loving her as only an elder brother could.

"Here, take this, dear." Grace had joined them. "Please, Jack," she whispered holding out the leather purse. "I could never take it all."

"I'll hear nothing of the sort, mother," he replied, feigning anger and pushing her hand gently from him. "I've said already that it's ours to be spent as we want and that's the end of the matter." He waved the bag away. "Something'll come along that's for sure." He stood and threw his cloak around his shoulders. A few minutes later, he was on his way, the sound of hooves on the track behind the cottage growing fainter.

※

The manor house at Simonsbath was alive with activity.

"The house will be full." Parker had called a meeting of the senior staff to go through John Knight's plans for the summer. "Mr Knight has a busy guest list, sometimes we'll be having more than twenty staying at once together with their staff." He had the attention of those around the table. "I need not stress that we'll be hard pressed to keep the house going…but," he raised a finger. "We have no option. Several great names will be gracing us with their presence." He was on his toes, hands on the lapels of his morning coat.

"There'll be the Naresmiths and the Piggots." Parker inclined his head. "Both

His Grace and his younger brother the Marquess of Bicester. They'll be followed by the Rutlands and the Latchfords." He took a deep breath and picked up the list in front of him. "But, before them, and most important of all, we have the Northboroughs again…His Grace and the rest of the family."

Even he was surprised at the list of names. "And I haven't yet mentioned the guests who live locally…those from Filleigh, Holnicote and so on." Mrs Appelton was away and Parker had taken his chance. "It goes without saying that I'll be expecting the very highest of standards in the house. I cannot speak for matters outside but I've no doubt Mr Knight will make plain his expectations to those concerned." Abbot, the head gardener nodded. There was a short silence then a chair scraped.

"You need not concern yourself about my domain, Mr Parker." The words cut across the room.

The butler caught his breath. "Thank you, Tucker," his voice was barely audible. "Such assuredness is rare indeed. I'll see Mr Knight is made aware of your confidence."

Throughout July, as the Knights entertained, the weather grew hotter. Fishing parties on the Barle and the Exe were organised for the men, together with conducted tours of his moorland domain. Elizabeth-Jane took her own guests to picnics and beach parties along the coast.

4.

The Piggots had gone, for which the yard was glad. Tempers had become frayed in the August heat, the more so when the Northboroughs arrived. Every box in the stables was taken, necessitating several horses to be kept out to grass. The already long hours for the lads grew longer, free time no more than a forlorn hope. Only when John Knight and Lord Northborough left for a few days on their own was Jack able to relax.

✳

"Down the Barle valley then, Master Frederic?" Jack looked across the scrubbed surface of the pine cleaning-table. "Aye, sir, should be no problem…they're getting a mite tired though, all of them."

"That's it, the old hill fort, just past the mines." Frederic nodded. "They're after taking a picnic there. It's a strange place, so it is…there's a presence down there of something or other." Frederic laughed at the memory of how Edward and his sisters had been so wary of the remote Iron Age hill fort, a wild and lonely spot, steeped in mystery and legend.

"Take good care of them all, Freddy," John Knight had warned before taking his leave. "It's beautiful down there, but the land's steep and we don't want any accidents. Mind what Tucker and the others say about the going…and watch the river. The water's as low as I've seen it, but it's still wide and deep down by the hutch…and the rapids are still bad when it's like that."

The plans changed as they often did. The day before, Elizabeth-Jane decided to take a party to Lynmouth, leaving the duke's two daughters to ride out with Frederic and James Acland. Jack would accompany them, a groom leading a packpony and two maids were to go ahead and prepare the picnic site.

"Yes, just the four of us," Frederic bent to let his fingers tussle with Scamp. "We won't hurry away in the morning…the heat's going to get us anyway, so we may as well leave at a decent hour." The two laughed for his father would have demanded preparations at dawn. "Bring some running collars…and a couple of canvas buckets. We'll try for some shade for the horses." Jack nodded. After Frederic had left, he returned to the business of polishing leather.

He remembered her ladyship, remembered her well. He remembered, too, how closely Kenton and Frederic had attended her every move but neither had he forgotten their ride along the river. How often had he idled away the time by recalling the sound of her voice as she questioned him, her bright laughter and the silences when they rode together side by side.

✳

By eight o'clock they could feel the heat in the yard and by ten the sun, now high over Shear Down, had forced the animals to seek cover. The two older yard dogs, lying on their sides panting and listless in the heat, barely lifted their heads. Only Scamp stood at the sound of the voices.

"*Jack.*" It was Frederic. He was hurrying and the yard gate slammed behind him. "I'll have to be gone. Mama needs me back at the house," he panted. "You're going to have to wait, I'm afraid. Get the ladies mounted and then hang on for a few minutes." Frederic wiped his brow. " I won't be long…Lady Katherine's on her way now, the others'll be down shortly."

The horse he was saddling looked up at the sound of the gate opening and shutting again. Whoever was coming now was approaching quietly but the gate had creaked, giving them away. He knew at once but bent low, away from the sun to be sure, with one arm shielding his eyes. She was taller than he remembered and was dressed elegantly in a light cream habit. The peak of her plumed hat was shading her eyes but he could see she was looking at him.

"Hullo, Jack. No need to bend double like that for me, I'm not royalty you know." Her soft voice and her laughter broke the spell. "But working away as ever, I see. They sent me on ahead and I thought I might find you here."

"That's fine, m'lady…an' very good to see you again, ma'am." He wiped his hands on the stable cloth. "More'n a year ago now…must be fer sure." As he took her hand, he caught her eye once again, returning her smile but knowing intuitively that she had come to find him.

"Yes," she chuckled. "D'you remember? How we put Lizzie in the cart and you rode back with me? I wasn't much company, I'm afraid."

"Not so, m'lady, not at all." Now away from the horse he could see her more clearly. "'Twas a great pleasure, ma'am an'...well, you were riding real fine. Nort to worry about."

"Spoken like the master horseman you are," she laughed again, coyly this time, flattered by his words. "They all say that, you know... 'Jack the master' and you're out with us today, I hear." She inclined her head impishly. "Well, you are, aren't you? I hope so, anyway."

"That's right, m'lady." He caught her look and their eyes held but, this time, he could feel himself beginning to colour and forced his mind back to the matter in hand. "Now then, ma'am, we've got Bracken for you today...in here, see." He held the door and followed her into the deep gloom of the box, standing back to allow her to examine her horse. Her shoulders were slimmer than he had first thought, her throat snow white like her neck where her hair was pinned up save for one stray lock. Almost immediately he caught the rich fragrance of her perfume, recognising at once it was the same as the year before.

"*Bracken*...that's a *she* isn't it? A mare? Goodness, she's huge." She moved forward to stroke the chestnut's blaze but he could see she was concerned.

"Very steady though, ma'am." Jack came up beside her. "Won't have no trouble with Bracken...eh, gal." He put one hand on the mare's withers. "There we are, see. Just about the right height...just right for you, I reckon." She watched him weighing her up, sizing her for the horse. She knew he would; it was his job to be sure but there was something personal and intimate about the way he was looking her up and down. "Aye, just right," he confirmed.

"Oops, help, I'm coming apart." The horse had nuzzled her and he waited respectfully as she unpinned her hat then reached round with both hands to adjust her auburn hair. "Always these pins," she muttered, half turning and causing her coat to strain against her body with the effort. He glanced away quickly but he had seen her. He could tell she was showing herself, showing him the fullness of the soft curves under her bodice. He kept his eyes away realising she had seen him watching her, and aware that she was flaunting herself. "Right...there we are." As she adjusted her cuffs, their eyes met again. "*There*, that's better," she smiled. "But, goodness, it's far too hot out there for all this."

"Katherine?" It was Frederic's voice.

165

"We're here, Master Frederic." Jack hurried to the door. "Just introducing her ladyship to Bracken, sir."

*

He rode ahead of the party. The Barle, he could see, was very low, everywhere the water seemed to be feeling its way sluggishly between the rocks whose coats of moss and lichen, usually half covered and slippery wet, were now baked hard by the sun. Sand and gravel banks forced what water there was to seek out the deepest channels. He could see the trout darting from cover to cover, nervous of the confined spaces left by the falling levels. Downstream a heron rose, beating heavily and urgently for height before settling into its slow, measured flight.

He kept his distance, only half aware of life around him, thinking only of that brief moment in the stables earlier. Why had she done that? Why had she come in ahead of the others to taunt him like that? She was a flirt, teasing him, knowing well that he was powerless to react. Were he so much as to return those looks she gave him, glance at her even, he would be before the master and out of the yard. She was cruel, playing with him as she did knowing he was helpless.

And yet...and yet. Her smile had been warm and enticing rather than some jesting smirk. She had sought him out privately so she could be with him alone rather than waiting to mock and taunt in front of the others. In fact she had shunned their company, he had seen it last year and again earlier this week. Why? What was behind it all? Why him?

What did she want...or was it nothing at all, simply his imagination because, deep down, he knew he was attracted to her as the lodestone between them had told him? Their eyes, the language of their bodies and all those tiny, invisible signs were telling them so. And she, too, must have seen it in him. Perhaps that was why he felt the way he did. But it was dangerous, deadly so, and he wanted none of it. All day long he brooded, preferring his own company and keeping well away from the party itself.

*

At the end of the day, he and the others worked on the horses that were still sweating freely from the day's work. They had washed them down then stood them in open doorways to catch whatever breeze there might be. Now they had rubbed them with whisks of straw and the yard, save for the chomping of feed and the odd stirring of hooves, was quiet.

It was as he was walking into the harness room that he felt her presence. He knew instinctively that she was there. "Jack, it's only me." He turned and saw her against the wall, out of sight of anyone who might come into the yard. He placed the saddles he was carrying on the rack then paused. In the distance he could hear laughter and voices but right outside it was silent.

"Can I see you again?" He froze, quite unable to move: only his heart was hammering furiously. A thrill of excitement surged through him but it was madness itself. Nothing like that could possibly happen...nothing, ever. What was on her mind?

"I have to see you Jack. There's time enough yet. We can meet..."

"*No!*" He turned sharply, shaking his head. "Beg pardon, m'lady, beg pardon for speaking like that but it's not possible...it's *madness.*" She could see the shock on his face. "You must never talk like...."

"Stop it," she whispered harshly, crossing the room. "Listen to me, Jack...listen" Her hand moved to brush the hair from his eyes.

"No m'lady...you mustn't." He caught her wrist then looked at their hands, suddenly alarmed at what he had done. He let her go, his eyes searching anxiously for movement outside. "'Tis wrong...dreadfully wrong. If anyone were to...."

"But I have to see you." She came closer and took his hand. "Jack," she whispered. "Please."

"No, m'lady...it can't be done." He took her hand from his. "It can't. If anyone should find out....."

"Freddy knows."

"*What*? Dear God, Master *Frederic*. That *can't* be so. Who else...who else, m'lady?"

"No one, only him." She put her hand to his cheek, but started back at his flinch. "Believe me...only him. He asked me outright when we were down by the river after lunch. Told me he had seen it as plain as day and I did not deny it." She shrugged and sighed. "I know...but he said he knew how I felt...that he could tell beyond doubt. I *could* not deny it...it was impossible. He just knew and that was that.

"It's all right, though." He could see she was smiling at the confusion on his face. "Don't worry. I'll ask him to see that we ride out together. I have to...leave it with me." And there she left him, leaning against the harness room wall.

∗

Later, as he walked between the boxes, Jack listened to the evening sounds. By now the sun had dipped behind the skyline. Shards of gold, orange and salmon pink touched the underside of the high clouds. The heat had gone out of the day at last, allowing the first damp of dew to moisten the grass in the meadows along the river bank.

Behind him, the blackbird that had nested in the honeysuckle beyond the haybarn was singing, answered shortly by another further away. Overhead a curlew was circling, calling softly as it went and, down by the river, snipe were drumming. He could hear noise and laughter coming from the manor gardens, and strained his ears to catch sound of her voice, but it was the sound of running feet that made him turn.

"Parker wants to see you, Jack." Abel Tarr was out of breath. "Says 'tis urgent," he gasped, wide-eyed with effort. "Says for you to come quick."

"Right, Abel. I'll be there." Tarr, he knew, had seen his irritation. "Away and tell the man I'm on my way."

He began to walk, surprised at the butler's urgency, but stopped. Why so? What was this about? Had someone spoken about what had transpired earlier? The thought chilled him yet he had done nothing of which he was ashamed, that was for sure. But somehow, someone had talked. Who and what had been said that resulted in this urgent summons? Frederic perhaps or Charles Acland...*her*? Had the maids seen something, had somebody gossiped? Jack knocked on the butler's door.

"Right, Tucker. Come with me," Parker stepped past him. "Mr Knight has asked to see you. He says it's urgent and wants to see you now, just as you are." Something had changed. It was Parker; the iciness had gone as had the arrogant hostility. He was walking more quickly than usual. Why this hurry, something was different.

"Just a moment please, Mr Parker," Jack caught his arm. "What it's all about? Is the master upset about something?"

"I can't say, Tucker. 'Tis none of my business, I'm afraid." The softened voice alarmed him. "He'll tell you himself soon enough." Jack waited, starting nervously at the butler's knock.

"Jack Tucker, sir," Parker announced, motioning him into the room before closing the door. Knight picked up a letter, rose from behind his desk and came round to face him.

Jack stared. It was news of some sort, there could be no doubt. "Look, Tucker." He could see the strain in the old man's face. The lines were hard but the eyes had saddened. "I've news from Molland. Here." He shook the letter. "It's not good, I'm afraid. It's bad, my boy...very bad."

"Sir?" Jack felt himself tense. The two men faced one another, barely three feet between them. "Can you tell me, sir? What 'tis about."

Knight glanced down, took a deep breath then looked up again. "This here's from Parson Froude." Jack felt a knot tighten deep in his stomach. Knight cleared his throat. "There's a disease about called cholera. It's bad... dangerous. Has been about for a time now, making its way out of the cities." The old man wiped his mouth, struggling to continue. "It's reached the country around and about and...Molland. I'm afraid, it's there, Tucker and...." his voice trailed off.

"Yes, sir?" The voice was calm, but his heart was pounding.

"It's at Luckworthy, Tucker...and it's with the family."

"My mother, sir?" The voice was raised.

"No, praise be to God. Well, not that we know of anyway." Knight glanced out of the window. He knew the words were going to hurt. "But your brother, Edward's down with it. The lad's in a bad way, in fact they fear for his very life."

Knight saw the line of his jaw and the deeply furrowed brow. "I sent the messenger back...he left a while ago. Told him to say you'd be on your way as soon as I'd seen you." The master put a hand on Jack's shoulder. "Take a horse," he growled. "The best there is, two if you want. Ride like hell, boy, and get to your mother's side. She'll be needing you just now."

Chapter Eleven

Edward died that evening. Dr Collyns had called twice during the day, the first time to bleed him and leave barberry bark. Brave though she was, Grace collapsed and wept when he warned her about what was likely to be. At dusk he called again unexpectedly; only later did the family learn that he had come directly from home, riding hard on his roan cob. Even so he was too late.

The youngster had been in a coma since midday, subsiding after a period of stomach cramp so severe that he had clung to his mother as he cried out in pain. She watched the doctor examining him, sensing, as mothers can, that there was little hope. For the last five days he had been unable to eat, his body had simply rejected any nourishment. Nursing him in turn, Grace and Hannah tried to get him to drink fresh cow's milk and water spiced with herbs but he spurned that also, retching violently, his empty stomach contracting again and again until he was exhausted.

A day later Hannah began to have pains. Not sharp at first, she kept them to herself, bending double and gasping on her own each time they returned. But the second night they worsened, Grace heard her cries and saw the sweat on her brow. Charlotte came from Tiverton and the two of them, in spite of Collyns warning them, took turns to sleep in the kitchen directly beneath her room.

Cholera, he had told them a few days earlier, had spread from the cities further east, Bristol in particular. Now reaching out to the countryside, the nearby flourmills at Yeo and Bottreaux had closed, as had The London Inn. Several farms had shut their gates to outsiders. The day before Edward died, the first victims were reported in South Molton, then more in Dulverton. Immediately he heard the news Parson Froude had sent a galloper to Simonsbath asking that Jack could be spared.

*

"I'm sorry," the doctor, dressed in a fine dark maroon coat over his green and vermillion patterned waistcoat, turned to Grace. "There's nothing more we can do. The boy's gone…passed away." She had been with him while he checked for life, feeling for the pulse then bending low to place his head against the boy's chest, before finally searching his eyes. There had been none and he led her gently from the room.

He then returned and stripped back the soiled sheets. As he turned the youthful frame, still fresh from life, the limbs and head flopped ungainly. He could see the body was spent, worn out by the helpless struggle. Pulling the legs straight, he folded the arms then lay the hands flat across the chest. Using the lower sheet as a shroud he quickly and skilfully wrapped the corpse before covering the body with a hair blanket.

Hannah was in the next room and he went to her immediately. As he sat at the edge of her cot, her eyes opened, wide and staring, before closing again as if she had returned to sleep. Even as he took up her wrist and felt her forehead, he knew. The pulse was slow and her brow paper dry. There was no moisture left in the body, just as he feared.

He rose cursing to himself. Stepping carefully down the narrow wooden stairs, he had to stoop and turn sideways to see his way and it was just as he was catching his breath at the bottom that the cottage door opened. It was Jack. Collyns saw the look of one desperate for news. "Ah, Jack," he said quietly. "I'm afraid...it's Edward." He paused, searching for words. "The lad's gone...he died an hour ago in his cot aloft there...I've seen to him." For a moment nobody spoke. In the silence all eyes turned to the one who had only just heard. Jack's face was grim, lined and hard but they could see the grief and watched as his eyes searched the doctor's.

"But Hannah, doctor?" He had noticed his sister was not with them and spoke with a sudden urgency. "What about her?

Collyns doctor sighed. "I'll be honest with you," he muttered despairingly, letting go of the post beam. "It's found the girl as well." The verdict was half whispered. "I'm certain of it. Still early days yet, of course, but I fear for her." He tried to smile reassuringly but his words had struck home. "So..." He sighed again and went to open his bag. "I've got some more herbs...here." He held up a bunch of silvery leaves before searching again. "Wormwood...right? And we must try the barberry as well...here look.

"Sometimes these things work and work well," he advised. "Even at this late stage. Crush the leaves into warm water and stir them, d'you hear?" Heads nodded. Charlotte had taken hold of her brother's hand. "And as for the barberry, remember to brew the bark in boiling water first. At least an hour, right? Boil everything before it's taken...*everything!*"

"That bad is it, doctor?" Jack's were wide with anxiety. "You say that but how poorly is she?"

"She's not well...not well at all." Collyns spoke gravely, looking from one to the other. "As I said it's the disease...however, while there's the very breath of life in the girl we've to do all we can. But first there's Edward...we've to get him from here immediately. I'm sorry, my dear," his hand went to Grace's arm. "It's vital we do that. I'll be away to the rectory then arrange for the carpenter."

The doctor pursed his lips. "And Wilmot's on his way already? Yes? Well then...once here he must stay," he ordered. "Stay until all danger's passed. I'll be back to see the maid again tomorrow." As he reached the door, he turned. "But be sure to do what I said...right away."

✳

It was when he was turning up the collar of his cloak against the wind that he heard the footsteps. "Doctor...forgive me...a minute of your time, sir." Jack had followed him out. "I'm here to help...Mr Knight's told me to stay as long I'm needed but what can a man do, sir? Where does this...this cholera come from, for Heaven's sake? Other people, animals or what?" He reached forward to open the garden gate. "Or does it ride on the wind even? If I knew, then maybe we'd have a chance."

Collyns tried to explain the mysteries. "*Water,*" Jack muttered, half to himself. "Water, so that's it. Then perhaps..."

"I told them to search for fresh...there must be some around here somewhere." He waved his hand in despair. "What they've got's as rancid as sin...every time they use the pump they're bringing up filth. It's the weather...the drought's the worst in years. 'Tis exactly the same wherever I've been."

"But they're already boiling everything, doctor...*and* straining it," Jack added. "We've always done that...always."

"Then keep at it, Jack. Redouble the effort. Make sure they do, especially for Hannah." He stopped at the mention of her name. "She's very weak and you're going to have to prepare yourself...be strong now." One hand took his, the other went to his shoulder. "I'll see you tomorrow," he said softly. "Do what you can."

Jack rested his head against the stable wall, watching the doctor until he was out of sight. He was exhausted, drained and his eyes closed. First Edward and now Hannah. Dear God alive, could it really be so...and where was it all going to end?

✳

He catnapped in the rocking chair by the hearth. Only when sleep finally overtook him did his head loll forward. Twice he jumped when she cried out. The second time, at daybreak, he took her the cracked earthenware pitcher. The water, although boiled was still discoloured and it stank but there was nothing else. She clutched at the glass, drinking greedily before falling back breathless. Minutes later she retched, throwing up what she had swallowed then cried out again as the pains returned. Her eyes he could see had sunk deep and were dulled with exhaustion. Her face was even paler than the pillow under her head.

"How're you feeling?" he asked quietly, smoothing hair back from her brow. But suddenly, with no warning at all, she was awake and at him. Both hands clutched at his arm, her fingers dug like claws into his shirt. She half sat, clinging wild eyed and afraid, as though the very demons of hell were after her. Even his great frame was pulled down by her strength.

"Help me, Jack," she whispered. "Please help me...I'm frightened." Now her voice was louder. "I'm so frightened...Edward's dead...and I'm going to die. I know I am…I just know it," she cried. "I saw the way he looked at me…the doctor. I could see it in his eyes."

He hushed her gently, rocking her head against him but once more her fingers dug into his arm. "I don't want to die, Jack…I don't. I love my life, I love it here…and mother, and you and…oh God, please help me. Why me?" she cried as her arms went round his neck. "Why me, Jack?" she whispered against his cheek.

Jack stared ahead, searching his mind desperately for something to say, for some way out. But there was nothing. Outside, as a soft orange glow was spreading across the last of the night sky, the first birds were beginning to sing. Yet below the farm the valley remained in half-light, the trees and hedgerows no more than dark smudges. Colour was flooding into the dawn landscape. Jack loved the hour but today it was as though nature was mocking him. It was as though she was taunting him with her beauty while his young sister, filthy, foul smelling and dying, lay clinging to him, terrified.

❋

As soon as she was asleep he went to the Loosemores. Wilmot had arrived in the night and they talked with the farmer. "There must've been other water, Fred," Jack turned to the older man. "Think now…can't be the first time we've had a drought like this. Where did they get water?"

"How does the pond fill?" Wilmot asked. "There's water there when every-thing else is bone dry…look at it. Something fills it…where's the source?" Jack saw the studious frown. "What about over there…over there, by the building?"

"The old wash house," Fred muttered dimly, following his gaze. "'Tis always damp in behind the back wall."

"Yes, but see here…it's higher than the pond. The same spring must fill them both…one feeding the other." Wilmot quickened his pace. "And look…if that's so then it's still running. What's behind those stones, Fred?" He had reached an area of rubble. "See here. The ground's wet, boggy even now." He stamped. "There's water here for sure…has to be."

"Aye, s'pose there is," Loosemore, still uncomprehending, pulled at the first stone. "Used to be an old stone trough in there. Father filled it in years back."

The three dug into the rubble, piling the stones and earth to one side until the hollowed stone trough was exposed. At first the water seeped slowly. As they dug further the flow increased until it was trickling into the trough, filling it and spilling over before twisting its way through the dust in the yard. "That's how't used to be," Fred Loosemore announced. "After rain, 'twas more or less a stream. Ran across to the pond then away down t'other side…down the combe."

Throughout the afternoon they worked at clearing a channel for the spring, scouring the trough clean until it was filled with fresh water, cold to the touch in the summer heat. The women cleaned the kitchen. "Scrub and scour everything," Jack urged. "Take out whatever there is...there's sand and grit by the pond. Use that with old cloths to get everything off...pots, pans, pitchers, jugs, everything." It was a race, a battle for life itself.

When Jack lit the fire in the open hearth he ordered the bedrooms upstairs to be shut off. Collecting damp grass, rosemary and lavender from the garden, he smoked the kitchen fiercely, clearing any last remnants of flies and cockroaches from the chinks and cracks. They worked with a grim resolve, driven on by fear, sweat running down their faces and rings of dried salt on the backs of their shirts.

∗

By nightfall the job was done but Hannah had worsened. Although the water she drank was crystal clear, freshened by mint and thyme, she could not hold it down, neither that nor the potions they held to her lips. The disease had worked its way too deep and by now it was too late.

Next morning her mind began to drift. Sometimes she appeared lost to the world, at other times she woke and lay mumbling deliriously as her memory drifted back to their childhood days. "Where's dada?" she asked half sitting, frowning and puzzled like a child that had been woken. For a moment, they dared to hope. "He should be here today," she went on. "He told me he was coming. He did...he promised me, ma'ma." But they knew they were wrong.

"He's had to go off awhile," Jack spoke gently, wiping her face with a damp cloth. "He's been called away but he'll be back, my love. He won't forget you...he promised me that."

"He's in his best uniform, isn't he," she whispered, suddenly coherent once more. "Did you see him last night, ma'ma?" Jack glanced round but there was nobody there. "He came to say goodbye...he did, you know. You saw him, Jack, didn't you?" She nodded eagerly, her eyes suddenly bright at the memory. "He stepped right over you, just there. He did...really." Even as he was laying her back her eyes were closing.

"Told me not to worry, that he'd be back...dada will be coming back," she murmured. He watched as her head turned to one side. He knew she was slipping away yet her hand still clung to his. There was life yet. He tiptoed to the door, ran downstairs and called the family to her room.

Hannah struggled on until the evening. Twice more she woke, smiling at the faces around the bed. The second time they could barely hear her. "Ma'ma," she called. "Here's Dada...he's there, look...and he's smiling, ma'ma. He's happy...so happy," she murmured. "He's so...so happy." Jack felt her hand

174

loosen its grip, only her eyes remained open and staring.

"She's gone," he whispered to no one in particular. "I can't believe it. Our little Hannah...oh, dear God, she's gone."

*

The funeral took place the following morning, attended by those who had come earlier for Edward's. She was buried next to her brother on the higher side of the churchyard at a spot where the lane could be seen winding its way down to the mill. There was none of the usual gathering after the service. Luckworthy was quiet and the family exhausted. Even so the Loosemores again took Grace into their care.

Jack accompanied Charlotte back to Tiverton. The two rode slowly, fording the river above the mills and made their way through the cobbled streets to her home. He never knew if she told him everything but she told him a lot, enough to fire his anger. Times, she said, were difficult. Amos, the child's father, had taken to drink and was beating her for not getting out to earn a living. There was never enough for her and the child. She was afraid for her boy, afraid sometimes for their very lives.

"Mother never said anything to me," Jack commented. "Mind you 'tis none of my business. I'm sorry, Lottie." It was the first time he had used her childhood name and she smiled.

"'Spect she thought it'd make you angry," she replied. "I mean, here am I in a right mess, what with no husband, no home...no nothing really." Jack's anger was confused but now he felt protective. Although she had always been different, a plump, dowdy girl with her hair cropped short, quite unlike her sisters, she was, nonetheless, their own flesh and blood as was her child.

"Go back to mother, Lottie," he urged. "Wilmot's almost away now. Emma and I've left home and...well, she'd give anything to have you around. And young Davey, here." He rocked the shallow wooden cradle where the toddler was sleeping. "That's where you should be...home...Molland."

*

He left her, called briefly at Luckworthy then rode on to Simonsbath. It was a strange, lonely journey back and, as he rode, he wondered why fate was treating him so. The last few days had seen terrible things but all that had now happened and there was nothing more he could do. Yet ahead of him he had a home, a safe job, more and more responsibility and the ear of a powerful man.

Simonsbath was fun, alive, a place where life was exciting. His friends were there. Things happened, people came and went – among them the Duke of Northborough and his family. As he rose in his stirrups, he lifted his face to the breeze.

175

2.

The grey-green water lapping against the quay was ruffled by a keen westerly. Most of the shipping had left earlier, catching the ebb tide and tacking their way out across Bideford Bar before the sandbanks were exposed. Gulls wheeled noisily, fighting for scraps of refuse drifting past Castle Quay while, beyond them, sandpipers and knots raced one another for the lugworms still burrowing into the mud banks.

Enid Chapple snatched at her strands of loose hair and turned up the collar of her coat. She hung on to rather than held Parker's arm, staring mournfully at the wagonette waiting where the North Walk track met the cobbles of Tully Street. Parker frowned. Even from where they stood he recognised the coachman and the slight figure of Dan Webber sitting hunched under the horse blanket. The butler knew they had seen him and he attempted to ease her arm away. "When d'you think you might be back?" she tried to sound indifferent but clung to him tighter than ever.

"Difficult." He shrugged disconsolately. At first he had enjoyed their time in Barnstaple. She had shown him the shops and the esplanade, even the grounds of Marwood House where she was working. But she had spoiled it by complaining too much about her new employers, moaning about the difficult children and the strange ways of Mr Daniel Stewart, her master. That had been irritating.

On the other hand, the room in The Rising Sun, where she had given him her attention, had been comfortable enough, and they had eaten well. "I'll have to see what's coming up. Perhaps in the spring...can't see it before then." He was not going to let her rush him.

"*Spring*?" Enid turned and pulled him into the warehouse doorway, her feet slipping on the damp cobbles in her effort. "*Spring*, Bernard? Surely before then, dear?" He could see her eyes beginning to water. She looked silly in the blue bonnet she had bought for the weekend, and sillier still when she stood all miserable like that, with her damp, red nose. He groaned inwardly; it was time to be gone.

"Please try, Bernard." Her fingers were squeezing the underside of his arm. "You know how...well, how I love our time together. And *you* enjoyed it didn't you...last night? Didn't you...my precious?"

Parker stretched to check those on the wagonette were not watching. Yes, it had been fun, great fun; the harder he had worked the more she seemed to enjoy it all. Her energy had surprised him but then no man could have been near her for weeks, months probably. Even after she cried out in pain, she came back for more. Twice he woke in the night when her thin body had climbed over him.

"What are you laughing at?" Now she was smiling as well, gazing up at him expectantly, waiting for the good news. "You will come, won't you...before then. Tell me you will, dearest." She shook his arm encouragingly. Somehow her dull, miserable face lit up and, for a brief moment, he wanted her there and then but it was no more than passing lust.

"I'll see." He straightened his shoulders and stepped back into the street ensuring that the two of them were walking apart as they approached the wagonette.

"Well, Miss Chapple, it's certainly been my pleasure." The formal farewell would be best so there would be no chance of her clinging to him all maudlin in front of the servants and making a scene. "I shall be writing...that is for certain. But now," he extended his hand. "I must away to Simonsbath and the master." He refrained from saying anything that might build up her hopes about a reunion, and most certainly nothing personal or endearing lest the others should hear. She looked miserable again but that was her fault.

"Farewell, Miss Chapple...and my thanks again." Her hand was limp but he let go of her quickly before she could get any closer. "I shall be passing on your news, you can be sure of that." The cart jerked forward and he glanced back briefly at the lone figure then settled to wrap the rug over his knees. Once comfortable he shivered suddenly before rubbing his hands together.

＊

"Oh, Mrs Appelton, just one minute please." The cook reached the house-keeper at the door that led to the staff room. It was three o'clock, lunch had been cleared and the two women were alone. "You haven't changed your mind, have you?" Mrs Strong looked up at the taller woman, knowing well what the answer would be.

"Certainly not, Mrs Strong. What, pray, made you think that I might have done so?" She knew the cook had come to plead for the man. She could see it all over her face.

"Well, it's just that he's been here so long now...*part* of the place, so he is." Mrs Strong glanced round, listening carefully. Her face under her white mobcap was creased with worry. "You see...well he's got nowhere to go. He's a lonely man really and he's too old to start afresh. D'you think that, maybe, there's...."

"No I do not." The housekeeper was adamant. "I've warned him often enough...he's been inebriated more times than I care to remember. You know that...as do the servants." Mrs Appelton had sent word via the cook as soon as he returned from his weekend and she had pleaded then. The half bottle of gin lay where she had found it but there had been no sign of the six missing from the cellar. "I respect your loyalty, Mrs Strong, but the matter has come to a head...it's not going to be pleasant, but that is my duty." Her head rose defiantly.

"Look," Mrs Strong, now that her glasses were off, blinked in the light. "Look,

Mrs Appelton...just one more chance." Her voice was raised. "Let me talk to him...I know him better than anyone...."

"Thank you, Mrs Strong, but no." Janet Appelton made to move past the cook. "My mind's made up and I'm going to deal with it now...thank you. Excuse me, please."

The cook could hear their voices even before the door of the staff room closed. Concern now turned to anger; Mabel Strong had known Bernard Parker too long for this, far too long. She stamped her foot then marched to her chair in the kitchen where she dumped herself frumpily like a child in a rage. A moment later she was up, the papers that had been lying on the cushion dashed to the floor. She was certain the two of them would know who slammed the door so she pulled it as hard as she could behind her.

*

"So that's your last word?" Parker adjusted his cuffs. "A drunkard you say, Mrs Appelton...so I'm a man of the bottle, am I?" He had watched unmoved as she opened the door of the dresser and produced her evidence.

"I did not say that." The two were facing each other. Parker, calm and cold, could see she was apprehensive. He was taller than her and let her know it. "What I said was that I had come across you worse off for drink on numerous occasions, that I had warned you and that you had chosen to ignore me."

He turned to the window. The woman had decided to make her move and had probably been to the master already. That would have been typical of her. He had never liked the interfering, self-important busybody and was not going to make it easy for her now.

"Tell me Mrs Appelton," he spoke slowly, bending forward as if to check something in the driveway. "When has it ever come to your attention that my work, as first butler and steward, has been anything but of the highest order? Mmm?" He paused before turning back to face her. "Difficult to answer, Mrs Appelton, very difficult, no doubt. Well, let me tell you...there has never once been any cause for complaint either from the master, his good lady or the household. Has there now? What say you to that?" Now he was glaring.

"Your performance at work is not in doubt...you've quite missed the point." Mrs Appelton tossed her head dismissively. The man was offensive, and guilty as sin. Anyone could see it. "It's your personal conduct, Mr Parker. As head butler you should be setting the standards you wish the remainder of the staff to maintain...*you* know that and *I* know that. And I can smell it even now." She took a step back. "*Gin*, on your breath. It's...it's horrible, dis*graceful*."

"Oh for God's sake, woman why...."

"That...is...enough. How *dare* you speak to me like that."

Parker could see the anger; she had gone white. It was too late now but he had enjoyed cursing her and it made him feel better. "Mr Knight is going to see us and you can start thinking about the discrepancies in the cellar account, as well. No doubt he will be interested to hear your comments on *that.* Kindly remain here and await my call."

*

John Knight was irritated. The moment she had asked for an interview yester-day he sniffed trouble. Usually she went to Elizabeth-Jane who dealt with these matters. Domestics were none of his business and it was only when she mentioned Parker that he asked her to explain herself.

He had heard her out, seeing at once how it had come to this. She was a haughty creature, and that would have annoyed the man. As she stated her case, he took notes as was his custom. It made anyone in front of him choose their words carefully, and it gave him time to think. A mere raising of the quill feather would bring proceedings to a halt. However, the woman had a point and it was going to be difficult.

But Parker, the Parker of old? He liked the man and always had. He was loyal, he kept the staff on their toes and his master well briefed about everything and everybody, even the guests when his opinion was asked. He knew the man would have preferred to stay in Worcestershire but he had come to Exmoor nonetheless, as loyal as ever. He had heard about this woman of his, too. Knight grinned to himself. And why not? Good luck to the man.

Now they were in front of him; she with her notebook, all stuffy and piqued, he all starched and scrubbed. No love, there. But they could both remain stand-ing, it would do them good. "Is that so, Parker?" Knight looked up, mouth open in anticipation.

"Sir?" The butler's thumbs were pressed down the seams of his trousers.

"Drinking? Swigging from a bottle...and during working hours?"

"On occasions, sir...from time to time."

"Hmmph." Knight scratched at his hair. "That's bad...shouldn't be done. Can't have that," he frowned. What the devil was he supposed to say for goodness sake? "Hmmph." As he felt for his shoulder, he scowled darkly. "Any incidents of...loss of performance, Mrs Appelton?" He stared impassively at the buckle of her belt, no longer caring if the housekeeper read his mind or not. "Any complaints?"

"Not that I can recall, Mr Knight." She made a pretence of looking through her book. "It's the matter of *example*, sir. If it goes on at the top then the younger and more impressionable ones...."

"Thank you, Mrs Appelton. I can do without the lecture." Parker stared at some point on the wall behind his master, the housekeeper at her hands. "Hmmph...and what's this about gin, Parker? A bottle or more of the stuff going missing...what's all that about?"

"Nothing to say, sir."

"What d'you mean...*nothing to say?* Come on, man, you can do better than that. What the devil's bin going on out there?" Parker remained silent, simply rising on his toes and returning his gaze to the spot on the wall. Mrs Appelton coughed politely. "Right...stay where you are, the pair of you." Knight pulled himself to his feet and walked to the window. Lifting the shoulder of his frock coat, he rubbed gently.

The bracket clock on the mantelpiece behind his desk chimed the hour, answered, a moment later, by the deep strike of the walnut longcase in the hall. Parker should go, there was no doubt about it. Drinking his master's drink while on duty would see him out, and see him crippled at that. He would never work again, no recommendation, no grace and favour, no charitable handshake, nothing. The man would be broken, and unemployable. No one would touch him.

But, set against what the woman had reported was his twenty-five years service. *Twenty-five* years. He remembered how the callow, lank-haired young footman at Lea Castle used to stay up half the night waiting for him then cover for any indiscretions, supporting him whatever he was told to say. He remembered how Old Tom, the butler, and Drew, the house steward, had threatened the young Parker but he had stood his ground. The man, then no more than a lad, had never let him down.

He would stay...the man was worth more to him than these petty charges; far more. So then the Appelton woman would go. She was the sort that would leave on principle. First she would go running to Elizabeth-Jane, setting master against wife, then storm away in a huff with her head held high. Well, let her, the wretched creature.

"Thank you, Mrs Appelton." Knight had returned to his chair and sat heavily. "Thank you...you may go. Not you, Parker."

"Are you not satisfied, Mr Knight?" Janet Appelton let her arms drop in a show of exasperation sure to be noticed.

"Thank you, Mrs Appelton." Knight waved towards the door, watching her as she went. His hands returned to the desk and clasped one another. "Look at me." The voice was quiet. "I said look at me, man." Parker's eyes moved.

"You should know the ways of women by now, for God's sake." Parker thought he saw the hint of a twinkle. "What the bloody hell're you up to? Eh? Yer damn fool." Knight paused. "All right, so she's not your cup of tea but she runs the place and you don't go around performing like that...giving her the chance of a lifetime." The master lowered his head to rub one side of his temple. "Watch your step, man. No more of it...d'you hear or you'll be gone, I'll have no choice."

"Sir." Parker's eyes had already returned to his spot on the wall.

"Cut it out, d'you hear? No more of it. I need you here sober and sharp as an old fox...there's work to be done." Knight tore the page from his book. "Anyway...away now and get me the seating plan for tonight...and the wine list. Oh...and Parker."

"Sir?"

"Keep out of her sight. Get out of her hair and stay out of it."

"Sir." He chose not to return what he thought was a smile for he might have been wrong.

Mrs Appelton resigned and left a week later, as Knight said she would. Her replacement, Peterkin, the house steward, arrived at the end of the month from Powderham Castle.

3.

"I can see your concern...quite see it." Sir Thomas Acland nodded and crossed his legs then smiled benevolently. "But life's full of surprises...take *me*, for goodness sake." He shrugged and laughed, going on to explain how the Reform Bill had split the Commons earlier in the year. First it had been passed only to be defeated later in committee. Now a re-draft was in the offing but it was *he*, Acland, one of the last to speak, who had been cast as the devil incarnate, finishing up with enemies on both sides of the House. "And that's not much fun either, I can tell you," he joked.

Frederic, now worried about his father's business, had sought the meeting. Lady Acland, for years a close friend of his mother, had arranged luncheon at Holnicote, the excuse being that Charles, their son, would soon be joining his ship. Sir Thomas, the tenth baronet, family patriarch and good friend of John Knight, always enjoyed Frederic's company.

The youngster, barely twenty-two, had inherited much of his father's fire and drive yet there was a more sensitive side to his nature which Acland found interesting. He was delighted whenever Frederic sought him out, taking their exchanges as a compliment, occasions for which he always found time.

His eyes went to the long drawing room windows against which the November rain was buffeting, driven hard by a gusting wind. Since the family had taken up residence again, Lydia had poured affection into the place, the great fire, fifty years before, having all but destroyed the old house. The bright lemon curtains and pale silk wallpaper caught whatever light was available to balance the dark oriental rugs. He had thought that the lightness of the new elm floor would have been adequate but she had been right. Even today the room managed an air of bright gaiety. Holnicote was a happy house and he, now free of parliamentary responsibilities, was never happier than when here.

*

"I don't think the mines are going to work." Frederic, chin on his thumbs, regarded his mentor gloomily. "I've been out to see Havers twice now and he's nothing to show for it...absolutely nothing." He laughed cynically. "It just does *not* add up...even father can't go on like that." Thomas Acland nodded for he had heard it himself. Swayne, his Cornish land agent had been told by the miners when he saw them at Cornham.

"Snuff?" Acland pushed the two silver and onyx boxes across the cloth. "Nutmeg...in that one, or Turkish Ginger." Frederic shook his head then watched as his host took a pinch into the crook of his thumb.

"D'you think your father realises this, Freddy?" Thomas Acland drew out his green handkerchief and blew heavily. He knew Knight well but hesitated to press the matter. The industrialist, now nearer seventy than sixty, had his moods, famous even in London, and some things were best left unsaid. He sat back, wrinkling his nose and stretched his long legs. "It's a bit difficult, don't you think? I'd tell him myself but I've a feeling he's got a pretty fair idea...dangerous to press on that particular sore."

Frederic waited until the nose had been blown again. "Then why doesn't he stop, sir...cut his losses?" He bent to adjust the collar of his velvet jacket. The fire was hot and he shuffled his chair, before moving the vase of dried flowers to see his host better. "There's enough work with the farms...twelve at the last count and more in his head, would you believe."

Acland bowed appreciatively, then frowned. A King's ransom was being poured into the moor and there was nothing coming back thus far, nothing to show for it all. Little wonder the family were worried. "A gamble perhaps?" Their eyes met. "It's always a risky game, this mining. Nobody's ever quite sure what's down there. To be honest, I *am* a little surprised he's still exploring."

"And cutting his lines...for the railway and canal," Frederic interjected. "Honestly, sir," he shrugged despairingly. "I just wish he'd call a halt...stop for now at least and take stock." Sir Thomas's eyebrows flickered but he knew he was right.

"He's a very proud man...your father, and fear of failure hangs heavily over the proud. Vanity, stubbornness, call it what you will, it's always difficult to get that sort of person to face reality...and your father's not always the easiest of men." Both laughed. "But what *about* the farms, Freddy?" Acland tapped his teeth. "I hear several are coming along well. In fact I can see progress myself every time I'm up there."

"Indeed, and thank God for them. Honeymead, Cloven Rocks and Emmet's...they're all well on the way. That's something to fall back on." The two sat in silence. Once the butler came in to replace the decanter. Once an extra strong blast of wind made them both start when even the fire smoked.

Acland knew how lucky he had been to miss ownership of the moor. What he would have done with the land he had no idea; his farms near Exeter were difficult enough. John Knight could not go on much longer; already his son was waiting in the wings, young and energetic but cautious and that had to be good. "What about your other plans, Freddy?" He took snuff again. "Charles tells me you've spoken...the military, didn't he say?" Acland laughed at the confused flush. "Well...and why not? Nothing to be ashamed of, that's for sure an' you're the right sort of age."

"Can't make up my mind, sir." Frederic toyed with the lace cloth. "On the one hand I'd give anything to join you in London...one day that is." Their conversation at Arlington Court a month earlier was still fresh in his mind. "I'd love that. There's so much coming up...all these new laws for instance. Parliament's the place to be but I'd have to stand in Worcestershire and, goodness, all that's years away yet."

Acland pulled a face. It would be difficult, especially from Exmoor. "I know and there's so much to be done here."

Frederic rocked back in his chair, hands behind his head. But the idea still appealed and he brightened at the thought. "Either the Dragoons or the Yeomanry...not sure which...the Yeomanry more likely."

Both turned as the door opened. "Tea, sir...Mr Knight." The footman inclined his head then turned to open both doors. "Lady Acland is ready, sir...in the salon."

*

It had all seemed rather a silly little affair at the time but not any more. Frederic, head bowed into the breeze and with his cloak buttoned high under his chin, urged his horse towards Berry Castle and the Exford track. At first the night had been black, any light hidden by low cloud. But they were lucky. As they climbed out of Porlock Vale, the rain eased and the clouds lifted. By the time they reached the Roman camp, the first stars were visible. Moon by eleven, Coward had predicted but they should be home by then.

Frederic Knight looked older than his years, anyone who saw him that evening would have agreed. The dark, deep-set eyes behind the hawk nose gave a piratical look. His black whiskers, so carefully cultivated and turned under his chin only added to the image, as did the thick black cloak. Tall and slim, the young master-to-be rode hunched, sitting well forward in the saddle as the brass butt of his pistol reminded his ribs of what was there. His horse, black also, save for two white socks, was a handsome animal. Fifty yards ahead of him, Hector Coward and one of the new grooms cleared the way as the three of them rode steadily into the night.

Sir Thomas had been right. The mines were unlikely to repay much of the time and money spent prospecting, if anything at all. It would have to be the farms alone which would bring in money but his father had yet to see it that way. Before he left they had discussed Maxwell's ideas for breaking and reclaiming the land and how best to set about finding tenants.

Local men, Acland had warned, would be wary of taking on such a venture. Too canny by half he had joked. Those close to the moor steered well clear of the place. Everyone apart from the summer shepherds was distrustful of the harsh winters. His father would have to advertise further afield, but who would answer the call? And would they be able to take on the challenge? That alone was another risk to be addressed.

Lydia Acland had sat quietly over tea, letting the men have their say. Frederic knew she was studying him closely, listening carefully to his points of view. Hardly a word from her, though, just a tut here and there or a nod was enough. He had always liked her, she seemed to understand his ways, almost how he thought. Then, tea cleared away and Sir Thomas out of the room, the two of them had talked. What were his plans, she had wanted to know? Where was he going to go and when, and *who*, she asked, had he in mind?

There he had stalled. There was no one, seriously, but he could see the expression on her face. "Come, come," she had feigned surprise. "A handsome, well connected young man like you. There must be somebody in mind...somebody, surely? Katherine Darcy, perhaps, or Lizzie? Such attractive young things", she reminded him, "and a *won*derful family." The questions had come softly, cleverly, as they were making their way towards the front door. He had half expected it, but there were no such thoughts about himself on his mind. He dare not even consider the situation for it had all become such a terrible muddle.

For weeks he had waited, listening anxiously with his ears ever alert to hear that somebody other than he knew what was afoot but nobody else, it seemed, appeared to know. However Katherine, the lovely, elegant, headstrong Katherine, was risking everything. And poor Jack, trapped and helpless, had not said a word. My God, if ever it became known.

But Lizzie was different. She was calmer and steadier with none of her sister's fire. Were either ever to interest him, it should be her. Yet it was not. It was her sister, Katherine, who still held his mind. Too late though. It had indeed seemed a silly little affair at the time, but no longer. Katherine had seen to that and the whole dreadful business now filled him with a deep foreboding.

By now his horse was blowing, so he eased to a walk and let the reins drop.

Chapter Twelve

The signpost at the junction of the main Barnstaple road was still at the same drunken angle it had been for over a year. Beyond the mud and puddles etched in the road lay the remains of a cooking fire, beaten flat by somebody but still smouldering. It was the magpies fleeing from the scene that made his horse start.

"I'll be damned…that's a fair brave sight." Hector's mouth remained agape. The two riders, now well ahead of the others, pulled up and stood looking down the long slope towards South Molton. "See they horses working…eh?" he remarked appreciatively. "*Massive* things, they coaches. Must be at least six inside and eight or ten up top an' all. And don't 'alf crack along, too." Jack, only a few feet further on, backed his horse away from the edge of the road. Lurching from one side of the road to the other as the coachman tried to avoid the worst of the ruts, the maroon and black Exeter Mail rattled past on the last leg of its journey. The guard-in-charge, a red-faced fellow resplendent in his maroon frock coat edged with gold, glowered suspiciously.

The four heavy horses, matching dapple-greys, were working hard. Jack noticed how each pair, their flanks steaming in the sharp air, worked in unison as they leant into the slope at a brisk trot. Yet, no sooner had they crested the Aller rise than the coachman flicked at the reins, urging the team into a canter. Those travelling on top, their collars turned up against the chill of the November day, braced themselves as the stage picked up speed.

"Aye," Jack waved at the youngest of the three riders behind the coach. "They've got to crack on yer know…ten miles in the hour, every hour, no matter what. An' that's with the stops an' all…fairly press on they do." Both stood to watch the coach disappear on its way. "Master says he wants to get from Lynton to Tiverton then on to London in less than a day'n night…two hundred miles or more."

✳

For weeks Frederic had been looking forward to the break. Twice each year, in the spring and late autumn, sportsmen from as far as Barnstaple and Bridgwater met in South Molton. It was the gathering of the select Hunt Club, when every available room in and around the old market town was taken by masters and their servants, every stable and kennel filled. Various packs of hounds were invited to meet in the square and shoots were organised at Filleigh and Whitechapel and other country houses. The members themselves stayed at The George which, for those two hectic weeks, became the centre of their world.

Frederic Knight, top hat perched at a jaunty angle, was gesticulating expansively. The Acland brothers and Roger Bamfylde, with their reins hanging loose and their feet dangling beside empty stirrups, listened intently before shouting with laughter. "They'm at it again," Jack grinned. Collecting up the horse he was leading, he nodded back towards the party. "They lot. C'mon...let's get on down."

✳

It was also the time of the South Molton sheep fair and, as the party rode down Barnstaple Street, they fell in with others. Some were mounted on an assortment of animals but many were on foot, several carrying bundles slung over their shoulders or pulling handcarts. There was an air of merriment and excitement: everyone, it seemed, was converging on the town centre. Ahead they could see that Broad Street and the square in front of the Guildhall were packed with traders' stalls. Suddenly, in the space of a few minutes, everything had changed; gone was the peace and quiet of the ride from Simonsbath. Instead they found themselves in the centre of a mass of pushing, jostling people where the air was filled with shouts and curses, with whistles and hawkers' cries, with laughter and banter.

Further along Broad Street, beyond the white-fronted George Hotel, cattle were bellowing in the livestock market. Either side of the wide street, row upon row of tethered beasts awaited their fate, some standing forlornly others lying quietly on their own chewing their cud. Then there were the sheep, hundreds of them, mostly in pens but some loose with their drovers.

Between them all, dealers were bargaining and haggling. Back in the main square parties of smock-clad farmers stood in groups with their heads pressed together. Their wives, dressed in best bonnets and shawls, gathered in clusters, some grouped around yet more women sitting in lines of wooden benches with poultry at their feet. Chickens, most tied in bundles, waited patiently for the next hand to examine them while guinea fowl, ducks and geese lay passively, their minds closed to the noise around them.

Gossip seemed to be the business of the day. Some, oblivious to events around them, were locked in earnest debate, others exploded with laughter, time and again slapping their thighs as the stories wore on. For months they had not seen each other and digesting such news was not to be missed. Food and vegetable stalls lined the sides of the square where the merchandise was arranged in colourful rows. Behind them vendors brayed hoarsely. In front of The Barnstaple Bank, two women fought savagely, cheered on by a mob. One, without her shoes, was hopping from foot to foot while the other, doubled over by her skirt pulled over her head, screeched and cursed.

Elsewhere hawkers bantered with the crowd, showing off their cheap clothes, their boots and wooden clogs. Tinkers hovered around piles of tin and copperware while gypsies sat quietly behind baskets of pegs and cages of small songbirds. Outside the corn exchange a fiddler played while his monkey, no bigger than a large kitten, danced on a cloth-covered fruit box dressed in its waistcoat and hat. Buyers crowded around stalls of pies and pasties kept warm by braziers of hot coals. The waft of hot pie-crust caught the air vying with the stench of dung and sweat and the smoke from a hundred coal fires. Everywhere, urchins squabbled and fought noisily: beggars, dirty and dishevelled pestered anyone they could.

It was difficult for the newcomers to remain together for, even where the square was at its widest, the crowds were packed tight. But they were mounted: they could see over the heads and it was Hector who saw them first. Swinging his horse round and scattering those too close he pointed towards the Guildhall where two redcoats from The North Devon Militia stood resplendent in their scarlet tunics with white cross straps and their black shakos. Beside the infanteers, and mounted on their well-groomed bays, sat an officer and trooper dressed in the black and gold of the hussars.

*

Frederic Knight doffed his top hat in reply to the salutes from the militiamen. "Good day, sergeant and my thanks to you," he nodded politely and rode on to the hussars.

"And a very good day to you, sir." Somewhat older than the others, the lean-faced officer cast a knowing eye over Knight's horse and smiled appreciatively. "A fine looking animal you've got there, sir. We could do with a few more like that in the Royal North Devon's, y'know." He spoke in a friendly manner, quite unashamed of the job he had to do that day. "Not thinking of coming our way, I suppose?"

"Could be," Frederic replied thoughtfully. "Could just be. I'm undecided as yet but we've been reading about your exploits. That shipwreck...over at Bideford, and all these civil disturbances." He paused then removed his right glove. "But here, I must apologise, sir... Knight's the name, Frederic Knight of Simonsbath and Lynton."

"Your servant, sir. Captain Edgar Porter. Then pray, why don't we talk away from this mayhem? Yes? I suggest this way...if you would care to follow me." At this the captain turned his charger. Frederic could see he rode well. He saw, too, how the boots gleamed liked oiled ebony and how the white cockade above the helmet swung as the animal moved. Without stopping to think, he followed, the sounds of his own horse's hooves adding to the echoes of the other on the cobbles under the archway that lead through to the courtyard behind.

*

"Well, I've done it now." Frederic was smiling. He had been away an hour before rejoining them in the stables behind The George. "The good captain and

188

I've been talking out there and I've given my word to go along to the hussars...The Royal North Devons themselves."

"'Tis a bit sudden, Master Frederic." Knight made room on the bench as his groom made to sit next to him. For a moment his announcement had been greeted with silence. "That means you'll be leaving us, sir? Eh? Goin' off with they lot?" Hector Coward scratched at his tousled head.

"'Tis what yer father was telling you about, the other day, Master Frederic, ain't it?" Jack, too, moved a bit closer, suddenly curious at what the reply might be. "Remember you was telling us how he was worried 'bout all the trouble up north."

"That's it, really." As Jack folded a patched horse rug and sat facing them, Frederic picked at a blade of straw. "He's been pushing me a bit, I suppose...but then, I reckon somebody has to do something. And it's not only up *there*," Frederic continued. "Take the Bristol riots last year for instance. Then there's all this going on in the countryside as well. Not here yet, although we've had the trouble in Bideford, but right across the south...Norwich, Winchester, Salisbury, wherever you look in fact. So it's up to this lot to keep the peace...the Yeomanry and Militia."

The three fell silent, each contemplating what Frederic had said. "There's more'n more of it...trouble over work and food mainly. An' it's getting worse...take Dorset. Hundreds have been arrested there alone. Deported, too, and some of 'em hanged even. I can see why father's so worried. He's after bringing down all the latest machinery...ploughs, threshing machines and all that kind of thing. He's worried about how people'll are going to react and I don't blame him."

"What's his worry then, sir?" Hector frowned.

"Jobs," came the immediate reply. "All these new machines are taking jobs and the labourers're scared stiff. I can understand it up there perhaps but there's no need to worry down here. I've tried to tell him...we need every pair of hands we can find and there's no way we'll be putting people out of work."

"So you're not joking then, Master Frederic? You're goin' to join 'em, like?" Hector's eyebrows remained raised. "An' d'you reckon there'd be room for us? Jack an' me? To come along with you, like?" Jack laughed. He had been about to ask but his friend spoke first.

"Well, that's why I've brought you in here out of the way. So we can talk." Frederic eased his back. "Father's hoping some of us at Simonsbath'll join, so we're seen to be doing our bit as it were. There's not much money involved but he's promised to keep the wages going for anyone who signs on. Supply the horses as well." He half turned to Jack. "What d'you reckon, eh? Might not be quite so easy, I suppose...the family might not be too keen."

Jack shrugged. He had stood up to stretch. "Oh, that's all way back now, sir. No...bain't a bad idea at all. Hector and I've bin talking. Father would've been proud...proud as anything." He thought for a moment. "Aye, an' reckon mother'll come round to the idea soon enough. Not as though we're goin' to have to be out of the country or be gone for months at a time."

"That's true." Frederic paused then stood as well. "Right then," he announced grinning cheerily. "We'll go for it...all of us. I'll see father and tell him the plan."

2.

Elizabeth-Jane took a last look through the deep bay window before turning at the sound of footsteps crossing the hall. The weather had been wild, even for an Exmoor December. During the night it had rained with great sheets of water falling from the heavens, but now it had stopped. Outside it was still, as though the downpour had drawn the sting from the wind.

She could see that the tops of the beeches down by the bridge were barely moving. Since dawn, the river had dropped, even so the mud-brown water still raced under the arches, breaking angrily against the stonework. She watched as two drovers trudged past the gate at the end of the garden, huddled under their sacks, the heads of their sheep barely visible above the low bank. The weather looked set for the winter; it was raw and she shivered.

✳

"Ready for the wilderness?" Elizabeth-Jane knew how Morgan disliked being away from his soft luxuries and laughed at the figure in front of her wrapped in cloak and muffler. "Oh dear," she groaned. "It's all very sad really and I shouldn't be laughing today. You'll be gentle with him, Durnford. It's going to hurt terribly, you know."

Morgan nodded. "I know. We've all been dreading it coming to this. Even London have been on their knees praying for a strike somewhere. Is Frederic out with them?"

"Yes. He and Maxwell have been out looking at the farms. He can see it all clearly enough, thank goodness, so perhaps he's the best one to handle his father...once the dust has settled, that is. But now then." She walked around the rosewood sofa table and came up to him. "I suppose you'll be away soon...before Christmas anyway? Mmm?" Her fingers reached out to straighten his collar. Even dressed as he was, the banker remained wildly attractive. The hair had thinned a little and the sideburns were flecked wiry-grey but his eyes were the same: bright, inquisitive and always laughing.

"Indeed that's so...but not for long. Sir James has arranged to switch funding from mining to agriculture. Some clever ruse dreamed up by Crispin Barclay.

If I may, I shall be taking your leave at the weekend."

"Still here for a few days then?"

"Still here for a while...yes." His voice had softened. Last night after dinner she had played for them and it had been just as he first remembered her. She looked so different by candlelight in her midnight-blue velvet gown trimmed with lace. They had retired late but now she was as fresh as though she had slept through the night like a child. How any mother of six, and the eldest a grown man, could remain like that he would never understand.

"What are you thinking about?" She knew, of course, and her smile showed her appreciation.

"Nothing...because you've gone and emptied my head as you always do." Morgan grinned mischievously. "Anyway, whatever it was in there's vanished...and I must away too or I'll be in trouble. Don't worry about today though, dear lady, I have a feeling the master already knows the decision that has to be made. We'll make it look as though it was his...it's best that way and easier for everyone." He inclined his head to take his leave.

"Durnford." Elizabeth-Jane followed him. "Listen. You said you'd be away in a few days but when do you think we might see you again?"

"Goodness." The scarlet lining of his cloak billowed as he turned. "Early after Christmas, I suppose. When our man Maxwell has got his figures together, and then again in the spring...Easter, when this mountain fastness of yours has some warmth in its stones. But when I do come back, I'll be lodging in Barnstaple again."

"Oh." The tone in her voice told him she found the news disappointing.

"Nearer the bank. It's much easier that way, isn't it? Perhaps easier for everybody." She had moved closer and he could see the rise and fall of her apple-green day dress. For a moment she frowned confused, even when he caught her eye.

"*Easier*, Durnford?" She sounded puzzled. "And easier for *everybody*? Well, not quite, surely. I mean...will it really be such a good idea to be so far away? In Barnstaple?"

"I thought it might be better that way." Morgan raised an eyebrow. "If we're honest...and perhaps make life seem a mite more straight forward as well. No? At least that's what I thought." He bent and kissed her hand.

"Oh, I see," she murmured, not moving as he turned to go.

"My hope is that I have judged the situation...the situation between us

191

correctly." He turned towards her but continued on his way walking backwards. "Difficult for us in other ways, perhaps," he shrugged apologetically. "But then not so complicated either." She watched him turn back again and stride from the room, then closed her eyes and smiled.

*

It did not take long. Knight had asked him to be there at midday, and he was in good time. Mercifully, for the wind had risen again, the meeting was to be in the blacksmith's shop near the Cornham drift. As soon as he crested the ridge, he could see the grey coal-smoke of the forge. John Knight would still be in the mine, either there or at Hangley Cleeve.

They had found the vein at forty-five feet and begun an adit, lifting more than twenty tons of minerals but the lode had run dry, as had those at Blue Gate and Deer Park where Rogers had gone down even further. He remembered how their spirits had soared when the first good quality ore came up but that vein had died too and the shaft had to be closed. It had been hard on them all but it had hurt the master most.

Maxwell was there, as brusque and businesslike as ever. The workshop had been cleared, save for the fire that glowed orange as soon as the boy worked the bellows. Chairs and a table had been set, rugs and tarpaulins placed over the machinery. Frederic came in first, followed by Havers then Knight himself. As lunch was served so cloaks and coats came off. Faces, fresh from the cold, flushed hot in the warmth.

No sooner had Knight begun to speak than Morgan sensed an air of relief rather than the despair they had been dreading. Perhaps he had known for sometime that there was little hope. Perhaps, deep underground, he and Havers had talked by the light of a guttering candle, standing together with water up to their calves and their heads stooped under the low roof. Wherever it was and however it had been done, John Knight had somehow learned the truth and overcome the disappointment that would have broken a lesser man.

"Just the two of them, eh Havers? Blue Gate and Deer Park? All the others dead."

"That's it, sir...well three with Hangley Cleeve. Trouble is the lodes ran dry...got down to sixty feet, like we did at Picked Stones. 'Tis easier enough to get that far but from then on the cost increases...bigger engines, lifting gear, more powerful pumps and so on. And with nothing to show I could hardly come begging again." The Northerner looked at Knight apologetically, his sunken eyes all but hidden by the black eyebrows. As he waited, he sniffed.

"And the others....Blacklands and all them?"

"Not even there, sir. You saw Whitfield Down the other day. Thought we had copper there but…" he grimaced. "Here, too. The Ulverston Company has done us proud though. Really thought we were on to something…but the old workings had us all hoodwinked." The miner checked himself and looked down. "Dreadful sorry, sir…we all are. You could see it yourself…the men hate it when it goes like this…hate it bad so they do."

Knight sat staring at the hot coals, his hair as tangled a mane as ever. As he did so his eyes widened slowly, mesmerised by the heat and glow that made them shine. The others knew that his moment had come and waited, respectful of the one who had to make the final decision. "You've done well, Havers. All of you have done me well…*but*, enough is enough. *Pah*…'tis one of those things…just one of those things. An' you reckon it's still there…down there somewhere?" For a moment his eyes glinted.

"No doubt, sir," Havers nodded sagely. "The whole place has the feel about it. It's down there somewhere that's fer sure."

"Your job one day, Freddy." He reached out behind him for his son's arm. "You know what's what and if you've a mind to have a go, and a damned good go at that; you know what your chances are. Right then…Maxwell, Morgan…Havers, all of you, that's it. Work stops." His hand came down on the table. "That's one decision…now the farms. Where do we stand?"

Raimond Maxwell was more fortunate, like all those whose privilege it is to bring welcome news. The roads would be cut, banked and surfaced within the coming year, so he reported, as would the tracks into the first of the farms. Thus far they had sited fifteen, over seven thousand acres in all. As the rough moorland was broken down and ploughed, so the first of the buildings would go up. Two hundred labourers would join the workforce in the spring. The land agent looked pleased. Knight sat slumped as though the report bored him.

"How long?"

"Three years, sir…perhaps two for the first three or four homesteads."

"Too long…far too long," Knight turned in his chair. "I'll be dead by then, dead an' gone. Why so?"

"Breaking the land, sir. That's what takes the time. 'Tis devilish hard for the ploughs. Then there're the hedges as well, nearly twenty miles of them and that's only the big enclosures."

"Hmmph…not going to be beaten am I? Beaten by nature again? Once is enough, you know."

Morgan saw the usual signs. "We can guarantee the project, sir." Knight swung round at his intrusion. The banker could see he had been stung by what he had just heard and cleared his throat. "Now you've given us the word we can boost the agricultural fund…just as Sir Crispin said. That'll give Maxwell far better resources and that's bound to speed things along."

"Is that so?"

"No doubt at all, sir." Maxwell sounded as relieved as he felt, for he, too, knew his master's moods. Knight might not have shown his displeasure but they all knew his pride had been wounded. It had happened before, when good men who had taken him for granted had been destroyed by the sudden wrath. The inside of a blacksmith's shop was no place to challenge John Knight.

"I would recommend you put everything into getting the first few up and running, sir." Morgan saw his chance to dispel any remaining doubt. "Concentrate our assets there then establish the others more slowly."

Knight rose, followed by the others. "Well, there we are. Seems reasonable enough." His hands were on the table. "I'll see it through, see these changes through…then stop and have a think." He paused then turned and lowered his shoulder so Maxwell could throw his cloak over his back. It was a little more hunched than hitherto, Morgan thought. Neither was the turn quite so swift, and the rasp in the voice had lost its edge.

3.

Jack was tired. The ride back from Dulverton with the two colts had been difficult, for the unbroken one was nervous and had played up throughout. He lay on his cot and glanced at the silhouette of his father that the tinker had painted for him the year Edward was born. The two locks of his hair that Emma had plaited were still tied to the frame. He undid them and blew off the dust then rubbed them against his cheek before replacing them carefully.

The room was comfortable, at least he could stand upright and the corner window had a view down to the river. The staircase, half-roofed over, was built inconveniently against the outside wall but Jenny Squires thought he would like the extra privacy and had offered him the room. Indeed he did, in particular because the sound of footsteps on the wooden stairs outside gave him plenty of warning. Everyone's steps were different and it was not long before he recognised whose they were, even what sort of mood they were in.

He half turned, still lying, and stretched out to feel the mud he and Hector had thumbed into the two cracks under the bulge in the plaster. It was solid, not even a sign of the damp that had left the green mark. The floorboards by the door had been more difficult. In the end, Dermot Ransom, the younger of the two carpenters, had replaced them but it had cost him nine pence. Abel Tarr had found him some carpet and an oak dresser with a broken leg which Ransom had mended. He was comfortable enough.

*

His mind went back to the time Dan Webber had come to see him before Christmas. Some time ago now but he remembered the conversation clearly. "'Tis that young Kenton Knight again, Jack." He had recognised his friend's boots on the stairs and had shouted for him to come in before he had time to knock. "Took a horse out without any of us knowing, not just once but twice now." Webber sat slumped in Jack's only chair. "Fairwind it was...brought him back lame and in one hell of a state. God knows what he'd been doing out there."

Jack had felt his anger rising. "What did you do about it?" he had asked.

Webber had shrugged and shifted uncomfortably. "Not much, I'm afraid. What could I do, man? Started last week...I asked him to check with me first. Like you said...so we'd have time to get things ready. Asked him proper, I did...no shoutin' nor nuthin'. Man just laughed at me." The groom had looked up help-lessly. "Laughed right in my face, then started getting all mouthy. So, I took it to Parker. Fat lot of help *he* was...told me 'twas none of his business and to see you." He had paused. "Watch out for that Kenton, Jack," he warned. "I can't take him. He's poison, he is."

*

Jack knew that Dan Webber was right. He knew all along but it had started to slip from his mind: maybe Dan had been exaggerating a bit or maybe he really had found the man difficult as well. Whatever, for months now, peace in the yard had been the order and already the New Year was in. Frederic had left for a month in London and there was still no sniff of trouble. Kenton Knight, it seemed, had learned at last.

But he had not. People like that never do and everyone must have heard the sudden dreadful commotion outside in the yard. A horse was struggling on the cobbles, plunging and kicking out. A voice was shouting, then another. Jack leapt from his bunk and ran.

"Will you bloody well...*stand still*" It was Kenton and he was lashing out wildly. "Damn you!" he lashed again at the horse's head. "Damn you!" Still the blows rained down. The animal reared up at the sting of the whip. "Stand *still*, you bastard," he yelled, tugging cruelly at the horse's mouth. "I said stand still you brute." Even now his whip was raised as he prepared to strike again.

"Stop that." Jack leapt at him, wrestling him away from the horse and twisting the whip from his grasp. Blood was welling from a cut at the base of the gelding's ear and the eye underneath had started to close. There were more angry cuts across the sweat soaked neck and shoulders. The animal was shiv-ering, snorting with fright. Its eyes were rolling.

"What the *devil* are you doing, man?" Kenton Knight half turned to answer but the animal lunged back and he was pulled round again.

195

"Get off me, Tucker." The words were spat as he tried to wrestle himself away. As he did so the horse broke free and bolted. "*Get* your filthy hands off me, damn you." He struck backwards with his elbows and kicked out but he was held easily.

Jack turned. "Get after Nero," he called over his shoulder to the lads with his arms still locked around the struggling figure. "Get away after him, quick...up the Exford track. Never mind saddling up," he shouted. "Just get out there quick." He had a mind to hurl the youth to the ground but released him instead.

"No horse ever deserved a thrashing like that, Master Kenton. What the devil was all that about?"

"Mind your own goddamned business," Kenton Knight backed away straightening his jacket. Jack could see the malice and hate. "How *dare* you manhandle me like that? How *dare* you?" he yelled. He continued to back off, deaf to any form of reason. "*That's it*...I've had enough of you throwing your weight around here." Now he was gasping for breath. "Why don't you get the hell out of here. Get out of here and back where you belong. Get out, damn you...you *peasant*."

The cruel insult stung and Jack wiped his mouth where Knight's oiled hair had brushed against him. Everywhere eyes were on them for the disturbance had drawn onlookers. More stable lads had come running and were gathered by the stalls. Two of them made light of something or other and one laughed out loud. From the corner of his eye, he could see figures in cottage doorways, somewhere a window had been thrown wide.

"This *is* my place, Master Kenton," he said in a measured tone. "I'm here on orders from your father and it's to him that I'll be speaking about this matter. Right now, sir...right now." He made to move then stopped. "And I don't know what the devil you lot are staring at either," he snapped at those watching. "Get on with your work. *Go on.*" he yelled. "*Now!*"

"Oh, to hell with you, Tucker." The words rang in Jack's ears but he ignored them. Swooping low to throw open the yard gate he strode purposefully towards the back of the manor. The scullery door crashed open causing the maids washing dishes to jump back as he stormed past and on into the kitchen where he stopped, white-faced and furiously incensed, just as Mrs Strong and two girls leapt from their chairs.

"Why, Jack, what the...."

"Thank you Mrs Strong but I need to see Mr Peterkin and see him now. Him or Mr Parker," Jack glared about him wildly with his chest heaving. "Where are they? *Come on, come on,*" his voice had risen angrily. One of the maids ran from the room.

"They're off, Jack, both of them...off until dinner." Mrs Strong's voice rose louder than his. "But what's all this about, for goodness sake? What's goin' on, Jack?"

Jack strode towards the hall door. "Right, then I'll see the Master himself. I'll soon...."

"*No!*" The sudden shout made him hesitate. A chair crashed to the floor as she dashed in front of him. "*Stop it*, Jack," she was desperate. "*Stop it this instant.* You *can't*...you can't just go running around in there like this. What d'you think they'd say? *Look* at you...look at your face. What's happened for good-ness sake? Tell me," her voice dropped.

"'Tis Master Kenton, Mrs Strong. I've had enough o' the man. Time and time again he does whatever he wants with the horses. Never tells us, never asks, just takes, takes, takes...and leaves 'em in a right old state. And just now I caught him whipping one of them. A right murderous thrashing it was too." He paused, struggling for breath. "Over my dead body does anyone do that to my horses. And then, and then," he gulped. "Then he turned on me swearing and cussing in front of the others. 'Tis him or me Mrs Strong, him or me. Why the rotten..."

"*Shhhh....*" The little cook put a hand on his arm. "Now *stop* it, Jack. That's no way to carry on. There's no need for it," she said quietly. "Don't go rushing in there like that. You'll only go saying things you'll regret and once said, they're said." She put her arm through his and led him towards the back door. "Best to let things calm a bit," she soothed. "I'll tell them what happened and that you want to see Mr Knight, proper like."

"'Tis no good us doing anything like that, Mrs Strong." His voice was raised again. "Don't know about the new man but Parker and that Kenton, Master Kenton...they see things together, they do. Eye to eye they are." He looked down at her. "I won't get nowhere like that...honest, I won't. That'll do no good, Mrs Strong."

"Oh yes it will," the tiny woman puffed herself up. "If he won't see Mr Knight, Jack, then *I will*. I'll make sure you get to see him, all right." They walked down the back steps together. "Now go steady, dear," she cautioned. "Don't go doing nothing silly, now. Nothing you'll regret later.

＊

Jack saw Mr Knight the following day. Knight had told Parker to remain in the room and the two listened as Jack told the sorry tale. It was the same as before and no easier this time but he told the whole story. The time had come. He missed nothing and could see it pained the father to hear the facts. The old man sat rock-like, staring down with his hair swinging free and his hands clasped together like a man in prayer. From time to time he nodded slowly, as if he knew already or at least that he understood. By the time Jack had finished, Knight's chin was resting on his hands.

"All right, Tucker...thank you," he said quietly, lifting his head. "I thought something like this would come to pass sooner or later...I'll see the boy." He rose from his chair. "Right, Tucker...Parker, thank you." The butler followed Jack from the study and closed the door behind them.

"So, Tucker," Parker turned in the dark passageway. "You said your piece and you didn't spare the Master's feelings, did you?" The two men walked on. "But don't go pushing your luck too far, Tucker. That's my advice...and I wouldn't forget it either."

"When I need your advice, Mr Parker, I'll ask for it." Jack strode on, ignoring the shout that came after him.

4.

Tom Sargent, the short, bald butler at Holnicote, the one who looked like a pompous carp, closed the double doors then turned back to face the long mahogany table. Adjusting his cuffs and shrugging at his collar, he glanced round, satisfying himself that everything was in order. Only then did he nod to the staff.

Lydia Acland had given much thought to the occasion. Combining the requirements of a winter evening with the celebration of Saint Valentine's night, she remembered also that it was the birthday of Harriet Amesbury. Furthermore, the Northboroughs were staying with the Knights and it was her turn to entertain she explained to Elizabeth-Jane. And this she had done, inviting them to stay together with the Amesburys and Westhams.

The silver had been a good idea. Just right for the occasion, she thought, but Sargent had foreseen a problem. The early Georgian plate did not hold the heat, thus extra staff had been brought from Exeter to facilitate the journey from the kitchens. As the liveried footmen moved behind the chairs to place cups of Bouillon en Tasse in front of the diners, so Sargent stalked imperiously from vantage point to vantage point. Lydia Acland fingered her sapphires again. She couldn't resist it for they were lovely, her best, and the fact that Amelia Northborough had been admiring them made her feel better still.

Elizabeth-Jane found herself between her host, Sir Thomas Acland, and one of his visitors. Viscount Amesbury, older, fatter and more grizzled than the others, with grey, curly hair and brown teeth, was on her left. Arthur, as he beseeched her to call him, rested his hand on her thigh just long enough for his intentions to become plain.

John Knight looked across at his wife and she smiled back at his wink. Both knew at once that the other was recalling the moments of tenderness in their room earlier when he had professed his love and she had responded. It was a sly, affectionate wink almost boyishly cheeky of him and it made her blush. She looked down hurriedly knowing exactly what was on his mind but her smile remained.

Amesbury, though, was persistent, the fingers of his crab-like hand forcing her to reach under the table to deal with the intrusion. She could tell her husband had noticed and her heart sank as his face began to darken. It was going to spoil their evening but the music came to their rescue, giving her the excuse to throw up her hands in delight and to twist herself free from his grasp.

Steeling himself by pulling one of his more miserable faces, her husband unfolded his spectacles before reaching out. Still frowning, as though the taste in his mouth was bitter, he picked up the programme of music, lifted his head to see better and glanced wearily at what it had to say but with no idea as to what it was all about. Elizabeth-Jane, he knew, was watching him and their eyes met again. One smiled then the other but it was the ugly face he pulled that made her laugh with relief.

✳

Music Programme
Holnicote House
Tuesday 14th February 1834.

To be played whilst Dinner is served.

1. Boccherini   Opus 13, Number 5 for strings.
2. Schubert   Quintet in A, Fourth Movement "The Trout."
3. Beethoven   Piano sonata Opus 24. "Spring."
4. Haydn   Songs "My mother bids me bind my hair."
5. Rossini   Songs "La Danza."
6. Sea Shanties A selection in honour of the promotion of Lieutenant Charles Acland R.N.

✳

Following the bouillon came plump roast partridges and woodcock from the estate together with chicken and lobster pies and scalloped pigeon, all in preparation for the main course of the evening – a haunch of venison taken from Horner Woods. Lydia Acland had overseen the preparation herself, watching closely as the cook marinated the meat in claret and fresh vegetables where it lay for more than a day before being committed to the open fire. There it was to be roasted in the time-honoured fashion, she ordained, well larded and basted repeatedly with a sauce of junipers, mixed peppers and herbs. Lemon sherbert, oranges and quinces in jelly concluded the meal along with raspberries in redcurrant water-ice, damsons and morello cherries.

✳

Less than an hour after the meal, when the menfolk had rejoined the ladies in the south drawing room, the music master presented himself and the dancing began, once again organised by their hostess. Frederic, rather than Kenton, approached Katherine first and yes, she most certainly would be pleased to accept his hand.

First came the gaillard and the pavane followed by the more modern minuets and gavottes and finally, as a special treat, the outrageously daring new waltz from Vienna. The young, Lydia Acland surmised, would love it and she had arranged for the music master to call out the turns and the drills in time. Everyone, she had decreed, would have to dance. There could be no exceptions, it was simply a must.

"Enough, Freddy, enough...I'm roasting." Katherine's arms dropped by her side. "It's so hot, gracious it is...*too* hot. Let's get some air...out in the cool."

Soon they were alone and walked slowly together down the hall past where the musicians were taking their break and then on and into the gallery. Nobody but a footman passed them. "Well," Katherine, with her arm through Frederic's glanced behind her. "Have you seen him?" she asked. "Jack, I mean." The breeze came from somewhere and she brushed at her hair.

"Yes, of course," he gave a little laugh. "I see him every day up at Simonsbath."

"Don't laugh at me, Freddy," she squeezed his arm. "Please don't. I'd love to see him and I can't help it. You know I do, I told you so months ago." For a time they were silent. "Even if only for a few minutes...and tonight, here...of all nights." She stopped and pulled away from him, then turned.   "Freddy, it's awful." One hand reached out for his arm. "How can I possibly wait 'til spring. I mean, we're not coming down again until May...*May* for goodness sake. How can I contact him? Just to let him know how I feel...to let him know how much I long to see him again?" Her face was searching his and her look caused him to pause. Then he nodded slowly, yet still he hesitated.

"Katherine...listen," he begged at last. "Just listen to me." He had pulled her closer. "Are you sure? Really sure about all this? No, no, don't get like that." He raised his hand. "Listen...I know how you feel and I understand. At least I think I do. But the others...your mother, and father. For Heaven's *sake*...even if they were to hear such thoughts the world would go mad. The Heavens themselves would simply fall in. It would be the end...you *must* see that."

"I know, I know, I know...yes, I do know." Katherine nodded, then drew in her breath. "You're right," she sighed. "I know you are. Dear, dear Freddy, you've been so good and so kind. But...it's hopeless." Her eyes were appealing for help. "I adore him, Freddy," she whispered. "Don't ask me why or how. It's not just that he's such a madly attractive man. It's not that, not at all," she insisted before checking herself again. "I've never felt like this before...never have I been so certain. I can't explain it...and most likely never will."

"But how *can* you tell...how can you *possibly* say you know, like that? Give yourself time...time to think...to be sure. A year or so, perhaps. Now Florence...you talked about going there," Frederic knew it was no good. "Just a year or so, to see how you feel...to think...to compare him with others you'll meet...to give yourself more time." Even as he was speaking her head was shaking. "Please, Katherine. Can't you see...see the danger?"

"No Freddy...I couldn't wait. I could never do that. I love him...I really do."

"But listen...love is something that has to endure...and *last*, for Heaven's sake. D'you think that *this* will last, I mean stand the test when people find out...as they must. What then?" he asked ducking forward until he could see into her eyes. "Will you be able to stay with him then...go through all the terrible strife." He paused. "D'you realise all this, Katherine...really and honestly? You will be an outcast."

"Yes, I do Freddy...really and honestly. It's been months now, years since I knew. I haven't looked at anyone else, haven't wanted to...I couldn't bear it. It's him and only him...honestly."

"Then write to him." It was a desperate idea but anything to buy time. "Why not send him a note?" He watched as she checked herself, for a moment still in thought, before looking up. He could see the gleam of hope. "That'll bring you a bit closer," he continued. "I mean he'll know it's you. He'll know it was your hand which scrolled the words, *your* hand that held the paper." Frederic had his hands on hers. "It's not exactly as though you'll be there with him, not the same but...but it's next best. If you write a note, a little 'bon mot,' I'll see he gets it."

"Why not?" Katherine bit her lip. "Why not indeed? Listen. There's paper and ink in the salon. Next to the library...over there. I know it's there for I've seen Delia at the desk." She put a hand on his chest. "But, listen. Go back and see what's happening. See if anyone's missing us. I'll take this lamp. Now then," she was half talking to herself. "It won't take long, just a few lines to tell him...oh, I don't know...just that I'm thinking of him."

It took him no time at all. Nobody, as far as he could see, could have cared less about their absence. The musicians were back in the orangerie waiting for the order to start. His brothers were talking to Herbert Preston and barely looked up as he passed them while his mother was in the drawing room with Lydia Acland and Daphne Westham. When he passed the door of the hunting room, he heard the duke's voice and his father's laugh, no doubt admiring the Acland hunting trophies and portraits. They sounded well settled and would be there for some time. Everybody, as far as he could see, was happily disposed and only when they gathered again to dance would he and Katherine be missed. There was time but he needed to be quick.

She was at the desk, the light from the lamp falling across her face. Frederic watched as she paused, tickling the end of her nose with the quill before dipping it back into the silver inkwell once more. She wrote slowly and methodically, biting her lip and with her head low over her work as she concentrated. "I won't use the sand, it'll make a mess, but I can't find the wax or signet block." She went on writing without looking up. "Have a look in the drawers for me."

"Better not the wax," he replied. "The smoke'll give us away. Just fold it and trust me."

"I've got to anyway, haven't I?" she laughed, glancing up. "I mean if anything happens and this get's found," she shook her head slowly. " Phew...oh dear...as you said, they'd go mad, all of them...quite, quite mad." She waved the paper gently and blew. "It'll dry in a minute. Here...you might as well see what I've written." She watched as he read quickly and saw him gasp.

"*Freddy...Freddy...Katherine.*" Kenton Knight's voice rang out in the gallery. "Where the devil are you?" As he made his way towards them, his footsteps rang out on the tiled floor.

"Here...quick." Frederic snatched at the note, folded it hurriedly and put it in his inside pocket.

"A-ha, so...surprise, surprise. What's all this then? And what *have* we got here?" Kenton stood in the doorway. His white tie was askew. He was hot and flushed yet his eyes were gleaming in triumph. "And *what*, might I ask, are you two up to? Tucking ourselves away in the library are we, brother dear? And what next, might I ask, sweet Kate?"

"Oh, for God's sake Kenton..." Frederic gritted his teeth.

"Don't be so childish, Kenton," Katherine chided, relieved that his suspicions ran thus. "Anyway, why *can't* I have a few minutes with Freddy? What's it got to do with you?" But she laughed gaily and moved closer to adjust a dress stud on the newcomer's shirt. "Come Kenton, I can assure you your brother's behaviour has been beyond reproach...entirely befitting the gentleman he is." Still smiling she patted his cheek affectionately and the music began.

"In that case you'll just have to take this dance with me," Kenton reached out for her hand. "Excuse us, dear boy."

"My pleasure." Frederic returned his bow and watched them go, wondering at the mind of this beautiful woman who was so determined and who seemed so set on throwing everything away. She had so much to offer. He had seen that and he, too, had been drawn by her beauty and that wonderful carefree spirit. He reached for the note but checked himself. Envy, he knew, was something he was going to have to battle against; it was a powerful emotion better left dormant rather than roused and inflamed.

Chapter Thirteen

Kenton Knight was in an excellent mood. The last few days had been a success and only yesterday a letter from Viscount Amesbury had arrived inviting him to join their house party for the Derby. How much more preferable to stay and be pampered at Walton Grange where everything would be organised, rather than having to take sordid lodgings with his friends. But, even better, were the sweet memories of the Holnicote party.

Both Katherine and Lizzie Darcy had danced beautifully and told him how much they were looking forward to their visit in the spring. They had enjoyed his company, of that he was sure, and Katherine had given the clearest of signals that she was grateful to have been rescued from his brother.

Nothing had been said but he remembered the soft touch of her hand as they danced the second pavane, how she had held his hand when turning away, and how quickly she had taken it up again and...*how* she had enjoyed it all. Even now he could hear her laughter. Once, as they came together, their bodies had brushed, only briefly and gently but he saw by the look in her eyes that she had noticed it. Yes, she *had* noticed, he knew she had, and had enjoyed the encounter.

And then there had been the waltz. Only a few knew the steps and they had led, turning and turning in time to the music with his brother and her father among those watching. The duke had nodded encouragingly, his face beaming with pleasure. Suddenly the Spring looked fun. Frederic, always the man of the moment at house parties, would have to take account of his younger brother.

Although Lizzie was not so keen, Kenton knew Katherine loved to ride out. He would see to it that they did so together for the moor abounded with wonderful, secret valleys and hollows where they could picnic together. He was seized with the desire to see her alone, where she would, at last, be free to demonstrate her affection. Where this would lead them he had no idea but the thought of the two of them together once more filled him with a sudden yearning.

*

Kenton rubbed his hands together but the tinkling chime of his French mantel clock made him start. They were late. "Dale...Dale! Where are you for God's sake?" Dressed in nothing more than an open, collarless shirt and his breeches and stockings, he stood in the bedroom doorway. Cursing impatiently, he ignored the neat bob of a parlour maid as she slipped past, her eyes averted respectfully. "Dale," he shouted, walking across the landing.

"Coming right away Master Kenton, " John Dale, his valet, looked up from the hall. "Just checking your boxes, sir," he called.

"Well come on, man. Jump to it. We're away shortly. And make sure my evening dress is pressed and packed."

Minutes later Dale knocked on the bedroom door. "Beggin' your pardon, sir. But I'm afraid your set of tails are not ready yet...still very wet after last night and your second pair's still at the tailors. Can't have you taking them like that, sir." He thought for a moment, aware of the likely response. "Why not borrow Master Frederic's, like you did a month back? He never minds, sir...besides, he took his old set off to Portsmouth, last week, so 'e did."

"Right, let's have them...but I'll need to check them first. Then get the rest of the things together and packed. Now hold on." He paused. "Tell Lord Preston's man that we should be away on the hour, no later."

"Very good, sir."

Kenton stood while Dale helped him into his brother's coat then walked over to the mirror and swung round, looking down at the lie of the tails behind him. "Mmm, they seem right enough. I'll call when I'm ready. That's all."

He turned back to face the mirror once more, adjusting the lapels and cuffs. Without thinking he slipped his hand inside. It was there, in the small left hand inside pocket. Frowning and curious, he opened the paper and walked towards the bay window seat where the light was better, reading as he went.

Half way across the room he stopped dead, standing as if carved from stone.

The note was short and well written. He read it quickly, raced through it a second time, then again, this time more slowly. "Ye *gods*," he gasped. "What is this? It *can*not be so...*can*not be so." But he recognised her writing. "Dear God alive," he wiped his mouth. "It's just not possible." He raised the letter to his nose recognising instantly her delicate perfume then let his hand fall. Still unable to believe himself he read the letter yet again, this time by the open window. His heart was pumping furiously.

✳

Holnicote House,
Selworthy,

Dear Jack,

Tonight, Saint Valentine's, finds us so close but not, dear man, close enough. Since I first saw you that day at Simonsbath, I have thought of little else and knew at once it was fate - that we were destined to meet. Our lives, our lineage and upbringing in this world are entirely different yet I believe our future lies together. Each time we meet I feel more certain.

When fate strikes like this, it is as if some unseen, incomprehensible power guides us, but from which we cannot escape. Our future has been preordained and we must accept it as such.

I cannot explain why this is so, merely beg you to understand that my heart yearns for us to be together again. This comes with my deepest regard, my affection and my love.

Katherine.

*

"My God, woman, you're *mad*, quite, quite mad…and as for you…why, you jumped-up, scheming *bastard!*" He raised his hands as if to crunch the letter into a ball then stopped. "Ohhh…no," he chuckled grimly. "Ohh…no, no, no. That's far too kind. Far, far too kind."

He crossed to his bed and sat heavily, toying with the letter, now consumed by a wild, burning rage. No *wonder* Katherine Darcy had flirted with him. No *wonder* she had danced so provocatively and given him the glad-eye. She had been drawing him away from his brother and their wretched, filthy little plot. She had used him, played on his best intentions. How dare she…how *dare* she do that. What a fool he had been, how naïve. But now the tables were turned.

Kenton knew he had his faults. Ever since he could remember he had been at the centre of family disputes, of rows with the staff, and the object of his father's wrath. When he was small they had to prise him away from Freddy or Charles after he had flown at them, kicking and biting, or rescue Margaret and Isabella from his taunts. He had grown into a lonely child, bitter, jealous and unloved.

Time and again at Charterhouse, they had come for him, making him pay dearly for his sudden outbursts of rage and his sharp tongue. The older boys had held him down and whipped him for his high opinions of himself and his arrogance. But he had ridden the storms until he was in the senior house: then he had hit back.

The fags and junior boys were terrified of him and that was satisfying. A beating by Knight in the locker room was something to be feared, the mere threat gave him a sense of power. The sight of the younger boys in the washroom or dormitories showing the cuts where his cane had bitten deeply, gratified him. He knew it was cruel and that was the way he was.

But, through it all, he had learned the meaning of caution, to watch carefully those on whom he sought to impose his will, to plot with precision before the hunt began. Only very occasionally these days did his temper get the better of him as it did the other day with Tucker in the yard. He had cursed himself for that but, this time, there would be no rush to confrontation. He would wait, savouring this piece of luck. He had the upper hand. It thrilled and it was an opportunity not to be wasted.

His options were numerous, the possibilities endless but he would take his time, moving only when he was ready. He read the letter again, the tiny valentine hearts she had drawn churning his stomach, then he folded it carefully and reached out for the leather-bound bible by his bed. Inside the back cover, the thick paper next to the binding board had become detached and he slipped the note between. Once, years previously, he had hidden a note from a younger boy there, in which the youth had professed his undying love. It had never been found.

*

"Damn and blast…the wretched animal's cast a shoe." They were a mile out of Exford, on the high ground to the west. Herbert Preston pulled up, dismounted and picked up the near foreleg. "By the saints…look at that." He wrestled with the shoe, which had but one nail remaining and held it up. "Off, clean as a whistle."

"Well, get back up," Kenton said impatiently. "We need to trot on, we're behind as it is."

"Steady on," Preston's owl-like face looked up from where he was bending over the hoof. "That's asking for trouble. No…I'll walk or the brute'll go dead lame. Honestly. Send the lads on ahead to clear the way…tell them to warn the farrier then we'll take a bite at The White Horse."

It was the middle of a working day so the taproom was not crowded. The few who were gathered around the open fire fell silent, immediately curious at the two finely dressed strangers now removing their cloaks. "Who's there? Hullo, hullo." Kenton Knight banged the flat of his hand on the counter then swung round and smirked. His look was more of a challenge than a greeting to those watching, causing heads to turn away in embarrassment. The silence that followed was waiting to be broken.

The newcomers, now with their coats open and elbows on the bar, surveyed their companions and the sparsely furnished surroundings. The room smelt of wood ash and wet dogs but there were none to be seen. Although noon, it was difficult to see clearly for the tiny, latticed windows let in little of the winter gloom.

The light from the fire flickered against the smoke-stained plaster and the faces of the ones nearest the chimney. Two men, the taller and heavier dressed in a drover's smock, the other thin and stooped, both now uncomfortable with this sudden invasion, eased their way self-consciously past the outstretched legs.

Kenton ignored them, rather he leaned forward.

"Don't I know you?" he asked. The woman, youngish and dark haired, and dressed in her drab working smock was sitting by the bread oven. Her shawl had seen better days, as had her clogs that she had removed leaving her bare feet, earthy and bone-hard, as near to the fire as the heat would allow.

"You worked at Simonsbath? At the manor...surely? In the kitchens, with Mrs Strong. Yes?" Kenton remained where he was, pleased with himself for creating the suddenly uncomfortable atmosphere. The woman had kept silent hoping not to be recognised but, now trapped, she whispered hurriedly to the man behind her and rose. "I've seen your face before," Kenton persisted. "I know I have."

"Meg's the name, sir, if it pleases you." Now the centre of attraction, she blushed at the sound of her own voice. "Meg Braddon as was, sir, when I were at Simonsbath," she laughed nervously. "Now I'm Smales, Meg Smales, sir. Me and Tom was married and live down 'ere now."

"Ah, yes," Kenton nodded, every eye back on him once more. "I see, I see. Well now." For a moment he appeared undecided. "That's good to hear...and this is your man, here...you, sir?" The figure crouched by the fire ignored him. If anything he turned closer to the wall.

"No, sir, no." Meg chuckled throatily, glancing round for some form of help. One, a fair-headed youngster, sniggered but nobody else moved. "'Tis not Tom, sir...he's away. 'Tis my brother here, sir. Josiah...Josie Braddon."

Kenton stepped forward. "Your acquaintance, my good...."

"Beg pardon, sir," Meg moved between the two. "Pardon me, like, but Josie's a bit...well," she paused, glancing warily at the seated figure. "Sometimes, he feels a bit shamed when he's with strangers, sir, a bit awkward like."

"Away with yer, maid." As it growled, so the figure, short and wiry, twisted itself up from the stool. Those watching saw the glint of a thick, gold watch chain swinging from his tattered waistcoat, once yellow and patterned but now dirty and torn. The black frock coat was patched and thread bare. He reached above his head, clasping hold of a leather strop nailed to a beam for just such a purpose. Now steady, he turned and stared at the man who had disturbed him.

Kenton shrank. His jaw dropped and his eyes bulged. The deep, purple scar began high above the stump of his right ear. It traversed the forehead as a furrow might cross a field, disappeared under the eye patch, then reappeared on the cheek, now empty of flesh. It crossed both lips to finish star-shaped on the chin. The whole side of his head had been scalped clean and his mouth sliced open. The two regarded each other in silence.

"Ye Gods." Kenton stammered weakly. "Oh, I do beg your pardon, sir. My...my most sincere apologies...I'm so sorry."

"Be not sorry, sir." He lifted his stubbled face high so his one good eye could see more clearly. "Never be sorry," he chortled. His audience waited while he cleared his throat then further while he caught his breath. "But be well advised by what you see here. 'Tis the mark of a sabre, sir. Delivered by a wild ruffian high up on the moors above Sandyway. Years back now...but's taken its time to mend."

"Tell me about it if you will." Kenton reached for his tankard. "Quite took my breath away, sir. But tell me...one hears tales of such things. Perhaps it's something we should know about."

✳

By the time the party set out for Tiverton, the weather had closed in. The wind had risen and flurries of snow swept round them as they leant into the steep climb out of Exford, spurring on their horses to a brisk trot.

"I've heard of that fellow," Kenton held on to his top hat, shouting through his upturned collar. "I'll wager he's the one. The one they all talk about. The one who worked the Sandyway road...between here and North Molton. A nasty fella to all accounts...used to give his victims a hard time, so they say. But listen, Herbert. Listen, I'll tell you something else."

Kenton chuckled at the idea. "If he had that done to him all those years ago and it happened where he said...hey, d'you hear?" He pulled down his collar and shouted above the wind. "I said if that's the case then I'm pretty sure I know who did it...I remember the talk at home about the staff clashing with high-waymen." They were riding close, side-by-side, heads down. Kenton paused, it was indeed a good idea.

"I'm damned sure I know who did it and I'm damned sure the fella and his friends back there would like to know as well. Come on."

2.

Amos Naylor sat back in the tattered armchair and stretched his legs. Unsure whether his tankard was empty or not he turned it slowly until it was upside down. It was and he swore. The stone jar with the rest of the ale was across the room on top of the broken-legged dresser. He considered a refill, his piggy eyes staring blearily as he weighed it up, but slothfulness won. He could not summon the energy and remained slumped, irritated at having to go without.

He belched, pulled the shirt from his leather belt and scratched deep inside his trousers, down below his white belly to the hairs where the lice were restless. Upstairs he could hear her putting the child to bed. Amos hawked, hawked a second time and swilled the phlegm around his mouth while he thought. She was an idle cow, he decided, good enough for one thing only and not much else. He kicked out at the mess of dirty clothes and broken clogs around him. Shaking his head in disgust he swore again and spat into the fire then watched as the thick ball of spittle sizzled in the embers.

Problems at the Tiverton mill were getting worse. Orders had fallen and the workforce had dwindled, several leaving to seek better wages in Exeter and the dockyards at Plymouth. Wages had been cut and he had had to throw his weight around to get the daily schedule finished. Amos, a great bull of a man, shrugged. His job was secure and if others were suffering that was their concern.

He and two others ran the floors of the mill, and they ran it as it should be run. A bit of muscle never hurt. Amos Naylor, Reg Carver and Zachy Hamer kept the place going and everyone knew it. Either people *kept* out of their way or were *kicked* out of their way. The manager had demanded more from them, told them to drive harder and they had obliged. Reg and Zachy had their ways and Amos Naylor had his. The back of his plate-sized hands or a tickle from the leather soon had the idlers and latecomers jumping. Everyone, from the looms and bobbins on the fifth floor down to the sorting shed, knew Amos. He scratched the back of his neck and frowned. It had been quite a day.

*

Much earlier he had been called into the manager's office. "You're in for a move, Naylor." Mr Avebury, the manager, wheezed as he struggled for breath. He nodded at the second man in the room. "Mr Jowett here's from the new lace factory." Naylor was on guard. He sensed trouble and watched the manager closely.

To him all managers needed watching, especially Avebury. There was something about his scrawny little body that revolted him. Perhaps it was his wheeze or his unhappy face. Amos did not like managers and this one in particular. He was a sickly creature, a runt of a man, the mere sight of him was enough. Decisions were made behind his door that made or broke those on the work floor. Amos was never going to be a manager, they had told him that. Something was amiss and he scowled.

"A move, Mr Avebury?" Naylor's ginger eyebrows ran into one another. "Not sure I understand?"

"Not your job to understand the whys and wherefores." Avebury sucked more air into his lungs and surveyed the buckle of the belt in front of him. "*Why* we're moving you, Naylor, is of no concern to you but Mr Jowett here has asked us for help. The Leat Street factory needs a new floor manager...a foreman of works."

Amos Naylor squinted, his little eyes flitting from one to the other as he struggled with the news. "But I thought you needed me here, Mr Avebury." He stepped forward and pointed at the floor. "Ain't we got problems enough 'ere? Falling orders, men going absent and that? Wanted the place kept moving, that's what you said."

It was not easy to smile at Naylor's pock-marked face but Jowett, the other man, tried. "It's all right, Mr Naylor, there's no need for alarm. It's you I'm after," he smiled disarmingly. "Both Mr Avebury and I've discussed the matter with the owners...Mr Swayne and his brothers are happy to release you. We're all agreed that Carver and Hamer can run things here. Isn't that so, Mr Avebury?" He nodded, confirming his own statement. "Yes, you see...Mr Heathcoat's new lace factory's been difficult to get off the ground and I need your help. That's why I'm here and that's what this is all about." Naylor frowned at nothing in particular and began to pick at one of his ears.

That afternoon he toured the lace factory with Jowett. It was a mess. The machinery in the weaving rooms was dirty. The floors were unswept and the storerooms ran with water. He lost count of how many empty chairs and silent looms he saw. Jowett asked what he thought and he told him. The place wanted tightening up. It was sloppy and it needed a firm hand.

"Can you do it?" Jowett asked. "I can tell you now, I've paid good money for your services and I'll pay you well, too." The manager pursed his lips and fiddled with the papers on his desk. The presence of Naylor was uncomfortable. "I'll double yer mill salary, Naylor, and I'll find yer a decent house. But I want that floor sorted. D'yer hear? That's the bargain...sort the place, no questions. Just get it straightened and moving. Yer start Monday morning, bobbin nets open by five."

※

Amos Naylor sat up in his chair, spat again and looked at his stone jar. Just time for one more before he went out. Oh yes, the day had been different that was for sure. Wait until Carver and Hamer heard about it. "Can I do it?" he muttered, heaving himself out of the chair. "Can I bloody do it? What does Jowett know about graft...fat little sod. Come Monday and I'll show 'em.

"'Ere," he yelled, scratching his back. "Come down 'ere woman ...an' clean up this mess. Place stinks...look at the state of it. Come *on*," he bellowed. "Get down 'ere, I want a word, I do...now."

Charlotte came down the stairs. She stepped ponderously, her clogs clumping on the bare boards as she picked her way. Naylor sneered. She was pregnant again making her short, dumpy figure look worse than ever. "Look at the state of this," Amos kicked at a pile of clothes. "And the table here...*hell's teeth*." His hand swept the remnants of supper to the floor. A milk jug smashed as it hit the hearth, the sour, curdled contents flooding into the ash.

"Come on woman, for Christ's sake." She held up an arm to ward off the blow but it was too heavy and she sank to the floor. She made no attempt to move, just sat there with one arm supporting herself, the other holding her head where Naylor's hand had struck.

"Get up, you black slag." He bent down and hauled her back to her feet. "Get this bloody tip cleared up," he shouted. "It's filthy...stinks it does." Charlotte cowered, now crying quietly.

"Sorry, Amos," she whimpered. "I'm sorry. I was going to do it once Davey was down...honestly."

"*Damn* him," he cursed. "*Who* comes first here? 'Im or me? 'Oo brings the money home, eh? 'Oo goes out and grafts away twelve hours a day, eh? And what do I find when I get back? This," he kicked a shoe across the room. "If it weren't for me, you'd be nowhere, *nowhere*." His thick finger jabbed her chest time and again until she gasped and caught her breath. "I got you out of that farm hovel, didn't I? Knee deep in muck it was. Brought you here, put a roof over your head and filled your belly. Look at the state of the place. Sort it out, woman."

*

Later that night, as the cottage door slammed, Davey Tucker woke with a start. The little boy could hear everything. There was stumbling and cursing and the sound of someone being sick, then the heavy footsteps on the stairs. The floor-boards on the other side of the thin wall creaked. He heard voices, quiet at first, then his father's raised in anger. He could hear his mother's soft tone as she answered him, then, her voice too, was raised. But she was pleading with him, begging. Then came the first slap of the heavy belt, then another. Terrified, he screwed his eyes tight shut and balled his fists, willing the noise to go away.

3.

Kenton Knight sat at the leather-tooled mahogany desk in his room: he had been there since breakfast. The late February sun had barely risen above the high ground beyond the stable block and his sitting room was gloomy. He had found it difficult to work so had called for the lamps to be lit then told the servants to leave him in peace.

Katherine Darcy's letter was on the desk as was a sheaf of paper, a number of quills and his silver Italian inkstand, garishly decorated with hunting dogs. His immediate reaction had been to destroy the letter then wait for events to unfold as the Darcy sisters – he had no doubt that Lizzie was involved as well – sought to reopen contact.

She would hardly be stupid enough to write directly to Tucker, although the tone of her letter suggested she might do anything. Rather she would be far more likely to use Frederic as courier again. In that case, Parker, he knew, could be relied upon to advise him if any mail arrived for his brother bearing the Northborough seal. The problem was that there were too many imponderables and, unless he was careful, he would lose control of the situation.

His next idea, and it had been the one that amused him most, was to substitute the letter for one composed and written by himself, twisting events and emotions. Such a letter might convey Katherine's affection far more passionately, enough to encourage Tucker to respond boldly when they met. *That* would cause chaos when the family visited. Conversely he could write expressing her severe displeasure at his over-familiarity, warning him in no uncertain terms to mind his place.

He had sat for hours copying her hand writing, checking the loops and practising the cross strokes and pressures. Time and again he had begun but the right play on words eluded him, the balls of paper at his feet bearing testimony to his efforts. The more he struggled the more he realised how impractical such an idea was. Subsequent events would be almost impossible to control and there was always a danger that such a letter might rebound. But the possibilities fascinated him and he had returned to the idea again before finally discarding it.

In the end he decided to make a copy of Jane's letter and allow it to run, but to seal it so the secret could not be revealed. He had considered this the day before, on his way back from seeing Herbert Preston on to the stage at Tiverton. It was the simplest solution and would absolve him of guilt. He would be able to monitor Tucker's reaction, alerting Parker to look out for any subsequent mail, and he would have time to prepare himself for the Northboroughs' Spring visit. Then, at a time and place of his choosing, he would unmask the affair. Frederic was involved already and would inevitably be drawn in more deeply, but the principal casualties would be the groom and Katherine Darcy herself.

He glanced out of the window and watched idly as a heavy-laden timber cart approached the narrow bridge over the Barle. One of the woodmen jumped down and ran ahead to direct the driver between the parapets. Pushed forward by the weight of timber, the six dun-coloured oxen ambled down the slope before taking the strain again for the last steep climb away from the river and on to the sawmill. As the carter's two dogs chased a cat into one of the hay barns, he stood to get a better view.

Settling back once more, he took up his quill and scribbled on some rough paper until he was satisfied with the flow of ink, then made a copy of her letter, word for word. He assumed that Tucker had not seen her writing before, nonetheless he took pains to copy her hand. The thought that the man could read at all irritated him. Why his mother had decided to educate the staff he had no idea. It was dangerous…they shouldn't be taught to think. Far better to leave them as the simple illiterate peasants they had always been.

When he had finished he folded it carefully, lit a candle and allowed several drops of scarlet wax to fall where the edges of the letter met. Taking his own signet block, he wet it with his tongue then pressed gently into the wax. Before lifting the seal he gave it a twist to erase any impression of the Knight arms then repeated the exercise. Folding the original letter, he slipped it back into the space at the back of his bible. "Finished!" he exclaimed, waving the letter to dry the seals. "Huzzah!" he stood up, stretched and kissed the letter.

*

"Ah, Dale," Kenton turned to his valet who had responded to the bell. "Take my shirt and the beige pantaloons and give them a clean. And the black boots as well."

"Very good, sir." The manservant collected the clothes and backed towards the door. "Will that be all, Master Kenton?"

"Thank you, Dale." He waited until the valet had left the room then called nonchalantly. "Oh, one other thing." Without turning he held out the letter. "Get this across to the stables, will you. It's for Tucker…came from Holnicote with a whole lot of stuff about hunting and so on. Probably to do with the horses…let Tarr sort it out."

"Very good, sir."

*

An hour later Jack had the letter in his hand. When Abel Tarr told him that it had come from Holnicote he felt his heart jump. Whether that had been the sudden thrill of expectation or the chill of fear, or just plain surprise he was unable to tell. Whatever the reason his fingers fumbled as he broke open the seals.

For several days after his mind was in turmoil. It was beyond his comprehension but there was nobody in whom he could confide. His one hope, Master Frederic, was away when the mail packet from Holnicote arrived and would know nothing about it. He dared not go to Holnicote, even under the pretext of being sent there, and ask the staff. Even if they had been privy, he would be sent packing for daring to broach such a subject. Worse still, if they knew nothing about it, he would have betrayed Katherine.

"Come on Jack dear, eat up." Jenny Squires fussed over him. "Not been yerself at all these last few days."

"Love…that's what 'tis." Stan, her husband, sitting hunched over his plate, glanced up. "One of they kitchen maids round the back of the main 'ouse, I'll be bound." He chewed stolidly and took a long swig from his tankard. "'Ere," he paused, before swallowing and wiping his mouth. "'Ere, now…not got one of 'em into trouble or nuthin' 'ave yer?" Stan Squires, with one eyebrow raised in curiosity, glanced at his wife and grinned mishievously.

"Stop talking like that Stanley Squires. They're very nice girls...they are." Jenny took his plate and brushed away the crumbs. "Anyways, Jack's not like that. Are you, dear? There's no need to go thinking like that."

"No, 'tis none of that," Jack shook his head and grinned ruefully. "'Tis nothing, Jen. Just not meself today...that's all 'tis."

*

The soft glow of the lamp was barely enough for him to read the letter one more time before he let his hand fall onto the cot mattress. He looked up at the ceiling and sighed, the fingers of his other hand tickling the back of Scamp's neck. Even now he was unable to identify his true emotions. He should have been scared, terrified of the dangers of which there were many. To be caught even looking at such a high-born lady was asking to be horsewhipped and thrown out.

And this young woman, writing like she did and suggesting goodness knows what, was from one of England's great families...one of *the* greatest. He had seen the pomp and the might, the lifestyle and the sheer power of these people, not to mention the vast, unbelievable wealth...the clothes, the jewels, the finery and the horses. It was a different world as Parker had once told him and he grimaced at the memory. It was a world where they behaved differently, thought differently and spoke differently. A world where they knew nothing about dirt or graft and sweat.

He should have been trembling but he was not. There was an extraordinary sensuality about the woman that would have captivated men of all ages. There was grace and beauty, power and riches, all of that in abundance but there was a softness about her too, a gentleness he had not seen in her sort before. For sure he had wanted her, and when he had seen that expression in her eyes and had felt her against him, it had been like resisting the very devil himself. But resist her he had, and it was not fear alone that had put a hand on his shoulder. There had been something rare and precious about her that had struck a deep chord.

What, he wondered, had been going through her mind all these months to make her write like this. Surely to goodness she had suitors galore; elegant dandies, titled noblemen, dashing army officers...the Aclands, Frobishers, Bamfyldes – the Knights themselves. What was wrong there? Could it be possible that she had forsaken all of them for *him*, a humble, low-born groom hidden away in the wilds of Exmoor?

It made no sense, no sense at all, yet he had lived long enough to realise that many things in life made little sense. Perhaps she really did feel for him. Perhaps it was something more than a moment of earthy lust on a warm summer evening. Perhaps, perhaps...he could go on forever but if those were indeed her feelings then he was not afraid. Wary, yes. Very wary, but not afraid.

4.

Dogs darted out then scuttled back to bark from a safer distance as Frederic and Jack, followed closely by Leonard and Hector Coward trotted briskly up Barnstaple's Boutport Street. The noisy clatter of hooves on cobbles ceased suddenly as they turned onto the sand of Bear Street and headed north.

After waiting months, they had set out the day before, spending the night with Parson Russell at Swimbridge. Today they had risen long before the Spring dawn, stopping briefly for oatcakes and ale at The Barley Mow further down the street. Even now the early May sun had barely climbed above the far rooftops and the streets were still empty save for the homeless, huddled in doorways under what cover they could pull over themselves.

Ebberley Lawn barracks was different. Even as they slowed to walk their horses the last few yards they could hear shouts and the call of bugles. Cavalry troopers leading strings of horses were leaving the camp through the tall, metal gates. Soldiers were hurrying in for duty and the appearance of a gig or brougham signalled the arrival of somebody important.

The guard, a trooper dressed in a scarlet jacket and white breeches, and wearing a tall, green-plumed shako, lowered his sabre from his shoulder and walked towards them. "Attestation, gentlemen?" he asked, barring their way.

"That's right," Frederic replied. "We've come about The Royal North Devon Hussars, the Swimbridge troop." Jack, Hector and Leonard Grant pulled up behind, studying the man closely as he gave directions. The peak of his shako, held steady by the brass chinstrap, half covered his eyes forcing him to hold his head higher than he would otherwise have done. Jack noticed that the heavy silver epaulettes on his shoulders matched the silver lace on his high collar and the chain lace on his jacket and sleeves. A regimental badge adorned his white crossbelt, another shone from the brass buckle on his belt. On his left breast three medals hung beneath their assorted coloured ribbons. His black cavalry boots were burnished to a gleam save where the silver swan-necked spurs were fastened with chains.

As he took a short pace backwards, the sentry's sword scabbard scraped sharply on the stones, making the horses start. Jack watched how he came to attention and swept the hilt of the sabre to his lips in a salute.

"Over 'ere you lot," a second soldier shouted from the grass beyond the hard packed parade ground. Behind him, where he was pointing, a crowd had gathered and were milling around as if waiting for hounds before a day's hunting. They were a fine assortment and the new arrivals studied them closely, wondering how they would fit in.

Some were finely dressed and handsomely mounted, some not so well turned out and had brought their workhorses or ponies along. They came from all walks of life – the gentry, farmers, business men, working men, even a number of vagrants. A few were chatting together, looking for all the world as if they had done this sort of thing before. Several sat by themselves, keeping their own counsel, one or two slept, some read sitting propped against the low wall while three, all drunk, argued noisily. One man had brought his wife and several dogs wandered in and out of the gathering.

*

For the next three hours those applying to join the Royal North Devons were subjected to a bewildering variety of interviews and tests. The horses were examined by the Regimental Veterinary officer no less thoroughly than the Regimental Surgeon examined their owners.

"We need men 'ere," a corporal announced, stalking coldly between them as they stood naked, apart from their breeches, awaiting the surgeon's verdict. "We need men what can face the King's henemies…and fight 'em, too. Men what can 'andle themselves." Master Frederic was taking it all in his stride, Jack could see that. He had found somebody to talk to and even the corporal seemed to know he was a mighty sharp cut above the rest of them. Still, it wasn't right for him, Hector and Leonard to be undressed like this in front of their master, and him half naked too. Not right, it wasn't.

They had lunch together in the mess hall and even that didn't seem right. Then they paraded again but the numbers had dropped. Less than half remained. "That's it," the corporal announced after he and another had pushed them into lines. "That's got rid of the rabble and you're what's left. Now, pay attention to Sergeant Fanshawe before the Colonel speaks."

Later on they laughed about it, happy to be away from the man. Life on this earth was difficult enough without Sergeant Fanshawe.

*

"*Stand up,*" the sergeant screamed although they were on their feet already. "Oi hate soldiers, I do," the gravely voice rasped. Fanshawe paraded himself slowly down the lines of recruits peering malevolently into the faces in front of him. His eyes glittered and his nose twitched like an animal scenting its prey.

"Oi hate them….oi do. Hate them." The eyes, small, menacing and bloodshot, flickered from one to the other as the tips of his waxed moustache twitched. " Bleedin' scum, they are…an' they don't like me neither." Fanshawe climbed the few wooden steps to the low balcony where he prowled and swaggered as he surveyed the faces below him. That he did not like them at all was plain enough.

He rolled his shoulders, pulled himself up to his full height and began to unbutton his jacket. Behind him the corporal stood waiting, his face expressionless. "Know what they call me?" Fanshawe's theatrical whisper was heard by the furthest man. "Know what? Eh?" The last button was undone and he removed his jacket, sweeping it back to the man behind him without taking his eyes off those in front. His chest was bare.

"*Flogger*," he yelled. "That's what they call me...*Flogger Fanshawe*, I am." Only a few in the front rank noticed the scars on the right side of the lean ribcage. "Yes, Flogger Fanshawe and that's why." He spun round and stood with his back to them, grinning at their gasps. There was no skin. The flesh, ruffled like folds of cloth without shape or form, was pitted and discoloured into thick mauve and white ripples. "Nigh on a hundred lashes there," he cried. "And you know why?" he turned back to face them his face twitching.

"Late on parade they were...four rotten, stinkin' troopers. Late for roll call, they was...before the battle of Orthez. My men...they were...my own *bleedin'* men." His fist pounded his chest. "Two dozen lashes each one of the bastards cost me...two dozen lashes each, an' my corporal's tapes as well." His shoulders rolled as he put his jacket on and redid the buttons.

"But when the Lord God Almighty made us all, he made summat worse even than troopers. Oh yes," he crowed. "Oh yes 'e did, bless 'im. He made an awful, 'orrible thing called a civvy. And if oi hate troopers, oi verily detest civvies. *Deteeeest 'em* I do." Fanshawe, now dressed again, waved his sabre at those in front of him. "And that's you lot.

"Ain't got no discipline, no pride...no sod all," he growled. "Dirty, stinkin' flesh. Dirty clothes...I detest 'em, I do. *Lookayoulot*," he shrieked, jumping at the balcony handrail. "Just bloody look at you. But if the Colonel hi'self, an' the precious, sweet Jesus 'ave decided it's my job to change you filthy, stinkin' ruffians into good King's men then, God bless 'im, I will."

Fanshawe was enjoying himself. As he barked and cursed so his red face jerked, the points of his moustache twitched urgently. "An' if it's to be my little lot to sort you bleedin' wasters out and make good, honest soldiers out of you...then *I'll do it*," he yelled. "I'll do it...I'll bleedin' do it, d'yer hear?" They did.

"Remember that an' remember that you're *in*....you've signed on. You're mine now, all mine, an' there's no escape. Oh no...next time you're back 'ere, Flogger Fanshawe'll be waitin' for you. And it's goin' to hurt...oh, yes, dearie me, upon my soul it's goin' to bleedin' hurt."

✳

"What d'you reckon," Master Frederic?" Hector glanced across. "D'you s'pose the man's soft in the 'ead or what?" Simonsbath was in sight and they were glad for it was hot.

"Difficult to say," Frederic laughed and turned to the others. "And to think we've got ten days of him in the summer. *Ten days of Fanshawe!*" The four roared with laughter then rode on in silence. "Anyway it's back to the real world right now. Father's going mad about the roads and there're already stories of these Irish he's brought over. Exford's banned them and there's been fighting up at Mole's Chamber."

"Send for Flogger," Leonard Grant mimicked the scream.

"Anyway," Frederic raised his voice above the laughter. "Anyway, more to the point, we've got the Northboroughs coming in a week's time. They're all coming and that includes the duke himself and Lord Preston. Father's getting worked up about it all and I'll have to see what he wants."

Chapter Fourteen

"Very good to see you again, Mrs Tucker." Dr Collyns swept off his hat. "And looking so much better than last time." He left his cloak and top hat on the pile of logs in the porch and stooped low through the doorway before taking her hand.

"And you, too, doctor," Grace beamed with delight. "Come in, come in, I won't be a minute." Standing back, he watched closely as she fussed around the bread oven. She looked frail, to be sure, and he detected a stiffness in her neck as she turned back to the table with the plate of warm scones, but there was a spring in her step that heartened him. Just a month earlier she had been laid low by an infection which had reached her lungs. The Loosemores had called him, sending Isaac, their youngest, with the message.

"Oh, I'm sorry, do take a seat." She brushed an untidy wisp of grey hair from her face and stretched for a chair. Knowing that he was due to call, she had been hurriedly tidying, removing her flower-patterned pinafore only when she heard the farm dogs. Now she pulled up a second chair and sat beside him, warmed and comforted by his presence. She looked at him affectionately. "Yes, doctor, I'm fine thank you, much better now. It's been a long winter, though, and there's been many in the village far worse than me."

Collyns sighed and raised his eyebrows. "Aye," he murmured. "Sometimes the good Lord works in a mysterious way and there's precious little us mortals can do about it. But now...come, come," he looked at Grace and smiled. "Enough of that sad talk. I've come with some *good* news." He reached out and squeezed her wrist.

"I've heard from your young Wilmot and he's doing very well...by jove he is." The doctor pulled a letter from his inside pocket. "It came from Cambridge just a couple of days ago and I thought I'd bring it along for you. Here, look" He moved his chair closer to hers.

"Says he's enjoying his studies...see, here we are." Knowing she was unable to read, he pointed to the writing in the letter. "Says here that he's finding the physics hard work." He saw her frown and laughed. "Oh, physics...that means studying the nature of matter, such things as heat and light, sound, the mechanics of things and so on. All that sort of stuff."

He waited until she nodded, knowing full well she was none the wiser, then read on. "Says he's made any number of friends, from all over the country, and some from as far off as Germany and France. That's marvellous, isn't it? And he finishes by telling me that he's even managed a couple of days with the hounds up there. Now that's grand."

Grace shook her head. "It's wonderful, doctor. There he is talking like a fine, educated man, so worldly and sure about life." Her mouth pulled a brave smile. "We can never thank you enough, never."

"Come now," Collyns chided. "The pleasure's all mine, really it is. Nothing pleases me more than when a youngster grabs hold of a chance like that. Nothing...nothing at all. It's marvellous and the boy'll go far you know. Only a few months more now and he'll be making his way. Anyway I hear young Jack's doing well, too."

"Oh, did you?" Grace smiled brightly, thrilled at the news. "I'd love to see him again."

"Parson Russell passed on word of the lad...saw him a week back. Told me that Mr Knight's singing his praises very highly. He's got great faith in your boy and he's put him in charge of the stables at Simonsbath. Joined the army, too."

"What?" A hand flew to her mouth and she sat back. "The *army*, doctor?"

"Aha now, don't go worrying yourself." Collyns grinned at the look on her face. "He, young Freddy Knight and a couple of the others stopped over with Parson Jack on their way to enlist with The Royal North Devon Hussars in Barnstaple. They're the yeomanry, part-time soldiers...nothing like the regulars. Nothing like Lionel," he assured her. "Just a couple of weeks or so each year. Freddy got them to go along with him and volunteer. It's a fine thing to do, you know...and the girls'll be mighty impressed."

They both laughed. "And what news of Emma?"

"I'm a granny again," Grace beamed proudly. "They were here just a fortnight ago, after the snow. The coachman at Filleigh got hold of a little dogcart from one of the keepers. Ever so smart it was." She went on to tell how Emma and Troy had arrived unannounced to show them their baby daughter and had stayed for the day.

"But that's wonderful news, wonderful," Collyns got up and walked to the window. "They've done well, all of them...no doubt about that." He paused. "Yes," he muttered more to himself as he looked down the garden. "No doubt at all."

But then he frowned, thinking hard and pursing his lips. "All that's great news," he said turning back. "But, I have to say there's just one thing I'm *not* quite so happy about, Mrs Tucker." Grace glanced up sharply. "I was in Tiverton last Thursday and called in to see your Charlotte." Collyns noticed how she caught her breath. "Just thought I'd see where she was and what she was up to." Grace rested her chin in her hands and nodded. "I'm none too sure things are going well there." He went on to explain that the little boy had clung to his mother's skirts and it was fear not shyness that made him stick so close. When eventually the wee mite spoke he stammered badly and cried.

What the doctor did not tell her was about the purple bruises on Charlotte's arms and the marks around her throat. "I'll see if we can get her back here for a few days. Perhaps the little lad could stay on a bit longer…he'd love it out here on the farm." He could tell that Grace knew what was behind his remarks. "It might be easier for all concerned. Did you know she's with child again?"

"Oh, for mercy's sake." Grace looked out of the door. "What ever next, doctor? She should leave the man."

"I know, I know," he soothed. "But now then, Wilmot'll be home before long. Perhaps Jack can come over and you can arrange something between you all. It's been hard for me to bring this news but I'm happier now you know my thoughts."

2.

Frederic hooked his foot around the leg of the low wicker table and pulled it towards him. He was feeling lazy. Lunch with his mother at Castle Heights had been a hurried affair but Tarr had done them well. He half sat and snatched at Maxwell's latest report before falling back again. One glance at the columns of figures was enough and he let it drop on to the terrace, preferring the comfort of the high-backed armchair and the warmth of the afternoon sun.

It had been his mother's idea to split the forthcoming visit of the Northboroughs between Simonsbath and Lynton and they had been discussing it. Hunting for the season had long since ended and the schooner his father had taken for the two weeks would be moored off Lynmouth. Before that, though, talk had been of Jessica Orchard of Hartland, a new and interesting acquaintance who had strayed into his path at Filleigh a month earlier.

✳

"Tell me about them, dear…the Orchards." Luncheon over, the two were sitting together: they had an hour before the coach was due to collect them and Elizabeth-Jane returned to the subject. "Your father's hardly heard of them. I have though and so's Lydia Acland…Surrey aren't they? Isn't that where they're from?"

"Hampshire, mother…originally anyway. Near Petersfield apparently but now they're at Hartland…some distance away though. The Northborough's know them or at least the girls know Jessica." Elizabeth-Jane toyed with the velvet sash of her blue day dress, the one with black and white stripes then lifted her chin, mulling over this new information.

"Timber, mother," Frederic laughed. "I bet you were going to ask me what they do. Timber from the Baltic…Sweden mainly, and very nicely too. They've just ordered three more ships. Apparently Hartland Abbey's quite beautiful. A bit remote according to Marcus…but in a wonderful setting."

"Will she be down again? I mean…would you like her to come and stay? You know she can."

"I really don't know, mother. I only saw her twice this time but she's due back in August then for good, I believe. So…who knows? Perhaps then."

"My goodness you young are lucky." She swatted at a wasp and adjusted her straw hat, reaching up to check the trailing silk ribbons. "So much coming and going, and all these new faces. Your father told me that Exmoor would be like Kerry but there's *much* more going on here…and next week's almost upon us." He knew she had been worried about the visit.

"I daresay, but they all love it here." Sitting back and putting his arms behind his head he closed his eyes. "And we've got stacks to do. The Aclands are home and the Luttrells have asked us over to Dunster. Then there's this man o' war that father's arranged…so that's half their stay already."

"And how *about* the girls, dear? We thought Katherine was looking very special back in February. She does seem to be rather fond of you…."

"Don't think so mother." He remembered, at once, how closely she had been watching them. "She's quite enchanting and I love her dearly…both of them but that's that. She…" Frederic paused. "Katherine's enormous fun but she's got a way of her own, y'know. She can be desperately stubborn…really digs in when she's a mind to. But Kenton's yer man there. You should be asking him about her."

"Yes, I remember them together at Holnicote. They looked very handsome together and, goodness, how they danced that new waltz…round and round and round." Elizabeth-Jane looked at her son. "D'you think they're really that fond of one another…father and I thought you'd be the one. The one for Katherine, I mean," she added.

"No mother. Not me, honestly." Frederic sat up, suddenly conscious of what he was saying. He'd thought of it often enough, even yearned for her affection but her eyes and her heart were elsewhere. She was beautiful and joyous, they revelled in each other's company and confided in one another but, beyond that, it was difficult to know quite how he felt.

"Oh, I know what I wanted to ask you." Elizabeth- Jane sat as well, blinking and shading her eyes. "Goodness, it's bright. The Royal North Devons, dear…father's terribly pleased about it, I heard him telling Giles Chichester the other day. But he did go on a bit…made it sound as though you were commanding everything."

"A mere humble trooper at this stage, mother, that's all. Parson Jack urged me to go straight for a commission, said it would be far easier that way. But I'm not so sure and in any case, it'd take up much more time. I want to settle in

222

first…feel my way then, maybe, they'll invite me." For a moment the two were silent. "Anyway mother," he rolled out of his chair and stood, buttoning his waistcoat. "I'll go and get the coach organised. What say you…ten minutes? That sufficient?" He bent and kissed her cheek.

✳

The track between Lynton and Brendon Common was as troublesome as ever. Frederic ordered the two dogcarts to close up on his mother's double brougham and made sure all three moved together. Shamble Way, the name of the track they were on, rose sharply out of the valley to cross Lyn Down before dropping down, as steeply again, to where it forded the next river. It was a distance of barely two miles but he never liked that part of the journey.

When the going had been soft, cartwheels had bitten deeply into the soil but today the old ruts were bone hard making movement difficult. And it was a desolate spot at the best of times, a point not lost on highwaymen and he was glad of the two outriders. Had he been on his own he would have ridden hard for the moor, going straight up one of the many narrow tracks and on to the open ground. As it was, he sat with the coachman until they were clear of the woods before calling a halt to give the horses a blow.

✳

Mother and son were reunited once more, sitting together in the shade at Scobhill Gate, under the four rowans that the wind and weather had twisted together. "Did you see Durnford away yesterday?" Her question came suddenly but boldly and with none of the caution he used to expect.

He knew the banker delighted in her company but, in the early days, he had been angered and protective of her as any son might. His instincts had told him that Morgan's attentions were closer than was proper, that mischief was afoot, and he had been angrier still when he sensed his father had noticed as well. It was as though the patriarch had seen his position challenged, as though the old grey muzzle was no longer able to see off the young intruders as it once could. Instinct told him also that it was *his* job as heir apparent to head off the usurper, if necessary to confront him and see him away.

But he, Frederic, had been hurt as well. Could it really have been that his mother, whom he adored, had eyes for this man who had come into her life so suddenly, and that *she* had been trailing her coat? Could it be also that his father, older and no longer so vigorous, might not have been able to keep hold of his beautiful wife? As he grew older himself so Frederic began to understand life's ways, how people thought and behaved when thrown together and it had been painful to realise that his own mother, like any other mortal, might have been tempted. After all, no matter how high the pedestal on which he and the others had placed her, she was human and vulnerable like everyone else, as was his father…as was Morgan.

But his fears had come to nothing. If the banker had ever chanced his hand as so many would have done, and if his mother had once been tempted, the moment had passed. There remained a friendship between them that was too open to be anything other than pure. It bore a freshness and innocence that would never have been had the relationship been deeper, and he rejoiced in it.

"Yes, I saw him away and he'll be gone for months," he replied. A year ago he could never have faced her like this. Back then his thoughts had been black. "He's fun, clever too…and he adores my mother." Frederic put his arm around her and pulled her into his shoulder.

"Oh, away with you now…I'm too old for all that, far too old." She was laughing but there was a hint of a blush, just under the eyes. "He's a lovely man…time he was married again."

"*Again*, mother? "D'you mean he…" Frederic paused searching for words.

"Yes, he was once but she died…the baby as well. It was terribly sad, he told me in Barnstaple. It all happened years ago and I tried to tell him that life should move on, that he had everything a woman could want. But…."

"But what?"

"Told me he wasn't ready. That however long ago it was, the memory of her, Fanny…yes, that was her name, the memory was still too fresh, too raw and he couldn't find anyone like her."

"And is that why he was showing such interest in you? I told you before that I thought his intentions were a little too…well, that he was taking liberties where he should never have done. Why didn't you tell me then?"

"Because he confided in me, dear. Asked me not to talk about it." Elizabeth-Jane looked at her son. "Believe me, Freddy. He begged me to keep everything to myself. Told me how much it helped him to be able to talk, how it eased the pain."

"And you *believed* him?"

"But of course, dear. When you have conversations like that you get to know if something's true or not. All the details kept coming back, time and again. Little things I remembered him telling me earlier, little insignificant things. Nobody could make up a tale like that and keep to it year after year." She paused for a while and their silence seemed right.

"Come, dear." Elizabeth-Jane rose as the coachman came to collect the rugs. "No, poor Durnford. He was terribly, terribly hurt by it all. He's a lovely man, a treasure but…well, it's a very sad story."

"Dear mother." Frederic put his arm around her shoulder. "They…we all come to you, don't we. Why is it, I wonder?" He opened the brougham door and held his hand for hers as she climbed in. Only when she was comfortable did he clamber up beside the coachman once more.

3.

"Come on, get a move on, we haven't all night. *Harvey*." As usual The Duke of Northborough was bellowing. "*Harvey*, where the devil are you…ah, right. I want you to remain here until I call for you. You've got a lot of work to do on the wagons and we'll get word to you in a day or so."

"Very good, my lord." The tall, liveried footman bowed and turned back to the bustle of activity behind him.

"Right, Freddy." The Duke was still shouting. "Let's be on our way." As he kicked his horse into life and turned towards the coach entrance, his elbows and knees were flapping in frustration.. "Let's get up the hill and see what your father's got for us."

Frederic had foreseen that the heavy wagons would get no further than Exford so, for the last three days he had been arranging the reception at The White Horse. Half the village had turned out to watch the leading carriage, in the silver and powder blue Northborough livery, swing into the stage yard. A second carriage and two wagonettes followed, leaving the remainder to follow on the next day.

Earlier the family had taken tea and then changed in the three rooms he had booked for them. Only then, and after the Duchess had turned down two horses before she was satisfied, were they ready.

❊

An hour later Katherine and Lizzie followed their mother up the steps of Simonsbath Manor and through the front door. On their way, a gentle wind had risen, blowing across the moor beneath the unseasonably grey skies. It had been enough to make them stop at the entrance to Cloven Rocks, a sharp, bleak corner, where they put on their cloaks. Just before they set off again, Katherine left the party and stood looking back down the road. She could see the pack-train slowly cresting the high ground almost a mile away and she studied the distant figures. One was detached from the rest, riding in front and off the road as if leading. It might have been him but she could not be sure. She looked again then wheeled her horse round and caught up with the others.

"Hullo, Sarah." She acknowledged the curtsey and turned to let her maid take her cloak. "You got here safely, then?"

"Yes thank you, m'lady. Lovely it is." The young maid had arrived with the baggage the previous day and had been learning the ways of the household at the manor. "The room's ready, ma'am. Like to come with me?" Katherine followed her up the main staircase from where the stags' heads still glared down imperiously at those in the hall below. Her room was large and airy with a high ceiling, one she had not used before. As she walked towards the window, her boots rang out on the boards.

"It's lovely here, m'lady, real wild. They say smugglers an' highwaymen used to come here. Spooky at night tho'."

"I know," she laughed. It was the girl's first visit. "They used to frighten Lizzie and me with stories. Now then…last time I was in the other wing and didn't have a view anything like this." She leant over the dressing table then stood on tiptoe to see better. "There're the stables, over there…beyond the hedge. I remember now…and there's the clock tower."

"That's right, m'lady. Got 'undreds of 'orses here. Can't get no carriages up yet, well, no big ones, not 'til the roads are done." She paused watching her mistress who was still looking out of the window. "Beggin' yer pardon, m'lady, but I've laid out your things." Sarah pointed to the chaise longue. "Over here.

"Put your pink walking dress ready for you, the one with the satin edging. That's here, look." Katherine remained by the window. "Then for dinner, seein' it's the first night, I've put yer full dress with the train…the cream an' white one you like…an' the buff gloves. Makes you look lovely, that one does. Shall I bring your water now?"

"Mmm?" Katherine turned back from the window. "Oh yes, thank you Sarah. Tell them I'll be down in about an hour."

She took off her boots and riding habit then lay back on the bed and closed her eyes. It had been a long day and she should have been tired but her body felt alive. He was here, so close, just across the lawn behind the tall beech hedge. She had longed to catch a glimpse of him earlier at Exford but it had been impossible with Freddy and Kenton rushing about organising everyone. But tomorrow she would make a point of letting him know she was here and that nothing had changed.

It had been almost a year but she could still see him now as he stood looking at her in the yard. His face had been burnished to a deep tan by the wind and summer sun. She remembered his finely chiselled features. His blond hair, bleached almost the colour of straw and too long by today's fashion, had been swept back over his ears and tied with a black ribbon. It must be darker now, she thought, as dark as his eyebrows which gave his grey-blue eyes their piercing look. Only when she had come up to him in the stable did she realise how tall he was.

She smiled to herself at the memory and hugged her body, allowing her fingers to trail softly along the outside of her arms. In a sudden moment of desire her hands had gone to her breasts and her legs had pressed tightly together as the rich warmth of passion flowed through her.

Jack was twenty-seven, Freddy had told her that. A man in his physical prime, a man on whom any woman's eyes would linger, one about whom many women would dream. But there was an indefinable quality about him also, an inner strength, a confidence she had seen as he walked and talked with the Knights and her own family. There was a calmness and dignity; he was a man who neither feared nor wanted for anything. The first time they had ridden together she had sensed it, as she had when they were alone in the stables.

Later she dressed, turned down her lamp and walked to the window. Daylight had almost gone allowing a glimmer of lamplight to filter through the hedge at the end of the garden. She knew he would be there, tending the animals and seeing all was well before walking along the narrow path he had shown them, to his room in the cottage. There he would be on his own, most likely lying back in his cot with one arm across his face, thinking of what had been done and what tomorrow would bring. Thinking of her perhaps? Wondering what she would be doing, wondering if she was thinking of him. She was so close, so agonisingly close, yet unable to reach out and stroke his forehead or slip her arm through his.

*

Next morning, as soon as she dared, she searched but in vain for he had been sent away by Knight and would not be back before dark. And it was the same the following day and for two more after that. Twice only had she seen him, once busy in the yard talking with strangers, the second time alone on a young horse when she had been afraid to call out. She rode with the others across the moor to Ilfracombe where they had taken a boat for the day and watched as the mackerel fishermen hauled in their catch. The next day they had ridden to Lynmouth, this time going out with the Knights and her parents to the seals off Foreland Point. Time was beginning to slip by.

Then the weather changed and it was John Knight who took charge. "Take Herbert, Kenton...Herbert and the girls," he instructed them at dinner. "Get away early and make the most of the day." The idea of them setting off early amused him and he chortled over his port. "Head off south, somewhere along the river...you all know it well enough. Pick a good spot, the moor's lovely just now. "I'll need Tucker and Coward for a mail run, so get Floyd to go out with the house staff." Katherine listened in dismay. "Freddy'll be back in the evening so the four of you are on your own. Look after yerselves, mind." She managed to return Kenton's smile.

"It'll be a lovely party," Katherine looked down at Elizabeth-Jane's hand on her wrist. "Tell Parker about the lunch, Kenton dear, and he'll get Tarr to have things ready."

*

227

"Now then, Tucker," Knight was pressing his signet block into the red sealing wax. "This has got to get off today. We're too late for the South Molton stage but there's a mail going out of Withypool…soon after midday. Take the track down by the river to Landacre bridge then up around the higher side of the farmland." There he paused, frowning at a sudden thought. "What's the news about men on the road?" he asked, before nodding soberly as Jack told him.

"Hmmph," Knight toyed with the packet. "Well, this is important," he announced, cocking an eyebrow. "It's got to get to London…and fast. Make sure you're well armed and if they get in the way don't spare 'em. Let me know when you're back."

✳

They had been riding for almost an hour and had crossed the river before climbing the steep slopes of the old hill fort from where they hoped to pass the picnic party. Other than a pile of hampers, rugs and over clothes, there was no sign. They must have ridden on.

It was Hector who saw them. "Hey, Jack…wait a minute. Down there, look. What's that?" He was pointing. "Way down there, by the river. Summats up." Jack followed his arm. "That's them," Hector was standing in his stirrups. "An' I reckon someone's in trouble, by Heavens. And look, there, two of them's running…looks like the two maids."

"It's the Great Deep." Jack had pulled up alongside. "My *God*. The bog, Hector. The Great Deep at Ferny Ball…the stupid, clodhopping fools. Someone's gone in…caught up by the looks. *Come on*, man, quick. If they are…*Jesus!* Come on.

"No wait," he shouted suddenly. "Grab whatever rugs an' blankets are here…quick as you can." He turned again. "Get over at the ford, above the rapids…then up over the steep. Fast as you can." Jack took off, straight down the hillside, his horse taking great bounds then sliding for yards before launching itself again. At the ford he met Dick Floyd.

"Capstan's going down," the groom yelled. "Lady Katherine's caught as well…she tried to get him out and got caught herself."

"Get back and bring men and ropes. Take whatever horses you can," Jack had already passed him. "Hector and I'll get the girl, then try and keep him afloat. Ride fast, Dick."

"Dear God, please don't let it be. Please," he muttered to himself. Hector crashed down the slope behind him and the two drove hard together.

"The very devil, Jack," Hector shouted across to him. As they raced towards the edge of the great bog their heads were only a few feet apart. "Look at that…she's in a bad way an' all. Up to her waist already." Jack made out the figure of Lord Preston standing at the edge of the bog. He was trying to reach out for her but it was hopeless. Even from where they were, they could see her face and clothes were covered in mud and water where she had been struggling. Kenton was further away, trying to cross the surface of the bog. He, too, was getting nowhere.

Jack cursed in disgust. "You'll never do it like that, yer damn fool," he swore. Suddenly he could see old Orwell Govier. *"Got to get yer body flat on the surface if you're in and the ground's shaking all around you,"* he had cautioned. *'Lie down and spread your weight, or the bog'll open and swallow you.'*

"Here, hold my horse," Jack shouted at Herbert Preston. "Get out of there and let's have your shirt. Quick, man, come on…let's have it. Might still be time. *Master Kenton,*" he yelled. "*Master Kenton,* get over here and let's have your shirt. Hector, I'm going for the girl first…lets have some rugs, two'll do. Get the shirts into a rope." Jack tore his off and threw it to Hector."

"Hey, I say, there." Preston was hurrying across.

"Just do as I say," he snapped. "Capstan looks a gonner but I'm going for the girl. Give Hector a hand…just get on with it. *Get on with it man.*" He threw the two blankets down and waded into the bog. Every time he moved he could see the surface shaking. She had sunk further and was whimpering in fear for, by now, the bog had closed over her waist.

"I can't move," she cried. "It's pulling me down…please hurry."

"Don't worry…I'm coming. Don't move…put your arms out to hold yourself up." He turned. "Hector…a blanket, quick, man. I'm going out," he yelled. "Let me have the rope when I'm ready."

He heard Capstan whinny and saw the horse had sunk to its withers. As the animal struggled so it reared up and its forelegs struck out but it slipped back again. The bog was closing round him. Jack eased himself across one blanket, his weight spread over the surface. All around him the green sphagnum bubbled and trembled. "Don't struggle," he called to her. "One more of these and I'll be with you."

He turned slowly. Already the foul, icy bog-water was gurgling onto the blanket. "Just give me one chance," he muttered. "Just one chance." Straining as hard as he could, he raised himself and threw the second blanket between them. She had sunk further and was crying out in desperation like a frightened child. "Hurry," she gasped. "Please…hurry."

"Let's have the rope Hector," Jack half turned and raised his hand. As he did so, the knotted shirts fell across him. "Right," he yelled and moved forward again. The bog trembled. Around her the sundews and bell flowers were bobbing and nodding. From the corner of his eye he could see the bog grasses were shaking as well, as though the thin crust of the surface lay over a huge, bottomless jelly.

"I'm coming," he muttered, spitting out water. Their fingers touched. "Hold on, girl, hold on." He eased himself forward and felt her fingers gripping his hand, but they slipped from his grasp. "A bit further," he muttered.

Now he was alongside her and could hear her breath coming in gasps as the bog squeezed ever tighter. "I'll put this around you, under your shoulders and tie it." As the horse struggled nearby, whinnying and snorting in fear, he felt the whole bog quiver. Large, black bubbles gurgled as they burst on the surface around them. The bog was moving. It was alive and it was hungry.

"The horse?" she gasped. "Capstan...."

"In a minute...soon as you're out." He looked back under his arm. "Right," he yelled. "Take it up, but slowly for God's sake." He turned back to Katherine. "Hang on, Kate...hang on, girl. Keep your arms tucked in, your legs together." He had called her by her name, her pet name only her father ever used but it had slipped out as naturally and easily as if it made no odds. The shirt tightened. "Right, slowly," he called.

"Stop," he yelled suddenly. The knotted shirts had ridden up over her head, forcing her face into the water. "All right, try again. Slowly now." The shirts rode over her head again.

"Get it right under yer arms," he shouted at her. "Then trap it there fer mercy's sake. Go on, girl...right under yer arms and hold 'em there." He turned and raised his hand. *"Right, try again."*

This time the shirt held. Slowly, with the bog bubbling and sucking, she was clear. "Keep your legs still and your body flat," he whispered. Suddenly he bent forward and kissed the matted hair above her ear.

"Told you," he whispered again. "We're going to be fine." She was dragged to the bank sobbing with relief. Her hair was plastered flat, her body and clothes drenched through and black with slime. Jack followed, swimming his body over the half submerged blankets.

"*Capstan, Jack*," Hector shouted. Jack turned to see the great horse slipping further down. By now the bog water was up to his neck. There was no hope.

"My pistol, Hector," he called. "I'm going back for him. Can't let him suffer like that...never." By the time he reached the horse, the desperate animal had churned the bog around him into a black, watery mud. But his time had come. Capstan, one of the great favourites of the stable, was staring skywards. His eyes were rolling in terror, his head thrown back in one last desperate attempt to escape the bog. Even as Jack watched he slipped further down, his breathing now coming in short, rasping gulps.

"Steady, old friend," he whispered coming alongside the still proud head. "All right my lovely, I'll not let you go under. Shhh…there now, boy. There now" the muzzle of the pistol was pressed under his jaw pointing upwards to the brain. "God speed, dear friend." He fired and saw the head jerk back. As the lifeblood spurted from the wound, the horse shuddered and slipped further away, now lifeless.

By the time Jack reached the bank, Capstan had gone. For a long time no one spoke, the silence broken only by Jack's gasps for air and the sobs of the two women.

✳

"You did *what*," John Knight glared at Kenton. His face was white with shock. The arrogance and confidence in his son had gone. The eyes that met his were baleful, more than that they were afraid. For a moment, one brief moment only, Knight felt contempt for the creature in front of him. Whether his own or not, nobody bearing his name should cower like that.

"Father, I tried to warn her but it was…."

"*Warn…her*," Knight's voice was little more than a whisper. "*Warn…her*, for Heaven's sake, man. You shouldn't have been anywhere near that godforsaken place. How was she to know? And anyway, stop trying to shift the blame…you were in charge. I ordered you to be so. The Great Deep's the worst bog on the moor. It's a killer, we all know that. And look what happened to Capstan." He glared at his son and squared his jaw.

"You're a fool, Kenton. A damn stupid, young fool. By the grace of God, Tucker and Coward were passing and saved the girl." He meant it and took satisfaction in seeing his words strike home. "Her father's sore vexed, and I don't blame him." Knight stood up behind his desk and ran his hand through his grey mane. "But he's a man of the world, too, and knows you're fond of the girl."

He had said enough. He had humbled his own son and had no wish to break him. "All right…all right, what's happened's happened. You might not care for Tucker but if it wasn't for him…."

He came round the desk and walked up to his son. "If it wasn't for him, there'd be a funeral to arrange…or a memorial service if there was anything to bury," he added grimly. "Can you imagine that? Well…can you?" Even now his breath came heavily. "Learn from it, Kenton," he growled. Learn from it and mark it well." He nodded for his son to follow and they left the room together.

✳

231

Life at Simonsbath was not easy but the fine weather continued and the household, determined to put the tragedy behind them, began to enjoy themselves again, led by the master himself. Elizabeth-Jane arranged for a group of musicians from Taunton to come for the day, organising a garden party in the grounds during the long midday interval. Supper parties were held for the young. Charles Acland, home on leave from his ship, brought a fiddler and two sailors who danced hornpipes. Later, after tea, the master brought the household together to sing sea shanties. Edward Chichester, a friend of Frederic's, came with two falconers and the company rode out to watch the birds work above the Foreland cliffs.

4.

Two days before the Northboroughs left, Katherine announced she wanted to ride out again. She asked to go on her own but John Knight refused to countenance such an idea so Frederic offered to accompany her. Plans were made for them to explore the mysterious valley of Badgeworthy to the north, about which so many tales were told.

"It's quite a place," he warned her at dinner. "There're all manner of tales and rumours about the valley. It's strange…definitely a presence of something down there." He thought for a moment. "Without doubt it has a sort of silent eeriness…the ghosts of the Doones," he quipped. "But it's beautiful…a wonderful place."

The morning of the ride Frederic was called away to Barnstaple. A letter from the Yeomanry had arrived demanding his presence and it was a summons he dare not ignore. Kenton claimed to have other plans and John Knight refused to allow the younger children to accompany her. "You'll take Tucker, my dear," he patted her shoulder. "I'd have given him to you first of all but you'd have preferred someone to chat with. Anyhow, he knows the moor better than most. Tucker's your man for today."

✳

The two horses trotted easily up the track towards the gates on the Lynton road. Nothing had been said in the yard, nothing at all but Jack sensed her mood. She had been too ebullient back there, too light-hearted. She had chatted and joked a little too much with her sister who had come to see her off and it was not like her. While they were getting ready, she had kept her distance from him, two or three times he had caught her eye only to see her toss her head. Lady Katherine Darcy, so she was telling all who might care to be watching, had little time for the company she had been invited to keep that day. She had expressed a wish to be on her own and would have preferred it that way. Servants and staff, therefore, should keep their place.

He rode several lengths behind her, as beholden of an escort, for he knew those in the yard would be watching, simply interested to see how he would go. Had they left riding side by side, it would have given cause for comment. But also, he told himself, there might still be some misunderstanding, some dreadful mistake or cruel trick and he should take care to treat her with the respect her position demanded.

For a while they rode in silence, each willing the other to break into the conversation they knew had to come. Eventually she tired of the game and fell back to join him, questioning him studiously about life around them, about how the land lay, about the foxgloves in the hedgerow and the call of wild birds. She even sought his views on the few clouds that were above them.

Once through the gates at the entrance to Brendon Common, Jack swung off the track and followed Knight's wall until they reached the head of the valley where they began their descent. Gradually at first, then more steeply, the long combe deepened, turning north and twisting as it went.

They rode down the narrow sheep track in single file, she behind him, until they reached the bottom of a great, wide bowl where another stream joined the one they were following, and from where the heather and bracken-covered slopes rose for hundreds of feet above them. They were alone and the silence, save for the occasional cry of a bird, bore heavily while overhead the midday sun beat down relentlessly.

"Let's stop for a bit...over there, look," she pointed. The clump of wizened oaks, ancient and covered in grey lichen, crowded the edges of the narrow glade as if linking arms to hold back any who wished to trespass onto the spring grass underneath. Except for where the sunlight had forced its way through the shield of young leaves, the ground lay in shadow, dappled and deep. "By those trees over there...it's far too hot in the sun."

Jack dismounted and walked over to hold her horse. "Here, take my hand, m'lady. It's quite a step and you don't want to slip." He felt her fingers tighten around his, squeezing him as she slid from her saddle. He relaxed his grip but hers remained, so he drew back forcing her to release her hold but without causing offence.

"I'll see to the horses, ma'am, then I'll bring my saddle roll." He stepped back. "You must tell me where you'd like to sit and I'll make sure things're comfortable."

She had been watching him tether the animals and unstrapping his roll but now, as he returned, she laughed with one hand to her mouth. "D'you know," she said. "I've just realised I haven't brought anything to eat. Honestly, I thought I'd ask them to prepare something for me." She laughed again, shyly this time. "They must have forgotten, or perhaps I did...oh well, never mind."

He was forced to look at her but it didn't matter for talk about such simple things made it easier rather than more difficult. "Only bread an' cheese and an apple here, I'm afraid, ma'am…and a small jar of cider." He was bending over, unpacking his bag. "Not much, I'm afraid but you're more'n welcome. Jenny makes enough for two, three sometimes," he joked. Their eyes met again and they smiled then, suddenly and for no particular reason, they laughed out loud together.

Hurriedly, and as if to try and break this sudden unity, he spread the rug, throwing it high before letting it fall gently to the grass. He smoothed it and stood then reached out for her hand to steady her as she sat. For a moment, he watched, checking she was comfortable, as she tucked her skirts under her knees.

"I'll be with the horses, ma'am," he announced, stepping back.

"No," she replied turning and looking up at him. "Don't be so silly. Here." She patted the rug beside her. "Come and sit with me for goodness sake…and leave all that formality well alone." So, although he should never have done, he sat beside her. Such an act of disrespect anywhere else would have been outrageous, unthinkable and he would have been chased away. But now, at this moment, he knew it was expected of him. Even so, he kept his distance, making certain there was more than half the rug between them. The silence was difficult but he dare not speak for he would have had to turn and face her. He thought of making some excuse to go back to the horses in order to get well clear of her, then take a walk up the stream beyond the trees. But he could not bring himself to move; he knew he had to stay.

He could see her from the corner of his eye. She had taken off her jacket and was lying back, making much of settling herself on the uneven ground. He noticed, too, that they were closer than before. She had moved herself nearer, twisting and turning as if to get comfortable. "Jack look. What's that? That bird up there?" One hand was pointing, the other shielding her eyes from the sunlight filtering through the leaves. "Up there, look. And there's another, over there…a pair of them, soaring and wheeling together. Right up there."

"Buzzards, ma'am." He had glanced up but now half turned towards her. "Beautiful birds, they are. Hear them calling? Mew like kittens, they do…there," he held up a finger. "Hark to the pair of 'em."

They listened in silence together. The sudden stillness troubled him and he was about to say more, when she spoke again, more quietly this time. "They're circling one another. Round and round…gliding, almost as if they're dancing, flirting perhaps. D'you think they are, Jack? D'you think they're in love?" He eased further onto his side and looked up, holding his hand to shield the light. It was then that he felt her hand.

She had reached out for him and her fingers were on the back of his neck. From there they went to his hair then back again, caressing him gently. "D'you like that?" she whispered. He said nothing but leant further back moving himself slowly from side to side against her fingers.

"Tell me something." Her voice was louder. "Why did you kiss me the other day, when you were rescuing me?" She felt his shrug.

"Dunno really. Seemed natural…just so happy to've got you out alive." He kept his back to her, afraid the rise and fall of his chest would give him away.

"That all?" she sounded hurt but he made no reply. "And you called me by my name…Kate, didn't you? When your face was next to mine." She paused. "Nobody does that, y'know. Nobody except papa. Everybody else calls me Katherine."

"Yes, and I beg pardon for that, m'lady, really I do." His head dropped. "It just sort of slipped out…I couldn't help meself. Didn't mean no disrespect nor nothing."

"Jack." He half turned at his name, glancing back over his shoulder. "Jack." This time her hand was trying to pull him round to face her. "Make love to me," she whispered. His body tensed, the muscles under her fingers now as tight as whip cord. She could see the blood coursing through the veins on his neck. Still he did not move. "Jack, look at me."

He didn't move. "You're mad," he whispered hoarsely, clearing his throat.

"I'm not…I'm not mad at all. Look at me." She pulled at him again but still he resisted.

"D'you realise what you're saying, m'lady? *Me*? Me…and you? It's madness. Really. *Here…*" He struggled to rise. "We ought to get back before…."

"*No!*" Her fingers tightened on his shoulder and this time she pulled him down beside her, wriggling half on top of him before he could move away. "Jack, listen," she whispered, one finger trailing down his face. "Just Listen. You got my letter, didn't you?" He nodded but made no reply. "I said it all then and nothing's changed…nothing at all." She stroked his cheek just as she had been longing to do.

"I'll never be able to explain it but…well, ever since I saw you two years ago, I've never even looked at another man or thought of anyone else. D'you know what that means?" He glanced away, knowing the answer but unable to give it. When he did look back, his eyes dare not meet hers, rather they rested on the amber pendant around her neck.

"It means I love you, Jack," her fingers traced a pattern on his throat. "Love you more than words can describe. I'm not a little girl, you know. I'm a woman and I know exactly what I'm doing and what I want." She paused and looked down, slowly shaking her head in wonder.

"Don't worry, dear man," she whispered. I know what I'm throwing away, what I'm leaving behind. I know what they'll all say and what they'll think. Can't you understand that I've thought about all that?" She bent forward and touched his lips with hers. "But I don't care," she murmured. "I honestly, really don't care…I just want to be with you. That's all I want. I can't let you go, you must realise that. I never will." She rolled away from him and onto her back.

"Please, Jack," she whispered, then leant over to pull him towards her. "Please."

Jack bent over her, his mouth gently finding hers. Slowly and surely his fingers began to unbutton her blouse.

Chapter Fifteen

"So." Kenton snapped the telescope shut. "So…that's enough of that. Come on Dale, leave the horses and follow me. Keep quiet and do exactly as I say…and remember *everything.*" It took them a little over five minutes to leave the copse, cross the open ground under the ridge and push their way through the high bracken, even so Kenton was panting with exertion.

"Well…well…well," he crowed. "And now we have it all. Look…at…*that.* '*In flagrante delicto*' as they say" He brushed aside the undergrowth and stood in front of them. Katherine sat, then rolled away in an attempt to cover herself. "Just look at that. The lovely Lady Darcy rutting with the groom."

"Damn you, Kenton Knight. Damn you, damn you and damn you again," Katherine twisted around for her clothes. "What a filthy, dirty trick to play. How dare you?"

"Because you double crossed me, dear lady, that's why," he jeered. "And as for *you,*" he sneered at the look on Jack's face. "You Tucker, you've crossed your Rubicon, and how. You've done it now and my God you're going to pay. *Dale,*" he shouted for his valet. "Dale, come here. I want you to take note of every-thing. Look at them. Look at their clothes, look at their nakedness. *Everything,* and that's an order. Move yourself and remember what you see…remember everything."

"Oh, shut up." Jack leapt to his feet. "Shut up you miserable, whining little man. Spy on me if you have to but don't start throwing your weight around here, mocking us like that. You're a bitter and twisted man, Kenton Knight…always have been and always will be." His breeches were on.

"Tomorrow, for me and the rest of us, will be another day but for you it'll be the same – jealousy, bitterness and spite…and detested by everyone…*loathed* and despised. And you'll be like that 'til they throw you into your grave. Now, do what the hell you must and get out of here. Go on," he shouted. "And take yer man, Dale, with yer before I break every bone in your body."

✳

When they returned Frederic met them at the stables where he broke the news. They had an idea the story would be out already for they had seen Kenton and Dale galloping away towards Simonsbath while they had chosen not to hurry. John Knight put word out that he wanted to see Jack immediately he returned and that he was waiting for him. Frederic's face alone confirmed their fears.

"Come on, Jack." His hand fell on the other's shoulder. "I'm afraid we're both in this and I'm coming with you."

"Look, Master Frederic, there's no need to...."

"I'm coming, Jack, and that's that. Kenton, damn his eyes, has had his say with father and they're going to hear my side."

The kitchen was empty save for Parker. "Right Tucker. Get yourself over here, just as you are and follow me."

"I'll go first, thank you, Parker," Frederic pushed past the butler.

"But, Master Frederic...."

"I said, I'll lead the way, thank you."

✳

The Duke of Northborough and John Knight, side by side at the window, turned together. None of those entering the panelled study saw Kenton sitting behind the drop-leaf table in the shadow of the high bookcase. As soon as he moved, however, Jack saw him. From then on, like a predator fixed on his prey, his eyes rarely left the man. Knight motioned him to the front of the desk and for Parker to leave the room.

For a second nobody moved, then John Knight began to speak. But he stopped, suddenly, and leant on his desk. His eyes were closed and he was breathing heavily. Frederic started forward but Knight, head bowed, waved him back then glared unblinking at his head groom. The face was grey, stone-hard with anger, his body hunched well forward. Jack, his hands behind him, stared back.

"What in God's name do you think you've been up to?" Knight reached for Katherine's letter that Kenton had produced to support what he had reported earlier. As he held it up his eyebrows furrowed. "And don't think I don't know what's been going on." His voice was getting louder, his anger worsened by the fact the man in front of him seemed neither afraid nor moved by the confrontation. He expected submission but here was defiance, staring back at him.

"What, in the name of God the Father Almighty, have you got to say for your-self, man? I trust you with the safety of a guest of mine...a young woman at that. Eh?" By now the voice was grating harshly. "Eh? And you seduce her, putting yourself upon her like that. A titled lady...."

Knight pushed himself up and came around the desk. For his age he moved swiftly, raising his hand as if to strike the man in front of him. Jack half closed his eyes, ready for the blow. His own mind was in turmoil, cursing himself for having caused his master, the man he worshipped, such grief and rage. He had seen him like this with others and swore never to allow himself to be the object of his wrath, and now he was. A beating he could take and he willed the blows to fall, happy enough to stand there allowing the old man to expend his fury. If that was all then he would be more than pleased but, even if it came to that, he knew there had to be more; that it could not end there.

"*Father*," Frederic leapt between them. "*Father*, for God's sake. This was no seduction, no mad moment of passion."

"Then what the devil was it?" The Duke's hoarse bellow burst upon them as he moved in from where he had been standing. For a moment, he hesitated, scowling darkly as he muddled his words. "What the devil were you doing to my daughter out there? What the hell were you doing?" Jack took a deep breath. "Damn you, man...answer me, now...at once."

"Master Kenton will have told you everything, my lord." His eyes were on the Duke's but he ducked away and nodded across the room. "Hiding over there, my lord, in the shadows, like he hid from me in the grass. I've no doubt he's spoken out...no doubt at all." He saw the figure draw back as eyes were turned his way. Jack knew he would remain hidden in shadow, gloating quietly yet not daring to meet him man to man. The very thought gave him strength.

"*Damned* if he did," came the reply. "And what he told me was *outrageous...quite outrageous*. Nothing more than pure bloody lust, ravaging my daughter like that. My *God*...you savage...you vandal." He hesitated, breathless and red-faced. "I've asked Knight here to deal with you and when he's done I don't want you ever to communicate with or set eyes on Lady Katherine Darcy again... or any of my family ever...*ever*. D'you hear?" The Duke was bellowing, wide-eyed and puce.

"I can't promise you that, my lord." He looked from one to the other but both men, stunned by his reply, simply stared back. And why *should* he? She had made her choice, decided for herself how she wished her life to be rather than submitting meekly to her father's demands. She had thrown up everything for him and the choice was hers. She had told him again and again and, for that, he would never let her down.

"Oh yes, you damn well will," Knight interjected. "You give your word to his lordship right here and now...right now, d'you hear."

"*Listen*," Frederic's shout cut across any reply. He picked Katherine's letter from his father's desk and glanced at it. "Listen, father. I can only imagine how this came into your hand." He turned but Kenton avoided him. "Yes...there you see, just as I thought, but I was there when it was written. I've no idea how he came to possess it but I was the one entrusted with it...and I failed to honour the agreement. It was I who failed her."

He turned to the Duke. "Sir, there's no lust or sudden desire here. Upon my word this is not some matter of the moment, rather it is something that's endured...two whole years at least, three almost if I'm not wrong. What has happened, Your Grace, has happened. Whether you or father can bear it or not…the moment has passed." Jack watched Frederic from out of the corner of his eye. He had not asked for this but the friend he needed was there, by his side.

"That's enough of all that, Frederic," Knight held up his hand.

"Please, just one moment more, father, if I may. If what Jack's done is so wrong in your eyes then so be it, but the man has committed no crime, no law has been broken." He caught his breath, now aware that he had their attention. "So…before you pass sentence on what you might consider to be wholly unacceptable, spare a thought for the man you're condemning. He's given his very life and soul to us for twenty years…taught myself and the others everything we know, remained faithful and true to the family. And I'll ask you not to forget last week, neither of you, when he alone so bravely saved dear Katherine…and it's something none of us should ever forget."

Knight calmed, as if suddenly proud of his son's stout defence. The very same thoughts had gone through his mind earlier but he had been given no choice. "I hear all that, Freddy, and I've considered it too, but my mind's made up…Tucker will leave. He'll not set foot here again except on business and, as His Grace has requested, he'll not have any more dealings with Katherine. That's it and that's the end of the matter."

He turned to Jack. "I'll not forget this, Tucker. I don't care what you or Lady Katherine have to say…it was nothing less than an outrage, an insult to His Grace and the family. And it's put me and my own family into a dreadful position…*dreadful*." He took a deep breath, blew hard and swept his hand across the desk in exasperation. "You'll be away from here directly. You'll go to Lynton and work there for the Slocombes at West Lyn Farm. You'll work as a farm hand and be paid as a farm hand. No more of this…" Knight waved his hand in the air and came up close.

"It's *gone*, over…*finished*," he cried. The two men looked at each other. Frederic watched as Jack held his father's gaze. He saw his father nod as though, even then, he understood the man in front of him and was telling those watching that he knew. Then, and only then, did he lower his head and look away. "And you can think yourself damn lucky my son spoke up for you…damn lucky. You may go."

The door shut and there was silence. Anger and raw tension filled the room. As Knight left with his guest, so Kenton got up to follow but Frederic barred his way.

"You swine," he whispered hoarsely, holding him back with the flat of his hand. "You filthy, miserable, scheming swine. You'll never find a better man than that. Never, no matter how hard you search…but perhaps that's why you did it." Kenton stared, sneered contemptuously then looked away.

2.

Her eyes were red as though the kitchen range had been smoking again. Parker steadied himself against the sideboard and watched as the cook slumped disconsolately into her chair. She sighed then took off her glasses and huffed on the lenses before holding them up to the light. But her heavy tread on the stairs a few moments ago told him she had been in her room and nowhere near the kitchen fire. "Come now, Mabel." He spoke quietly. "It had to be done, y'know…had to be done. The master had no choice."

"Should never have come to all this, so it shouldn't." There were just the two of them in the senior staff room and the butler could see she was still feeling the effects of the last few days. "Just don't know whatever it was that came over them both…carryin' on like that. What ever do they think they were doin', an' she an 'igh born lady like she is."

"That Tucker's as much at fault." Parker straightened his tie and walked to the window. "Should 'ave kept his distance and had *nothing* to do with it." His hand swept through the air. "He should have kept himself a mile away, pretended he'd no idea what she was playing at. That's what…he should 'ave seen it coming."

"Oh come, come, Bernard," she sniffed. "What's a man like that s'posed to do, for Heaven's sake? Can't go pretending he doesn't know what's what when a woman gets all like that. I mean…Jack's not a fool y'know, he's not a boy. What would any young man do if…if, well…."

"Well…he's not so young either." Parker's voice sharpened. "Trouble with Tucker is that he's never known his place…never knows when to step back and mind his peace. And I've told him that often enough." Parker wagged a finger. "Never had any thanks from anyone for my trouble, neither, mind you." The two were silent. Simonsbath and Lynton were alive with gossip. Already the butler had been forced to call the staff together and order the whispering to stop, but the chatter persisted.

"And to think I remember him down at Castle Heights…when him an' his sister first came. Just a lonely little lad so 'e was, bless 'im."

"Bless nothing, Mrs Strong," Parker snapped, now speaking formally as he thought fit. "The man's dragged Mister Knight's good name through the mire and back again." He straightened his jacket and felt for his braces. The mere thought of his master being called to account infuriated him. No matter what, neither the Duke of Northborough nor anyone else should be given an excuse to run the family down. Nobody should, let alone when a mere groom was behind it all.

"Can you imagine the talk in the grand houses up country and around the dinner tables, places where Mr and Mrs Knight are well known? Why, *poof.*"

He puffed his cheeks and raised his eyebrows. "Every butler and footman in the country'll hear word of the goings on at Simonsbath. Think of the sniggering and jesting out in the kitchens?" Parker rose on his toes then pulled roughly at his cuffs. "No, I'm sorry, Mrs Strong. I know you like the man but he's always had something brewing in him...but never *this* for mercy's sake." Parker coughed and she could hear him muttering again.

"I'd have had the man thrashed." He glared at her defiantly. "Happened up at Lea, y'know. Old Mister Knight had a pair o' footmen given a damned good hiding. An' for far less than this, I can tell you. Just nosing around the ladies' bedrooms so they were. Gave 'em what for an' threw 'em out." He grimaced and pushed back a lock of black hair. "Anyway, enough's been said...*too* much and that's the end o' the matter." He picked the silver tray from the table and dusted the heavily engraved surface with his cuff. "I'll be away to do the wines for luncheon, Mrs Strong." Having had his say and feeling the better for it, the butler lifted his chin. "And I daresay you've got enough to keep you from worrying too much."

✳

On her own once more, the little cook raised her glasses and buried her face in her hands. It was that Kenton man and she shivered at the thought. She had never been able to take to him, not like Bernard had. Always arguing or boasting he was, or in trouble with something or other, forever causing his stepfather upset. And now this. How could the man do such a thing? How *could* he? Master Frederic had been right all along; the man was jealous mad. He'd never fitted; there'd always been trouble and now there always would be.

She sighed and pulled herself up, glancing at the wall clock. She remembered how the ladies had decided to leave straight after breakfast the following morning and it had been Mrs Knight who had come and ordered the hampers. She could see how upset she was, the poor dear, and had wanted to console her but it would have been wrong. It'd be better once they'd all gone...cleared off and given things a chance to settle. She checked herself in the mirror, licked her finger and dabbed at her eyes before turning to go. It was all very wrong.

3.

Elizabeth-Jane stood by the bow window. There was not a cloud in the sky and already it was hot, too hot. For a moment she paused, watching as Aitken, the new gardener, cleared molehills from the bottom lawn. Leaning forward to see better she rested her hands on the back of the window seat and laughed out loud at the sight of his terrier puppy chasing pied wagtails. It would crouch, preparing to pounce but the clever little birds anticipated what was coming and flitted away to settle a few yards further on where their bobbing tails mocked its efforts.

She lifted her eyes to beyond the bridge and on up to the heights of Shear

Down. As she did so her smile faded. It was Katherine: she could not get her out of her mind. She should have seen the signs a week ago, long before the terrible drama at Ferny Ball when poor Capstan was lost. Almost from the start of their visit, Freddy had been unusually quiet as though something pressing was on his mind. She shook her head. In spite of what he had told her, she had been sure there was something between them, so sure that she had discussed it with Amelia Northborough. Now, of course, she knew the truth.

What a fool she had been: what a blind, stupid fool! And Freddy had been party to the plot. All the while, when the two of them had taken those long walks down by the river, they had been scheming. She knew how Freddy adored Jack and had lost count of the times he had stood up for the man against Parker and Kenton. It was always Freddy who led the stories about his horsemanship or his skill with the sword and gun. Jack this and Jack that. Poor, dear Freddy had been loyal to the end and, now, thanks to Kenton unmasking their secret, it had all gone horribly wrong.

She ought to have been thankful that this mad affair had been exposed, grateful for what her stepson had done, but she wasn't. She would never be able to condone the malice in the man and yet, only now was she seeing in him what the others had seen so long ago.

Time and again, since that dreadful shouting match in the study, she had searched her mind, asking herself why she felt like she did. She should have been cursing the guilty pair for their madness; she should have treated young Miss Darcy with icy contempt for disgracing herself and the good name of her family. She should have shunned her, heaped misery on the shame and guilt that was there already. And, as for Tucker, he should have been dismissed there and then. She should have insisted on it, demanding to deal instead with one of the others – Grant or Webber, even that new boy from Challacombe. Anyone but the man who had dared to even *think* of behaving like he did.

But she had not. She could not bring herself to condemn them. In fact she found herself forgiving them their sins, excusing their scandalous behaviour. Gossip had filled the house like flood water that remained in every corner long after the storm had passed and which then rose higher and higher all the while contaminating everything in its path. Everywhere she went, chattering or whispering chambermaids and footmen sprang back, bobbing or scraping as she passed only to huddle together again once she had gone on her way.

She remembered, too, how she had stopped by the sewing room door that one of the maids had left ajar. Katherine's clothes, washed and ironed and ready for packing, were hanging out to air. She found herself looking around guiltily before going into the room and closing the door behind her. Then, quite unaccountably, she pressed the silk shirts to her cheek before letting her fingers trail down the fabric of the riding bodice where they toyed with the pearl buttons. It was here that other fingers, his, had been before and she undid them slowly, one by one, just as he must have done.

What, she wondered, would he have been saying to her as he opened her clothes to lay her bare, and what might have been her reply? Had she simply lain back or had she encouraged him to take her lustily like animals? How had she felt, she wondered, as his hands sought out her hidden body and how had she responded? As she stood there, a thrill of excitement coursed through her, as though she had been present, a silent witness to what had taken place.

It was not until the chill, dark hour before dawn the following morning that she knew. For a while she had lain unmoving, her body as still as the blackness around her while she listened for the creak of boards or the soft groan of the closing door that would tell her he was there. At first she had believed herself but the dream had faded. Although she had willed him desperately to stay, he had drifted away like the mist. Earlier, as he bent towards her, she had seen his face so clearly and it had been her, with her own soft, manicured hands, that had reached out and caught hold of his flaxen hair before pulling him down. His eyes, those of a boy barely older than her sons, had never left hers even as he was taking her. But now he had gone. She knew she had called out his name just before she woke but he had moved on and it was then that she knew she could never blame them for what they had done.

✳

She shivered involuntarily, hugging her arms to her sides, then turned at the sound of his footsteps. "I'm away with Freddy, m'dear." John Knight's riding boots rang out on the drawing room floor. "We'll be out at one of the new farms. Something about the roof, so they say."

"Don't be too late, dear. Remember Dr Collyns and Parson Jack are due here before seven." Elizabeth-Jane straightened her husband's cravat then bent forward to kiss his cheek. "They're going to stay...you remember, don't you? I reminded you yesterday."

"Hmmph." Knight scratched at his mane of hair. "And thank the Lord for that." He rolled his shoulder then scratched again. "A touch of sanity about the place at last. None of this...this...."

"Shush." Elizabeth-Jane touched his lips. "It's over, dear. All over and there's nothing more to be done...nothing that *can* be done. George Northborough was very good about it in the end."

"In the end, yes," Knight grumbled, frowning at the arrangement of dried flowers in the hearth. "But it took some doing, y'know and Amelia went off with a face like Boadicea." The two were silent. "You're right though...you always are." The frown had gone and he chuckled. "But never again, so help me God." He turned to go then paused. "Tucker's off at dawn, by the way. I've had him working out at Honeymead with the cattle these last few days...well away from them all. But that's it now. He's been paid and he's on his way." Knight rolled his shoulder. "He'll survive, never fear of that." He sounded optimistic almost admiringly so. She sensed he was about to say something else but he stopped, no doubt thinking better of it.

Once he had gone, she turned back to the window with her head bowed listening to the footfalls fading on the flagstones until a door slammed. All of them were going to miss him but none more than her husband.

4.

"Don't move." Nancy Coward, standing behind her husband, leant forward and nuzzled her cheek against his face. "Over there...by the tub." The little field mouse sat up and tested the air before dropping down to continue his search among the chive seeds. "Dear little thing...there 'e goes."

"Not long out of the nest, 'e's not." Hector leant back on the wooden bench they had put outside the cottage door. He could feel the warm softness of his wife's body against his back and caught hold of the white arms that encircled him. "Ears still pink, an' all. Don't give 'e much of a chance if 'e starts runnin' aroun' like that tho'...not in broad daylight." He kicked off his clogs and wriggled his toes then turned to look up at his wife.

She returned his smile. "Tired, love?" As she spoke so her arms tightened around him.

"Not so bad really." It had been almost three months since John Knight had put him in charge of the gardens at Castle Heights. The first few weeks had been hard as he and the new men struggled to put the neglected gardens together. All had gone quietly until last week when one of the housemaids came into the potting shed with the news from Simonsbath.

He and Nancy had worried about their friend until they heard he had been sent to work at West Lyn. The farm, bought by John Knight to keep the household at Castle Heights, sat high on the hill behind their cottage. The thought of him being so close had cheered them. Hector looked up at his wife again. "Jack'll be 'ere tomorrow, y'know. Fancy you'll be seeing 'im? Up at the farm, like?"

Nancy had been working at West Lyn for over a year, walking up the steep cliff path every morning. First it had been to help Joshua Slocombe with the flock at lambing time but now she did the milking as well. She had heard the elderly farmer complaining in his slow, mournful voice about this man from Simonsbath who had been sent to the farm in disgrace. "A sinful, iniquitous man who's yet to find our Lord," he had grumbled. His sentiments had not surprised her for she often came across Joshua and his wife bent over their Bibles in the farm kitchen and she knew he would have something to say. "Touched by Satan himself, that's what," she had mimicked to Hector. "The devil has visited him and cast aside his soul. He's left the path of true righteousness, gone astray and needs the bright, guiding light of salvation to bring him back to the fold. May the Good Lord have mercy on his soul."

"Oh, aye." She wrinkled her nose at the thought of having to live there, then stood and brushed back her long, sandy curls. "But the poor love's not goin' to find it easy, that's fer sure. That old Joshua Slocombe gives I the creeps. Always on about the Good Book. Never lets up. A right old misery-guts so 'e is...an' tight as they come as well."

"But anything fer Jack to get away from Simonsbath." Hector stood and stretched. Placing one foot on the bench he began examining his toes. "'Es had enough up there. Feels terrible about it."

"'Twasn't his fault." The sharpness in her voice made him look up. "Honest to God, Hector, they can't go blaming poor Jack for what happened. 'Twas them both, y'know...one just as bad as t'other. Anyways, listen, you." Nancy pushed his foot away and sat down. "'Tis fine for they lot to run around misbehavin' like we hears they do, but when it's done with one of us, I mean like with Jack or someone then 'tis merry hell to pay. 'Bain't right. An' what's so *wrong* if they love one another? Why can't they?"

"Bain't like that." Hector walked to the door. "'Tis all right for the men folk to...well, you know, but the ladies not s'posed to do nothing like that...not with us sorts anyhow, an' never someone like Lady Katherine. 'Ers a real lady. Cuh," he paused. "Can just imagine the state of it all up at the big house...bet 'twas right old thunder an' lightning."

"Well, 'tis done now and they can't do nort about it." Nancy scowled, still smouldering at the thought of Jack taking the blame. "Anyhows, us'll see to 'im...can't have him all miserable up with they Slocombes wi' their Bibles an' praying." She picked at the stain on his shirt. "Reckon 'e still loves her?" Nancy craned her neck to look up the cliff path across the valley to where the bracken met with the fields just below the farm. "Sad if he does, mind...she's real nice. Wonder if they'll ever meet again...see each other." Intrigued by the thought, she fell silent and looked down at her hands.

5.

The taller of the two men stood with his hand resting on the saddle. He had been up since before dawn.

Although it was high summer, a number of horses had been kept in overnight ready for the morning ride and he had begun the day by feeding them, moving from box to box in the half-light. Each time he opened a door the occupant would whinny quietly and move towards him, legs brushing through the deep straw, before turning and following him to the manger where its muzzle would push hungrily against the bucket in his hand.

This morning he had given them an extra handful of crushed oats and forked a little more hay into the racks. While on his way round, he had stopped to spend a bit of time with each one, running his hands gently across the withers and down the flanks. He had hoped to finish long before any of the others had risen but now, just as he was saddling up to go, he had company.

The second man, shorter and younger, and already dressed for riding, leant against the stable door with his frock coat hanging open. Jack patted the mare. "'Tis ever so kind of you, Master Frederic, but he'll be missed, y'know. The master'll soon see 'e's not here."

"And so?" Frederic pushed himself away from the door and stepped into the box. "Listen. Remus is mine and I can do what I like with him. And in any case, father doesn't go near him any more, he's far too lively for the old man. Don't suppose he's set eyes on him in months."

"Well, sir." Jack thought quickly. Remus, the dark bay in the next box, had been one of Frederic's favourites and now he was pressing the gelding on him, claiming that he would need a good horse at West Lyn. "Let's just say that you'll be loaning him, like, and if ever you feel the need for 'im then you'd...."

"Oh, no." Frederic shook his head. "No, no...you're the one who'll be needing him, Jack, and you must bank on him being available, not worrying about if he's going to be there or not."

"Well, sir." Jack shook his head slowly, searching for the right words "'Tis ever so good of you, really it is...I'll get the saddle changed right away." The two were silent. Both knew that the moment had come and that it was going to be difficult. "S'pose I'd best be getting on my way then, sir. It'll take a good couple of hours an' more and old Joshua's expecting me early so I hear." As he undid the girth, the grey mare half turned and nuzzled his chest, forcing him to take a step back. "Dunno what to say right now, sir...just that, well, t'was such a dreadful shame you were caught up in it all."

"Stop." Frederic held up a hand. "Listen, that's enough. Come on, now. Honestly Jack, we've had this out time and again. Really we have. To be honest I'm sick of the whole damn business and I never want to hear another word of it." He paused. "We were in it together and that's that...that's *it*." He raised his arms and let them fall again, standing awkwardly as though uncertain what to do next.

"Aye, sir. Well...."

But wait a moment." Frederic put a hand on his shoulder. "Look, there's just one thing more...it's something I have to say."

"Listen, sir." Jack interrupted him. "Beg pardon but whatever 'tis, then perhaps it's best not said. Not now." He waited, studying the other's face against the dawn light.

"No, I must," Frederic persisted, a note of urgency now in his voice. "It's been on my mind to tell you but I've found it…well, up to now I've not found the moment right."

"All right then. Go on, sir." He was speaking quietly. "Please speak your mind."

"It's just that…and I tell you this only because I'm so fond of you both." The words, both men could tell, were tumbling out. "It cannot go on, y'know…you and Lady Katherine that is. It really cannot and I fear for you both, Jack. I've told her myself like I'm telling you now. The world out there would tear you apart, finish you…destroy you both."

Jack pursed his lips then, slowly, shook his head. "Trouble is, sir, I've told her so myself. Told her to forget me…forget all about me. She *must*, I said. What's done's done and she has to move on."

"Well then?"

Their eyes met. "Said she couldn't sir. Said she would never leave me. No matter how long it'd take and no matter whatever might happen…she'd always be there waiting."

"And?"

"Same with me, sir." Jack took a deep breath. "After she told me, we swore we'd wait for each other, no matter what. And that's it, sir. That's the way it has to be."

Frederic said nothing, merely held his friend's steady gaze. Eventually he smiled. "I knew it," he whispered. "I knew it in my heart but I had to let you know my thoughts. I owed you that, my friend." Then, almost hesitantly, he held out his hand as though he was seeking Jack's but clasped hold of him with both arms instead and felt the strength of his embrace in return. He paused fleetingly, feeling the friendship between them before pushing himself away again. Glancing briefly at the man, he turned quickly and walked from the yard not daring to look back.

Jack stood alone. Time would tell, that was for sure. The day ahead, he knew, would be long and hard but he had nothing to fear from life, nothing at all.

THE END